THEY STOOPED TO FOLLY.

A Comedy of Morals

Books by

ELLEN GLASGOW

ELLEN GLASGOW

THEY STOOPED TO FOLLY

A Comedy of Morals

MCMXXIX

THE LITERARY GUILD

NEW YORK

"When lovely woman stoops to folly,
And finds too late that men betray,
What charm can soothe her melancholy?
What art can wash her guilt away?"

Contents

Part First

MR. LITTLEPAGE

I

MR. VIRGINIUS CURLE LITTLEPAGE, who had his reason apart from the weather for a melancholy view of life, stood at the window of his law office and looked out upon a depressing afternoon in November. Against blown sheets of rain his large, benign head was dimly etched by the fire-light. At fifty-seven, his dark hair was still thick and only a little gray on the temples; his ruddy Georgian features were still noble in contour; and his short, well-fed figure, though a trifle stout at the waist, was still imposing in carriage. For he was one of those Virginian pillars of society that are held upright less by singleness of heart than by the firm support of woman's influence.

Without, he saw clouds, rain, mist, a few scudding yellow leaves from a tormented elm, and all the uniform ugliness of a commercial invasion. Within, illumined by the sunken fire of his youth, he looked back upon the creditable years of his life, and felt that he hated them. When had he really lived? When, in all his successful career, had he reached after happiness? When, even for an hour, had he taken the thing that he wanted? Gazing down on the flooded High Street in Queenborough, he told himself that he had learned to bridle his impulses from the hour of his birth. He had respected convention; he had deferred to tradition. Yet to-day, by this dying flare of the years, all the sober pleasures he had known appeared as worthless as cinders. "What is the meaning of it?" he asked, with a start of dismay. "Is it middle age? Is it the fatal inadequacy of all human experience? Or is it merely that I have become a disappointed idealist?"

A philosopher by habit of mind, he persisted in his search for the cause beneath his disenchantment with life. "I've had more than most men," he continued precisely. "I've been successful beyond my deserts. I was born with the things for which other men sacrifice pleasure and health, and I've gone as far, at least in Virginia, as my profession can take me. Moreover, I've one of the best wives in the world, and no man could ask for three finer children. Duncan, to be sure, contracted a form of moral dyspepsia in the war; but any father ought to be satisfied with so normal a son as Curle. Common, perhaps, in spite of his blood, though a taint of vulgarity, as Marmaduke would say, helps a man to feel at home in his world. And Mary Victoria! A girl like Mary Victoria, blessed with beauty, sense, character, and determination, scarcely needed a world at war and a white veil to turn her into a heroine. True, she stayed abroad too long when she went back after the armistice. But in a few hours she will be home again, and we shall soon have forgotten how we've missed her. . . . Yes, my children are all right, and so, of course, is their mother. When I think of the nervous and nagging wives that drive men to despair, I ought to be thankful that Victoria has never lost control of herself since she married me. No, it is not that. Something else must be wrong. I seem to have had everything, yet I feel—I've felt for months—as if I'd never had anything that I wanted. The war, I suppose. But the war has been over for five years, and I've had time enough to grow used to the changes. Unless," he drew his breath in horror, "I've all along missed the excitement we lived in." Though he told himself that the memory of the war had sunk in a black chill to the very pit of his soul, he knew that nothing else could be compared in vehemence with that witches' sabbath of released desires. "For once we were natural," he thought, while the sensation of cold nausea crept from its retreat and invaded his mind. "We were trying to be too superior, and it was a relief, even to the women, especially to the women, when the savage hunger broke through the thin crust we call civilization. It was a relief to us all, no doubt, to be able to think murder and call it idealism. But the war wasn't the worst thing," he concluded grimly. "The worst thing is this sense of having lost our way in the universe. The worst thing is that the war has made peace seem so futile. It is just as if the bottom had dropped out of idealism . . ."

Behind him the door opened and shut. Without turning, he was aware that the younger of his two secretaries laid a pile of letters in front of the immense ebony inkstand, shaped like an elephant, which his wife had given him on his birthday a few weeks before. While he looked at the rain, he could see the ivory and dusk of the girl in the firelight. Her name was Milly Burden, and he had found her attractive enough to arrest his attention without unsettling the stable equilibrium of his emotions. For nearly six years she had remained more or less of a mystery; and though she had remained more or less of a mystery, he had always respected her. In the beginning his ideals had restrained him; and after he had lost his ideals, an obscure aversion, familiar to him as the instincts of a gentleman, had adequately taken their place. He pitied her; he had become sincerely attached to her; but all modern youth was too hard, too flippant, too brazen, he felt, to awaken romantic desire. Had he been capable of desire without romance, he would still have harboured a prejudice in favour of severe virtue in women. Not all his

affection for Milly Burden, not all his admiration for her
courage and the flowerlike blue of her eyes, could blind
him to the fact that she had once forgotten her modesty.
Other women, it is true, had forgotten their modesty even
in Queenborough, where modesty, though artfully preserved, was by no means invulnerable. But these other
women, though one of them was his own poor Aunt Agatha
and another was his attractive, if unfortunate neighbour,
Mrs. Dalrymple, were all safely provided for either by
the code of a gentleman or by the wages of sin. With Milly
Burden, however, there was a difference. From the beginning of their acquaintance she had treated the feminine
sense of sin with the casual modern—or was it merely the
casual masculine touch? Ever since the unhappy occasion near the end of the war, when she had become involved in those troubles that overtake women who are
more generous than prudent, he had waited in vain for
the first sign of repentance. She had, he knew, suffered
desperately. Not even poor Aunt Agatha, wrapped in her
sense of sin as in perpetual widow's weeds, had loved more
unwisely than Milly. The difference, he perceived reluctantly, was less in the measure than in the nature of their
guilty passions. While poor Aunt Agatha, condemned
by the precepts of beautiful behaviour to her third-story
back bedroom, had mourned the loss of her virtue, Milly
Burden, typing his letters with light fingers and a despairing heart, had mourned only the loss of her lover. The
war had taken him away from her; and, with a dark and
bitter passion, she had hated the war and all the contagious war idealism which had swept Mary Victoria, like
a winged victory in a Red Cross uniform, as far as the
distressed but animated Balkan kingdoms. Though he had
disapproved of Milly, it was pleasant to remember now

that he had protected her. Her youth, her gallantry, and her imprudent passion, had stirred him more deeply than he had ever dared to confess. Assisted by his wife, he had helped the girl in her trouble, and, opposed by his wife, he had received her again when her trouble was over. Her story was common enough, but he was sufficiently discerning to realize that Milly herself was unusual. Her indifference to what in a Victorian lady he would have called her frailty, appeared in some incredible fashion to redeem her character. "After all, is it the sense of sin that makes the fallen woman?" he asked himself in serious disturbance of mind.

This had occurred more than five years before, and while he had meditated on the painful nature of her problems, Milly had looked up at him with disaster and yet something stronger than disaster in her deep blue eyes.

"Does he know of—of this?" Mr. Littlepage had asked with sternness.

"I haven't told him. He couldn't do anything, and besides he is miserable. He isn't a fighter. He was always afraid of life. Some men are, you know. That makes it harder for me. I am living with his fear all the time."

"And not with your own?"

"Oh, I'm not like that. I haven't enough imagination. I take what comes, but I don't go out looking for trouble. Martin does."

"Is his name Martin?"

"Martin Welding. Do you know him?"

"I am not sure. Was his mother an Annersley?" Vaguely he had remembered that one of the obscure Annersley girls had married a Welding, who had proved worthless and finally taken to drink.

"Yes. She is dead now."

"What does he do?"

"He was in a bank. There wasn't much in that, but he was trying to write. He is only twenty-two."

Twenty-two, and Milly, at the time, was not yet nineteen! "Well, if I were you, my dear, I should let him know of this," he had said gently, while Milly wept with a violence that penetrated his heart.

"I am not thinking about this. I am thinking that I may never see him again," she had sobbed, as she dried her eyes.

Whether she had told Martin or not, Mr. Littlepage had never discovered. By the time she came out of the hospital, where the child, blighted by Mrs. Burden's moral sense, had withered immediately, the war was already over, and he had thought it wiser as well as kinder to ask no questions. Then, three years later, she had broken through her reserve in the hope that his daughter, who was employed in the reconstruction of Europe, might help to find Martin Welding.

"But the war has been over for almost three years, my dear. Where has he been all this time?"

"He was sent home in a hospital ship. For six months they kept him in St. Elizabeth's. I went there every Sunday when they would let me see him."

"And you said nothing about it?"

"What was there to say? I saved all my money for those trips. I never spent a penny on myself."

"So that was why——" Overwhelmed by the discovery, Mr. Littlepage had gazed at her through an iridescent film of emotion. That was why she had appeared so much shabbier than Miss Dorset, who was independent in means and superior to men.

"Yes, that was why."

"And I never suspected."

"There wasn't anything to suspect."

"In all that time did you tell him?"

A look of agony, which he had never forgotten, convulsed her thin features. "How could I? They said in the hospital that we must tell him nothing depressing. I always hoped that when he was well again everything would be just as it was before. Love can keep alive on so little hope."

"But didn't you see him after he left the hospital?"

"Not often. After he got his discharge, he tried to find work in New York. That was too far for me to go, and he could not afford to come home. Then suddenly he went back to France."

"Didn't he see you before he sailed?"

"No, he wrote from the ship. He was at the end of his luck, he said. Everything had failed him, and he had had to borrow money to go back in the steerage. He hated America, and he hoped that, if he went back to France, he might be able to write what he felt about it. If he ever got on his feet again, he said, he would send for me, and he added that but for me he should have given up hope. When he was in the hospital he wanted to kill himself."

An unmitigated cad, Mr. Littlepage had reflected; and while he watched her stricken eyes (the eyes of a dying hope, he thought sentimentally), he had mused upon the singular power that masculine cads exercise over the feminine mind.

"Did he write after he went back to France?"

"Only in the beginning. At first he was lonely and miserable, and he seemed eager for me to write to him. Then his letters stopped suddenly. It has been almost six months since I heard from him. I want to find out the truth. Even if he is dead, even if he has killed himself, I must find out the truth. Anything is better than this suspense."

"Well, I'll see what I can do, my child." Mr. Littlepage had promised readily, for he had one of the kindest hearts in the world; and before going to bed that night, he had written a vague but urgent letter to his daughter. If anything could be done, he assured himself in distress, Mary Victoria, who had a firm hand with an emergency, would be equal to the occasion. Not only was Milly as dear, by this time, as a second and less formidable daughter, but he was sentimental enough to deal mildly with love when it did not endanger either his peace or his prospects. That Mary Victoria was more than equal to the event was proved, within a reasonable space of time, by a triumphant cable which announced that Martin Welding had been found in a provincial French hospital. He was suffering, the message briefly divulged, from "a nervous collapse," and this was followed by the encouraging words, "we are helping him." Several months later she had written that Martin was out of the hospital, but still subject to attacks of depression, and unwilling to return to America because he felt he had made a failure of life. "We have offered him the position of secretary in our orphanage," she had concluded, "and he may go back with us to the Balkans. It seems the best thing for him to do." Two years had passed since that letter, but there had been no other mention of Martin. Though Mr. Littlepage had asked many questions, Mary Victoria had neglected to answer them. Apparently the young man with the inadequate nervous system had dropped out of her noble and active life, and she seemed to be occupied with more important affairs.

II

"I WONDER why Mary Victoria never told us what happened," he mused this afternoon, while his mind turned back to the silence and anxiety of all the years since the war. "Did something occur that she couldn't bear writing us? Is it possible that the chap went out of his mind or even made away with himself?" Well, whatever had happened, he could do no good by beginning this futile speculation all over again. In a few hours, unless there had been a delay with the customs, his daughter would be in his arms and could no longer evade a reply. Suspense had been hard; but it was unfair to expect Mary Victoria to realize the slow torture of a deferred catastrophe. Meanwhile, the best way was to put Milly's anxiety out of his thoughts. . . . Should he go on to his club in the hope of diversion? Or would it be easier, as well as more prudent, to wait, as he had promised, until Victoria stopped by for him? . . .

Through his slow but thorough mind there floated a disquieting vision of his favourite club. Shivering in the chill dawn of prohibition, he watched a few timid drinkers (Ah, degenerate scions of the Virginian throats of hickory!) measure out their evening thimblefuls of old Bourbon. "No, there's nothing in that for me," he thought gloomily, and decided that it would be wiser to wait until his wife picked him up on her way home from a lecture.

Victoria, he knew, could be trusted to come early.

Though she had found time, since the children were grown, to take part in several major reforms, she had never failed to put the duties of marriage above the urgent needs of philanthropy. There was, too, this other reason to expect promptness to-day, since their only daughter, and the youngest of their three fine children, was coming home after a long absence. Having gone abroad with the Red Cross in the last year of the war, she had returned after the armistice to do her independent duty by the Balkan Peninsula. A girl of much character, which she had inherited from her mother, handsome, capable, high-minded, and almost automatically inspiring, she was one of those earnest women who are designed to curb the lower nature of man. Even at a tender age, when she had left her play to guide her blind uncle Stephen Brooke through the decorous shadows of Washington Street, she had inclined her infant ear by choice rather than compulsion to the Stern Daughter of the Voice of God. At seventeen she had become engaged, against the wishes of her parents, to a youthful missionary, Episcopal but devout, who had been indiscreetly assigned to the Congo. From this mistaken sacrifice she was saved only by the invasion of Belgium; and Mr. Littlepage had become ignobly reconciled to a world conflict that diverted Mary Victoria's mission from the Congo, where faces are incurably black, to the Balkan kingdoms, where, he charitably assumed, they are merely sallow. But it was a relief, nevertheless, to find how all the romantic satyrs of the Balkans were repulsed by Mary Victoria's moral idealism. After all, there was more than a grain of truth in that favourite proverb of the Southern gentleman, "A woman's virtue is its best defense." Though he had missed her sadly, for he was a devoted father, he had been prevented by a legal conference from meeting her on the dock, and in his place he had sent Curle, a popular young man, without charm, but as loud and bright and brisk as the New South. In spite of Mr. Littlepage's love for his daughter, and his sincere pride in her achievements abroad (were not her boxes filled with glittering decorations bestowed by those countries that are content to honour rather than imitate altruism?), he was unable, when he thought of her, to dismiss a feeling of paternal inadequacy. For Mary Victoria deserved, he felt, a more celebrated father; a father who had distinguished himself, if not in war, which is an exclusive field, at least in the less favourable path of private virtue. She deserved a second parent after the finer pattern of her mother, who was, as Mr. Littlepage had every reason to know, a match for any moral necessity.

After thirty years of married happiness, he could still remind himself that Victoria was endowed with every charm except the thrilling touch of human frailty. Though her perfection discouraged pleasures, especially the pleasures of love, he had learned in time to feel the pride of a husband in her natural frigidity. For he still clung, amid the decay of moral platitudes, to the discredited ideal of chivalry. In his youth the world was suffused with the afterglow of the long Victorian age, and a graceful feminine style had softened the manners, if not the natures, of men. At the end of that interesting epoch, when womanhood was exalted from a biological fact into a miraculous power, Virginius Littlepage, the younger son of an old and affluent family, had married Victoria Brooke, the granddaughter of a tobacco planter, who had made a satisfactory fortune by forsaking his plantation and converting tobacco into cigarettes. While Virginius had been trained by stern tradition to respect every woman who had not stooped to folly, the virtue peculiar to her sex was

among the least of his reasons for admiring Victoria. She
was not only modest, which was usual in the 'nineties, but
she was beautiful, which is unusual in any decade. In
the beginning of their acquaintance he had gone even further and ascribed intellect to her; but a few months of
marriage had shown this to be merely one of the many
delusions created by perfect features and a noble expression. Everything about her had been smooth and definite,
even the tones of her voice and the way her light brown
hair, which she wore à la Pompadour, was rolled stiffly
back from her forehead and coiled in a burnished rope on
the top of her head. A serious young man, ambitious to
attain a place in the world more brilliant than the secluded
seat of his ancestors, he had been impressed at their first
meeting by the compactness and precision of Victoria's
orderly mind. For in that earnest period the minds, as
well as the emotions, of lovers were orderly. It was an age
when eager young men flocked to church on Sunday morning, and eloquent divines discoursed upon the Victorian
poets in the middle of the week. He could afford to smile
now when he recalled the solemn Browning class in which
he had first lost his heart. How passionately he had admired Victoria's virginal features! How fervently he had
envied her competent but caressing way with the poet! Incredible as it seemed to him now, he had fallen in love
with her while she recited from the more ponderous pas-
sages in *The Ring and the Book*. He had fallen in love
with her then, though he had never really enjoyed Browning, and it had been a relief to him when the Unseen, in company with its illustrious poet, had at last gone out of fashion. Yet, since he was disposed to admire all the qualities
he did not possess, he had never ceased to respect the firmness with which Victoria continued to deal in other forms
with the Absolute. As the placid years passed, and she

came to rely less upon her virginal features, it seemed to him that the ripe opinions of her youth began to shrink and flatten as fruit does that has hung too long on the tree. She had never changed, he realized, since he had first known her; she had become merely riper, softer, and sweeter in nature. Her advantage rested where advantage never fails to rest, in moral fervour. To be invariably right was her single wifely failing. For his wife, he sighed, with the vague unrest of a husband whose infidelities are imaginary, was a genuinely good woman. She was as far removed from pretense as she was from the posturing virtues that flourish in the credulous world of the drama. The pity of it was that even the least exacting husband should so often desire something more piquant than goodness.

Although he had been contented with Victoria, he could not deny that there had been troubled periods when he had craved something more than marriage. This was nobody's fault, he assured himself; least of all was it the fault of his wife. What it meant, he supposed, was simply that marriage, like life itself, is not superior to the migratory impulses of spring and autumn. And if he had suffered from his thwarted longings, it was a comfort to remember that he had made Victoria perfectly happy. It was a comfort to remember that, like all pure women everywhere, she was satisfied with monogamy.

In his own vagrant seasons, since the nature of man is more urgent, he had found himself thinking wistfully of Mrs. Dalrymple, who, when she was not repairing her charms or her reputation in Europe, lived on the opposite corner of Washington Street. Too alluring for her widow's weeds, to which she imparted a festive air by the summer bloom in her cheeks, he remembered her as one of those fair, fond, clinging women whom men long either to pro-

tect or to ruin. Frivolous, no doubt, yet how appealing,
how fascinating, how feminine, in her light-hearted
bereavement! Why is it, he had often wondered, that not
only a wife but even a widow appears more attractive
when she is adorned with a sprightly demeanour? When he
thought of Amy Dalrymple in his hours of leisure (the
only hours in which he permitted himself to think sentimentally of any woman), there was a motion, a surge, a
buried whirlpool, far below in some primeval flood of
his being. For the last ten years (while Mrs. Dalrymple
found her widow's ruche becoming and continued to wear
it lightly), he had asked himself, in those vagabond moods
that visit husbands in April and November, if he might
have been happier with a woman who was sometimes indis-
creet but always amusing. It was true, he conceded reluctantly, that Amy Dalrymple was very far indeed from what
in Victorian days they had called an inspiring example. Before her fortunate second marriage, and even more fortunate widowhood, she was the heroine of a scandal that had
shaken the canons of refined conduct to their solid foundation. While her husband, conforming to the dramatic style
of the period, had promptly transfixed her by a divorce,
her lover, a practical rather than a theoretical exponent
of chivalry, had discreetly married a lady of sober views
and impeccable conduct. Moved by her youth, her loneliness, her amber-coloured hair, and the drenched brown
velvet of her eyes, Mr. Littlepage, though he usually
avoided the divorce court, had consented to act as her
counsel. Victoria, who was unfashionable enough to be
called a "woman's woman," had stood by him steadfastly,
and had even appeared in the street with his amiable client.
Yes, Victoria had been wonderful from the beginning to
the end of that trying experience. Only the public conviction that she was too frigid to harbour designs on the

male sex in general had enabled her to emerge unspotted from her noble behaviour. "She never liked Amy Paget," mused Mr. Littlepage now. "She never liked her, yet she was at her side when all the fair-weather friends fell away. Strange, how often in the last few months that one generous act had commanded his loyalty. Fifteen years ago, and it seemed only yesterday! At the time Amy Paget, though a ruined woman, was still young and beautiful, and nobody was astonished when, within the next five years, she married Peter Dalrymple in Paris and safely buried him in Père Lachaise. Mr. Littlepage had visited the imposing marble tomb in that wilderness of lost illusions, and he had been favourably impressed by the style, as well as by the substance, of Mrs. Dalrymple's grief. "Fortunately her heart was too light to sink," he thought now, with tender compassion. "After all, she was deeply wronged, poor lady." Attired in her soft French mourning, she had continued to flit airily between Paris and Queenborough, until, on one of her summer flights to her old home, Mr. Littlepage was tempted to become more than a friend though, perhaps, a little less than an advocate.

Many sober years had come and gone since that August evening when he had lingered beside Mrs. Dalrymple on the vine-draped veranda at the back of her house. His home had seemed empty while Victoria and the children completed an art pilgrimage in Europe; and swayed by a fluttering impulse of curiosity, he had wandered through the darkness toward the friendly light in Mrs. Dalrymple's window. A business matter, she explained, had brought her back in the dull season, which was the only season that encouraged her to defy the gossips of Queenborough. Then she had slipped through the French window, out under the dark and fragrant grape-leaves, where the moonlight clustered like flowers over her blue dress. They had talked casually of many subjects, and not until she touched on the past had that sweet and perilous emotion rushed like a burning wine through his senses. Still glowing, still intoxicated, he had followed her when she fled into the dimly lighted hall, and enfolded her in his arms. After ten years and a world war, he could see again the way her white lids closed like flowers over her dark eyes and her red lips (at a period when a scarlet mouth was a badge of shame) parted with the quivering sound of her breath. All those years and all that conflict between them! Yet only a few hours before he had watched her cross the pavement and step into her car, and he had suffered again the dull ache of unsatisfied longing. That one glimpse after her long absence (for she also had obeyed the summons to world service) had shown him that she was still youthful, still seductive, though her once shapely figure was now severely repressed and her lustrous hair was flattened in shallow waves over her ears. Just the sight of her in the street had made him feel suddenly ardent within, as if that flitting view of charms he might once have possessed was a reminder that he was not yet too old for temptation. For he had not forgotten that beneath those Bacchic garlands he might have been, but was not, a conqueror. Even to-day the memory vibrated in his steady nerves, while he felt that some remembered delight awakened a faint echo of rapture. Of all his tender recollections this, he told himself, was the only one that aroused a reminiscent emotion. This was the only one, too, that he had been able to bury away from Victoria. Other secrets he had kept, but they were all of an innocent nature. He had, it is true, suppressed the obscure indiscretions of railways; he had even suppressed the simple indiscretions of secretaries; but his share in these hidden misdemeanours had been invariably blameless.

After the rapture of that August evening why, he wondered now, had he awakened 'the next morning with diminished ardour? Why had his desire, with the innate perversity that makes desire so unsound as a guide to behaviour, dissolved into a mixture of bitterness and regret? Where was that hidden flaw in his nature which made it harder for him to commit a pleasure than to perform a duty, which compelled him to hesitate and fail in the hour of adventure? Where was the moral scruple that commanded him to give up Mrs. Dalrymple before he had fallen in love with her? The following evening, though he knew that she waited for him, he had taken a heartless satisfaction in the thought of her disappointment. While he wrote a long and unusually demonstrative letter to Victoria, he had been astonished to find that even an imaginary infidelity had restored his relish for the temperate joys of marriage. To-day he could reflect, with the surprise of a husband and the complacency of a philosopher, that he loved Victoria the more because he had been so nearly unfaithful. Such, he meditated deeply, are the inscrutable contradictions of passion. Such are the concessions to nature in the code of a gentleman. Was modern youth, he asked despondently, capable of these logical inconsistencies and these swift recoils? Was there, after all, so great a disparity between two social epochs as people liked to pretend? Women appeared different on the surface; but had they actually changed beneath their figures? Was the heart in Milly's flat little chest still as erratic as the heart in Mrs. Dalrymple's once opulent bosom? For even Mrs. Dalrymple's bosom, he had not failed to observe, was no longer opulent. Almost insensibly this led him to a deeper and more delicate specu-

lation. Could she have changed also within? Had her
ardent temperament decreased with her diminishing
shape? For was it reasonable to imagine that a flat bosom
could contain all the true womanliness provided by the
ample curves of the 'nineties?

A few weeks after his old desertion of her Amy Dalrymple had closed her house and sailed for Europe.
Before he heard of her again his wife and children had
returned with improved opinions and modest but fashion-
able appearances. Dulness has no right to grow middle-
aged, he had mused the first evening at dinner, while he
listened to the opinions that Victoria had assembled as
methodically as Curle had supplied his album with postage
stamps. Then, aided by his disastrous adventure, his marriage had relapsed into the serene monotony that so
often wears the aspect of happiness. He had believed himself to be contented until the war in Europe had inflamed
all those repressions that it failed to set free, and the
Peace of Versailles had extended more important fron-
tiers than physical boundaries. Presently, when the flood
of war idealism had subsided, he discovered that Mrs.
Dalrymple's indiscretion had diminished in size. New and
perhaps ignoble standards had emerged from the conflict.
For the decadence of Europe was slowly undermining
Virginian tradition, and even the Southern gentleman, he
told himself, was beginning to suspect that the ruined
woman is an invention of man. Was it possible, Mr. Littlepage inquired, fearfully but hopefully, that there was
something wrong with the past? Deeper than law,
sharper than logic, this corroding doubt penetrated
his mind. Was there a fatal flaw even in the Episcopal
Church? Was the ideal of pure womanhood infested with
moth and decay? Beneath these derisive questions, it
seemed to him that the stern but noble features of the

categorical imperative had been battered beyond recognition. How often in his youth had he heard his father lament somebody's "loss of faith," as if such a deprivation were a calamity. Yet he himself had found that a world without earnest conviction could be far from uncomfortable. It afforded, among other luxuries, ample leisure to regret all the pleasant opportunities that one had missed in the past. And gradually, as he grew more relaxed in principle, he began to sweeten disapproval with tenderness when he thought of Amy Dalrymple's frailty.

III

"Mr. Littlepage, you have forgotten to sign your letters."

The voice was reproachful, and he glanced round with a whimsical apology in his soft brown eyes. "I'm sorry, Milly. I am not often so careless. You must find excuses for me to-day," he added in the playful tone he reserved for sentiment. "I am as useless as an expectant lover."

Milly looked at him with the composed tolerance of modern youth. "Your daughter has been away a long time."

"She went the week you came. That, I think, is one of the reasons I've always felt you were related to me."

"Well, it wouldn't have made any difference. You couldn't have been kinder."

"There were perhaps better ways, but I was too stupid to think of them. Whenever you looked unhappy I thought of Mary Victoria in the Balkans—or even in Paris."

"She wasn't obliged to go back, was she?" There was an accent of derision in Milly's voice.

He smiled indulgently, for his sense of humour, unlike Victoria's, embraced not only his wife and himself but his children as well. "She thought so. You see, the war didn't last long enough to exhaust her moral energy. She was obliged to use up a good deal that was left over. She remembered the distress in the Balkans, and of course there is always Armenia."

"Anyhow, I'm glad for your sake that she is coming home."

"Yes, I'm glad, of course, but—I may as well admit it— I'm a little afraid——"

"Afraid? You mean she may have changed?"

"It isn't only that. I suppose I've missed her too much. Are you waiting for these letters?"

"No, I'll come back after I've got my coat. Everyone else has gone."

As the girl left the room, he turned back to his desk, while his whole being was swept by paternal solicitude. Was Victoria, he wondered, suffering from this anxious expectancy? Could even a mother have hungered more acutely for the sight of a daughter? All day it had been impossible to govern his mind properly when he remembered that every hour, every minute, was bringing Mary Victoria nearer his arms. Ever since she had cabled him the date of her sailing, he had awaited her return with a curious mingling of delight and reluctance. Hope and fear were so blended that he had long ago ceased to distinguish between the conflicting emotions. Whenever he thought of Mary Victoria, it seemed to him that his heart dissolved into a rainbow mist, and flowered anew in the vision of a little girl wearing a short white frock with starched frills and a blue sash tied in a big bow at the back of her waist. Always she came to him like this; never older, never younger, than she had looked at the age of seven. He saw again her shining auburn curls, confined by a blue ribbon, her innocent gray eyes beneath winged eyebrows, her sturdy sunburned legs in white socks that were ribbed at the top, and her blunt childish feet in black kid slippers with prim straps at the ankles. Nothing in his whole life, not Victoria in her bridal veil, not Curle in his soldier's uniform, not Mary Victoria marching in a Red

Cross parade, had ever touched him so deeply as the image of those helpless feet in white socks and black slippers. The living Mary Victoria had outgrown his protection. She had advanced so far ahead of him that her nearness as a daughter had diminished while her stature as a philanthropist increased with the distance. What remained to him, he sometimes felt, was only a vision painted on air of a child with clustering curls, eyes as innocent as stars, and bare sunburned knees above the ribbed bands of her socks.

Having signed the letters, he lighted a cigar and sat nervously smoking until Milly returned.

"You've been working too hard," he remarked as he looked up at her.

She shook her head. "No, it isn't that. It isn't work." Her face looked pale and tired; her usually smooth dark hair had drifted down in a mist over her forehead; her dress, an old one that she wore on wet days, was faded and unbecoming; but her eyes, large, deep, radiantly blue, were burning with life. Judged by the waxen ideal of the 'nineties, he knew that she was not beautiful. Beside Mrs. Dalrymple's rose-leaf bloom and texture, Milly's face, he reflected, would appear almost wasted. There were hollows in her thin cheeks and her small white teeth were uneven; yet these hollows and this unevenness became, when she smiled, a part of her indescribable charm. Months went by, since few men were less predatory, when he was scarcely aware of her presence. Then, suddenly, without warning, the recollection of his absent daughter would bring Milly into his mind, and he would awaken to the bright audacity in her laugh, or to the look of wistful expectancy in her April eyes. For an instant he would become intensely alive to her gaiety, her suffering, and her defiant courage. "Is it possible," he would ask himself with a start, "that a woman can be noble without goodness or good without virtue?"

"If it isn't work," he said gently, "it must be worry, Milly."

The corners of her lips quivered. "Well, you can't help worrying, can you?"

"I am not sure. People who don't worry tell us we can."

"Then they've never been in love. I sometimes think love isn't anything else."

"Are you still unhappy, my dear?"

Her eyes darkened with pain. "I want Martin. I've always wanted him."

"I had hoped you were getting over the worst."

"No, I haven't got over it. I haven't got over it even a little."

"Perhaps you will when you hear something definite. I'll ask my daughter as soon as I can see her alone. But don't hope for too much. It is a mistake to hope for too much or you are sure to be disappointed. If there had been good news, Mary Victoria would have told us."

"You said just the opposite a year ago."

"Then I was trying to keep up your courage. Now I am preparing you for a blow."

"Well, I shan't have long to wait. But the last hours are the hardest."

"I'll call you up as soon as I speak to her. No, I'll come to see you, that will be better. I'll have a talk with her to-night, and if it isn't too late, I'll come straight to see you."

"If anything has happened to Martin, I don't want to live, I don't want to live."

"Do you still care as much as that?"

"As much as that?" Her tears were brimming over. "I love him. I've loved him since the first minute."

"How old were you then?"

"I wasn't eighteen until August, but I knew what I wanted."

"Well, you can't blame your mother for thinking you were too young."

"She hated Martin. She never had happiness and she could not bear the thought of my having it."

"You must not say things like that, Milly."

"But it is true." She looked at him defiantly. "What good comes of lying about things? People used to believe in lying, but we don't any longer."

"Do you believe in anything now, Milly?"

"Not in shams. I have a right to my own happiness as long as I play the game fairly."

"And you think that you have played the game fairly?"

"Haven't I?" Her eyes were like blue flames. "My life is my own. I haven't hurt anybody but myself."

"Are you sure of that, Milly? You must have brought pain to your mother."

"It was her own fault. She tried to manage my life. She tried to make me into what she was at my age."

"Can you blame her for that? She believed it was best for you."

"No, it wasn't that. She simply couldn't bear my having a life of my own. She has always thought happiness immoral. That was why I had to run out to Martin at night after she went to bed. She never let me see him at home. She never let me see anybody."

"I suppose she thought she was right."

"She has always thought that. Her thinking that drove Father away from home."

He looked at her sternly. Oh, modern youth, modern youth! "You must control yourself, Milly."

"Would you rather I'd be deceitful?"

"I'd rather you'd show proper respect for your mother."

"Do you want me to say I love her? I don't. I don't even like her. She has ruined my life. I had a right to my life, and she has ruined it."

"Other people can't ruin our lives."

"You wouldn't say that if you knew Mother better. She could ruin anybody's life. She was afraid that I'd be like Father if I once found out that there is such a thing as happiness."

"She was mistaken in that. You must remember, however, that her own life had been tragic. She had lost her other children, and your father had deserted her."

"She drove him to it. I never blamed Father."

Nor, if the truth must be told, could Mr. Littlepage, who was imperfectly acquainted with Mrs. Burden, find it in his heart to blame the fugitive husband. There are human rights, he mused sadly, that should be respected even in marriage. There are virtues so prickly that no mortal thing, not even a husband, could be expected to live in the house with them. "No, I may be wrong in principle and deficient in moral constitution, but I have never felt that I could blame him." Erring, no doubt; yet how human, how comprehensible, how heroic, some desertions appear to a philosopher! In spite of his own happy marriage, he had suffered all his life from a secret leaning toward faithless husbands and other undesirable acquaintances. Vainly he had tried to trample down these low but vigorous impulses. Vainly he had endeavoured to prefer the right-minded and to pity only the deserving. But something stronger than his will—was it a secret pulse of wildness in his heart?—had urged him to an irregular alliance with the obscure and the profligate. How much of this, he had often speculated, was owing to his childish admiration for his elder brother, Marmaduke, who, after

driving an ambulance under fire, and leaving a sturdy right
leg in the war zone, had climbed as high as the picturesque
attic of Mrs. Burden's lodging house? Not that Marmaduke was impoverished; merely that he was more or less
disreputable in his opinions. Had the repressed longings of
their mother, whose nervous temperament had overflowed
into water colour, achieved a more or less permanent form
in Marmaduke's pictures? Or was it merely the prevailing
fashion of fancy-work, as his father pretended, which
had festooned their French mirrors with wild roses
and decorated their satin sofa pillows with snowy
landscapes? Marmaduke, because of his turn for painting and his zest for experience, had been in childhood his mother's favourite; and there were glimpses of
her still in the reformed romantic, who now occupied, with
the hilarity that recollections of a well-spent life so seldom afford, a dormered room overlooking the sunsets on
James River. Beneath this once imposing though now ram-
shackle roof, in an obscure street, which had been as conspicuous for fashion as it was now safe for bootlegging,
Marmaduke painted with vehemence in firm strokes of
red, blue, and yellow. As if, Mr. Littlepage had reasoned
sadly, an artist could be sincere only in primary colours.
Devoted as he was to his brother, Marmaduke's pictures
had always seemed to Virginius too unpleasant to be
natural, and too—yes, even if he did sound like Curle and
the New South—too un-American to be really modern.
For if Marmaduke had stayed in America, and painted the
outside instead of the inside of his subjects, he might have
won by now an enviable reputation, and probably have sold
his more flattering portraits of women. Even in Queenborough, where, until recent years, conversation had been
the favourite and almost the only art patronized by the
best circles, wealthy citizens were beginning to realize that,

if books look well in a library, pictures lend even more emphatically the right note in decoration to the walls of a drawing-room. All this and even more Marmaduke had forfeited by his light conduct and his intemperate opinions. . . . And the worst of it was that Virginius found it impossible to blame either the hostilities in Europe or the bad example of the German army for the profligate disposition of his elder brother. Many evils he held against them, but, being a just man, he could not charge them with this one. Milly's wildness, he felt, might have sprung, however indirectly, from the invasion of Belgium; but he must look deeper and perhaps further, he knew, to find the source of Marmaduke's moral infirmity.

While he meditated he had almost forgotten that Milly was waiting, a small black hat pushed down over her eyebrows and a purple umbrella swinging by a cord from her hand. Beneath the dark cloud of hair, her eyes were starry and watchful.

"How long has it been since you heard from Martin?" he asked suddenly.

"Oh, an age! He was going to the Balkans, he wrote, because it was either that or starvation. Relief work made him sick but there wasn't anything else ahead of him. He told me he wasn't worth thinking about and I'd better forget him. As if I could!" she added passionately. "As if I could forget him just because he is a failure!"

"It is a pity you can't, my dear."

"But I don't want to. I don't want to forget him."

"Well, that's even more of a pity."

"For a time I tried not to think of him. Everything but a part of me seemed to forget."

"Was that the best part of you?"

"It was the deepest part. It was the little hard kernel of memory that makes a sore all round its edge." Her features, swept by tremulous wings of longing, were rapt and enkindled. How could any man who had been loved like that have forgotten her? Was the fellow mad? Or was he already dead and well out of the way?

"It was a pity you never told him about—about your trouble, Milly."

"I tried to spare him." At her voice, which was a mere thread of emotion, he turned to her quickly. "I never told him because I wanted him to have only happy memories. Even if he ceased to care, I wanted him to have only happy memories."

Looking at her, as she stood there in her youth and her despairing passion, which was the youngest thing, he reflected, about her, Mr. Littlepage reminded himself for the hundredth time that it was impossible for a man to understand women. The firm ones were necessarily less difficult to comprehend than the frail; but even the firm ones were not so easy to understand as they used to be. In the old days, Mr. Littlepage admitted, a man had only himself to blame if he did not soon discover at least where he stood with a woman. He thought of his father, a Virginia gentleman of Georgian morals but Victorian manners, who had found it less embarrassing to commit adultery than to pronounce the word in the presence of a lady. Well, it was fortunate, no doubt, that he had not survived the decorous nineteenth century. Certainly the conversation, if not the conduct, of the post-war age would have been the end of him. For the modern revolt, Mr. Littlepage was beginning to realize, was less immoral than experimental. The change was not merely a breaking away, as in the case of poor Aunt Agatha or even of Mrs. Dalrymple, from social conventions that one still respected and Sabbath observances in which one still believed. No, the saddest thing about Milly's past, he mused, was that she had been able to leave it so lightly behind her. Considered merely as the sort of impediment that had figured depressingly in *fin de siècle* drama, Milly's wild oats looked as small and almost as harmless as canary seed.

"If her life had not been spoiled, she would have made some man a fine wife," he meditated regretfully. Though he considered a passive attitude in love more feminine, and preferred an amiable softness to a tragic intensity, he felt that a man who was unacquainted with Mrs. Dalrymple might surrender to the sheer variety of Milly's charm. What a pity it was, indeed, to discover that charm is so often divorced from the cardinal virtues. What a pity it was that deserving characters, who made the most excellent wives by daylight, should be so frequently denied the magic that works best in darkness. There was, for example, Victoria's closest friend, Louisa Goddard, an admirable spinster, who would have made the reputation of any man she had chosen to marry. Tall, majestic, silver-haired, and as subdued in bosom as she was emphatic in gesture, Louisa was scarcely less distinguished than Mrs. Dalrymple—but with what a difference! He admired Louisa cordially; he even liked her, though she held what he still called "advanced opinions," and lectured upon the obscure morals of civilizations that have crumbled to dust and are therefore safe topics. Conspicuous in her youth for sound sense, a handsome figure, and discreet manners, she had developed an intrepid intellect in later years, and since the war she had discoursed publicly but prudently upon the more interesting theories of social reform. In this enterprise, to his mild astonishment, Victoria, who thought evil of no persons and of few reforms, supported her friend. "It is so important to look at these subjects from the right moral angle," his wife had explained with her usual generous simplicity, "and if there is a woman in Queenborough capable of doing this, surely it is Louisa." To-day, after a lecture upon the Morals of Babylon, Louisa, who was wealthy by inheritance but saving by constitution, would certainly drive home in Victoria's car. In common with other men Virginius admired frugality in woman almost as fervently as he respected chastity, and even when, as in the case of Louisa (who could never spend her income but refused to employ a chauffeur), economy approached the border of avarice, he felt that the fault was merely a defect in a sterling virtue. And what a mind she possessed! It was almost incredible, he had confided to Victoria after an informing talk with Louisa, how much you could learn about human depravity without vital contact with life. Not, of course, that she was ever indelicate. She was, on the contrary, refined enough in tone to satisfy Marmaduke, who had the fastidious taste in such matters of a confirmed libertine. That, Mr. Littlepage assured himself, was a reasonable explanation not only of Marmaduke's loose living but of his prolonged absence from the fleshpots of Europe. He was still hoping, with the sanguine temper peculiar, his brother had observed, to reformers and reprobates, that Louisa, who had refused him at twenty and thirty, would relent at fifty and supply him with a good and sufficient excuse for mending his habits.

IV

MILLY had slipped away while he meditated, and from the window a little later he watched her purple umbrella tossed about by the flying gusts in the street. How slender she looked against the driving rain! How slender and helpless and yet how determined! It was almost six years since she had first come to him, and in those years, though he deplored her liberal behaviour, he had become deeply attached to her. "I wonder if it is possible to be kind to a woman without growing fond of her?" he thought, for his mood was indulgent. Then, since there was still no sign of Victoria, he turned back to his chair and diverted his mind by moralizing upon Milly's unfortunate past. . . .

She had come to him on a stormy afternoon in that dreadful last winter of the war, while Victoria was divided between the Red Cross and an epidemic of influenza, and Mary Victoria was inspiring the American Army in France. Why, he wondered, was that winter fantastically associated in his mind with wild roses in water colour and snowy landscapes on satin sofa pillows? At the time Milly had barely recovered from influenza, and she was still suffering from poverty and frustrated desire. Yet he had felt her charm even then. He had felt her charm in spite of her thinness, her pallor, the heavy circles under her romantic eyes, and the pitiably neglected state of her clothes. After he had engaged her (for good typists, being of adventurous disposition, were scarcer than munition workers that winter), she had fainted from weakness, and he had felt strangely chivalrous and paternal. Not until spring had he discovered that her trouble was as real as her poverty; and by that time the war and contact with loose-living Europe had broadened the sympathies, or softened the moral fibre, of Queenborough. Was it really the war, he asked himself, that had at last loosened the bonds of tradition? Was it the haunting thought of Mary Victoria, lovely and alone, among the predatory males of Europe? Or was it the visit he had endured from a genteel lady in weeds, who broke to him in mournful accents that she was Milly's respectable but unhappy mother?

"I am sure I don't know where she gets her character, sir."

"It is easy to believe that, Mrs. Burden."

"She was always brought up as proper as proper."

"I am sure of it."

"I sent her to Sunday school as soon as she could lisp. I took her with me to church and to missionary societies and prayer meetings whenever I had a decent dress to put on. Those were the only amusements she ever had as a child, except sewing for one of the little converts in Africa. She never ran out at night like other girls, and it isn't my fault if she found there were wild sorts of pleasure. I declare I don't know what the world is coming to now, but it isn't as bad of course as if I had any cause to reproach myself. I've been a good mother, and I was a good wife, even if I wasn't treated as well as I ought to have been. However, I didn't hold that against Albert after he died. I've worn mourning for him now going on thirteen years or more."

Such, incredible as it sounded in memory, was the nature of Mrs. Burden's complaint. Though she had lived the

better part of three generations, she had remained mentally arrested in the God-fearing posture of evangelical
piety. Her long sallow face, hopelessly flattened out by
life, had worn an expression of resigned but uninspired
martyrdom. Above invisible eyebrows her yellowish-gray
hair was plastered down on her forehead, and her pale,
tight lips were as rigid, he had said to himself, as a
clothespin. That she should be Milly's mother had seemed
to him as incomprehensible as almost everything else in
the age. Drab features, drab voice, drab spirits. Estimable, in character, no doubt, estimable, but depressing
to any husband who had not lost the active instincts of a
vertebrate.

"I hope your daughter has been considerate of you," he
had remarked, with the sharp recoil every sentimentalist
feels in the presence of a repugnant fact.

"She ought to be, sir. I've done my duty by her, if I do
say it."

"I am sure she realizes that."

"You'd never know it if she does, sir. I sometimes think
she was born without family feeling, like her father before
her."

"Indeed!" Mr. Littlepage felt helpless, and wondered
why you could be so much more indulgent to human nature
when it was not in the room with you. At a reasonable distance, across the street for instance, he had felt compassionate toward Mrs. Burden, and had been disposed to
blame Milly for a deficiency in filial respect. "She seems
to be a warm-blooded girl," he had added impressively.

"She is where you don't expect it of her," Mrs. Burden
had sighed, while she sank dejectedly into her crape. "That
was her father's way too. He would always pass over the
persons who had a right to expect feeling from him and
fling himself away on somebody without the shadow of a

claim to his affection. And it has been the same with Milly. All this would never have happened if she had inherited a proper sense of duty."

"No, I suppose not. But is this young Welding the only one?"

"You'd think one was enough, sir, if you'd heard the way she took on when he went abroad. That was the first time I knew things were not what they should be between them. It wasn't until three months after he had sailed that I found out she'd gone wrong, and then I begged her on my bended knees to let me write and tell him what I thought of him. I'd have done it without asking her, but I knew if she ever suspected it, she would desert me just as her father did after I had him sent to gaol for his own good."

"Do you know whether she writes to this young man?"

Mrs. Burden had broken into eloquent tears. "Only cheerful letters, she says, only cheerful letters that won't make him reproach himself."

This was indeed a fresh point of view, and a questionable one even to the tolerant masculine mind. Modern, perhaps; yet he felt sure that Mary Victoria, who was as advanced as Milly though in an opposite direction, would have indignantly repudiated such moral evasion. In his youth reproach had been the natural, if by no means the only, weapon of pure womanhood, and he disliked seeing it discarded so easily by a girl who was, to put it mildly, no longer a shining honour to either sex. Still, since he was unpolemical by disposition, he had remarked gently:

"That seems an unfeminine attitude. What is her reason?"

"How do I know? She never tells me anything. When I question her, all she ever answers is that I have no right to interfere with her life. No right to interfere! If I haven't a right to interfere with her, is there anybody who has, sir?"

"Perhaps not. Well, it is a sad case, Mrs. Burden, a very sad case. You have my sympathy. I will talk to your daughter, though she will doubtless consider it an interference, and I will see what can be done for her."

What he could do proved to be, in the end, more than he had hoped, though scarcely less than he had expected. He had talked mildly but gravely to Milly that afternoon, and finding her tragic, mocking, and scornful of the conventions that he esteemed, he had surprised in his heart some deep pulsation of sympathy. Though he had been prepared to counsel the erring, he was soon bewildered not so much by Milly's unrepentant attitude as by the perilous response in his own nature. It was, he had recognized reluctantly, his duty to discharge her; and he had intended, after making suitable provision, to fulfil this moral obligation. For the sake of his other secretary, the impeccable Miss Dorset, for the sake of Victoria, for the sake of his own unsullied reputation, he told himself, it was undesirable that Milly should remain in his office. Several particulars, nevertheless, he had failed to consider. He had weighed respectability, but not human relations; genteel conduct he had taken for granted; but he had overlooked the fatal indulgence of the paternal heart, and the softening influence of a daughter who is as far away as the Balkans.

"Your mother has been to see me," he had begun sternly.

Light had rippled into Milly's changeable face, and it seemed to him that the sadness in her eyes sparkled with laughter. "I am sorry," she had answered mockingly, "I tried to spare you."

"She is greatly disturbed about you."

"Poor Mother. She is obliged to be disturbed about

something. If it isn't about me, it will be about public morals."

"You are making her unhappy."

"I don't make her so. She was born that way."

"She tells me," he had said severely, "that you have been very wild."

Though her voice was defiant when she answered, there was, he remembered, a springtime freshness in her eyes. "Well, we are all wild together, aren't we? There's murder in the air."

"I don't like your levity, Milly. In spite of your manner, I refuse to believe that you are incorrigible." So little, he reflected, had she resembled the proverbial lost woman that Goldsmith himself would scarcely have known her for what she was. It is true that her clothes had harmonized better with the institutional than the romantic idea of a life of sin. Her dress, he had observed, was cheap, faded, and carelessly worn, and her shoes had borne, to his attentive eye, every sign of having trodden the downward path. Touched by her evident poverty, Mr. Littlepage had thought of his daughter, and had felt his harshness dissolve. Many things had softened his heart, but most of all the memory of Mary Victoria as she had looked as a child. In the end, he had decided to reprimand Milly instead of washing his hands of her. Any good woman would have dismissed her without regret; but men, he mused now, pricked by a sensation of guilt, are softer by nature—or is it merely more brittle?

"She tells me you are in trouble," he had said.

"I suppose she would call it that," Milly had retorted, with the flippancy he feared and expected.

"What do you call it?" How unfeminine she was beneath that perverse gaiety!

"I haven't had it long enough to know. I may call it trouble, too, before it is over."

"Why didn't you marry him, Milly?"

"How could I when we hadn't any money and there was Mother to look after?"

"If you couldn't marry him, why didn't you wait?"

An inward storm had darkened her eyes. "I have a right to my life."

No lady of the nineteenth century, neither poor Aunt Agatha, who had been completely crushed, nor Mrs. Dalrymple, who had been merely tarnished, by betrayal, would have asserted an inalienable right to her life. Yet this fantastic notion appeared to be the solitary principle that modern youth was willing to embrace. Even Mary Victoria, who would have been an inspiring example in any period, had taken a firm stand in defense of her natural right to do as she pleased. The difference appeared to be that, while Milly was satisfied with the right to her own life, Mary Victoria demanded, from the purest motives, the right of moral encroachment upon the lives of others. Had duty, which in his youth meant violence to his appetite, become to-day merely a label for unbridled impulse?

"As long as you know what you want most, what do you ever get by waiting?" Milly had asked, turning upon him the unembarrassed scrutiny with which her intrepid age regarded vital statistics. "Look at Mother. She waited for Father until she had dried up to a husk. Of course, if you aren't in love," she added presently, "it is different. But, if you are in love, then you know that nothing else really matters."

He had looked at her attentively. Was there, after all, something more than selfishness in Milly's outlook on life? Unfortunate as her lapse from virtue appeared, he could

not deny that she wore the confident air which makes a
settled point of view more respectable than a vagrant
emotion. Independence of character had acquired, on the
surface at least, all the lustre he associated with conversion from sin. It was impossible to imagine Milly
either crushed like poor Aunt Agatha or tarnished like
Mrs. Dalrymple. In demanding the right to sin she had,
he told himself disconsolately, elevated an improper act
into a mistaken theory of conduct. Was not this, after all,
the superior advantage attained by the present vocal
generation over the reticent feminine mode of the 'nineties? To reduce behaviour to a formula, however wanton,
appeared miraculously to invest it with the dignity of an
intellectual habitation and a name.

"I refuse to argue with you, Milly," he had said sternly.
"I can only tell you that you have opened the door to
regret."

He had expected contradiction, but she had astonished
him, after a thoughtful pause, by a gesture of agreement.
"Oh, well, I should have regretted either way, shouldn't
I? I am always regretting things. But the regret for what
you have had doesn't last nearly so long as the regret for
what you have missed. Life isn't forever. What is the fun
of dying before you have lived?"

"The trouble is that you have learned nothing from the
past—nothing from the experience of other women."

"From Mother, you mean?"

"Not only from your mother, but from all women
everywhere. You have set out to demolish conventions
before you have tested them."

Her eyes had mocked him. "But you have tested them,
haven't you? And where have they led you? Could anything that we do or think end in a greater calamity? No,
we'll have to learn the truth for ourselves. Nothing that

the older generation can tell us will do any good. We refuse to accept your theories because we saw them all break to pieces. The truth is we are determined to think for ourselves and to make our own sort of ideals. Even if everything you say to me is true, I shouldn't consent to take my experience from you second-hand. I want to find out for myself. I want the freedom to live my life as I please. I want to choose the things I believe in. . . ."

Delusion? Sophistry? Or the simple moonstruck folly of youth? Is it possible to reason, he had asked himself helplessly, with frustrated desire? Useless to argue. Useless either to advise or admonish. Since he was as generous as he was tolerant, what could he do but invoke the forsaken ideal of chivalry and protect her, as far as he was able, from the errors of her own undisciplined heart?

V

THE wind whipped a spray of rain in his face, and through the scattering mist he distinguished the fine presence of Louisa Goddard in the back of the car. A handsome woman, notwithstanding her years, with stiffly waved gray hair, a high flush in her thin cheeks, and the sharpened nose that so often accompanies virginity. Why, he speculated idly as he made his way to the car, could not virginity preserve the figures of spinsters without sharpening their noses? Yet, in spite of her aquiline features, Louisa was more attractive, he admitted, than she had been as a girl. She was one of those rare women who improve with age and become active instead of apathetic as they grow older. Gray hair, which he disliked as heartily as most men, had done a great deal, he acknowledged reluctantly, for her appearance, while the lecture platform, which he disliked even more than most men, had done quite as much for her manner. Behind the footlights, she had acquired the courage of an evangelist and the attitudes of a Shakespearian actress.

As he entered the car, she leaned forward, and he met her lively hazel eyes behind the rimless glasses which, he had decided, were becoming as long as she did not expect him to kiss her.

"Where is Victoria?" he asked when he had taken her gloved hand. "Has anything happened?"

Louisa shook her head, and the light flickered from her

glasses to the reddened tip of her nose. "She was not feeling well. She has gone home to lie down before Mary Victoria comes."

"Not well? I am sorry. She overtaxes her strength."

"Yes, she never considers herself. It is impossible to make her remember that she isn't so strong as she used to be. She has never been the same since that attack of pneumonia."

While Louisa responded, he looked at her gravely and wondered where her conversation was leading. Like so many women who have missed romantic happiness, she was extravagantly fond, he felt indulgently, of minor mysteries. With her bright flush, which had come with middle age, her lively glance, and her vivacious expression, she appeared to carry her years bravely. Beneath her small black velvet hat, with the new high crown, which she wore slightly tilted, the scalloped line of her hair gleamed like polished silver. She dressed better than Victoria did and on less money; but, then, he had long ago decided that unattached women or widows, however afflicted, always manage to dress better than matrons. Singular as it was, he had noticed that the less reason women have for keeping up an appearance, the more time and energy they lavish upon the effort. Take widow's weeds, for example. What garments, especially what bonnets, could be more fetching, more coquettish even, than the ones Mrs. Dalrymple had worn in her bereavement? Yet she had been genuinely distressed, he knew. Her heart, as she had so often assured him, was buried in Peter Dalrymple's grave. Only she had not buried her dark eyes and her amber hair behind the flowing crape of her veil. He could still see the way her widow's ruche had intensified the brightness of her hair, the velvet dusk of her eyes, and the bloom of her lips. Twelve years

ago, and yet—and yet—— Well, she was back in Queenborough again for the first time since the war. A little
tarnished, perhaps. Not ruined, of course, like poor Aunt
Agatha (we were not living in the 'seventies, thank God!),
but still a trifle damaged by the unsavoury, or at least
indelicate, character of her past. . . .

Sadly but firmly dismissing the subject, he turned back
to Louisa, who was still occupied, he could see, with her
mystery. Whatever it was, he decided after a minute,
she was equally competent to discuss or dispose of it. Had
it anything to do, he asked anxiously, with Victoria? Or
was it merely one of those unpleasant moral dilemmas
that beset the slippery paths of philanthropists? In
Louisa's youth, while Marmaduke courted her with all
the ardour exacted by that romantic period, Virginius
had wondered at the fascination she exercised. There
was, he had thought, and his mother had agreed with
him, something masculine in her prominent features
and her pronounced opinions upon public affairs. Thirty-
one years ago, he meditated sorrowfully, neither prominent features nor pronounced opinions in women commanded admiration from the opposite sex. How much
of Marmaduke's long faithfulness was owing, Mr.
Littlepage had once asked himself, to that truculent
temperament which keeps the artist in perpetual conflict
with destiny? But in the last few years, and especially in
the years since the war, he had realized that, after all,
there are attractions more enduring, if less delightful,
than physical charm. There is, he admitted, with all the
distaste of a chivalrous mind, the pleasure afforded by an
intelligent interest in life. Though he was inclined to regard any spinster as a being blighted by fate, he
was obliged to acknowledge that Louisa had attained the
perfect sophistication which finds social misdemeanours

less exciting than the imponderable sins of psychology. He glanced at her composed features (it was a pity that the tip of her nose reddened so easily in cold weather), and from her features to her flat bosom, firmly encased, beneath her sealskin coat, in moral principle. Yes, decidedly a sterling character. A trifle dictatorial, to be sure, and frigid, no doubt, in temperament. Only by regarding Louisa as frigid in temperament could he explain her old rejection of Marmaduke, who had been a promising suitor in the 'nineties, before he lost his leg and adopted the French view of sex. Yet, in her case at least, frigidity had not, apparently, interfered with enjoyment of life. At fifty-odd (he was not sure of her exact age) she was the happiest and the most industrious woman of his acquaintance.

Turning suddenly, she leaned toward him with an alert birdlike movement, as if she were about to peck at a succulent morsel. While he waited patiently enough he hoped that she was not occupied with the mouldy problems of Babylon; for, though he preferred ancient history to modern, he disliked and resented the platform manner in women. Victoria, the perfect wife, reformed by inspiration alone; but Louisa, who possessed a more active mind, undertook to do so by both example and precept.

"I hope I didn't keep you waiting," she began crisply, as if she were determined to overlook anything that he had said.

"Well, a little while, but I left off working earlier than usual. I dare say I am impatient. Mary Victoria doesn't come home every day from the Balkans."

Louisa smiled. "Victoria says that Mary Victoria is the romance of your life."

"That is because Victoria forgets herself," he returned gallantly.

"Yes, that is just what I said to her. I told her also that she ought to be the one to prepare you."

"To prepare me?" From the bottom of his masculine soul he hated mysteries and disliked having them broken to him.

"Victoria was not feeling well, but the real reason she went home straight from the club was to have the blue guest room put in order."

"The blue guest room? Isn't Mary Victoria's old room big enough to hold her and her Balkan decorations?"

"We thought so yesterday. But while Victoria was at the club, she talked over the telephone with Curle in New York. It seems that Mary Victoria is bringing a surprise with her. She is not alone."

"Not alone? Has she adopted a war orphan?" Though he spoke in stolid tones, he wondered if Louisa could fail to hear the fluttering sound of his heart. For the war, as he assured himself, was well over, and even in Queenborough, war orphans had diminished in public esteem. It was, of course, conceivable that Mary Victoria's orphan was not only indigent but of royal descent. Such a combination, he had heard, was far from unusual in the countries in which she had exercised her benevolence. But, even so, he was inclined to think that the blue guest room, which Victoria had recently had done over at great expense, was too good for a refugee.

Louisa raised her lashes and studied him with her sympathetic, amused, and faintly ironic expression.

"It isn't an orphan, Virginius," she answered slowly, while the lively hazel of her eyes softened and darkened, "though I confess that would have astonished me less when you consider all the thousands of them she must have held in her arms. You never," she added reproachfully, "did justice to Mary Victoria's wonderful work with her orphanage."

"If it isn't an orphan, then—well——" He looked at her imploringly. "It isn't a Russian, Louisa?" For it seemed to him that, whatever the sex or parentage of Mary Victoria's surprise, he could bear anything better than its being a Russian.

"Oh, no, Virginius." Louisa, who had a masculine sense of humour, was actually laughing. "What an imagination you have! No, it isn't any kind of orphan, my dear friend, though I am not sure that mightn't be better. It is a husband."

"A husband!" As he gasped out the word, he felt that the worst he had expected would have been better than this. "A husband and a refugee?"

Louisa shook her head. Her manner was as composed as ever, and it occurred to him resentfully that she was enjoying the sensation she created. "There isn't but one, and I didn't say he was a refugee, even a left-over one. No, Mary Victoria might sympathize with refugees, but she is hardly the kind of girl to marry one."

"Tell me all." The words were swept out on a sigh of relief. "Don't break anything to me. Nothing can be so bad as suspense."

Though he could see that she was disappointed, she was too human at the core to resist his appeal. "As well as I can understand she has been interested in this young man for several years. It was all very confused over the telephone, and you can imagine what a shock it was to Victoria. But she is quite positive that Curle said it wasn't a recent affair. It seems they were married five, or maybe it was four, months ago."

"Four months ago, and she never told us a word of it!"

"I suppose there must have been what seemed to her a good reason. Anyhow, Curle says he is not at all bad-looking and seems to have a mind of his own. Mary Victoria met him first, several years ago, in a hospital. He was, Curle said, in a terrible state when she found him, though he had not apparently lost his appearance. Besides, Mary Victoria feels that she saved his life—and you can understand what that would mean to a high-minded girl."

"You haven't told me his name." Fear was crawling round his thoughts like a caterpillar on the edge of a leaf.

"Well, Victoria took that more to heart than anything else. I mean his coming from Queenborough and our never having heard of him. However, as I told her, that makes very little difference to-day when few people can afford to marry into the best families because they are all so impoverished. Blood is the last thing I'd think about, and, after all, he is so obscure that he may have descended from a Colonial governor."

"You haven't told me his name," he repeated, and there was the rasping sound of suspense in his voice.

"Welding. Martin Welding." She paused to drive it in, and then added brightly, "I am sure it has a very distinguished sound. There used to be a family of that name in the Northern Neck, and even if he doesn't belong to them—well, sound is really more important to-day than anything else, except, of course, money, which he doesn't appear to possess."

Mr. Littlepage breathed with difficulty. Was it possible, he wondered, collecting his faculties, that he was on the point of having a stroke? "I don't care about the family," he rejoined presently. "I don't care about the money—damn it! I beg your pardon, Louisa, I must have forgotten myself. But—but this is worse than anything I imagined. Mary Victoria had no right. She must have

known, or at least suspected the truth——" He broke off
and choked back his words, arrested by the thought that
Louisa was ignorant, unless Victoria had told her, of poor
Milly's disaster.

"The truth, Virginius?"

A feeling of prostration, of inexpressible futility,
rushed over him. What an unfair advantage life could
take of the young, of the poor, of the generous in heart!
That Mary Victoria, his own daughter, his noble, earnest,
high-minded daughter, so eager to sacrifice herself in
[what now appeared to him as an inaccurate and abomi-
nable phrase], world service—that Mary Victoria should
have been involved in this moral catastrophe! "That is the
young man I asked her to make inquiries about in Paris,"
he said thickly. "I know very little about him, but the little
I know I dislike."

"You mean that there is something to his discredit?"

"Decidedly." He felt that mute rage would strangle
him.

"I hope it is nothing about a woman," Louisa observed,
with a competent air. "I hate discreditable things in con-
nection with women."

For a moment Mr. Littlepage hesitated; then indignation triumphed over prudence. "I happen to know that
he was—well, deeply interested in another young woman
before he was sent to France."

"Not a girl we know?"

"Well, not a girl you know."

"But a good girl?"

"That depends upon what you mean." There were
moments when Louisa exasperated him.

"I mean a moral one."

"I take that for granted." He hesitated, and then added
firmly, "Yes, she is a good girl."

Though he knew that Louisa had one of the kindest
hearts in the world, he resented her unaffected enjoyment
of picturesque scandal. "I suppose I oughtn't to have told
her," his legal instinct admonished, "but I can't help it
if my temper gets the better of my caution once in a blue
moon." Horror had fastened upon him, and not horror
alone, but an anguish of indignation and pity. He knew
now that Victoria was right when she said that his daughter had been the romance of his life. In his misery he heard
the beating of the rain on the closed windows of the car,
and it seemed to him that it was the sound of an inward
desolation which flooded his soul. Through the November
dusk there flashed now and then, like a sinister warning,
the headlights of a car, or the wet gleam on the rubber
coat of a policeman. He had almost forgotten that Louisa
was still beside him when she broke into his reverie with
one of her pointed questions.

"Do you mean that he was engaged to her?"

"I couldn't mean anything less."

As she leaned toward him with an emphatic gesture,
her rimless glasses dropped from her nose and he looked
straight into the unsullied depths of her eyes. "Virginius,
this is very serious," she said in an urgent voice.

"Yes, I suppose it is—or it would have been considered
so when I was young."

"At all costs we must keep it from Mary Victoria.
After all, she is my godchild and I feel that I share your
responsibility."

"Perhaps she knows." He didn't mean that, not really,
he told himself, but Louisa's suppressed excitement ruffled
his nerves.

"Not Mary Victoria! Can you imagine her taking a
man away from another woman?"

"No, I cannot. But you must remember that she has

spent five years in Europe. They do things differently in Europe."

Louisa assented brightly as if she enjoyed it. "You can't go over every summer without discovering that." Holding her glasses in the tips of her fingers, she firmly replaced them on her nose. "I feel, however," she continued presently, while she straightened the platinum chain studded with seed pearls which she wore attached by a gold safety pin to her bosom, "that Mary Victoria is superior to any temptation."

With this he was in sympathetic accord. "Yes, she takes after her mother."

Louisa's face softened and flushed, as it always did when she spoke of Victoria. Even as children they had been inseparable, and marriage, which destroys so many earnest friendships, had only sealed their devotion into an indestructible bond. While most of Mr. Littlepage's intimate associations with men had gradually weakened and melted away, it seemed to him at times that Louisa had been drawn into his marriage and had become a central part of his placid life with Victoria. Though he had always admired rather than enjoyed her, he respected her talent for making herself indispensable in a crisis. At the birth of every child Louisa had sat all night, without unfastening a button, near the foot of Victoria's bed, ready, at the nurse's fateful whisper, to fetch whatever was needed or telephone for the physician. It was Louisa who had brought him the news of his first son, and it was Louisa who had murmured to him the inspiring name "Mary Victoria." She had been near at birth, and she was nearer still when death had taken, first two of his children, and then his father, whom he had worshipped, and Victoria's mother, whom he had esteemed and disliked. It was impossible to think of his children without remember-

ing the mornings when, still erect and trim in appearance,
Louisa had poured his coffee, while Victoria looked more
virginal than ever beneath the sky-blue canopy over her
bed. It was impossible even to recall the house of mourning without a grateful memory of Louisa's capable dealing
with funerals. As she grew older, it is true, her interest
in what she called "the new psychology" became tedious
to his imperfect sophistication. "Poor Louisa," he had
once sighed to Victoria. "If she ever falls from virtue how
disappointed she will be to find that there is so little in it."

The car had reached his door, and Louisa, thrilled by
the secret between them, was urging him to let her go
alone to the station while he waited at home with Victoria.
"Victoria needs you," she reminded him impressively.
"There are things that you ought to talk over together
before you see Mary Victoria. After all," she repeated in
a faintly sepulchral tone, "I am her godmother, and she is
almost as dear to me as she is to you."

In the beginning he had resisted; but it was useless to
oppose Louisa when she had definitely made up her mind.
"Perhaps you are right," he admitted at last. "I confess
it has been a blow to me. Maybe I'd better get braced up
a bit."

"You are very sensible, Virginius." From her manner no
one would have suspected that the suggestion had come
from her. "It is much better to accustom yourself to the
idea before you see Mary Victoria with her husband. If
I go alone to meet them, you and Victoria will have time
to collect yourselves and arrange your plans. Since you
have confided to me what you know of this young man, I
feel more strongly than ever that you should have time
for discussion."

He looked at her keenly. "Is it necessary to tell Victoria
this? I spoke imprudently to you."

She looked hurt but magnanimous. "Not to me, Virginius. You could not speak imprudently to me." Then, after a thoughtful pause, she added with gentle sagacity, "No, it is not necessary to tell Victoria, but it will be natural."

"You mean I can't keep a secret?"

"I mean you can't keep that kind of secrēt."

"Victoria has high ideals."

"All of us have high ideals, my dear friend. There aren't any low ones."

Cool, composed, mistress of herself and her destiny, she drove on and left him gazing after her more in respect than admiration. Yes, Louisa was a brick; and if like all other bricks, whether they are composed of baked clay or valiant dust, she was deficient in charm, he could not, he decided, as he ascended the baronial steps of his house, imagine a well-regulated world that existed without her.

VI

FORTY years ago, the Brooke mansion, as it was respectfully called, embodied all the culture to be derived from a fortune safely invested in Northern securities. Built by old Silas Woolley, who had died in the comfort of his shirt-sleeves, the dwelling had passed to his granddaughter, Victoria Brooke. As a young husband, Mr. Littlepage had been proud of living in a house that was pointed out to visitors as "the finest example of improved Colonial." After all, "improved Colonial" may mean anything, even Victorian gloom, if one is sufficiently liberal in one's ideas. Unhappily, the malice of the years, which is so often diverted by architecture, had subdued the innocent pleasure with which Virginius had once regarded the imposing façade. Nothing, however, could impair his respect for the refined taste and unerring tact of his wife, who appeared to have inherited only her fortune and her house from her grandfather. "It is nonsense to pretend that blood is a match for money in the second generation," Mr. Littlepage mused. "Notwithstanding an ancestor in the Susan Constant, to say nothing of a Colonial governor and a British general thrown in, I am raw material when you compare me with old Silas Woolley's granddaughter."

In the spacious hall, which he never entered without the feeling that he comprised a whole invading army, he found his elder son, Duncan, a dark, morose, and inscrutable young man. In France, where he had served with ardour in the last year of the war, Duncan had lost not only his health, but all the amiable pretenses which had made life supportable. Even the armistice, which had left so many relief workers unsatisfied, had come too late to save him from that singular French decadence which only the Latin mind is able to find piquant. At thirty, he was as cynical as Marmaduke, and far more depressing. For Marmaduke's cynicism, however unwholesome, preserved the Attic salt that imparts a relish to the stalest philosophy. But, after all, Marmaduke was past sixty, and at sixty it is possible to disbelieve in life and love and yet find them amusing. Though Duncan was as trying in the house as other philosophers, Mr. Littlepage preferred his nocturnal moods to the morning brightness of Curle. Even as a baby Curle had annoyed him by his inordinate zest for living. Nothing, not even his first tooth, had been able to dampen his spirits; and he had actually appeared to enjoy teething almost as much as he enjoyed a world war some twenty-odd years later.

"Have you seen your mother?" Mr. Littlepage inquired with an anxious frown.

Duncan turned on him a long sallow face, which was good-looking in a saturnine fashion. "You look as if you'd heard of Mary Victoria's final reform."

"I am very much distressed, my son."

"What did you expect? We can't have a world war every day."

"If you take that tone, Duncan, I cannot discuss it."

"I am sorry, sir." There were occasions when Duncan dropped back, whether from reverence or ridicule his father had never discovered, into the ceremonial usages of the past. "I was hoping you would look at it philosophically. After all, as Curle remarks so accurately, everything might have been worse. It might have been, considering Mary Victoria's thoroughness, a whole asylum instead of a husband."

"I cannot understand why she married him."

"Perhaps she wanted to make an honest man of him."

"I must repeat, my son, that your tone is offensive."

"Oh, I beg your pardon, Dad. I didn't mean to be offensive. I was merely trying to be cheerful."

"You needn't. God knows I get enough of that from Curle."

"Mother has had a little too much of it, I imagine, over the telephone. Poor Mother! If only she could realize that life isn't spent either in Heaven or Hell, but in the sultry isthmus of Purgatory!"

"I am sorry she took the message. Do you know what Curle told her?"

"She was too agitated to repeat it, but it seems to have been hopeful enough to depress her."

"Yes, it will go hard with her. She expected so much of Mary Victoria."

Duncan smiled in derision. "Well, she got a little more than she expected."

"All of us aren't so cynical, my son. You must remember that your mother, like most good women, is an idealist. My father used to say there is only one thing more incorrigible than an idealist, and that is a predestinarian."

"You'd think the war would have cured anybody, even those who were so unfortunate as to be left out of it."

Mr. Littlepage smiled sadly. "Well, you must try to pity rather than censure the old fogies who still believe that anything makes a difference. After all, as Marmaduke will tell you, if there were no ideals there would be nothing left for us to kill each other about."

"There's no need to tell me. You'd better tell Mother and Aunt Louisa." The children had been brought up to call Louisa "aunt."

"Well, we needn't argue about that. What we must do now is to help your mother bear a great disappointment."

This time it was Duncan who smiled, though he was, as his father said to himself, in no smiling mood. "It seems to me, sir, that the one who really needs help is this poor devil of a husband. Do you know anything of him?"

"Very little, and that little, I am sorry to say, is not to his credit. But we must try to suspend judgment."

"Well, that sounds encouraging. I didn't know Mary Victoria had so much human nature."

"Your jesting is in bad taste. Where is your mother?"

"I left her in her bedroom a few minutes ago. Poor Mother! She would find life so much more livable if she could only give up being happy."

"She couldn't, Duncan, even if she wanted to. It is more than her religion, it is her very nature to keep hoping for the best and trying to make the world better. Think of all she must have suffered with you in the army, Curle in a training camp, and Mary Victoria in the Balkans. That must have tried not only her faith but her cheerfulness."

"Yes, I suppose that turned her optimism into a nervous habit. I sometimes think the muscles of her face have never relaxed since the war."

"You can't blame her for that. It wasn't easy to keep smiling."

"But why the devil did you have to keep smiling? What is there so heroic in pretending the world is what it isn't? It's like the everlasting Holy Rolling of American politics. That's what makes me sick about Curle."

"Don't be too hard on your brother. The noise he makes may be only a whistling to keep up his courage."

There was a sneering note in Duncan's rejoinder. "Well, if he doesn't look out, he will whistle himself into office. He is as average as a President."

"Curle keeps up with the procession, my son, and we do not. Even though we may object to his special brand of democracy, we cannot deny that he is one of the men who are responsible for our whole march of progress."

Duncan laughed almost naturally. "Yes, I'm ready to admit that. By the way, Mother doesn't wish us to drink anything more cheering than grape juice at dinner. She hopes, for the first night, anyway, until she has had a chance to inform herself about the habits of Mary Victoria's husband, that you will follow Curle's example and turn your back when you drink."

A cloud passed without settling over Mr. Littlepage's genial features. "Well, join me in the library before dinner," he responded gloomily; and reflected that he could forgive Victoria all the good she had ever done him if only she would occasionally appear to be in the wrong.

"Thank you, sir, but it seems to me a trifle hard on the poor devil. All I can hope is that he has been prudent enough to provide against our habit of reforming everybody but ourselves."

Turning away, with the uncomfortable sensation that Duncan was more than a match for him, Mr. Littlepage ascended the wide staircase and entered the very simple and expensive bedroom he shared with Victoria. From the portrait of one of his least prudish ancestresses by Sir Peter Lely, which hung over the Adam mantelpiece, to the delicate acanthus leaves on the fluted posts of the twin beds, and the flowered brocade of the Duncan Phyfe sewing-stand, the room had always impressed him as being, in some extraordinary fashion, less real than it appeared on the surface.

When he entered, Victoria, who had slipped into a tea-gown of violet velvet, turned her cheek for his kiss with her usual wifely composure. Though she had lost long ago her virginal loveliness, she had ripened at middle age into a handsome and fruitful-looking woman. Her complexion was still fine in texture, but she flushed easily and there were tiny clusters of veins in her smooth round cheeks. In the last year, after her severe illness, her brown hair had begun to turn gray in patches, while her limpid eyes had been ruffled by a look of apprehension—or was it merely a startled wonder at life? What she had never lost, what she could never lose, he felt, as long as she remained herself, was the expression of unselfish goodness that quivered in an edge of light about her pale full lips and imparted firmness and nobility to her features.

"I suppose Louisa told you," she began, while she lifted her arms to fasten a necklace of amethysts. Her hair, which was thick and soft but without lustre, was piled high on the crown of her head after a fashion of the early 'nineties.

"Yes, she told me, but I could scarcely believe my ears," he answered in a discouraged tone. He saw at once that she had been weeping, and though, like most other men, he resented tears when they were shed in earnest, he was touched by the sight of Victoria's reddened eyelids. "It must have been a shock to you," he continued, kissing her again with deeper tenderness but diminished enthusiasm. "Curle ought to have telephoned me first."

"He tried to, but you were in that conference. I wish you could have met them."

"I am not sure that I do. It seems to me just a little too much."

A sob quivered in Victoria's voice. "I could have believed it of anybody sooner than of Mary Victoria."

"Well, what was her excuse?" he broke out indignantly. "Why did she do it?"

"We'll never know unless she tells us. In another girl I should call it an infatuation. But Mary Victoria! Can you imagine Mary Victoria infatuated?"

"Things happen every day that I cannot imagine."

"Not things like this. Not to girls like Mary Victoria."

"Don't you suppose every parent must feel that way?"

"It isn't feeling only, Virginius. Think of Mary Victoria's record for world service. Think of all her independent work in the Balkans. Think of the way she refused to desert those friendless orphans after the war."

"Oh, world service!" he groaned, and felt that the syllables smacked of hypocrisy. "After all, even the best war records do not make good peace programmes," he continued presently. "And I prefer, on the whole, not to think of the Balkans."

"You don't mean to imply that Mary Victoria has been unsettled in—in . . ." The question, which had begun bravely enough, trailed off to a whisper.

"Well, I shouldn't be too sure of anything to-day, not even of my own daughter. I don't mean, of course, that her moral principle has been undermined. It would take more than an idea, it would take an axe, to undermine Mary Victoria's principles. Still she has been subjected to long contact with the Balkan temperament . . ."

"I am positive," Victoria insisted gently, "that no amount of immorality could shake Mary Victoria's ideals. What disturbs me is the thought that this young man may have worked upon the child's nobler impulses."

"Yes, I've thought of that." He appeared anxious and distressed, as indeed he was. "But it seems fairer to suspend judgment."

At this Victoria beamed upon him with more than wifely sweetness. "You couldn't be unfair, Virginius, if you tried," she responded, which was, Mr. Littlepage felt, as much as any husband has a right to expect. "Yes, it is more charitable to suspend judgment. And we must remember," she concluded in a brighter tone, "that whatever his past has been, he will have a wonderful influence in Mary Victoria."

In the severe discipline of marriage Mr. Littlepage had cultivated the habit of looking at his wife without seeing her. It was only in those rare intervals when his evasive idealism was transfixed by the sharp flash of reality that he perceived how time—or was it marriage? —had altered his vision. The wonder of it, he felt, while the actual Victoria stood imprisoned between the pointed beams of fancy and fact, was that he could ever, even in the flower of her girlhood, have found her exciting. That he had fallen in love with her features was less astonishing to-day than that he was once interested in her opinions. Even now he could see that she was one of those women who might still be beautiful if they had less confidence in the fidelity of their husbands. But her mind, which must have matured with years, could scarcely have been more interesting at twenty than it was at fifty. To be sure, he found himself insisting, she had been a perfect wife to him, and as a husband rather than a human being, he was still faithful, he was even devoted. Was it merely, he asked himself, that he had grown older and more settled in spirit? Yet there were moments in spring and autumn, when he was still young enough to feel that a thwarted buccaneer ranged in his soul, while the quiet air about him was charged with the bloom of the wild grape or the magic of drying vines. And in these moments, before this frail rapture broke, he would grasp again the perilous illusion of desire without end.

"I've had the two guest rooms put in order," Victoria was saying, for her practical mind could always find comfort in the details of living. "I couldn't bear the idea of putting a strange man in Mary Victoria's room."

He remembered the care with which she had just had her daughter's room papered and painted in ivory. Only yesterday she had shown him the yellow organdie curtains and the sea-blue glazed chintz for the furniture. After all, it was harder on Victoria, he told himself, because she had no outside profession into which she could retreat.

"Well, perhaps she is used to him by now," he remarked with gentle derision. "We are in danger of forgetting that he is her husband, not ours."

On her dressing-table, in an oval frame of ivory, there was a miniature of Mary Victoria, which her mother had had painted in Florence. Crossing the room, he studied the prim little features and the tight auburn curls gathered back above the delicately arched eyebrows and fastened by the familiar bow of blue ribbon. The nose and chin were firm for a child, and the lovely slate-coloured eyes were too serious for laughter. Yes, it was impossible to deny that Mary Victoria's character was as humourless as her war record. "Marmaduke is right," Mr. Littlepage thought dejectedly, "our lack of genuine gaiety was proved even before we invented the pompous farce of prohibition. No civilization with a true sense of humour could afford to take so seriously the feminine instinct and throw to the winds the gay masculine devil of compromise."

"This is the hardest blow we've ever had from one of

our children," Victoria was saying. "Even Duncan, with his unsound views, has never distressed me so much."

"What did Curle say to you?"

"Oh, he spoke as if it were a pleasant surprise. You know how Curle is."

"Yes, I know," he assented with weariness.

"I asked him how it had happened, and he said that Mary Victoria had saved this young man's life. As if that were a sufficient reason for marrying him."

"It might be for Mary Victoria. Most women seem to feel that way; but it is unfortunate that there are so many worthless lives to be saved. It is nothing less than a criminal assault upon the law of the Survival of the Fittest."

"Don't be flippant, Virginius. It isn't a laughing matter."

"I was never more serious, my dear."

"Your tone doesn't sound like it. Curle said that Martin Welding called her his good angel. I suppose he was speaking the truth."

"No doubt. Gordon Crabbe, you remember, called her that also. Think how desperately we opposed that marriage; yet God may have known best if only we had not interfered."

"Even disappointment, Virginius, will not excuse levity. Besides, that marriage would have taken Mary Victoria to Africa. Anything, it seems to me, is better than that."

"I am not sure. At least Gordon Crabbe had a fine character and came of good stock."

"Well, she never cared about family."

"I know. She is like Curle." If he had uttered his entire thought, he might have added, "After all, what are the Woolleys?" but it was not for nothing, he reflected, that he had bridled his inquiring mind in the early days of the Browning class. Moreover, prudence warned him that no

American stock is common enough to be plebeian to its descendants. So he said merely, "Louisa went to the station."

"I sometimes wonder what we should do without her. She is so helpful in trouble."

He looked with distrust at the ornamental clock on the mantelpiece, and then drew out his watch. "They ought to be here now any minute. If you have nothing more to suggest, I think I'll brace myself with a highball. Duncan has warned me that there will be grape juice for dinner. It's a pity that I happen to be expecting my bootlegger this evening."

"Oh, Virginius, can't you manage to put him off?"

"It isn't easy to catch him, you know. But there isn't the slightest cause for anxiety. Socially, you must remember, he is more presentable than a parson. Have you forgotten that he is both a college graduate and a member of one of the oldest families in the Tidewater?"

Victoria gazed at him sadly but without reproach. All the more prominent pillars of the society in which she lived supported the institution of bootlegging; and custom, which breaks laws and makes morality, had reconciled her law-abiding instincts to this ubiquitous lawlessness.

"I must have an opportunity to talk to Mary Victoria. If drinking should be his weakness, surely you would not wish to subject him to temptation?"

"Surely not. But in that case we'd be prudent to turn him over to Marmaduke."

"If only you would treat serious subjects seriously, Virginius! Of course what I said was merely a surmise. Only —only——"

"I know, my dear, and after Marmaduke there must

be the deluge. However, this young man isn't expected to live with us, is he?"

"I hope not, but we must consider Mary Victoria. I can't tell anything until I have had a long talk with her."

"Then the best thing I can do is to keep out of it." Turning away with a sigh, he was enveloped immediately, it seemed to him, in the colourless atmosphere of an existence that he led without desire, without even volition.

VII

WITH outstretched arms and the smile of an eager but doubtful lover, Mr. Littlepage watched Mary Victoria float toward him on the drifts of rain between the two fire-coloured maples. His first thought was, "She is lovelier than I remembered her"; his second, "And happy! I have never seen her so happy." Had he really forgotten the direct carriage, the radiant energy of her figure, the dovelike grace of her small head, with its wings of bright auburn hair, the tranquil beauty of her pure and resolute features, the cool, serene depths of her gray eyes? As she melted into his arms, another idea sprang from confusion into vacancy. "She is her mother all over again, only there's more of her." More of her not only in height and beauty, but in character, in determination, and in moral purpose.

"Dear Father!" She kissed him tenderly before she drew away with a gesture of pride and protection. "This is Martin, my husband. I wanted to bring him to you as a surprise, but Curle insisted upon telephoning Mother this morning."

When she passed on to her mother, Mr. Littlepage reluctantly held out his hand to his son-in-law. Not a bad-looking chap, he repeated to himself, while he struggled in vain to think of some phrase that would sound adequate when spoken aloud. To his dismay, a single rebellious sentence drummed passionately in his mind, and he heard

over and over the question, "Why did you betray Milly
Burden?" Well, he could scarcely, at the very beginning
of their acquaintance, make the single inquiry that he
felt to be of vital significance. Men, he reflected, especially
men who were Southern gentlemen, had long ago agreed
to refrain among themselves from embarrassing questions. Interrogation, like reproach, was one of the minor
perquisites attached to the otherwise dubious privilege
of being a lady. A little later, upon a more appropriate
occasion, the question might proffer itself uninvited. A
little later—but not now, not in this first glorious hour of
Mary Victoria's return. While these thoughts spun rather
than slipped into his mind, he gazed, in a silence that he
tried to make hospitable, at the flat dark hair, the pallid
and somewhat too pointed features, and the burning hazel
eyes of the man whom Mary Victoria had chosen out of a
whole world, or at least a whole continent, of scarcely less
desirable males. Not bad-looking indeed, he assented almost in spite of himself. Better in appearance anyway
than that sanctimonious fellow, the missionary, who had
passed straight from world service to one of the more
exclusive tribes in the Congo. But there's something
wrong, he found himself observing the next instant, with
the startling eyes of this chap. Attractive no doubt to a
woman; but, in the judgment of a father-in-law, they appeared too bright and inscrutable, as if they had come
suddenly upon something that nobody ought to have seen.
Then Martin smiled at him; and this smile, very slow,
very winning, explained, he felt, the dangerous infatuation
of Milly Burden but not of Mary Victoria.

"Well, this is a surprise—a surprise indeed," repeated
Mr. Littlepage, with an animation which, he felt, was
excessive in buoyancy. "You must give us a little time before we are expected to call it a pleasure."

"Oh, I shall never expect that of you, Mr. Littlepage," Martin replied slowly; and his voice, smoothed down by a foreign accent, was agreeable in quality.

The pause might have been awkward if Curle had not plunged, with his sanguine courage, into the break. "Why shouldn't we decide to take no chances, Father, and call the marriage a success from the beginning?"

"Where is Louisa?" Mr. Littlepage inquired, glancing over the mountain of luggage. There was something wanting, he told himself, in a family crisis that failed to embrace Louisa.

"She stopped on the way. Aren't you going to ask us into the house?"

"I beg your pardon, my boy. Come in, come in." Glancing up the staircase, he saw Mary Victoria and her mother ascending, with arms interlocked, to the floor above. "Perhaps you'd like to stop for a moment in my library," he added, as cordially as the circumstances permitted. "Mary Victoria must want a talk with her mother."

"And you must want one with me." Well, you could pick no flaw, Mr. Littlepage admitted, in Martin's attitude. It was reasonable; it was encouraging; it was even correct. Looking at the young man, while he sank into one of the soft leather chairs, his reluctant father-in-law decided that he might have made a suitable, if not an ideal, husband for Milly Burden. For Milly Burden, but not for Mary Victoria, who, with her conquering loveliness and her secure fortune, had every right to demand the best that nature provided. And, after all, now that he confronted Martin Welding like an embodied retribution, how could he begin? What could he say to a son-in-law who had once been the lover and must remain, in Mr. Littlepage's thoughts, the perpetual seducer of trusting innocence, or —even if girls were no longer as innocent as they used to be—of trusting devotion. For he was one of those unusual men to whom betrayed devotion appears a deeper wrong than damaged innocence. He was fond of Milly, of course, and if he had not been fond of her, he should still have felt that he wanted to tell this attractive rotter with the burning eyes what he thought of him. Well, youth was not like that in the 'nineties. When he was young, a man thought twice before he seduced a woman of good family; and Mrs. Burden might be tiresome but she came of decent and respectable stock. He had, it was needless to remind himself sadly, known Southern gentlemen who were immoral; but they had been immoral, in the teeth of a severe code of honour, with discrimination. They were held accountable not only by a proper regard for religion and a true reverence for pure womanhood, but later, when all these defenses of virtue failed, by the precepts of chivalry and the point of the pistol. When they wished to misconduct themselves, they had, with such notorious exceptions as Colonel Bletheram, stepped down discreetly from their superior station in life; and in the ages of gallantry, which were undaunted by the perils of miscegenation, they had stepped down also from their superior shading in colour. These unpleasant truths, thought Mr. Littlepage, who had become resigned to the universe, are the facts of life that every man discovers and no man discusses. But in those robust epochs sin was sin, he mused, and not merely an inhibited pleasure.

His eyes roamed over the background of English calf, of red morocco, of beautifully tooled bindings, and finally came to rest, over the mantelpiece, upon the distinguished profile of the first Littlepage in Virginia. "Before you go upstairs is there anything I can do for you?" he inquired as he drew out his watch. "We dine usually at half-past seven."

The young man brightened into his agreeable smile. "Nothing, unless you can give me a drink. I feel as if I were giving way somewhere inside."

For the first time Mr. Littlepage observed that a royal decanter of old Bourbon still remained on the table. Duncan must have left it there when he fled at their approach. "I'll take one with you. Only you must give me your word that it isn't a habit."

"It used to be, but Mary Victoria doesn't allow habits in marriage."

While he scrupulously measured out his whisky, Mr. Littlepage glanced at his son-in-law with a stifled feeling of human—or was it merely of masculine?—solidarity. "I ought to know," he thought, without uttering the imprudent confession, "for I married her mother; and Mary Victoria is her mother all over again, only more so." Aloud he remarked lightly, "Anyhow, I promise not to tempt you too often." Holding his own glass to the light, with a sigh of supreme satisfaction, he reflected that only in his diminishing stock of Bourbon or Bumgartner could he still savour the lost bouquet of living.

"Oh, it's safe to tempt me," Martin retorted. "I've already fallen."

"Not too far to enlighten us, I hope, upon the reason— or at least the meaning of this surprise."

Again that wistful and slightly ironic smile. "Mary Victoria can answer that better than I can. I suspect, however, that she married me because she saved my life and didn't know what else to do with it. That is the nuisance of saving people's lives. They are on your hands and you've got to do something about them. I had the kind of claim upon her she couldn't ignore." After a barely perceptible pause, he added in a tone that was half tender and half satirical, "She has been my good angel."

Mr. Littlepage nodded. "I gathered that much from Curle."

"Well, I think it explains everything that Mary Victoria has done."

"Perhaps. And now, if you don't mind my putting the question so soon, what plans have you made for the future?"

"Absolutely none. I've nursed an incurable hope, you know, that I'd be spared any future." Having emptied his glass, he put it down and remarked with a laugh that reminded Mr. Littlepage of his elder and least successful son, "At the moment, however, fortified by this incomparable Bourbon, I am reconciled to the present."

"Am I to understand that you are making no effort to earn a livelihood?"

"It isn't so bad as that. I suppose I'll have to find something to do. I used to work, you see, but this damnable war stopped me. When they told me I was needed for killing, of course work had to go overboard."

An ominous frown gathered upon Mr. Littlepage's benign forehead. Not only did the Great War now occupy a position scarcely less honourable than the pedestal upon which he had placed the war for the Confederacy, but he was naturally suspicious of a husband who was not at the same time a conscientious provider. "What kind of work were you doing?" he asked in a more reserved tone of voice.

"In the beginning it was crockery, but after that I went into a bank. Crockery paid better, but the bank left me more time for writing. You see, I have always wanted to write."

Though the candour of the young man was disarming, it seemed incredible to Mr. Littlepage that Mary Victoria could have stooped to the obscure, if blameless, business of crockery. And worse even than the business of crockery, which, though inelegant in sound, retained its decent status in society, was the confession that his daughter's husband had been seriously "trying to write." For Mr. Littlepage was an ornament of that exclusive sphere in which literature, like sin, is respected only when it enlivens the worm-eaten pages of history.

"Well, I don't imagine there's much in that," he observed, and inquired immediately, "By the way, what first took you into the crockery business?"

"I had an uncle who kept a store on Broad Street. It seemed the easiest way to keep from starving while I learned to write. Then I went into the Metropolitan Bank. I was doing better with my writing when the war came. After it was over they put me in a hospital for a while, and as soon as I was out and free again, I went back to France. That was where I finally broke down and Mary Victoria found me in time to save my life."

This, even if one failed to consider the ironic tone, was far from what the most generous father-in-law could call promising. More and more, as the conversation followed its deplorable course, Mr. Littlepage wondered if Victoria would be able to take a cheerful view of the bare prospect. "You don't imagine, do you, that crockery and writing together would be sufficient to provide for a girl like Mary Victoria?"

Martin shook his head, and it occurred to Mr. Littlepage that he had never entirely collected his faculties since the surprise of his marriage. "Well, you see, Mary Victoria seemed to think we needn't worry. She didn't like the crockery business; but she had some idea of speaking to her cousin Daniel Woolley. He is president of a bank, isn't he?"

"And you think you're fitted for that kind of work?"

"I didn't think so even when I was doing it. But Mary Victoria has settled it in her mind. She has been, as I told you, my good angel, and I have a dread of disappointing her."

"I know," Mr. Littlepage assented. "But you must remember that Mary Victoria is an idealist. It is in the nature of an idealist to expect a great deal of other people."

Martin sighed while his thin, pale hand groped nervously toward the decanter and drew back without touching it. "That makes it all the worse to be obliged to disappoint her. She feels things so deeply. And do you know," he concluded, with a rush of confidence that the older man found both imprudent and appealing, "I have a fear of not measuring up to her standard. I know, of course, that I'm not half so big as I look to her. She insists on seeing me not as the utterly inadequate fellow I am in reality, but as a kind of fallen archangel. It isn't my fault, though nobody, least of all her father, will ever believe it. I never even in the beginning tried wilfully to deceive her. I've told her again and again that I am not worth half that she has done for me. But it isn't any use telling her. She is still convinced that she is right and I am wrong in my estimate."

All this was imprudent, reflected Mr. Littlepage; but it was as familiar and almost as stale as a sermon. For Victoria also had had her aspirations. No sooner had she fallen in love than she had tried, though with the gentlest touch imaginable, to make him into the sort of man he had never been and never could hope to become. He had suffered the painful process of being moulded into an ideal, as well as the far sharper pang of realizing the disappointment that must have attended her efforts. Too sincere for dissimulation, too magnanimous

for resentment, Victoria had steadfastly ignored her failure, and had persevered, with unaltered sweetness, in the
pretense that Virginius and marriage and human nature
in general were all exactly what she wished them to be.
"As noble as she is herself," Mr. Littlepage thought with
tenderness. For never, since that memorable evening in the
Browning class, had he felt the faintest disposition to
deny that Victoria was noble in character. Her goodness,
so far from being academic or acquired, was as natural
as her simple faith in the perfectibility of husbands.
All her life she had diffused love as other persons diffuse
selfishness; and even in those frequent moments when he
had felt that the sweetness of marriage cloyed his spirit, he
had never forgotten that he owed more to her generosity
than he could ever repay. Watching Martin's way with the
decanter, Mr. Littlepage told himself disconsolately that
only the substance was different, not the situation. To his
veracious mind, which prided itself, however inaccurately,
upon facing the facts of life, it was evident that Victoria had
had more plastic material to work upon than the character
of this inadequate young man afforded. Yet, with this finer
clay and ampler measure to her hand, all that Victoria had
achieved was the pattern of a contented citizen and a
successful attorney. Beyond this, he could discern no more
exalted stature than that of a presentable member of
Queenborough society, in which the custom of dining out
with a limited number of one's least interesting acquaintances moved in a monotonous circle from October to June.
Into this circle, which grew duller as time and tide encrusted
the conversational platitudes, there entered occasionally
a new member, whose prerogative of wealth only those
too poor to profit by it had ever disputed. Yet the only
person who might have irradiated the lustre of pleasure,
for him at least, had long ago ceased to appear in the

sluggish air of these gatherings. Not that Mrs. Dalrymple was excluded by her station in life from what was now an affluent and had been once an aristocratic society. Even her fall, had it been as ladylike as poor Aunt Agatha's, might have been forgotten by everybody except a few crystallized virgins and old Colonel Bletheram. But her imprudent behaviour in the divorce court, combined with the well-founded suspicion that she had committed other pleasures abroad, had debarred her, in the opinion of the best judges, from the privileges to which she was entitled by birth. Regrettable. Almost deplorable. For in the stiff and slightly pompous dignity of his middle years, only the ardent memory of Amy Dalrymple had fanned to life the flickering embers of youth. Nothing since his first love affair, not material prosperity, not communion beneath the stained-glass memorial windows in Saint Luke's Episcopal Church, not even the contagious idealism with which armies are mobilized, had ever exalted him to this starry altitude of the spirit. While the echo of this lost but unforgotten ecstasy awoke in his mind, he asked in a tone of sympathy rather than rebuke:

"May I inquire, without seeming impertinent, where your education began?"

"Exactly where it ended, in a public school. If you ever attended one, you know that the word 'education' is a euphemism of modern democracy. But I got a good deal out of books. I think I may say I got as much as any man could out of books."

Again Mr. Littlepage frowned while he studied his son-in-law. The reply, he told himself, left much to be desired; for literature as a pursuit was even less profitable, and scarcely more distinguished, than crockery as a business. The young man's tone, with its curling irony at the end of a sentence, reminded him of the disreputable

way Marmaduke talked in his attic, and he sighed to think
that Mary Victoria might have introduced a second artist
into the family.

"Well, I shouldn't put too much faith in literature, if I
were you," he said presently. "Without posing as an
authority, I may express the opinion that there isn't much
material in Virginia history that hasn't been already
exhausted."

For a moment there was silence, and in the flatness of
this silence, Mr. Littlepage had a queer sensation that
Martin was smiling within. Then, with an air of incredible
patience, the young man answered slowly, as if he were
speaking to a foreigner in words of one syllable. "But
historical novels are all tosh, you know. I am interested in
life, not in costume and scenery. I want to get at grips with
reality."

"Well, I shouldn't build my hopes on that kind of stuff,"
Mr. Littlepage remarked mildly but firmly; for the word
"reality" startled him whenever it was divorced from
philosophy and dragged into literature. In that uncomfortable moment, he was visited by the fear lest Mary
Victoria's husband should be afflicted with Marmaduke's
foreign taste for indecent psychology. Then remembering
that he himself had acquired, since the Great War, a cos-
mopolitan attitude toward Mrs. Dalrymple, he observed
simply, "I'm afraid there isn't much to be got out of
literature as a profession."

"Not in Queenborough. Why, you haven't even a
library, yet you people pretend to be civilized."

For the first time Mr. Littlepage allowed his exasperation to ooze into his tone. It annoyed him profoundly that
this young man of ignoble antecedents should belittle the
ancient and honourable culture of Queenborough. All the
learning required to make a Southern gentleman was com-

prised, as every Littlepage knew without being told, in
the calf-bound rows of classic authors and the Prayer-Book
of the Protestant Episcopal Church.

"Those of us who have leisure to read are able to provide our own libraries," he rejoined, with dignity. "Or if
we are too impoverished for that, we may always borrow
with credit from our friends who are better off." Glancing
upward at the volumes he had inherited from his father,
he congratulated himself upon the ease with which his
declaration had been justified by his surroundings.

"Yes, I see, of course. But you must remember that I
could neither buy nor borrow when I lived here. However,
I shan't be able to do much reading until I have proved to
Mary Victoria that you can make your way in the world
without being a mutton head. Do you know, by the way,
what has become of her?"

While he looked at his son-in-law, Mr. Littlepage's
liquid brown eyes became opaque with a frozen reserve.
"She went upstairs with her mother. They have probably
stopped to speak to poor Aunt Agatha."

"Poor Aunt Agatha? Is she an invalid?"

"Oh, no. That's merely a habit that we fell into a
generation ago. Her life was wrecked in early youth by an
unfortunate love affair from which she never recovered."

"Good God!" exclaimed Martin Welding, while a
startled horror swept over his thin face. "I remember now.
Mary Victoria told me about her."

VIII

"WHAT were your impressions, my dear?" inquired Mr.
Littlepage, in modest blue and white pyjamas, of Mrs.
Littlepage, in a prim nightgown of white nainsook beneath a lavender flannel wrapper. Around them, the familiar estate of marriage was preserved in the unruffled calm
of their bedroom as in an embalming fluid. Against the
rear wall, the twin beds with fluted columns were neatly
turned down to the exact margin of embroidered linen
sheets and fleecy satin-bordered blankets. On Mr. Littlepage's right side, a small Heppelwhite table held a sky-
blue tray bearing a thermos bottle, a glass, a box of
cough drops, and one of Mr. Strachey's disrespectful
biographies bound in a subdued colour. Beside Mrs. Littlepage, the companion table bore a lavender tray and
thermos bottle, a glass, a tube of veronal, and a well-worn
Bible, which opened with a book marker of purple satin,
and contained, in addition to the inspired print, a hetero-
geneous collection of pressed flowers and poems culled
from newspapers. Though Mr. and Mrs. Littlepage were
so opposite in character and disposition, they had achieved,
in thirty-one years of effortless living, an indissoluble union
of habit. And it was in obedience to this fast nuptial tie
that Mr. Littlepage, standing beside his downy twin bed,
asked this pregnant question of his wife, who lingered before her mahogany dressing-table, with her soft
ashen brown hair brushed severely back from her forehead

and a film of camphor ice over her smiling lips. Victoria was not a plain woman, and she might have been very pretty still. But she had either failed to employ or too soon relinquished all the arts invented by those women who, from an urgency of temperament or a pressure of economy, are dependent upon the uncertain favour of men. There had been moments in their earlier years when he had wondered if her mildness could be merely the outward expression of an indifference too passive to be resentful in nature. As they grew older, and especially since his frustrated affair with Mrs. Dalrymple, he had accepted Victoria's sweetness of disposition as gratefully as he enjoyed clement weather in autumn. It was in this thankful spirit that he now repeated suavely, "Well, what were your impressions, my dear?"

Pausing to rub the film of camphor ice into the firm but pleasant line of her mouth, Victoria cast an anxious glance about the large close room, which was as open and as unventilated as marriage. "I confess that I cannot understand Mary Victoria."

Mr. Littlepage sighed in agreement. "I wonder if she really understands herself. Everything must look different since she came back to America."

"Yes, I haven't a doubt that she is already beginning to ask herself why she married so suddenly."

"Then you share my—well, not altogether favourable opinion?"

For an instant, while Victoria gave her mind to the problem, her attractive features wore the look of a resigned yet wondering Madonna. "I cannot see that there is a single point of contact between them," she said presently.

"They seem to be still in love with each other. Being in love does establish some kind of congeniality, I suppose. But I agree with you that he isn't worthy of Mary Victoria. He is a good-looking chap in his way; but his manners are as ordinary as Curle's, and bad manners have a way of outlasting good looks."

"That was why Mary Victoria never took her eyes off him," Victoria remarked sadly. "She was nervous, I could see, lest he should make a wrong impression the first evening."

"That worried me too," Mr. Littlepage rejoined irritably. "If she keeps it up, she will end by making him afraid to open his mouth. Couldn't you advise her, very delicately of course, to leave him a little more at liberty to make mistakes?"

Mrs. Littlepage shook her head. "Poor child, she is trying her best to help him. Did you notice how lovely her face was when she watched him?"

Yes, he had observed this, and it had reminded him of Victoria's tender and protective way with the poets. Her manner of reciting Browning, as if she were trying so patiently to bring out the best in him, had been the attitude, in an earlier fashion, of Mary Victoria toward her husband. "It is obvious that she is in love with him," he admitted, while his expression hardened, and he remembered that he had failed in his promise to see Milly that evening. Well, fortunately to-morrow was Sunday, and Sunday appeared to be the day appointed by Providence for unwelcome arrivals. "She may, of course, if it is not too late," he added grimly, "be able to make something of him."

"It will be his own fault if she doesn't. No man could ask for a finer influence."

"Except myself," Mr. Littlepage remarked with a smile. "But that, you know, is exactly what makes me uneasy. All men do not react in the same way to an influence. They are not all blessed with my aptitude for perfectibility."

Victoria responded to this with a sigh. "Few men are like you, Virginius. But there was a time," she added regretfully, "when you would not have spoken flippantly of my influence in your life."

"I did not mean to speak flippantly, my dear. Whatever I am to-day, I may say honestly, is owing to your example more than to anything else." While Victoria brightened visibly, he proceeded with less assurance. "Only it crossed my mind that it really takes two to make an influence. Fortunately, I came to your hand at the right moment and in exactly the right mood for your experiment. The very air was thick with idealism in the 'nineties; but the moral hysteria of the war has degenerated now into a sort of bleak realism. Mary Victoria lacks one of the chief accessories to feminine influence, and that is a benign moisture in the atmosphere."

"I did not think of it as an experiment when we were married, Virginius, nor did you, I am sure."

"You are right, my dear. I thought of happiness, not of improvement."

"I shall never forget," Victoria murmured in her softest tone, "what your father said to me on the day of our wedding. 'Thank God, Victoria, that my son is marrying a true woman; for pure womanhood is the only thing that stands between man and the jungle.'"

Yes, he recognized the Georgian flavour of that phrase; and now, with the relentless veracity of the modern mind, he could ask himself if Marmaduke had been right when he said that hypocrisy was the only art that had reached its peak in America? For, like most professions of faith, his father's panegyrics had been addressed to an invisible power; and when, as occasionally happened, his wife interposed, she had assumed the eternal outline and the shimmering substance of an allegorical virtue. As a

child, the little Virginius had been deeply impressed by
the dramatic interludes in their family life. The nights
when he had lain awake to listen for his father's stumbling
footsteps had been followed, as naturally as darkness flows
into dawn, by the days when he was obliged to bring tribal
offerings of flowers and fruit to his mother. From the
moment of his father's return there had floated through
the open door of the nursery (for his mother was one of
those women who civilize the emotion of love but not the
maternal instinct) the dreary monotone of abject apology.
Even at that tender age he had discovered that one very
special branch of sin is able to assume at will all the trans-
ports of religious conversion. Why was it, for instance,
he had once inquired of his grandmother, that his father
became more devout, and apparently more affectionate,
to his mother whenever he was accused of drinking or
loving too freely on unlawful premises? "Lip-homage,"
pooh-poohed his grandmother, an old lady of rock-ribbed
constitution, who knew her world. Yet the boy had already
begun to suspect that this idolatrous lip-homage recom-
pensed his mother, in a measure at least, for the infidelities which had become an important part of the ritual.
Though her forgiveness had seldom failed to wait upon
sin, it was in the midst of these spiritual excesses that she
had scattered her snowy landscapes and strewn her sprays
of wild roses over the mirrors and sofa pillows. And observing, as he grew older, that art becomes the vehicle of
unhappiness almost as frequently as it becomes the medium
of indecency, he had been prepared for the promptness
with which Marmaduke's thwarted desire for Louisa had
oozed through his paint brush into fantastic forms of the
nude. Well, he was obliged to admit that the nude was less
reprehensible to-day, though it was certainly redder than it

had been in the 'nineties. Moreover, the present age, with
its liberal views of sin, had softened Mr. Littlepage's
judgment not only of Marmaduke's pictures but even of
poor Aunt Agatha's past.

With this thought in his mind, he remarked tolerantly,
"Did you notice that this young man was particularly
courteous to Aunt Agatha?"

Yes, Victoria had observed it, and she was of the
opinion that such politeness spoke well for their son-in-
law. "So few young men pay any attention to old ladies,"
she said. "That is one nice thing about Duncan. No wonder he is poor Aunt Agatha's favourite."

Mr. Littlepage pondered this idea. "Am I mistaken or
is Aunt Agatha really beginning to take a new interest in
life?"

Victoria nodded. "The war did a great deal for her,
Virginius," she answered in a sympathetic tone; for her
kind heart had never been reconciled to the harshness
with which the canon of refined conduct had dealt with
poor Aunt Agatha. Such measures, she had been told
as a bride, were necessary to safeguard divine institutions and preserve the jewel of chastity from the roving
instincts of man; but this explanation, though she accepted
it with docility, seemed to her far from convincing. Thirty-
one years ago, when she first learned of the fate of poor
Aunt Agatha, she had had her doubts in the matter; and
since then, especially as loose conduct became more general and less conspicuous, her doubts had multiplied and
finally settled into an incurable suspicion of the Victorian
ideal. "She has been a different woman," she added, "ever
since she was needed to make pyjamas."

"I am glad of that," Mr. Littlepage responded, and he
continued after a pause, "I have always felt that the world

was a little too hard upon poor Aunt Agatha. After all, she was very young, and I remember that my grandmother never concurred in the opinion that she was of an abnormal nature."

"But the doctors all thought so. Your mother told me, I remember, that the doctors said she was one of those unfortunate women who needed a man in her life. They never left her alone with a man after that or let her go out by herself. What I always thought, though of course I could not say so aloud, was that it was simply a disastrous passion for Colonel Bletheram. I have never," she added, with indignation, "been able to shake hands with old Colonel Bletheram, though he has had three wives since he ruined poor Aunt Agatha."

Mr. Littlepage flushed darkly. "Yes, it was all very sad, and I admire you for your spirit. If other women were like you, poor Aunt Agatha's life might have been different. But everyone at the time appeared to think that it was noble of her to shield her seducer. They seemed to feel that she was merely obeying some unwritten etiquette of seduction, and Aunt Agatha had always been a model of deportment. It is little short of astonishing the way manners and even morals can alter."

Injustice had never failed to ruffle the limpid shallows of Victoria's mind; and her long resentment had at last convinced Virginius that chivalry had fallen short in this particular instance. To be sure, his mother and his grandmother, conforming to the arrested psychology of tradition, had accepted the belief that nature assigned the passion, as well as the pleasure, of love to the masculine sex. In his childhood no one, not even his grandmother, had ever disputed this theory; and the whole feminine world of the 'seventies had connived at the practice of explaining away a moral infirmity. By some subtle process, whenever the desperate passion of love visited the curving bosom of a Southern lady, desire was transformed into a mental affliction. How many cheerful family physicians of the old school, Mr. Littlepage now wondered, had encouraged this moral, if melancholy, hypothesis? How inevitably the pressure of tradition had changed Aunt Agatha from a spirited girl into an elderly Magdalen, as vague and insubstantial as legend. "It was a cruel age, but all ages are cruel," he meditated, "and all ages call their own cruelties civilization. The singular part of it was that women embraced their martyrdom more firmly even than men inflicted it." Yes, it was useless to deny that poor Aunt Agatha had fallen like a perfect lady. No persuasion, no threats, not even the sinister one of an asylum, had compelled her to divulge the name of her seducer. Only inference and analogy had attributed her ruin to dashing Colonel Bletheram, who had imprudently set an example of gallantry. While poor Aunt Agatha immured herself for more than forty years in a third-story back bedroom, and flitted down, like a wistful apparition, to family meals when there were no important guests, Colonel Bletheram had lost three faithful wives but never missed a Christmas cotillion.

"She seems to be taking a great deal of interest in moving pictures," Mr. Littlepage remarked aloud.

"Aunt Agatha? Yes, she never misses a new one. Moving pictures and banana sundaes are her only pleasures in life. I encourage the movies; but I am very much afraid she will ruin her digestion with those dreadful mixtures. It seems a pity, too, that she always selects films with the most sensational titles. To-day it is 'Passion in the Purple' and yesterday it was 'A Scarlet Sin.' I wouldn't for the world say anything to dampen her spirit; but I sometimes think it would be more dignified if she could interest herself in a charity. I tried to make her do a little work for our refuge; but she appears to have taken a dislike to those unfortunate girls."

Victoria, who was endowed with a gentle aptitude for uplifting, had been for years the president of the Home for Unfortunates (named after the "Bridge of Sighs" by her mother-in-law, who was one of the founders). Assisted by the indefatigable Louisa and a few earnest philanthropists, she spent her Thursday and Saturday afternoons patiently extracting the honey from wingless daughters of joy. Though her enthusiasm for this charity, and indeed for all charities, had decreased since her severe illness last winter, she still conformed punctiliously to her old moral observances. Virginius, who had noticed her waning fervour, asked himself now if Victoria could really have become as indifferent to the higher life as she appeared? Some imponderable force (he could only feel, he could not define, the loss) was slowly diminishing. It is true that she used the same forms, she employed the same platitudes; but the sound of them reminded him of husks in which the seeds were beginning to rattle. There was comfort, however, in the thought that her sweetness of nature was still inexhaustible. After all, he had been disappointed in her temperament, not in her character, and as nineteenth century moralists had conclusively proved, the forces of character are more than a match for the follies of temperament.

"Well, you can hardly blame her, my dear, if, after her experience, she prefers a sensation to a reform. At her age, I suppose, she is safe from demoralization."

"I am glad you feel that way, Virginius. Of course I understand poor Aunt Agatha's recoil, but Louisa seemed to think that people may criticize." As her gentle voice trailed into silence, it occurred to him that her secret wisdom, though still patient and uncomplaining, had grown a little weary from contending with indestructible facts.

"Criticize? Good God!" he exclaimed resentfully. "Do you think by this time that she could feel any criticism more immaterial than a brick?" Then, dismissing the subject with a gesture of disgust, he remarked abruptly, "I am sorry that Mary Victoria married a man she feels obliged to make over."

Victoria assented. "But she is so much better prepared than most women to bring out the best in a man."

"That, my dear, is what makes me anxious. I am not sure that her experience in the Balkans has been the safest preparation for marriage. Nothing, not even moonshine, goes to the head quicker than saving democracy with other people's money. I am not sure that the war didn't turn as many heads as it crippled heels. However, to be practical, I do not envy Mary Victoria the job she has on her hands. I've more than an inkling of trouble ahead, and, unless I am mistaken, this young Martin will bear a good deal of improving."

"Have you heard anything else, Virginius, to his discredit?"

"It isn't what I've heard, my dear; it is what I know. What does Mary Victoria say?"

"Very little. She seems radiantly happy, and I believe she fell in love with him because she feels that she saved his life."

"I remember now that young Welding used that same expression. What do they mean when they say she saved his life?"

"Didn't he tell you?"

"Too vaguely for me to understand what it is all about. Wasn't he included in her general scheme of salvation?"

"Please try not to be flippant, Virginius."

"I was never less flippant, Victoria. Nor more disgusted. Then his, I gather, was a special act of redemption?"

"Please, Virginius—if you will not interrupt. It seems he had a complete nervous collapse after he found that his work was a failure. Of course, Mary Victoria would not wish us to speak of it, except to Louisa, but he was in a state of acute melancholia, and on the verge of suicide when she came into his life. That is why he calls her his good angel. I gather that she helped him in every way, even financially, until he was on his feet and out of the hospital. Then she got him this position as secretary in her orphanage; and she says that he did very well. He has quite a gift for writing, you know."

Mr. Littlepage frowned. "I've warned him not to build his hopes on that kind of thing. He'd better look for a practical job." The more he heard of Mary Victoria's husband, Virginius decided, the less he admired him. Moreover, he was beginning to suspect that in love at least Martin Welding was disposed to be what philosophers have called a pluralist; and from pluralism in love he recoiled almost as sharply as from polytheism in religion.

"Mary Victoria feels that very strongly. I have promised her to ask Daniel if he will take him into the bank. Martin, I gather from what she said, wished to stay in Paris and do his writing where living is cheaper and more interesting; but after they were married Mary Victoria felt it was her duty to return to America. Her chief interest now, after Martin, of course, is the outlawing of war——"

"Well, considering all she owes to the last one——"

"Owes to it, dear?"

"I mean not only a husband, for he seems to me to

be a featherweight in the scale, but all the extravagance and excitement she and so many other women were able to indulge in."

Victoria stared at him. "I sometimes wonder, Virginius, where you get your ideas. I am sure there is nothing in your blood to make you a cynic. Nobody could have had higher ideals than your father," she continued wearily, as if she were repeating a ritual, "or a more childlike faith in religion. In the last conversation I had with him, he told me that he was securely anchored to every letter in the Bible. If he began to doubt that the fish swallowed Jonah, he said, it would make him an infidel."

Mr. Littlepage remembered the words; and he recalled also that, with the natural agility so often displayed by the male in appealing from example to precept, his father had seldom failed to invoke the ancestral creed in a moral emergency. "Even if he has lived loosely," Virginius had once overheard his mother remark by way of apology, "it is a comfort to feel that Marmaduke has never lost his hold on the truths of religion."

"Well, life must have been easier for a believing generation," he replied, with a levity that astonished him. "It is fortunate that my dear old father passed away while the world was standing still in its orbit. The gift of self-deception has become a lost art."

"Yes, I suppose faith is more difficult than it used to be," Victoria sighed, whether in regret or relief it was impossible to tell from her voice. "That is why Mary Victoria thinks it is woman's mission to hand on the torch."

"The torch? Have they begun already to preach female incendiarism?"

"She means, of course, the belief in the ideal. I suppose it is natural for her to feel, after the inspiration she was in the Red Cross, that there is no end to her in-

fluence for good. She is so confident that it is difficult not
to catch fire, or at least warmth, from her earnestness. She
takes everything, even that old entanglement of Martin's,
in the most forgiving and beautiful spirit."

"Entanglement?" There was the faintest quiver of fear
in the word.

"Surely, Virginius, you know, that other woman?"

"Only one? There may have been a round dozen from
all I've heard of him." After all, had he destroyed Milly's
happiness when he tried to protect her? Would it have
been better as well as wiser if he had told the complete truth
instead of a poetic version of facts? "The hardest thing
I ever had to do in my life," he continued indignantly, "is
to receive this—this unspeakable cad into the family."

"Mary Victoria says that she tried with all her power
to make him go back to the other woman."

"Did she go so far, I wonder, as paying for his passage?"

"Virginius, I never knew you to be so bitter. After
all, you were the one who started her on the search for
him."

"Perhaps that is why I am bitter. I wanted her to find
him for Milly."

"You never told me," Victoria said gently, "but of
course I knew, and I even tried to warn Mary Victoria
against him. I believe that she really did try to make
him go back after he was well, but by that time he was
head over heels in love with her. I don't know exactly
what he told her about the affair; but a man in love can
seldom be trusted."

"Well, it seems to me, my dear, that a woman in reform can be trusted even less. It is always a blow to discover how little honour there is in the best feminine motives."

"Oh, Virginius, you don't mean that about Mary Victoria? It hasn't been a month since you told me that, even if other women stooped to deception, you knew that Mary Victoria was the soul of honour."

A sound between a laugh and a groan broke from Mr. Littlepage. "I thought that a month ago, which only proves what a fool a father can be. Naturally," he added grimly, "I have no intention of giving my daughter away. We shall have to stand by her."

"What else in the world could we do? Of course I am deeply distressed that the other woman is the girl we helped through her trouble. That makes it more painful for you and far more humiliating for Mary Victoria. But, after all, we must think first of our child."

"That is human, no doubt, but it seems to me grossly unfair."

"I can understand how you feel, dear. It is harder on you than it is on anyone else. For it isn't as if you had a choice in the matter."

"Do you honestly think that I haven't?"

"Why, how could you have, Virginius? Are there any circumstances on earth that would justify our spoiling Mary Victoria's happiness?"

"No, I dare say you're right. But if Mary Victoria has found the slightest excuse for herself, I should like to hear what it is."

For a moment Victoria pondered her answer. Then, in her softest voice, she replied slowly, "She said that she could tell from the very beginning that the other girl had made the wrong sort of appeal to him. Then, when Mary Victoria got to know him better, and I suppose after they had fallen a little in love, she discovered that his mother had died when he was a baby and he had never come under the influence of a really good woman. Later on, after she had done so much for him, she became convinced that it was her duty to—to——"

"To perfect him, I suppose——"

"Of course, I agree with you that she might not have felt the necessity had he been less attractive. Didn't you find him attractive?"

"Not disturbingly so, but then, you see, I am neither an act of God nor an instrument of salvation."

"There are times, Virginius, when you sound almost like Marmaduke."

"I am sorry. There are few Southern gentlemen I should not prefer to resemble."

"I don't mean in behaviour. No two men in the world could be more unlike in behaviour." She hesitated an instant, and then finished magnanimously, "I can never be thankful enough that I married a man who did not have that other side to his nature."

"I appreciate that, my dear, and now, if you are ready for bed, I will open the window."

Slipping into his dressing-gown, and tying the cord securely in the middle of his rotund waist, he stood watching Victoria, with mild astonishment, while she stepped out of her felt slippers, placed her lavender flannel wrapper at the foot of the bed, and stretched her unconfined body, in the nainsook nightgown, between the fleecy blankets and embroidered sheets. Was it for this, echoed a derisive voice in the hollowness of his mind, that the arboreal imagination of man had climbed down from the feathery tree-tops?

Turning away, he crossed the gray velvet carpet, and after raising the window, leaned out into the silence that had fallen between a retreating and an advancing storm. Overhead, beneath a closed sky, there was the fluttering of shredded mist; but toward the south and west a low range of clouds shone silver-black beneath the pale lustre of moonlight. Poised between the eternal illusions of time and space, the world appeared to hang suspended in the midst of an encompassing desolation. And out of this desolation, it seemed to him that a burden of futility poured like a shower of ashes into his soul. "What is the meaning of it all?" he asked himself despondently. "Where is it leading? What else is left in life after you have had happiness?"

Then, suddenly, as if in answer to his meaningless question, a single fiery star shone in Mrs. Dalrymple's window on the opposite corner. "So she is still there," he thought, with scarcely a flicker of longing. "I wonder if she is happy at last."

IX

THE next afternoon Mr. Littlepage, who disliked walking as much as other successful men, picked his way in the direction of Juniper Hill, where his brother Marmaduke occupied Mrs. Burden's third floor. Not only had walking appeared to him, on this occasion at least, the only means of avoiding helpful advice; but he was moved by the suspicion that persons of dubious reputation, such as Marmaduke and Milly Burden, were in the habit of putting a correct value upon privacy. Though he doubted the wisdom of seeing Milly so soon after Mary Victoria's triumphant return, it occurred to him that Marmaduke, from his long experience with women who were conspicuous for kind hearts rather than for character, might be the messenger appointed by destiny to break the news of Martin's desertion. After all, the sooner she relinquished the hope of him, the happier Milly would be in the present and the more useful, no doubt, she would become in the future.

Threading his way through noisy streams of children, he passed rows of dilapidated houses, until at last the odours of boiled cabbage and decaying fruits were dispelled by the lighter air of the river, and the street emerged upon the brow of a terraced hill, which presided over an ochre-coloured canal, a group of empty smokestacks, and the smothered fires of the sunset. Farther away, the sad-looking hill was enlivened by a bleached plot of

94

grass, a fantastic iron fountain, protected alike from man and beast by a green railing, and a scattered row of inhospitable benches. On the benches a few solitary old men were patiently waiting for happiness; and where the street came to an abrupt end over the gloomy canal, Mrs. Burden's house was perched as insecurely as the forsaken nest of a hawk. It was an endless source of mortification to Mr. Littlepage that his elder brother, the head of the house since the death from octogenarian excesses of his uncle Powhatan, should choose to present the appearance, when he had by no means reached the condition, of beggarly circumstances. Virginius had reasoned earnestly and fruitlessly upon the subject; but then, as he reflected despondently, all his arguments with Marmaduke were as fruitless as they were earnest. For a few weeks after his return to America, Marmaduke had taken temporary shelter with Virginius and Victoria; and on both sides of the family, this experiment had ended in one of those complete disillusionments which, as the refugee jocosely observed, "can be faced only by turning your back on them." Victoria, who admired art rather than artists, was disappointed to find that Marmaduke was a futurist in morals. Even this, trained as she was in the tradition of perfect behaviour, she might have been able less to excuse as a fault than to overlook as a fact; but no amount of practice in evading reality could blind her to the proof that he was far from spotless in his attire. It is true that a wooden leg excused, she felt, a measure of carelessness. Her sympathetic heart had almost accepted this substitute as a mute plea for indulgence, when she was saddened again by the discovery that Marmaduke, even without a leg, was too sure of his ancestors to be particular about his acquaintances. The struggle between the habit of refinement and the habit of not having habits continued to wear on Victoria's nerves without ruffling her sweetness of temper. She was attached to Marmaduke; she was sympathetic; she was even indulgent; but she could not shut her eyes to the unfortunate truth that he was bad for the children. Marmaduke, on the contrary, who was attached to nobody, respected, and within reason, as he was careful to explain, admired Victoria. "The institution of marriage was invented for her," he had remarked, "and you can't blame her for defending it against the invincible adversary. Some day, as even Victoria knows, her defenses will fall, and then what will become of her? But I'll say this for your wife," he had concluded, with a dash of enthusiasm in his voice, "there is less humbug in her morality than in most. She is the only woman I know who isn't two thirds sham, and I haven't forgotten Louisa."

At the end of the visit an armed truce was established; and an armed truce, Mr. Littlepage conceded, is more successful in maintaining a balance of power than in promoting tribal festivities. It was impossible to deny that Victoria had emerged from the conflict with flying colours; but when Virginius had attempted to deal logically with Marmaduke, he soon perceived that the head of the family displayed as little respect for logic as he had shown for legitimate ties. In one of his vagabond fancies (which Victoria had found more disconcerting than temper), Marmaduke had shaken civilization and regular hours from his shoulders, and had entrenched his disreputable habits in the attic on Juniper Hill. "How can there be any civilization without regular hours?" Victoria had inquired reasonably. "He eats only when he is hungry, and then without laying a cloth." Virginius, who agreed with Victoria, and felt that the order of the universe depended upon punctuality, had decided that a situation which contained a single artist and all the conventions, was crowded with difficulties. Yet, in the very hour of his defeat, while he concurred in Victoria's opinion that "you can't take art very seriously when it doesn't bring you a living," he was unhappily aware that the buccaneer in his blood was allied with his brother.

This early November afternoon, while he stepped briskly over the mat of coloured leaves on the hill, no observer would have suspected that a roving buccaneer was hidden beneath the cloak of his correct Sabbath attire. With his handsome though slightly pompous features, which wore the look of heroic complacency that makes all Southern gentlemen resemble one another in the eyes of a stranger, he looked, as indeed he was, except for his vagabond impulses, a perfect example of what money can do when it has good material to work upon. But in his perturbed mind he was thinking, "I wonder if anything can be wrong with me? Is it only that the war has made all the rest of life seem distorted and out of proportion? Or can it be that my liver is going against me?" For he belonged to that normal masculine breed whose emotions are firmly seated not in the soul but in the liver.

He had quickened his pace to avoid a perambulator pushed by an inattentive negro nurse, when the door of the house he was passing opened and shut, and a woman in a red hat and a moleskin coat descended the littered steps to the gate. As her luminous brown eyes swept his face, he came to a sudden stop, and stood waiting. "How little she has changed!" he thought, while it seemed to him that a faint drumming vibrated through the depths of his being. "How little she has changed, and yet there is a difference.", Her hair was still amber; the colour in her cheeks was still as ripe as the bloom on a peach; her queenly bosom, beneath the slim lines of her coat, was still opulent. At a distance he had thought her as straight as a pole; but he perceived now, with an admiration the modern figure never aroused in him, that only the fashion of her dress, not the perfect curves of the 'nineties, had altered.

"Why, Mrs. Dalrymple!" he exclaimed, and there was a thrill of pleasure in his voice as he held out his hand.

Before yielding her gloved hand, she hesitated an instant and looked up inquiringly from beneath darkened lashes. So the brown velvet of her gaze had caressed him on that August evening; and while his nerves quivered like the strings of a harp under sensitive fingers, he felt for the first time in months, for the first time in years, that he had not yet outlived the age of delight. With her over-ripe but still voluptuous beauty, the brilliant fairness of her complexion, and the glimmering dusk of her eyes, she had awakened, however briefly, that old torment of unsatisfied longing. He remembered her not only as the woman he might have loved, but even more poignantly as the woman he might have possessed. This, he told himself triumphantly, was the beauty that had the power to wreck homes and make history. In its late autumn season, he felt that Mrs. Dalrymple's charm was sweetened with a honey which only the full-bodied masculine taste of the 'nineties had known how to appreciate.

"What a fool I was!" he thought bitterly, so far had he travelled from the moral idealism of the nineteenth century. Well, in spite of moral idealism, men had known how to enjoy life in the long ages when women were weaker and whisky was Bourbon.

"You!" Mrs. Dalrymple breathed forgivingly; and the look in her deep dark eyes was as challenging, he told himself, as champagne to a prohibitionist. From a provincial and pretty widow, with a soft heart and a brittle character, she had been transformed by Europe and her war record into a bright, hard woman of the world, who had exchanged her birthright of modesty for a profitable understanding of men. That double-edged blessing for a Southern lady, an ardent thirst for life and capacity for enjoyment, had not, he suspected from her scarlet mouth and hearty manner, diminished. Her laugh was as kind and as exciting as ever; the rich curves of her cheek and lips were as tempting; and though her figure was too womanly for the scant fashions of the present, Mr. Little-page had matured in an era when restrained abundance rather than flatness unconfined appealed to the robust instincts of man.

"She is nearly fifty, and almost as handsome as ever," he decided. "Well, that is what Europe and widowhood can do for a woman."

Mrs. Dalrymple, who had been blessed with sex attraction, but would have preferred, as she grew older, a moderate amount of card sense or even a strong religious belief, could have enlightened him still further on the subjects of Europe and widowhood. Though he would have been among the last to suspect the truth, it is literal, if not poetic, to describe her as the helpless victim of circumstances. Endowed with much energy and little temperament, she might have remained as virtuous as Louisa had her figure been less pronounced or the field of woman's activities more varied. But in the late 'nineties, when she had flourished and fallen, an immense feminine vitality was confined with the narrow range of a wasp-waist and the exacting ritual of being a lady. A deceptive bosom, which inspired hope in men, and a naturally kind heart, which hesitated to dispense disappointment, had been, if not the occasion, at least the original cause, of her frailty. Never in her life had she deliberately harmed anyone, not even a woman; and the wonder grew, as she looked back over the past, that so little pleasure could

have produced so great a catastrophe. It is true that
when men were deceived by her ripe mouth and rich
bosom, her kind heart had made but a feeble show of
resistance; but these episodes, after they had happened,
invariably seemed to her to have occurred in her sleep.
Few women had profited more by the war. Even her
queenly figure had been subdued to the service of patriotism; and her renown for easy virtue had yielded, though
not without a struggle, to a reputation for heroic ex-
ploits. Twice, it was said, she had carried or dragged a
wounded soldier from under fire into safety; once she had
saved, or assisted in saving, all the inmates from a burning
field hospital; and three times she had received foreign
decorations for gallantry. Royalty, undeterred by her
sins, had welcomed her with encouraging requests for
both moral and financial support. Her picture, taken in the
peasant dress of Berengaria, as she presented an American bank cheque to the queen of that interesting kingdom,
had adorned the Sunday supplements of the American
press. In this exhilarating atmosphere, it is little wonder that coquetry became a means rather than an end
to adventure; or that the pursuit of sex appeared a mistaken, as well as an uncongenial, vocation. Even her notorious past, which was attached, she felt, by the merest
thread of an accident, had crumbled away and scattered
like pollen over the fertile soil of the war zone. After the
armistice, it is true, there came a vast emptiness. In an
hour, it seemed to her, the euphemistic Powers of Europe
had made of her life a desert and called it peace. Not, of
course, that she had wished the war to continue. Like many
other women she hated and feared war in general, and
worshipped it in the particular instance; and her kind heart
still suffered whenever she allowed herself to think of the
killed and the wounded. Nevertheless, so long as there

was a war, and she was as innocent as a babe in the matter, she thanked her stars, with a clear conscience, that she had not avoided this historic prelude to glory. Never, until she engaged in active combat, had she been able to understand how the sex that invented battle and murder and rape could have invented also, without a change of heart apparently, monogamy and the perfect lady and the Protestant Episcopal Church. In the end, since the war left her precisely as it had found her, with a vacant mind and a well-stored heart, her inexhaustible vitality was stranded among all the trifling occupations of peace. Again she made an honest effort to enjoy the moderate activities of a sphere in which there seemed to be increasingly little to do. If her preparation for life had been restricted, it appeared that her opportunities for exercise were even more limited. It was natural, it was perhaps inevitable, that she should have drifted back at last to her old happiness-hunting in moral preserves. What was left for a fallen lady, she had demanded almost passionately of the Everlasting Purpose, except the most ancient vocation? Though she nourished few illusions, and none of these dealt with the nature of man, she had not failed to observe that for a Southern lady in reduced circumstances and with an impaired reputation, love is the only available means of increasing an income. A wealthy marriage, she would have been the first to admit, was too much to expect. For, even though men are indulgent, an ample fortune, she realized, bargains shrewdly for at least a technical virtue; and toward marriage without an ample fortune she felt no inclination. But two marriages and one divorce for love had taught her, before the war and tributes to the crowned heads of Europe had depleted her substance, that even widowhood or the path of virtue may be made easy by a generous allowance.

"Never again!" she had resolved, as she meditated upon the natural trials of love and the inadequacy of men as lovers. "I've had more love than most women, I suppose, and what has it ever done for me in the past?" After a pause, in which she summed up the uncertain rewards of the passion, she had concluded, with that ripe wisdom which is so often the fruit of imperfect behaviour, "Nothing. Absolutely nothing that I can show for it. Nothing that will be worth a row of pins to me when I am old. If you're careful, card sense will stay by you when you need it, and sometimes put money in your pocket long after you have lost your looks. But presents, even if they are set in platinum, go out of fashion." Then, since she had been a realist from the beginning, before the bottom dropped out of idealism, she determined to be guided by prudence rather than generosity in every love affair that came after fifty. For it was not, she decided, as if she had ever benefited by what she dismissed, no doubt inaccurately, as the overrated pleasures of love. "Even when I was at my best, and especially when I was at my best, a love affair was sure to be over and done with just as I was beginning really to enjoy it." And it occurred to her, since, like many philosophers and not a few saints, she had approached the ascetic point of view by the downward path, that love, in common with other benefits to be derived from the prudent pleasures of men, invariably appears either too soon or too late. How often had she watched elderly ladies (who were more estimable than tempting) assemble with eager eyes round the card table, at the exact moment when they desired with all their souls to play bridge. How often, at such instants, had she sighed to herself: "If only they realized what it means to have found a solace that is there when you need it." For even this last resource of vacancy had been denied her by a

mind that had never been able to think twice about anything and a figure that had falsely advertised her as ardent.
"All the same," she was thinking not more than two
minutes before she recognized Mr. Littlepage, "if I had
my life to live over again, I'd know better than to put my
main dependence upon love." Then, while the thought fluttered in her mind as wildly as a swallow circles in an
empty barn, she looked ahead and saw a conventional
male figure approaching. Instantly, without effort, without purpose, the glow of amorous challenge shone in her
eyes, and the smile of provocative mystery wavered and
vanished and wavered again on her lips.

"You!" was the only word that escaped her; for experience had taught her the value of monosyllabic re-
sponses. Though he was not all that she could have wished,
she admitted reluctantly that he was more perhaps than
she had a right to expect. After all, though she had finished
with love, no wise and prudent woman, she knew, is ever
entirely finished with lovers.

"It has been very long," he said pensively, "since you
went away."

"Almost twelve years," she answered, with a sigh that
she tried to make cheerful, or at least not discouraging. For
after fifty, as she reminded herself for the hundredth
time, few women can afford to be depressing and none
can afford to be particular. "I was in Europe when the
war came, and I simply stayed on. I helped to open one
of the first hospitals in France."

"Yes, I heard of it. In fact I sent you a contribution.
My daughter heard of you everywhere, even in the Balkans. She wrote us that your war record was wonderful."

"I suppose everything seemed wonderful while the
war lasted." How clear her eyes were, how bright and
gay her smile for the possessor of a lost or even an im-

perfectly restored character! But he remembered now that she had always left a more vivid impression than anyone else, that her colour and gaiety had often rushed into his memory like a running fire in a November landscape.

"Yes, to those of us who stayed at home you appeared to have cornered all the adventure."

"And you never came over?"

"No, it is the greatest regret of my life. Wars for me have always come at the wrong age. I've either had to wave flags or roll bandages."

"Well, there isn't much fun in that." Was there the faintest tinge of mirth in her voice? "I've sometimes thought that the worst thing about the war was that so many of us who were not hurt really enjoyed it. When it was over, we had nothing to fall back on but bottomless futility. I didn't wish it to go on, of course," she added, with a shudder, and wondered if she were not becoming too serious, "but I missed the waiting for horrors when it was over. In the last five years or so I have had nothing to do but try to put time into a kind of twilight sleep." Then the look of anxious wonder was driven from her eyes by a sparkling infusion of coquetry. "I wasn't that way twelve years ago—but you must have forgotten."

A swift pulsation quivered and died in some elemental darkness. "No, I haven't forgotten. But why did you go away?" What a fool, what an egregious fool he had been twelve years ago, when she was in the flower of her beauty and that flower might have been his for the plucking!

"I went away," she answered slowly, "because I needed to learn about life."

"About life?"

"About life and love." Was she laughing at him? Was she deriding his former resistance? Or was she seriously leading him on? Twenty, even ten years ago, he would not have hesitated over the answer. But at that age he had still his ten, he had still his twenty years of vigour ahead of him. On this November afternoon it seemed to him that his retreating youth wore the aspect less of a fugitive season than of a perennial estate.

"I thought," he said, "that you knew all there was to be known about love." Though he tried to borrow her lightness of touch, he was aware that a fatuous expression was spreading like melted wax over his features.

She shook her head, and her lashes drooped while a pensive note crept into her caressing voice. "No, there was one thing I had never learned. I had never learned why there is so little kindness in love."

He looked at her in surprise. "Are you sure there is little?"

"I am seventy times sure. I have had love seventy times, but not once have I had loving-kindness." Her eyes softened into pathos, and he asked himself, with a stab of memory, if she had suffered all these years because he had been true to Victoria? Was it within the bounds of probability that Mrs. Dalrymple (who was still accessible) had cared for him more deeply than he had ever imagined?

"Perhaps you did not look for it," he urged gently. "If you had looked for it, you might have found it."

She shook her head, and it seemed to him that her dark eyes lost their challenge and were drowned in a plaintive sadness. "All my life I have looked for it. It may be that I needed it too much ever to find it. I sometimes think that loving-kindness, like chivalry, is saved for the women who do not need it."

For an instant, so vehement was his response to her voice and her wistful smile, it seemed to him that he was in peril of losing not only his heart but (and this was more important to his legal mind) his judgment as well. "Surely

you have forgotten," he answered tenderly, "surely you
have forgotten that I gave you kindness once when you
needed it."

A change passed over her face, as if it were suddenly
enkindled by the dying flare of the sunset. "You gave me
kindness, but not love," she breathed so softly that her
voice rather than her words invaded his senses.

A flush rose to his cheek, and while his features burned
with embarrassment—or was it pleasure?—he exclaimed
as impulsively as if time had reversed its process, and they
were standing again beneath those Bacchic garlands,
"Then you never knew! You never suspected!" In that
quivering light her face swam before him, and he wondered, with an inward tremor, if there were tears in the
unfathomable dusk of her eyes.

"Ah, I suffered too much to suspect anything!"

While the words still floated toward him, she turned
away and walked swiftly from the brow of the hill into
the approaching shadows of twilight. For an instant, with
a sensation of dizziness, he looked after her. Then, casting an involuntary glance over his shoulder, he straightened his figure and passed on with a confident stride. It was
true that she was still accessible. It was true also that,
after twelve unprofitable years, though she was no longer
young, all the drab world had come to life again
when he looked at her. Nothing, he realized now, had ever
assuaged the old torment of longing. Nothing had ever
moved him so deeply as that haunting promise of joy
deferred but not defeated which she exhaled like a perfume. "I suppose I've always wanted her," he thought,
"even when I was not thinking about her. The trouble
with her is that she makes all other women, even younger
and prettier women, appear only half animate." Yesterday, he had believed that passion ended with youth, or

lingered on in middle age as an antiquated survival. Now, he told himself, nothing mattered, least of all the fugitive moods of the young. Every age, he had discovered, has its own sphere of influence. Every age (there was comfort in this reflection) has its own peculiar ardours and indiscretions. After all, he was only fifty-seven, and at fifty-seven a man is still young enough to be tempted and to yield to temptation.

X

He opened Mrs. Burden's creaking gate, passed up the walk of sunken flagstones, and entered the hall, which was pervaded by a yellowish dusk and the smell of boiled cabbage. At the foot of the fine old staircase Milly Burden was standing, and it seemed to him that the light had gone out of her face and left it drained of expectancy. "She is wasted as if from a mortal illness," he thought, with a throb of compassion. "This is what happens to women who have neither religion nor the sense of duty to fall back upon. It isn't only love she has lost. It is everything. Everything," he amended presently, "except the right to live her own life." And it occurred to him, while he enfolded her hands in his grasp, that the right to live her own life was a frail support compared to a womanly trust in Omnipotence. Though he was by no means unacquainted with grief, and thirty years of the law had prepared him for the usual wages of sin, he told himself sadly that he had never seen a look of deeper despair. Other women had lost their lovers; other women had been betrayed and abandoned; but these other women had appeared always to have something left over, if it was nothing more than redemption. Poor Aunt Agatha, who had suffered as much as a woman could, had clung firmly, though submissively, not only to her simple trust in the Protestant Episcopal Church, but even to her maidenly faith in men. For it was impossible to deny that poor Aunt

Agatha had observed the superstitions as thoroughly as she had discarded the moral principle of the Victorian age. Ruined, she had still trusted. Her betrayal, which had broken her heart, spoiled her life, and irretrievably impaired her value, had failed apparently to ruffle the surface of her settled convictions. And there was Mrs. Dalrymple, he reminded himself, who had become a romantic rather than an intellectual iconoclast. In spite of her immodest activities, she was as little inclined to dispute the merit of the double standard as poor Aunt Agatha was to question the authority of Saint Paul's views upon feminine deportment. Their suffering, he realized, had been alleviated by reverence for the powers that afflicted them. But with Milly, and perhaps with others of her refractory generation, every pious support had been already demolished. What was left to her, he inquired, with merciless logic, after she had rejected alike the moral law and the expert testimony of experience?

"I see you have heard, my dear," he began gently, while he turned with her into the dusty living-room, which was filled with the last glimmer of daylight.

"Yes, I've heard. Your brother told me. He saw it in the paper, and he told me. He told me."

"Don't, my child, don't," Mr. Littlepage pleaded. He had been prepared for tears. He had been prepared for anything, he felt, except for eyes in which tears had frozen to ice.

"You must pluck up your courage, Milly. A cad like that isn't worth your little finger."

"I know," she breathed angrily. "You can't tell me anything worse than I know already. But that doesn't give me back my life. That doesn't give me back all the love I wasted." For an instant he thought that her frozen surface had broken and that she would melt into tears. Then, with a gesture of repudiation, she laughed again in the same toneless voice. "But I am not going to talk about it. Not even to you am I going to talk about it."

"That is the best way. You know, whatever happens, I am your friend."

She smiled without a trace of emotion. "Nothing will happen now. I've felt all I can feel."

"I wish I could help you."

"There isn't any help. There isn't anything but hollowness."

"Not now perhaps, but there will be later. You are too young for happiness to be over. One mistake doesn't seem so important to-day, I suppose, as it seemed before. We may build a better life on our regrets."

Her laugh stabbed his heart. "Oh, I haven't any regrets, not what you would call regrets. I had a right to my life, and if I spoiled it, that is my affair. Nobody else had anything in the world to do with my life. Nobody else, not you, not Mother, not Martin. Nobody else."

The air, which had seemed so stale and lifeless when he entered, was charged now with vitality, with passion, and with an emotion, so vehement, so despairing, that it could be only anguish. Her face was as expressionless as a mask; but beneath its waxen immobility, he felt, there was the frozen isolation of youth that believed nothing. Anything, he told himself, even Christian forgiveness, was better than this. Though he had been exasperated as a child by poor Aunt Agatha's wronged but unresentful attitude, he realized now that there was much to be said for a code of manners so influential that its authority was exerted over the frail and the fallen. So unstable, indeed, are contemporary verdicts that within the last five years Aunt Agatha had shown signs of becoming more of an ornament than a disgrace to genealogy. Having risen poetically to the test of sentimental tradition, she was pointed out by the younger generation as a classic example of antique betrayal. Well, no doubt there was an argument, if he could find it, in favour of the new freedom; and society was probably safer, though men were less so, since seducers had ceased to be anonymous and seductions had ceased to be private. According to ancient ritual the true woman in dishonour had preserved her guilty secret to her grave, except, of course, on the stage, where she was required, by public scruples and the exigencies of the drama, to babble about her past. To-day, or so it appeared to him, all that had changed; yet love, in its ecstasies, its cruelties, and its contradictions, had not altered. Love was still the creator and the devourer of life.

Suddenly he became aware that Milly was speaking in a tone of passionate anger—or was it passionate agony? "I gave everything I had. I waited. Through all those horrible years, I waited——"

"Yet you never told him?"

"It was for his sake. I knew he was unhappy—and, if I had, what could he have done? But I thought he loved me. Oh, I thought he loved me!" She flung out her arm in despair, while it seemed to Mr. Littlepage that the dusk was alive with her sobbing. The firelight had died down, but a single thin blue flame wavered and sank and wavered again in a flickering pattern. By this desolate light her face and even her hands looked as pallid and insubstantial as mist.

"We've agreed not to talk of it, Milly," he said tenderly. "The less we talk of it, the easier it will be for you to get over it."

"Oh, I know, I know." There was a buried sound in her voice, as if her sobs had turned to lumps of earth in her throat. "I am not going to talk of it."

"In a little while you will be able to put it out of your mind."

"Yes, I will put it out of my mind. In a little while, I will put it out of my mind. Everything but the hatred. I shall never get over the hatred——"

"But that is the worst part of it all. Can't you see that as long as you nurse hatred in your heart, you haven't got over it?"

"Yes, but I can't help hating. Hating is something you can't help any more than you can help loving. Did you ever hate anybody? Did you ever hate so bitterly that you wanted to kill?"

"My dear, my dear . . ." No, he had never in his life hated; nor, for the matter of that, had he indulged in any other vehement emotion. To be sure, he had been in love more than once; but when he looked back now, it seemed to him that his love had been woven of sentiment rather than passion. In every case, even in his brief infatuation for Mrs. Dalrymple, he had been able to wave a valedictory blessing after his departed romance. And if violence was incompatible with the character of a Virginia gentleman, how much more repugnant must it appear to the ideal of pure womanhood. In the mannerly past, as Mr. Littlepage reminded himself, even womanhood that had ceased to be pure turned naturally to a drooping melancholia instead of to the more active homicidal derangements. "You must not say such things. You must not allow them even to enter your mind," he urged with genuine distress.

"If you have never hated anybody, you don't know what it means," Milly replied, without tears but in a voice that was still eloquent with passion.

"How can you hate anyone you've loved so deeply, my child?"

"How could I hate him if I hadn't loved him?" she demanded. Yes, it was impossible for a logical mind to understand women, Mr. Littlepage mused despondently, and he asked himself a moment later how the Almighty could ever have expected men and women together to make the earth civilized?

"Well, we must forget all that, Milly," he said presently. "Remember you have promised me not to talk about it. No matter how bad things may be, it doesn't make them any worse to keep hoping for the best."

"There isn't any best."

"My dear, there is always a best," he answered; for this was the way they had drilled cheerfulness into the young in the nineteenth century.

"Then I don't want the best. I want happiness. I have a right to be happy."

A right to be happy! How far, indeed, had they travelled since poor Aunt Agatha's fall. Neither Aunt Agatha nor Mrs. Dalrymple had ever dared to advance the bold modern theory of "a right to happiness." In the nineteenth century, and indeed before and after the nineteenth century, human nature, particularly feminine human nature, had possessed no rights, only duties. Vividly, Mr. Littlepage recalled a discussion one dreary Sunday afternoon, when his father, feeling more Victorian than Georgian at the moment, had stoutly denied the mortal right to resist eternal damnation so long as that robust doctrine contributed to the greater glory of God. Well, mortal right had triumphed to-day over even more inflexible doctrines. Duty, when it survived at all in the mind of the young, had revolved into an alarming centrifugal force. Nobody, not even the most unbridled philanthropist, not even Louisa Goddard or Mary Victoria, spoke, except in moments of heated discussion, of his own private duty. Always, when this antiquated term was used, it referred either to the public duty of others or to some paternal activity of the Republic. In Mary Victoria's letters, though the word "duty" occurred as rhythmically and almost as inaccurately as it occurs in the beginning of a war or at the end of a love affair, it was used less in the feminine sense of the thing that one preferred not to do than as the more dignified masculine synonym for the easiest way. Well, if women had at last usurped the ancient prerogative of man, who, Mr. Littlepage inquired of his soul, was in a position to oppose them with safety?

"You must remember, my child, that happiness is not a right but a blessing," he said, after an anxious pause.

"Is it? Then I've a right to a blessing."

"Your tone hurts me, Milly. Don't let this one mistake make you bitter and hard."

She laughed with mirthless derision. "Oh, I want to be hard. I want to be hard and bitter."

"Don't, my dear. That doesn't sound like you. It doesn't sound——" His reactionary tongue (for, as most sermons and all politics prove, the tongue is a reactionary member and often trips up advanced opinions) was about to supply the word "womanly." Fortunately, however, experience rather than judgment warned him that this epithet, though still respectable, had ceased to be flattering. While he tried in vain to think of something to add, shreds of Louisa Goddard's lectures floated loosely about in his mind; but he dismissed these wisps of research as unimportant except to those who no longer needed conversion.

"Should you like to go away, Milly?" he asked abruptly, for this seemed to him the most promising suggestion that he could make. "Perhaps a change of scene would make it easier for you to put this unworthy object out of your thoughts."

She shook her head. "Not now. Not until I've fought it out on the spot. There's only one thing that would make it easier," she continued quietly, "and that is a vacation from Mother."

"Well, we might arrange that." He caught hopefully at the plan. "Let me send her to Florida for the winter."

"She wouldn't go. Her duty isn't in Florida, and nothing but a wedge could separate her from her duty. The worst of it is that I am her duty——"

"Suppose I talk to her?"

"You might as well argue with the weather."

He sighed. "Well, my dear, if there's any way I can help you, you know I'm only too willing."

"Yes, I know." Her voice was as unresponsive as her expression. Gratitude, like love, appeared to have died in her. "We've forgotten that we were not going to talk about it."

"After this, we'll remember. Now, if there's nothing I can do for you, I'll go up to the studio. But remember that I am eager to help you in any possible way. You know I shall always feel that I have been to blame."

As she followed him to the door, the gas jet in the hall threw an unsteady light on her features, and he told himself that there was a vein of iron beneath her bloom. The contour of her face had settled into a look of defiant composure, and her blue eyes, which he had once compared to April flowers, were now as hard and gemlike as lapis lazuli. "Her best days are over," he thought regretfully, "and she would have made some man a wonderful wife."

"You mean that you asked your daughter to find him?" she said in so low a voice that he was obliged to bend his ear before he could distinguish the words.

"If I had not," he answered slowly, "they would never have met."

"And this would not have happened."

"And this would not have happened."

Her eyes were wide open, staring up at the light, and he was so close to her that it seemed to him he could see tiny sparks in the blackness of the pupils. "But she knew that he was my lover."

"Yes, she knew, but she couldn't have understood. I blame myself. I blame myself bitterly."

"Oh, she understood! But women are like that."

A shadow stole over the flame in her eyes, and this shadow passed into Mr. Littlepage's face while he watched her. "Mary Victoria is different," he answered in a troubled tone. "She is high-minded and unselfish. She must have felt that she was doing right."

"I know. The right thing is always what she does."

His face flushed. "I can't listen to that, my dear. You must not criticize Mary Victoria to me." Surely standards had fallen, he told himself, if frailty in woman could defy triumphant virtue. Fugitive scenes from his early boyhood returned to him, and he remembered poor Aunt Agatha shrinking, with the immemorial gesture of the Magdalen, from the startled presence of chastity.

"Did she tell you why it happened?" Milly asked in a tone that was more scornful than meek.

"Yes, she said she did it to save that—that young fool——" the epithet burst out explosively.

"To save him?" Milly breathed. "You mean from me?"

"No, my dear, from destruction. You must remember that he was in—well, in severe straits when she found him."

"Didn't she find him for me?"

"I thought so. Certainly I asked her to look for him on

your account. Then they were thrown together too much,
I dare say. I believe he helped her with her orphanage in
the Balkans. After all, you must make allowances for their
falling in love. There never has been, and never will be,
fairness in love." He drove in this point with emphasis.
"But, even then, I am convinced that Mary Victoria would
never have married him if she had not felt she was doing
the right thing."

"Yes, it is easy to feel that. All it requires is a little
practice."

He frowned. "You would not say that if you knew my
daughter. Her whole life is devoted to doing good. She
was decorated over and over again for her war service.
It isn't her fault if she is the kind of woman who becomes
an inspiration to others." His voice increased in volume
as he went on. In the last few years he had repeated these
phrases so often that they had begun to sound as infallible
as a confession of faith.

"Is she really so beautiful?" Milly inquired in her
mocking tone.

"Well, of course, she can't help being beautiful any
more than men can keep from admiring beautiful women.
You know that yourself, my dear," he added indulgently.
"And now, before I go upstairs, promise me that you will
try to get over it."

"Oh, I'll get over it. Don't people always get over
things?"

With that derisive answer ringing in his ears, he left
the room and ascended the curving staircase to Marmaduke's studio. Yes, it was useless to deny that a sense of
duty, however infirm, had been an incalculable advantage
in dealing with women.

XI

AT THE top of the dusty staircase a door was open, and plumes of yellow lamplight streamed out into the passage. As Mr. Littlepage ascended, he heard the querulous whine of a confirmed widow, and knew that Mrs. Burden must have preceded him. "I shouldn't have come if I had known she was here," he thought ruefully. "How in the world is Marmaduke able to put up with her?"

"My advice is worth so little, my dear lady," Marmaduke was saying airily, "that I hesitate to inflict it upon you. If you need the opinion of a man of sense, you had better consult my brother Virginius."

That was Marmaduke always. Even without the mellifluous tones, Mr. Littlepage would have recognized the tincture of Marmaduke's irony. Though he was both an artist and a bachelor, two conditions of life that aroused immediate suspicion in Queenborough, the opportune loss of a leg in the war had restored him, in a measure at least, to public esteem.

"I keep reminding her that I have a right to her confidence," Mrs. Burden was wailing, "but it is no use. She never tells me anything."

"Well, here is Virginius. He ought to be able to condole with you," responded Marmaduke, who was drinking coffee beside a littered table upon which Mrs. Burden had just placed an untidy tray. Thirty years before, or even twenty for that matter, Marmaduke was one of the

118

handsomest men of his age; and undeterred by the theory
that the feminine eye is indifferent to beauty in the opposite
sex, he had made himself irresistible to every woman but
Louisa Goddard. Now, approaching sixty, he was still
distinguished; he was even impressive. His leonine head
was adorned by a picturesque mane of gray hair; his skin
was clear and ruddy; and his eyebrows, still dark and
thick, beetled over a pair of large, deep, and singularly
living blue eyes. Beneath his romantic nose, which had
been compared in his youth to Byron's, a short silvery
beard spread away from a mouth that was considered
"too fleshly for a refined taste." Even as long ago as
the last century, it had occurred to Mr. Littlepage that
a mouth like Marmaduke's was as fateful as destiny.
Could the most exemplary character have triumphed over
such unvegetarian, not to say carnal, lips? "I ought to
thank God for my escape," Virginius had frequently reminded himself; for, if he had lost much of the simple
piety of his youth, God was still the oldest and the most
venerated of his traditions.

Though Mr. Littlepage respected art, and was fond of
remarking that he liked any colour so long as it was red,
few occasions were more embarrassing to him than those
upon which he encountered a lady in Marmaduke's studio.
To be sure, the room was large, the disorder great, and
the four long windows presented a creditable view of
earth and sky. But even the thinnest apprehension could
scarcely retreat behind these defenses; and surrounded
by Marmaduke's improbable nudes, Virginius was
assailed afresh by the suspicion that every woman was
purple under her clothes. Directly in front of him, an
undraped female figure was standing beneath a florid sky,
with her feet buried in splashes of orange beach and
vermilion sea. On her right, another naked woman with

indelicate limbs was (of all unlikely occupations!) sewing a white seam in the midst of an apple-green hill, under the pink boughs of a flowering almond-tree. "What on earth!" Virginius thought, turning away. "Is the world going mad? Or is Marmaduke already demented?"

"I've done something new in this one," Marmaduke was saying in the jesting tone in which he talked of art to Virginius. "It isn't only the loosening of technique, though I've tried to see how far I could go that way. But you'll notice a new fluency both in the design and the brushwork. There's a kind of symphonic rhythm——"

No, Mr. Littlepage had not the remotest idea of his meaning. All that nonsense, he told himself angrily, might be the patter of modernism; but the only impression it made was to strengthen his innate belief that human flesh is in some way obscene. In the old days artists, if they were American, had painted decently, and had draped their figures either in classic raiment or in symbolical clouds. But the decorous symbols of Victorian art bore as little resemblance to Marmaduke's carnivorous nudes as a creamed cauliflower bears to an underdone beefsteak. Well, it was fruitless to regret; it was fruitless to reason; it was fruitless even to wonder. On the whole, he preferred to look at Mrs. Burden, who was depressing but decent in appearance, though she wore at the moment an agitated frown, as if her moral fibre had suddenly become unbuttoned.

"You must have discovered that I have as little taste for symphonic rhythms as I have for modern art," he observed brusquely, and added in a kinder tone, "Is there anything I can do for you, Mrs. Burden?"

Mrs. Burden, long, narrow, and faintly greenish in colour, turned upon him the tight mouth and the bleak stare of predestination. "It is about Milly, sir," she replied grimly. "I was reproaching Mr. Marmaduke before you came in——"

"Reproaching him?" Mr. Littlepage repeated in horror.

"Oh, no, sir. I didn't mean that." Mrs. Burden's cheek flushed to the mottled lavender of outraged virtue. "It is only that he encourages her attitude."

"But it seems to me, my dear lady, that her attitude is commendable."

"You speak like a citizen of the twentieth century, Virginius," Marmaduke observed, putting down his cup and searching among the bottles on his table for a half-empty decanter. "As far as I am able to make out, this good lady is shocked by what you and I regard as rational conduct."

Mrs. Burden, who had had her troubles but had never been unrefined, wiped her reddened eyelids on a black-bordered handkerchief. "I expected nothing less of Mr. Marmaduke," she said, "for artists are not bothered by moral convictions. But I shouldn't have believed that you also would encourage Milly."

"Encourage her? Why, I am doing my best to help her make something of her life."

"That, Virginius, is what Mrs. Burden holds against us," Marmaduke explained in a serious voice. "She feels that it is immodest to recover from a seduction. The moral taboo requires that she should remain, like poor Aunt Agatha, a ruin."

"If such a thing had ever happened to me," whimpered Mrs. Burden, "I am sure that I should never have held up my head again."

"Does she really mean that she wishes Milly to be marked for life?" Mr. Littlepage demanded incredulously of his brother.

Though Marmaduke wore a look of innocent gravity, Virginius suspected that he was enjoying rather than deriding Mrs. Burden's evangelical conscience.

"Well, after all, why should it surprise us? Haven't we Aunt Agatha as an awful example of the power of moral principle?"

"But she was a perfect lady, though fallen; and perfect ladies do not exist any longer except as perpetual ruins or specimens of primitive art."

"It all comes of the way girls run about by themselves," Mrs. Burden lamented. "I always said that short skirts and silk stockings would end in immorality. But I don't reproach myself for Milly's wildness any more than I do for Alfred's desertion of me. I told them both I had a right to know where they went; but I could never make them see what they owed to me. Nobody can say that I haven't always done the best that I could; but the more I told Alfred it was his Christian duty to love me, the more he seemed to go wrong out of pure contrariness. And it's the same with Milly now. Whenever I try to make her feel proper remorse, she tells me that if I enjoy remorse so much, I may have her share of it too."

"It seems to me, my dear lady," Mr. Littlepage admonished gently, "that you persist in taking too hopeless a view. I understand the shock Milly's misfortune must have been to you. But you must make allowances for a world at war and the agitated condition of the public mind."

Mrs. Burden looked at him with opaque conviction. "It would take more than a world at war to make me forget my behaviour, sir."

"I am sure of that, Mrs. Burden. Nevertheless, you must remember that standards are less severe than they were in our youth. Is it possible," he inquired in amazement, since he was still young enough and open-minded enough for surprise, "that you wish Milly to be dealt with more harshly?"

"It isn't what I wish, Mr. Littlepage, but what is right. I can't reconcile it with my religion not to feel repentance for sin."

"Nothing," Marmaduke commented gleefully, "short of eternal damnation will satisfy her."

"I was just telling your brother when you came in," Mrs. Burden whispered to Mr. Littlepage, "that there are few things too sacred for him to make fun of. It's living so long in Europe, I suppose, that has given him his loose way with morals."

"You must not believe all that he tells you, Mrs. Burden. But it seems to my unregenerate mind that the first consideration is your daughter's welfare."

Mrs. Burden set her thin lips so tightly that they dwindled to a lavender slit. "Her eternal welfare, Mr. Littlepage."

"You can't mean, my good lady, that you wish to see her suffer on earth?"

"It isn't that I wish to see her suffer on earth, sir. But I've kept the fear of the Lord in my heart, though so many others have lost it. Doesn't the Bible warn us that there is no salvation for the sinner except through repentance?"

"And what does Milly reply to all this?"

"What she says, sir, is that her life is her own and she has no regrets."

Mr. Littlepage frowned. "Such talk is little more than the froth and bubble that has spilled over from modern psychology," he rejoined with authority.

"We didn't talk like that when I was young. Then we were taught to call sin death, not life, sir."

"Well, labels change even more rapidly than ideas. I

confess that I am an old-fashioned man in many ways, and, like you, I find it difficult to move with the times when they appear to be slipping downhill. However, Marmaduke will tell you that the world is better off because it has discarded moral shams."

"I shouldn't like to take my views of life, sir, from an artist, especially from an artist who is so familiar with undraped figures."

"I respect your delicacy, dear madam, but remember that, even if Marmaduke is a scoffer, he left his best leg in the war zone."

"I am not begging indulgence for folly," Marmaduke interrupted. "I am only asking you to observe that by the time the worst of us have finished with life, we have suffered enough to pacify even Mrs. Burden's deity. Why in the world can't you both leave the poor girl alone?"

Mrs. Burden choked audibly before she could gather her breath for a reply. "You forget, Mr. Marmaduke, that I am her mother! Is there anybody who has a better right than a mother to a girl's confidence? I asked her this very question last night, and all she answered was that you knew her better than I did."

"Well, I'm not sure that I don't, Mrs. Burden. After all, there are stronger ties than the umbilical cord."

"Be careful, Marmaduke!" Mr. Littlepage warned sharply; for it seemed to him that his brother was becoming ribald in language. "It isn't fair to torment her when you can't turn her an inch."

"I am not thinking of her but of Milly. Hasn't the poor child been through enough?"

Picking up the coffee tray as firmly as if it were a moral principle, Mrs. Burden departed without the sacrifice of her dignity.

"There are occasions, Marmaduke," Mr. Littlepage

observed sternly, "when I should think twice before calling you a Southern gentleman."

"Well, I've accomplished that much!" Marmaduke retorted, with all the airiness that could be expected of a man who stood on one leg and even less reputation. Leaning heavily on his crutch, he moved to the window and gazed, with the eyes of a caged hawk, at the mournful horizon, where the autumn twilight was floating down like a blue shawl. "God in heaven, these good women!" he exclaimed under his breath.

"They are not all like that, Marmaduke. Mrs. Burden, I think, is an antiquated survival. There was our mother, for example, and there is Victoria."

"But look at Aunt Agatha. Life imprisonment, nothing less. A free spirit condemned to perpetual captivity in a ruin."

Put like that, Mr. Littlepage was obliged to admit that poor Aunt Agatha's story sounded depressing. "It was unfortunate," he said, "but you must remember that Grandfather died of a broken heart over Aunt Agatha's disgrace."

To Mr. Littlepage's horror Marmaduke answered with a whistle of incredulity. "Well, I like his nerve," he exclaimed in the idiom of the streets which his brother abhorred, "when you recall the gay bird he had been in his youth."

"Standards were different then. Even Mother, who had the tenderest heart in the world, never felt that Aunt Agatha had been treated too harshly. I confess that the idea never entered my mind until I married Victoria."

"Yes, I take off my hat to Victoria," Marmaduke replied generously. "If she always thinks the wrong thing, she never fails, except by accident, to do the right one. The truth is, though we seldom agree in our opinions, that

Victoria and I are the only pair of genuine idealists left alive."

Mr. Littlepage smiled. "An unmatched pair, you must admit."

"Perhaps. Not so unmatched, however, as you might suppose. The point we have in common is that we are both genuine. We are neither of us so beautiful as Mary Victoria nor so intelligent as Louisa Goddard; but we are more real as far as we go, which isn't, I grant you, so far as it might be. Our only difference arises when Victoria fails to accept the greatest modern discovery that nothing we do or say matters to the universe. She has never lost the primitive belief that the cosmos is her audience."

"Is there any reverence left in your nature, Marmaduke?"

"Very little. No genuine idealist who isn't as simpleminded as Victoria could reverence the conspiracy of evasion you optimists call civilization. Only a materialist like Mary Victoria is capable of that kind of duplicity."

"Whatever you hold against Mary Victoria," Mr. Littlepage rejoined tartly, "you must admit that she is, with all her faults, an idealist."

"On the contrary," Marmaduke chuckled, "she is as materialistic as big business or organized Christianity. Have you forgotten the way she patronized the war as if it were her favourite charity?"

Mr. Littlepage looked away and pondered the question.

"She wasn't alone in that attitude," he replied presently. "You were abroad so long that I don't suppose you realize the effect of war work upon Aunt Agatha. She had positively a second blooming in the Red Cross."

Marmaduke shrugged his shoulders after the French fashion which Virginius had always disliked. "Well, you can't blame her. It was the woman's year of jubilee. I, for one, don't hold that against women. The only thing I resent is the sacred fallacy that they dislike war. What they really dislike is the war that they haven't a finger in because it is saving some other stronghold of civilization."

"It is impossible to argue with you," Virginius returned, with more dignity than conviction. Unhappily, he could not deny that all the women of his acquaintance had been thrilled, at least in the beginning, by the long reverberations of the Great War. Mothers who lost sons were naturally an exception; but he had remarked that even mothers who lost sons were inspired, if not consoled, by the popular superstition that heaven lies within the shadow of the crossing swords, and that death in battle possesses some mysterious sanctity which is absent from the most heroic death in peace. For example, he knew that he himself (as well as Victoria and Aunt Agatha and Louise Goddard, who worked untiringly in peace to discover the cause of war) considered big guns and poison gas inadequate means of settling an argument, and regarded all wars as barbarous, except the Civil War and the Spanish War, about which he had had his doubts, and the Great War, which was fought not only to end war but to preserve a moral ideal. Yes, he could not forget that he, in company with all the other inhabitants of Queenborough (not including the few disreputable pacifists to whom they stopped speaking), had unanimously disapproved of all other wars as passionately as they approved of the one righteous war they were immediately waging.

"Don't imagine that I reproach the women," Marmaduke repeated. "The prime advantage of living in a decadent period is that you are able to shoulder your own infirmities, and are not obliged to hold either God or the

devil responsible. All we have to do is to reconcile ourselves to alternate attacks of civilization and savagery;
and in the interlude between two righteous wars to end
war, while we are recovering our exhausted idealism, it
doesn't do any harm to invent one more benevolent pretense."

"Well, it is a comfort to reflect that you are as incon-
sistent as the rest of us," Virginius replied sadly; for
Marmaduke's views, though of course unsound in principle, were in some sinister fashion impervious to logic. "If
you had lived up to your pessimistic doctrines, you would
have remained abroad instead of returning to Queenborough. Certainly, you would not have wished to marry
Louisa. It seems that you have preserved that one ideal
anyway."

Tossing his cigarette into the fire, Marmaduke shuffled
over to a cupboard in the corner and picked out his last
bottle of Bourbon. "I've still enough left for two high-
balls," he said slowly. Returning to the table, he measured
out precisely two equal parts of whisky, while he listened
gravely to his brother's reproachful, "Merely a thimbleful, Marmaduke. I'll bring you a bottle of old Baumgartner
to-morrow."

"Louisa isn't an ideal. She is a habit," was Marmaduke's
only comment. "And no ideal is so obstinate as a habit."

"I should think by this time you would have become
hopeless about her."

"Never until I see signs in her of weakening moral
fibre. I have got into the habit of unattainable desire. It
is the only permanent force left in the perpetual flux of
my universe."

"But suppose she should ever relent?"

"She won't. Make your mind easy. There is nothing
in it for her. Louisa is wedded to her importance as indis-

solubly as I am wedded to an unattainable desire. Don't, I beg you, seek to divorce either of us. We are both well mated in life."

Sipping his whisky and soda, Virginius mused despondently, "Yes, I must bring Marmaduke a bottle to-morrow. He was always an improvident fellow. Another man would have saved his last highball. A generous fellow, indeed. Too generous for his own advantage, though neither sound in his opinions nor reputable in his associations. Yet he must have enjoyed life. On the whole, he must have enjoyed life more than I have." A pulsation, which might have been but was not a spasm of envy, stirred the slumbering buccaneer in the decorous soul of Mr. Littlepage. "The difference is," he thought consolingly, "that I was faithful to my ideals—or was it merely to my pretenses?—while Marmaduke let nothing stand in the way of delight. I chose wealth, security, steadfast position, but Marmaduke gave all those things in exchange for liberation of spirit. He has been himself, however ignoble." Long ago, he remembered, in his first youth, he also had craved liberty; but it was always some liberty of to-morrow or the day after. "Next year, or when the children are grown. Or perhaps after I have established a fortune. Then I shall take my fling before it is too late to enjoy freedom." But Marmaduke, he saw with disapproving envy, had not compromised, had not waited for the opportune moment. He was shabby and untidy and disreputable, but he was also a free spirit. He had never been twisted into a conventional shape. "Isn't there at least a grain of truth in his charges?" Virginius asked himself gloomily. "I've spent all my life trying to conform to other people's ideals. Fear, not ambition, has been the mainspring of my character. Fear of the stock market, fear of public opinion, fear, most of all, of what people would think of me." Aloud he remarked, "Of course, you are an artist. Nobody expects much in the way of character from an artist. But my position was different. A lawyer is obliged to build up a reputation for integrity."

"Well, integrity is a fine thing, whatever you mean by it. Now, my integrity consists in being true to my own nature."

"And mine has been exactly the opposite. Integrity for me has meant being true to what other people expect of me."

"Yes, I see it in your face." After draining his glass, Marmaduke picked up the empty bottle and surveyed it with a mournful expression. "You are easily frightened, Virginius. Not that I blame you when I think how your nerves must have suffered in the artificial life you have led. Artificial conformity is, I believe, at the bottom of the chronic dyspepsia among American men. How can you digest your meals when you live in a protracted panic, and your whole philosophy of life is rooted in the fear of women? Rabbit souls, you are afraid of a shadow. That is why you are so eager to escape into the stock market or into a war, which is the only complete escape from civilization. Good Lord! But I don't wonder. I'd escape that way myself if I were imprisoned in this woman-ruled society. After making a republic, you men have not had sufficient courage to keep what you had won from women, who know nothing of freedom because they have embraced sacrifice as an ideal. And you are still too cowed to realize that you have turned the American Republic into an oligarchy of maternal instincts. For the belief in sacrifice is so firmly embedded in the minds of women that freedom means little more to them than an extended area of reform. Already they have obliterated the distinction between a willing and an unwilling martyrdom. It is only human, you must admit, that after centuries of successful self-sacrifice they should seize with genuine enthusiasm an opportunity to sacrifice the other half of the world. So complete a reversal of the situation doesn't often occur in human affairs."

Mr. Littlepage rose stiffly. Not only were his deepest convictions affronted, but his academic mind, subdued by the prevalent habits of tight thinking and loose living, resented bitterly what he regarded as an attack upon womanhood. Moreover, he told himself sternly, there were occasions when Marmaduke proved that a Southern gentleman who had lived abroad could become as obnoxious as any Turk.

"It is useless to remind you," he said sharply, "that some of us have retained a sense of moral obligation."

"My dear Virginius! Am I not reminded of it every time I feel a hopeless desire for Louisa? Am I not reminded every time I look at Milly Burden that Mary Victoria has preserved a sense of moral obligation?"

A look of distress darkened Mr. Littlepage's bright brown eyes. "I am deeply troubled," he confessed anxiously. "I can't rid myself of the feeling that in some way I am responsible. If I had told Mary Victoria the whole truth, she might never have married him."

"Ease your mind of that worry, Virginius. Nothing could have saved that poor devil after he once put himself in the way of Mary Victoria's sense of duty."

"You must not think that I judge her so harshly, Marmaduke. I have confidence enough in her character to feel sure that she acted from a noble—yes, from an unselfish motive. What I can't get over is the way this consummate cad has worked upon the child's belief that she was saving his life."

"Well, I am not so certain that her belief required

working upon. Mary Victoria seems to know her own
mind—or morals—as thoroughly as any woman I ever
encountered. What she craves—though I am not sure that
she herself is aware of it—is complete domination of the
world within reach of her influence. The wider her sphere
of inspiration becomes, the more flattering it is to her
vanity. And vanity, if you will pardon my irreverence, is
the controlling interest in most feminine efforts to improve
the nature of man. Now, Mary Victoria——"

"I cannot listen to this, Marmaduke. It is not Mary
Victoria's fault that she is one of those women who inspire
men."

"That is exactly what I am trying to tell you. Don't
imagine for a moment that I blame her for being herself.
I know as well as you do that inspirations, like village
idiots, are born, not made. After all, human nature has
not changed since we were young. Only the horizon, not
the outlook, has become broader."

Mr. Littlepage's mild expression stiffened into a frown.
"I sometimes think, Marmaduke, that you hold no sentiment above ridicule."

"If you complained that I hold no age above ridicule,
you would be nearer the truth. I am, I hope, a citizen of
eternity."

"Then you have a longer span than most of us. All I
seek to do," said Mr. Littlepage, and he meant it, "is
not to fall below the standards of the age in which I am
living. If we still cherish a sincere reverence for womanhood, as I prefer to think we do in Queenborough, it is
because we have kept our institutions free from contami-
nation. Nothing, for my part, has given me greater pleasure than the earnestness with which Mary Victoria
implanted American ideals in the Balkans. General Clin-
tocksy told me on Armistice Day that she was a beautiful

embodiment of the American spirit. A saving influence, he called her."

"And yet you are astonished when the influence summons her to save young Welding." Marmaduke's satirical tone softened. "Has it ever occurred to you, Virginius, that you are a bit of a fool? I suppose it is too soon to prophesy; but in the end you may find that the Great War has demolished you and your last scarecrow of aristocratic tradition. A class without tradition but with a plebeian appetite for corn is already swarming over your field."

Virginius rose in silence and slipped into his overcoat. A few hours before he would not have believed that he could feel such intense irritation at the sound of Marmaduke's voice. "He holds dangerous views, especially about sex," he thought with indignation. "I wonder if I ought to warn Mrs. Burden that he is an undesirable associate for her daughter."

XII

OUTSIDE, in the dusk, his resentment cooled while he reminded himself of his father, who had been menaced by a stroke of apoplexy whenever his opinion was challenged. It was, he felt, proof of an unbalanced temper to take Marmaduke seriously. Only in the last few years, since the end of the war, had he become morbidly sensitive to such ridicule. And not only Marmaduke but Victoria and Louisa and Duncan and Curle had, each in a different way, begun to wear on his nerves. An obscure emotion, rustling like dark wings in the twilight, fluttered across his usually sanguine mind. Pausing on the brow of the hill, he looked, beyond the sombre canal and the stark chimneys, to the faint glimmer of mother-of-pearl in the sky. At the moment, his own disenchantment with life was engulfed in a sense of universal futility. "Where is it driving us? What is the meaning of it all?" he thought vaguely. "Yes, I've missed it. Whatever it was that would have meant happiness, I have missed it in life." Yet he did not know what this fulfilment was that he had desired more than all else, and had lost without ever possessing. Was it merely that, with the rest of mankind, he had missed the ephemeral flower of delight? He had had, it is true, other blessings. All the favours that society holds in esteem had been his without effort. Honour among men, wealth, love —yes, he supposed he had had love—but joy he had never known in its fulness. He had had his years or his seasons, but never his moments. For delight, he realized with a flash of vision, lives only in moments. It is as fugitive as the wings of a butterfly, and as flamelike in colour. It has no years; it has no seasons; for it is circumscribed by the spirit alone. "Well, it is too late now," he thought, without bitterness. "It is too late now with this heavy load on my shoulders. And, even if I have missed happiness, I have accepted my obligations. I have been a good citizen and a faithful husband. I have never shirked my public duty, and I have been able to make Victoria happy."

Turning away, with this consoling thought in his mind, he crossed the street and ran against Milly Burden as she flitted out from the darkness into the light at the corner. For the second time in one evening she had changed almost miraculously; and while he gazed at her starry eyes and flushed cheeks, he asked himself in astonishment if the human heart could be more elastic to-day than it was when he was young and a lover? Her step was light, her smile was defiant, and there was the softness of a carnation bloom on her lips. It occurred to him that women, especially women he had thought of as fragile, had acquired a tremendous power of recovery. Even if the passion of love had not altered, it appeared to have lost, in a measure at least, its finality.

"You look as if you'd made a fresh start in life, Milly," he said approvingly.

"Oh, I have. I've made a fresh start."

"You must go straight ahead. Put the past out of your mind. After all, there isn't anything to worry about now."

"No, there isn't anything to worry about now."

"It depends upon you whether your life shall be ruined or not."

"Well, it shan't be ruined. Isn't that right?"

"Yes, that is right, but you mustn't be hard."

She laughed, and in spite of the effervescent sparkle in her face, he told himself that there was bitterness in her heart. "Oh, but it feels so nice to be hard! If I had known how nice it felt, I should have been hard all my life."

"That sounds as if you had not put the past out of your mind."

"But I have put it out. I have put it out of my mind and out of my reach. That is why I couldn't stay at home to-night and watch Mother reading the Bible. I've wasted too much time. Life goes before you know it, and then you're sorry for all the time you've wasted. I want to get all the pleasure I can before it is over and done with."

"Where are you going now?"

"Oh, anywhere! Anywhere is better than staying at home. I don't want ever to think again. I'm never, never, never going to think again."

"But you will, my dear. This mood won't last." Where in modern youth, he wondered regretfully, was the proverbial softness of the feminine nature? Where was the clinging modesty of all the lost but lovely ladies in Victorian novels? For an instant, he was afflicted by the vision of poor Aunt Agatha swooning in her "polonaise" upon a mahogany sofa, upholstered in horsehair, while her stern but merciful family bathed her forehead with camphor and forced a dose of sal volatile between her trembling lips. Only a little while ago, it seemed to him now. Yet here was Milly before him, neither clinging nor soft. Yes, customs had changed. But, even if customs had changed, was not morality still as invincible as it had appeared in his youth? Were there, as the consecrated verdict of the past had decided, right and wrong ideas of conduct? Were there right and wrong habits of thinking? Were there right and wrong ways of behaving? Were there, indeed, right and wrong manners?

"Have you forgotten that this is Sunday, Milly?" he asked gently. "You won't find anything open but churches."

"Well, there is out of doors, isn't there?"

"Not at night. You can't run about by yourself after dark."

She laughed. "Oh, I shan't run about. I'll go somewhere, if it's only to church. I can stand church better than Mother."

"But your mother may be there."

"I shan't go to that one." Her voice was so mocking that he asked himself if she were merely deriding him? "I'm looking for pleasure."

"That's a dangerous search, my dear."

"Not when you don't really believe in it. Nothing is dangerous, not even love, when you don't really believe in it."

"You will believe in it again, never fear."

"Not in love. Oh, never in love again. In pleasure, perhaps, but not in love—not, at least, in the kindness of love."

With a start, he remembered Mrs. Dalrymple. Were all women, at least all frail women, alike? And did all women, firm or frail, value loving-kindness more deeply than love?

"Some day you may find both together. You are very young."

She shook her head. "Can you find what you don't believe in?"

"I am not sure, but you'll find your faith again."

"I am not looking for faith. I have given up happiness, but even when you've given up happiness, pleasure is left."

"Be careful, Milly, be careful."

"Oh, I'll be careful. I'll be so careful that I shall never again mistake pleasure for love." They had reached the corner; and for an instant before parting, she looked up at him with a smile that was mocking, ironic, defiant, and mysteriously desolate. Then, after the lightest touch on his arm, she opened a gate and ran quickly up the steps of a house.

"I'd give my right arm if it hadn't happened," he thought miserably. "I'd give almost as much if I had never written that letter to Mary Victoria. The truth is that the world has never been fair to women. Men have never been fair to women." Looking straight overhead, he saw a bright and clement star shining through the powdery bloom of the dusk. The star reminded him of the lost sweetness of life, and the lost sweetness of life reminded him of Mrs. Dalrymple. Suddenly, with one of those swift alternations of mood, which were, he told himself, the best survival of youth, he felt hopeful again, he felt hopeful and young and expectant.

Part Second

MRS. LITTLEPAGE

I

IN HER upstairs sitting-room, which was the brightest and most private room in the house, Mrs. Littlepage was discussing the situation, as she discussed every event in life, with Louisa Goddard. From one of the four long windows, where a canary in a gilded cage was tunefully greeting the day, a band of pale sunshine streamed in a border of filmy lace over the maroon-coloured carpet. Louisa's chair was placed in the middle of the sunshine, and delicate fringes of light waved over her narrow hat of black satin and splintered back from her eyeglasses.

"I hated to bother you, Victoria," she was saying, while she inserted a programme into a large yellow envelope, "but the proper handling of child material seems to me the most important subject before us."

Mrs. Littlepage, who was looking pale and very tired, nodded with her smile of unselfish goodness. "Nothing, of course, is more important," she assented, and thought wearily of Mary Victoria. Her face, which Louisa had admired and loved since childhood, was graver and nobler than usual, and the lips she pressed firmly together showed a bluish tinge in the sunlight.

"Are you ill, Victoria?" her friend asked anxiously. "Is it time for your digitalis?"

Victoria shook her head, while a lock of graying hair slipped down over her clear forehead and the smooth pale curve of her cheek, which had the softness of old

velvet. "Not yet. There is nothing to worry about, Louisa."
She paused, moistened her dry lips, and added slowly, "I
have decided to say nothing to Virginius about my illness."

"Are you sure that is wise, dear?"

"It would only make him anxious and unhappy. He
would be afraid to ask me to lift a finger, and it would be
the same way with the children. It would mean spreading
my death over months instead of hours. Besides, I haven't
the strength for emotional scenes. Since Mary Victoria's
return, I feel that I have less strength than ever. I find
any agitation exhausting."

Taking Victoria's large, soft hand, Louisa held it
against her cheek while her eyes filled slowly with tears.
"I am sorry the doctor told you, Victoria."

"But I knew it, you see. Mother died that way, and I
knew all the symptoms. When my first heart attack came
after that spell of pneumonia, I knew at once what it
meant. Of course, he tried to deceive me; but I was so sure
that I had only a little while longer to live that at last he
told me the truth. It wasn't as if it had been such a terrible
shock. My chief fear was that Virginius and the children
might find it out. I did not wish to spoil their winter."

"But Dr. Buchanan said you might live for years."

"Yes, he told me so, but I am sure he didn't believe it."

"Oh, dearest, why not?"

Victoria sighed. "I can't explain even to you, Louisa.
You see, I went through it all with my mother, though
Dr. Buchanan declares that there's nothing in the idea of
heredity. He says that my having the same kind of heart
attacks is merely a coincidence——"

"He must know," Louisa interrupted emphatically.
"That is his specialty."

"Yes, I suppose he knows, but something tells me that
he is mistaken."

"Isn't it only that you allow yourself to take a depressing view?"

Again Victoria moistened her lips before she answered. Though she had grown heavier in figure since her illness, it seemed to Louisa that she had never recovered her look of abundant but sober vitality. For one thing the colour of her complexion had altered, and the vivid bloom in her cheeks had divided into tiny veins which were duller and tinged with purple. Even her eyes looked tired under the full white lids, with their pale lashes, and there were drooping lines beside her fine straight nose and at the corners of her mouth, which had not lost its serene smile. "Her expression is so lovely that it is not easy to tell how she is feeling," Louisa thought, holding Victoria's hand. "With a smile like hers, it doesn't matter whether you are ill or well. It doesn't matter even whether you are beautiful or plain."

"No, I haven't really felt depressed," Victoria was saying gently. "That is the strangest thing that has happened, and there isn't anyone but you in the world who could understand what I am trying to tell you. I never wished to die. I always thought, indeed, that it would be a shock to find out I had only a little while longer to live. Yet, now that it has really happened, it doesn't seem to make very much difference. It is so queer that I can't even try to explain it. I am so tired that it takes all the strength that I have left just to try to keep Virginius and the children from discovering the truth. That is the only thing I worry about. Every bit of my energy goes into pretending that I am better and trying not to spoil their winter before I am obliged to give up. I go on day after day just as if I were in the midst of a great tumult, a terrible soundless noise, and were waiting for it to stop."

"I have always said that you were too unselfish, Victoria." Releasing her friend's hand, Louisa found a handkerchief in her bag and wiped her eyes.

Victoria shook her head. "I am not sure that it is unselfishness, Louisa. The truth is that things never seemed as important to me as to other people. Life has never seemed so important. Often, when I gave up my pleasures as a girl and was praised for unselfishness, it meant simply that my wishes were not strong enough for me to make an effort about them. Sometimes I think I was born inert rather than active. I don't mean that I haven't been happy; but even happiness has never seemed so important to me. I've had a perfect marriage, and I think Virginius has never missed anything. The chief satisfaction in my life is the feeling that I have made Virginius happy——" Checking herself abruptly, she caught her lower lip between her teeth. Not even to Louisa could she confess that there had been moments, there had been hours, when she had longed for something more satisfying than marriage, for something more satisfying than any love Virginius was able to give.

"You have, my dearest." Louisa was crying into her handkerchief. "You have been a perfect wife to Virginius. No man has ever been happier." Wiping her eyes briskly, she added in a more cheerful tone while she polished her glasses, "If only you could convince yourself that Dr. Buchanan is right and you may yet live for years."

Victoria smiled and patted her friend's arm. "Well, perhaps he is. Even that doesn't seem so very important to me. What I mind most is this noise all about me—this noise that you can't hear with your ears, if you know what I mean. It is the loudest kind of confusion, and yet I know that it has no actual sound, that it has no actual existence. Some day, I suppose, it will have to stop."

"Of course it will stop, dear. It is nothing but your imagination."

"That is what Dr. Buchanan says, but I know better. I have so little imagination, you see, that I could never have invented a tumult like this. Do you know," she continued, smiling into the glitter of Louisa's eyeglasses, "I have at moments a ridiculous feeling that the tumult is all in some other dimension, that something beyond time and space is trying to reach me."

Louisa looked at her closely. "But you never felt the slightest interest in such things."

"I am not interested now. I am merely wondering how long this soundless noise will go on."

"Perhaps if the doctor gave you a sedative?"

"He has been giving me bromide, but I sleep well enough. The only thing that keeps me awake is anxiety about Mary Victoria."

"Her marriage may turn out better than we expect," Louisa rejoined, but her tone was far from emphatic. "Have you heard anything more to Martin's discredit?"

"Only what Virginius told us. He blames himself bitterly for his share in the matter."

"I hoped, dear, that he would not tell you."

"It disturbed him so much that he could not keep it to himself. We are making every effort now to save Mary Victoria's happiness. But we both feel distressed about that other girl. Far worse, indeed, because she has no family to protect her."

"Then it is Milly Burden," Louisa said slowly. "I suspected as much."

"That is why Virginius feels it so deeply."

Louisa, who had a frugal though not a narrow mind, gazed at her with sympathy. "It must have been a great sorrow to Virginius. Do you know, I sometimes wonder

how he could have lived to be fifty-seven and practised
law for more than thirty years, and yet never have lost
his illusions."

Victoria smiled tenderly. "I cannot be too grateful that
I married a man who hasn't that other side to his nature."

"I am sure that no man could have less of it," Louisa
rejoined. "You know, without my telling you, that there
isn't anybody in the world I admire more than Virginius.
But, just because he is so free from the weaknesses of other
men, do you think he may have been a little unjust to Mary
Victoria's husband?"

For a moment, Victoria brooded over the idea. Then
crossing the room, she searched in her desk for a memo-
randum she had promised to give Curle at lunch. "I am not
entirely satisfied about that," she replied presently, while
Louisa observed, as she had done so often before, that
Victoria's slightest gesture had a royal air of command,
of grave decision, of effortless virtue. "Mary Victoria
says only that he had never known the right kind of woman
until he met her." A shadow flitted, without settling,
across her serene features. "After all, what is the right
kind of woman? And why should any kind of woman be
responsible for the moral sense of a man?"

Louisa glowed with admiration. "I have always said,
Victoria, that you are too broad-minded to be a woman."

"Well, why shouldn't women be as broad-minded as
men?"

"I don't know why, but they are not. They are not—
usually."

"Well, you are, Louisa, and I am delighted to see that
your fine example is felt more and more every year in this
community."

The flush in Louisa's face spread upward to the waving
line of gray hair. She had worked hard to attain her intel-

lectual eminence, and she had reached the sanguine period of life when a tribute to her mind was as much enjoyed as a compliment to her appearance. Though she had little exact knowledge, that little was an elastic measure, and could be stretched, with thinning substance, over a variety of unfamiliar topics. Versatility combined with the manner of authority had elevated her to a position in the mental life of Queenborough which sound learning and a vast accumulation of knowledge could not have attained. The ease with which her well-oiled mind turned from antique manners to contemporary mannerless youth was respected in an epoch which would have preferred to order its culture, as it ordered its Battle Creek health foods, from the most convenient greengrocer.

"It is like you to say that, Victoria," she responded gratefully but with proper dignity. "You know that I could never have become what I am to-day without your friendship. I cannot begin to tell you what you and Virginius have meant to me." Choked by emotion, she glanced down at the large yellow envelope as if it were some mysterious talisman of success. Then, recovering herself with an effort, while her thin throat worked convulsively beneath the band of black velvet ribbon, she asked slowly, "You are sure, then, that Virginius has not been—well, the least bit unjust?"

"Nobody could be fairer than Virginius; but you know how vague he becomes when you try to get anything out of him."

Yes, Louisa knew. She had had her disappointments in life, and she was inclined, moreover, to place masculine vagueness among the minor trials of a woman's lot.

"All lawyers are secretive, I suppose," she remarked, "and Mary Victoria is still too much in love to be just, even if she knew the whole truth."

"She is still seraphic, poor child. Almost too much so, I sometimes tell myself; but girls in this age are far less reserved than we used to be. I should never have dreamed of putting my hand on Virginius before other people, except of course when I was obliged to take his arm in the street. That is why, I suppose, I can't get used to seeing Mary Victoria more demonstrative in public than I could ever have been even in private. Virginius cannot bear to watch them embrace each other so openly. He told me yesterday that he sometimes thought the worst man was more modest to-day than the best woman. It is impossible for him to understand that such freedom is merely the trend of the age."

"Certainly, it is the trend of the age," assented Louisa, who was an authority upon trends, ancient and modern, and had found them to be of inestimable value in the dissemination of culture. Ancient trends were naturally more instructive because they were less pushing than modern ones, but all were equally useful as warning examples. Never, indeed, in an historical survey, which, though adequate to her purpose, was brisk rather than thorough, had she been able to discover a trend that moved in a proper direction. All flowed, however rapidly or sluggishly, over an immovable obstacle, which was revealed by the ebbing tide of progress as a bulwark of the best minds. Take, for instance, this bold modern trend toward loose behaviour in love. To Louisa, who was nothing if not compact in principle, and who disapproved of looseness in any form, even in her attire, the present impetus toward indecency appeared far less pronounced than similar trends in Babylon (if you could judge a whole civilization by the biased ejaculations of prophets) or even in Rome, where one could rely, of course, upon the impregnable reputation of Gibbon.

"Surely it is needless to remind Virginius," she said presently, still contrasting the old with the new improprieties, "that Mary Victoria is never prompted by any but the highest motives."

Victoria sighed. "He understands that—or, at least, I hope he understands it. As I've told you so often, Mary Victoria has been the romance of his life. No, I don't mean that he hasn't been a perfect husband—only that there was something more than love in his adoration of Mary Victoria. It was a blow to him when she insisted upon going back to the Balkans. Though he said nothing to dissuade her, I could tell that she felt he could not enter into her motive."

"Well, she must feel it still more since her marriage."

"How can she help it? Why, to hear Virginius talk you would imagine that he had never been in love in his life. But men are like that," she added in a troubled tone.

"Yes, men are like that," Louisa agreed; and she continued merrily, after a pause in which she retreated from the daylight of history back into the gray dawn of evolution, "men and women are so different that I sometimes wonder how they could have sprung from the same trilobite."

"You would wonder more," Victoria rejoined, and she was not smiling, "if you had ever married."

"I am not sure." Louisa looked at her attentively. "Sometimes it seems to me that the spectator has a better perspective."

For she was an impartial observer rather than a censorious critic of the institution of marriage; and she had learned to sift her facts with the cool judgment and the ample leisure of science. Virginius, in common with many other men who find biology everywhere, even in such unlikely places as the minds of confirmed spinsters, had confused the scientific spirit with a repressed mating instinct. It is true that Louisa had a lively curiosity on the subject of sex; but her inquisitiveness was that of the mind alone. Her natural bias (had she not been singularly free from moral infirmities) would have been in the direction of avarice rather than impropriety. A guilty passion had always appeared to her, indeed, to be the most overrated of pleasures. To be sure, avarice was a less popular vice, and lent itself with difficulty to the cinema or even to the more serious drama; but in actual experience, you at least had something to show for it after it was well over. With illicit love, on the contrary, she had not failed to observe that its victims were frequently bereft not only of lovers but even of the ordinary comforts of life. And, after all was said and done by romantics, it was impossible to deny that the comforts of life were more sustaining in the end than the most illegal of love affairs.

With a spring, she rose and fastened the flaring collar of her lambskin coat. Then, turning to the mirror, she slanted her hat at the correct angle and adjusted her eyeglasses on the aristocratic arch of her nose. "For my part," she concluded indulgently, while she drew on her long gray gloves and picked up the yellow envelope, "I have great sympathy for Mary Victoria. Martin is very attractive, and it is easy to understand how she was swept away by her feeling."

"Swept away by her feeling," Victoria repeated, sinking back upon the flowered chintz of her couch. What did it mean, she wondered idly, to be swept away from one's anchor, to be swept out into the vast sunlit immensities of the universe? In all her life of fifty-five years, never for an instant, never for a single flaming point of time or eternity, had she forgotten herself and her duty to others.

Was it possible that she had missed some finer essence of living, some purer distillation of joy? Suppose she had once, only once in the cloudless innocence of her youth, forgotten everything but delight. Suppose she had lost herself for an instant only, as a swallow skims and sinks and darts and curves and is lost, utterly lost, in the radiant mist of the afterglow. Suppose Virginius, whom she had loved, had not been Virginius at all, but the intrepid lover, the young Lochinvar of the mind. There was a romantic and very silly dream which had returned to her often as a girl and once again in her young wifehood. While it lasted she had imagined herself to be in the midst of an immense level plain, caught up suddenly into the thunder of galloping horses. Far in the distance, she had first heard them approaching, while a liquid fire ran in her veins, and she had asked herself, "Is it he? Is he coming at last?" Then, in her sleep, she was lifted by an arm like the wind, and borne away, with the wild horses, over the rustling broomsedge, into a sunset that was like the fire at the heart of an opal. Well, that was only a dream. Outside of legend there were no young Lochinvars left in the world, and all the wild horses, she remembered with a pang, had been slaughtered. After the April dream had come the bloomless actuality. After the young Lochinvar of the mind had come the Southern gentleman as lover and husband. Life, even at its best, was never what you had dreamed, was seldom what you had expected. Never, in its imperfection, is it woven of the dawn and dusk that is legend; never is it enkindled with the burning sweetness of ecstasy. But she had been happy. It was not fair to Virginius, she thought, to imagine that she had missed something. It was not fair to Virginius to feel that marriage, however perfect, had left some secret core of her being still unsatisfied. "No, it is not fair to Virginius," she repeated firmly. A dart of remorse stabbed through her when she realized how hurt Virginius would be if he should ever discover that, in the complete surrender of marriage, she had held something back, that she had never yielded some inviolable sanctity of the spirit.

II

In the dining room Mrs. Littlepage found Curle, who had a punctual appetite though his manners at the table left much to the imagination. Well, if he never did anything worse, she said to herself, than bolt his food, there was sufficient cause to be thankful. Even as a baby he had given her few anxious hours, and for this reason, so illogical is the maternal heart, she had always preferred Duncan, who had been from his protracted birth a thorn in her bosom. For Duncan had quality, if he lacked character, and quality more than any other virtue endeared a human being to Victoria. In spite of the doleful cast of his features and his habit of expecting the worst, which seemed to make him an excellent prophet, he brightened the dullest room for his mother as soon as he entered it. Though he was young and lean and dark there were times when he reminded her of Marmaduke, who was stout and elderly and gray. But, then, it was astonishing how many dissimilar persons and objects reminded her of Marmaduke. And this was the more amazing when she recalled that she disapproved of Marmaduke as heartily as she could disapprove of a member of the Littlepage family. Not that she had ever been unjust to him. Not that she had ever failed to do her duty by Virginius's brother, and indeed by all of them, including poor Aunt Agatha, whom she had released, as far as she was able, from a solitary confinement of genteel tradition. For it was

Victoria who had dragged poor Aunt Agatha out into the benign shelter of the Red Cross and filled her nerveless hands with unmade pyjamas. Yes, that one good thing at least, Mrs. Littlepage reflected, had come out of the war. At sixty-five, poor Aunt Agatha had actually begun to put out a pale December blooming, and since the armistice she had displayed this fresh moral weakness for moving pictures. Taken all in all, Victoria decided, Aunt Agatha, in spite of the outraged morality of her youth, was surpassed by Marmaduke as a family trial in the present age. Was it possible that morality had become less brittle? Or was it merely that a sense of dishonour, like widow's weeds, had diminished in quantity? Nobody, least of all Victoria, could begrudge the price of moving pictures, or even of anything so indigestible as a banana sundae. Yes, it was easy to feel benevolent toward poor Aunt Agatha, and to dismiss her, without anxiety, as a case of settled, if frivolous, regeneration. But Marmaduke, being masculine, was a more difficult problem. He had, it was useless to deny, the fatal personality that overflows, pervades, and submerges. A poor painter, she had heard, in spite of his pretensions (for can an artist who has never been able to make a living, repeated incredulous Queenborough, be other than a poor painter?). Yet, poor and unrecognized, at least in Queenborough, which was careful in matters of reputation, he was cheerful, he was contented, he was even hilarious. "Strings are what make trouble, my dear Victoria," he had said at their parting, "and there are no strings to my soul. The sooner you and Virginius break your strings, the happier you will be in the next generation." As if she and Virginius were not happy together! As if, except for Virginius's chronic dyspepsia and her double pneumonia last winter, they were not the happiest married pair in their own or Marmaduke's circle!

"I asked your uncle Marmaduke to lunch," she said now to Curle, who was looking impatient, "but you can never depend on him."

"We aren't waiting for him, are we?"

"Oh, no, as soon as your father comes, we shall begin."

"Isn't Father here yet?"

"No, he is a little late. Mary Victoria is using his car, and she expected to stop by his office."

"I suppose she will pick up Martin at the same time. He started in the bank to-day, didn't he? You can't say that he is not trying to live up to Mary Victoria."

"Yes, I am very much pleased by the way he has gone straight to work. I imagined from the things he said to your father that he might just sit down and expect us to provide for him. So many writers are like that. It isn't," she continued thoughtfully, "as if he wished to write wholesome books that would make the world better. His ideas are all dreadfully morbid."

"Punk, that's what it is!" Curle chirped, while his mother shivered as if the word had slapped her on the cheek. Why was it, she asked herself, in sudden depression, that a sanguine temperament so often overflowed into vulgar ejaculations? Curle, she acknowledged gladly, was one of those fortunate natures who live in perfect harmony with the temper and tone of their age; and certainly he could not be blamed if the temper and tone of the present sounded shrill and mechanical. Standing there in the pale sunlight, which quivered like gauze over the dark red curtains, the Duncan Phyfe dining-table, the old English silver on the sideboard, and the rarest English mezzotints on the ivory walls—standing there, against that decorous Virginian background, Curle appeared, she told herself sadly, as inspiring and almost as loud as a regimental band. Short, thick, freckled, puffed up with

optimism, and fairly bursting with public spirit, he was the
kind of man, she decided, who never fails to make a poor
lover and a good husband. The trouble was that so few
women, even among those who desire everything else,
could possibly desire Curle as lover or husband. Already,
at twenty-eight, he was making a conspicuous success in
his business, which was real estate; and he was engaged
now in the project of dividing up some old cornfields into
avenues and boulevards. This daring exploit had been
magnified by owners of the local press (who happened
to own also several of the cornfields) into a brilliant
achievement. To the annoyance of Virginius, who had an
old-fashioned distaste for advertisement, Curle had
sprung in a single season from genteel privacy to vulgar
success. Within the last few months, since he had repre-
sented the wish-fulfilment of so many of his fellow citizens,
his opinions had been eagerly sought upon every subject,
from "the art of advertising" to the value of Christianity
as big business.

"I shall have to snatch a mouthful and run," he remarked, drawing out his watch, a massive tribute to his
ability from the National Get Acquainted Club, a branch
of which he had organized in Virginia. "To Curle Littlepage," read the inscription, "one of those public-spirited
Virginians who are helping to make our country what
it is."

"Well, if they aren't here in five minutes, we'll sit down,"
she answered wearily. "There's the car now. I hope Mary
Victoria remembered to stop for your father."

Curle laughed while his mother shivered again. "As if
Mary Victoria ever forgot anything!"

"She never used to, I know. But since her marriage she
has seemed to me a little—well, just a very little inclined
to be casual."

"She's over head and ears in love, if that's what you mean. However, take my word for it, that won't worry us long. Martin is a good-looking chap, but if I know anything about men, and I think I do, he lacks staying power."

Mrs. Littlepage sighed again. "She thinks he is a genius."

The front door opened and shut; there was a stir in the hall, an imperious step on the threshold; and Mary Victoria entered with a streamer of sunlight from the French window. Erect, fair, slender, in her knitted sport frock of pale green, she reminded her sentimental mother of a tall golden lily in its sheath of leaves. Yes, Mary Victoria was beautiful, too beautiful to have married a man who was unworthy in character as well as impoverished in circumstances. And it wasn't, of course, as if he had distinguished himself in the war, which seemed to her, as Marmaduke said, a flourishing hotbed of honours. It was true that a renown for heroism did not last to-day as well as it once lasted in the preserving fluid of Confederate memorials. Though it was only five years since the Great War, Victoria had already observed that glory, when it was not fortified by independent means, was beginning to languish. Even in Queenborough where, because of the military ideals of Southern gentlemen, the war had achieved a great reputation, wealth was abolishing gallantry as a title to fame. For the prosperous non-combatants were reluctant to provide a living for the saviours of that democracy which had been so well thought of while it was endangered. More than once, she had reflected that a parade of heroes in Granite Boulevard would melt away before a procession of millionaires; and that the men who had saved our country would receive scant applause in the presence of the men who were selling it. Yet, admitting that prosperity, not patriotism, is the democratic road to renown, she could not help regretting that Mary Victoria's husband had not so much as a medal to show for his service. Even a foreign decoration, which was as much, perhaps, as she ought to expect, would have proved at least that he had known the right people. But he had won no decoration; and though he was well-favoured, even the bountiful Queen of Berengaria had overlooked him when she distributed honours. Which only showed, Mrs. Littlepage concluded, while she returned Mary Victoria's kiss, that in war as in peace money is more important than anything else.

"I'm sorry we are late, Mother dear," Mary Victoria apologized in her clear, fluting tones. "But Cousin Daniel wished to have a talk with Martin."

"It doesn't matter a bit, darling. Has everything been arranged with Daniel?"

"Oh, yes, perfectly. I knew it would be all right with Cousin Daniel as soon as I explained the situation. Of course, it isn't the kind of work Martin prefers, but he is willing to take anything for a start. After all, being in a bank is ever so much better than the other place."

Martin, coming in immediately after her, looked fatigued but admiring; and Mrs. Littlepage, who lacked temperament but had had experience, wondered what would happen when fatigue at last triumphed over admiration. Attractive in his way, she mused, though she suspected that he was deficient in the qualities which she called determination and strength of character, though Curle, in his sprightly style, referred to them as "pluck and punch." Nevertheless, she decided that she must drop a word of warning to Mary Victoria; for even a weak man, especially when he is a failure as well, will not stand too much driving.

"Cousin Daniel was really lovely about it," Mary Victoria continued. "He was so glad to be able to give Martin a start in Queenborough, and he was as sympathetic as he could be when I told him all of our difficulties. I made him understand that Martin will be obliged to go slowly at first because of his illness."

"There is a great deal of good in Daniel," Mrs. Littlepage remarked, as she sank into her chair and glanced down the long table, with its delicate lace mats and glowing fruits and flowers. "You must remember, too, that you have always been his favourite."

"That's because I've tried to be nice to him," Mary Victoria rejoined. "Mother, don't you think Martin had better sit by me so I can keep an eye on him? You know the doctor at Vichy told me I must watch his diet carefully until he is quite well again."

Martin was smiling vaguely, with the dazed and blinking expression that came over him at moments, as if he had stumbled from the darkness into too strong a glare. Was Mary Victoria almost too much for him? Beautiful as she was, Mrs. Littlepage would not have called her daughter "a restful person," and surely Martin, with his harassed manner and burning eyes, looked as if he needed rest even more than he required inspiration.

"I think, if you don't mind, I'd like to sit by Aunt Agatha," he said in a jesting tone. "She is so quiet."

For an instant Mrs. Littlepage stared at him, while she asked herself anxiously if Mary Victoria had married a man who was not quite right in his head? Since that fatal hour, in the early 'seventies, when she had yielded too much, no man had ever been bold enough to solicit a favour from poor Aunt Agatha. No man, indeed, had ever dared to approach her; for poor Aunt Agatha had been a carefully guarded ruin, and Victoria was aware that Southern gentlemen of the great tradition visited such ruins only by moonlight. "Why, of course, you may sit by her," she answered at last.

"Is there a new moving picture?" Curle asked in the indulgent tone he used to the mentally or morally incompetent. Even when they were small, Victoria had exacted that the children should address at least one cheerful remark to poor Aunt Agatha at every meal.

Without turning her head, on which the silvery water waves were plastered down above an unwrinkled forehead, Aunt Agatha replied in an almost inaudible voice that she was going to a movie at half-past two o'clock, but she had forgotten the name of it.

While she answered, the idea crossed her still and shallow mind that she had missed a great deal of pleasure by being born at least fifty years too soon. Not that she envied either the world or her sex this new liberty, which appeared to her, indeed, to be sadly over-estimated. But an age in which no lady was too frail to attend a play alone and soda-fountains occupied the homes of a more masculine indulgence, seemed to her, on the whole, better worth living in than the ceremonious era that had witnessed her fall. Though she seldom thought about anything, and would have chosen almost any other subject sooner than moralize over her own tragedy, there were hours when, tirelessly knitting baby blankets of pink wool, she would ask herself, in the windy emptiness that so often inflates a reformed character, if the women of her generation had ever realized what the passing of Victoria had meant to them?

While she sat now between Martin and Mary Victoria, mincing her food after the fastidious manner of her girlhood, the twilight vacancy of her mind was engulfed in a stifling fog from the past. Out of this darkness, fragments

of memory appeared for an instant, whirling like wreckage
strewn on the waves of a torrent. "A lady always preferred
the wing of a chicken when I was young. Never the leg.
It would have been indelicate to prefer the leg, even if she
called it dark meat. But now dark or light makes no
difference. She may prefer any part, even the pope's nose,
without being considered indelicate . . . Mother used
to tell us about Great-aunt Matilda. She was considered
unrefined because, when she was asked what part of the
turkey she preferred, she always replied 'the pope's nose'
. . . But that was three generations ago . . . A great
deal may happen in less than three generations . . . He
hasn't a bad face, this young man . . . I like pointed features. They remind me of a fox . . . I always liked foxes.
It is horrible the way people hunt them with dogs. And
deer too. It is horrible to be hunted. When human beings
are civilized, they will stop hunting things to death. What
would they think of a God that hunted men with immortal hounds? Yet they hunt animals that way. For
pleasure—merely for pleasure. And women. They used
to hunt fallen women, and witches too, as cruelly as
they hunt animals now. But Duncan won't hurt foxes.
And Marmaduke says only savages enjoy tormenting
animals. He says even religion is not so cruel as it used
to be . . . But how can religion be cruel if God is a loving
Father? . . . Well, all that is too deep for a woman's
mind. Father used to say that a woman's mind is like a
flower, designed to shed fragrance, not sense. . . . I
wonder . . . I wonder if people really know any more
to-day than they used to? . . . That young man has nice
eyes too. I don't believe he would think me bold if I looked
straight at him. Not at my age. At my age men don't
think about you at all. Only when they need you to make
pyjamas. Only in a war. I don't like war, but I made nice

pyjamas. Yes, I made nice pyjamas. The other women thought I was silly to put in such fine stitches. They told me I was wasting my eyesight. 'Just so they will hold together, that's all we ask.' Who said that? It couldn't have been Victoria. No, it was Bessie Caldwell. 'Just so they will hold together.' That was the way she talked. 'More and worse is my motto,' she told me. And the others were that way too. I should never have put a wounded soldier in the pyjamas they made. And how did they know who would wear them? I used to hope they would send mine to the kind of young man I should have chosen. Tall, strong, fair (I never liked dark men). It's funny, at my age, but even now I don't like dark men. That was the reason I always took the blue material before the other women could get it. Never gray. I always hated gray because I've had to wear it so much. But blue I like. Blue is better even than pink for young men . . ."

Virginius and Duncan, who had lingered over a private refreshment in the library, appeared, with smiling faces and restored spirits, and inquired eagerly if Victoria had provided their favourite dishes for lunch? At this question, Victoria transferred her patient gaze from Aunt Agatha to her husband. Puzzled but uncomplaining, she wondered mildly why Virginius, who would cheerfully sacrifice his life for his country, had never consented to surrender his daily thimbleful of old Bourbon! To Victoria, whose apocalyptic vision of a well-ordered world was one in which masculine appetites were harnessed to the feminine ideal of service, nothing was easier than the sacrifice of her own or other people's freedom. As with most women in affluent circumstances, liberty was little more to her than an illustrious name for which heroic but restless men had died in the past.

"You are not often so hungry," she remarked, with smiling wifely firmness.

Though she addressed Virginius, it was Duncan who answered with his laugh of amiable indifference. "It isn't every day that Father prefers his thimbleful before lunch. Why didn't you join us, Martin?"

Martin looked up with startled eyes, as if he had been day-dreaming beside Aunt Agatha. "Nobody asked me."

"Why, I told Mary Victoria to send you after us."

"I knew whisky wasn't good for him," Mary Victoria explained, sweetly but firmly. "The doctor told me a glass of sherry with his meals would be more wholesome. I begged a bottle of Father's oldest Amontillado. Here is your glass, Martin. Randall put it at my place."

While she transferred the glass with her manner of bright competence, and watched Randall, the butler, fetch the bottle of sherry from the sideboard, her face wore its usual look of angelic patience. "A flame of loveliness," Mrs. Littlepage thought tenderly, and wondered where she had first heard the phrase that sprang into her mind. "Beauty like that is a flame of loveliness." Then, while the flash of irritation with which Martin glanced at his wife subsided into a dazed and smouldering worship, Victoria added shrewdly to herself, "Yet men are strange creatures, and even beauty wears dull and tarnished after too constant use. If only she will learn that husbands are safe to lead but dangerous to drive." And the thought lingered in her just and benevolent mind that relief work in devastated regions is not the best preparation for marriage.

III

BRACING herself with an effort, for she felt very tired and there was a warning pulse in her arteries, Victoria became aware that a luminous veil had dropped between her and life. While she sat there, beyond the lace and fruits and flowers, at the head of her table, it seemed to her that she had withdrawn from reality, and that time, like a shallow stream, flowed on without her. "After all," she thought, with a detachment that would have been incredible to her a few years before, "I have only a little while to live, and none of this is very important." Even sparing Virginius and the children did not seem to her any longer to matter supremely. Sparing them was a confirmed habit, and like all other confirmed habits, it was easier to obey than to break. But, while the slow minutes ticked away from her, she told herself that the whole century in which she had lived and suffered and believed in unimportant ideals, was scarcely more than a ripple in the current of being. "Scarcely more than a ripple," she repeated, "and yet we make so much needless trouble about letting it pass. Think of all the blood sacrifices that have been made to unimportant ideals. Even now I am brave enough to think these things merely because I am at the end, and I can see that it all really matters so little. It isn't worth the effort to cover oneself with the shreds and tatters of what we used to call duty . . ."

With this august term in her mind, her glance sprang

back to poor Aunt Agatha; for poor Aunt Agatha was an impressive example, she felt, of what an urgent sense of duty may accomplish.

"Women don't repent like that to-day," Victoria thought, watching her with a shudder of compassion. "I suppose there is too much else for them to do." And she asked herself if such expiation would have been possible even in the sedate 'seventies if the moving picture had been invented, to say nothing of the still more demoralizing radio, which one could enjoy even in the enforced privacy of a refuge for Magdalens. For a machine age seemed to her to encourage remorse almost as indifferently as it cherished virtue; and it was useless to deny, she sighed, with a singular lack of concern, that the grand manner had departed from seduction as from everything else. Even that last obligation of honour, which had impelled an erring woman to screen her betrayer, had been demolished in Queenborough by Mrs. Dalrymple's completely articulate scandal.

With this thought in her mind, she remarked considerately, "You must not let us make you late for your picture, Aunt Agatha. Everyone says this new film is well worth seeing."

Aunt Agatha, who laughed at moving pictures but never smiled at a man, raised her drooping lids for an instant. "If you will excuse me, my dear, I shall not wait for dessert."

"Of course you must not wait, but are you going alone? I am sorry we can't lend you the car."

A flush as pale as the glimmer of reflected shame stole over Aunt Agatha's face. "I like to go alone," she responded slowly, as if she were afraid of giving offense. Then, lowering her tone to a still softer note, she added, "but I met Amy Dalrymple in the street this morning, and she offered to drive me. I suppose it is quite safe. She drove an ambulance in the war."

"Yes, I know." The faintest chill hardened Victoria's voice. Just by nature, she had often regretted that she had never been able to like Mrs. Dalrymple, that she had never been able really to trust her. Besides, merely to compare her with poor Aunt Agatha would prove beyond a doubt that the younger woman had never sincerely repented. Repentance, after all, was the chief thing to consider; and Victoria had seen enough of fallen women on the stage, as well as in the Home for Unfortunates, to convince her that the first and longest step in repentance is the one that leads to the wiping away of every trace of make-up. No woman so well dressed and so skilfully repaired as Mrs. Dalrymple could ever, in Victoria's opinion, have endured the withering fires of remorse. "I helped her as long as I could," she reflected, "and I should have tried to do it still if Virginius had not become so blindly prejudiced in her favour."

Still hovering beside her chair, poor Aunt Agatha appeared to flicker out like a shadow in firelight, while Mary Victoria remarked crisply, "I didn't know Mrs. Dalrymple had come back from Paris. She was quite a toast in the war. All the French generals lost their hearts to her." Then lowering her voice, she added, "Her war record was splendid, but she spoiled it all by her imprudent conduct after the armistice."

"She said business brought her home," Aunt Agatha murmured. "As soon as she has straightened out her affairs she expects to return."

"I am sure she would find it more congenial abroad," Victoria observed kindly enough. "I don't see how she could ever be happy in Queenborough."

"Is anybody happy here?" Martin asked so suddenly that they started and looked at him in astonishment.

Though his manner was more capricious than rude, he spoke as if he expected an answer; and Victoria told herself that such a question should not have come from any Virginian who had so little reason to be satisfied with his progenitors. The truth was that, after two weeks of earnest but futile effort to be indulgent to her son-in-law, she was ready to confess that he was beginning to wear on her nerves and that Mary Victoria's infatuation became more incomprehensible to her every day that she lived.

"We have always been very happy," she answered mildly, but with the faintest accent of reprimand in her tone. Then her face softened, and she turned with a caressing manner to poor Aunt Agatha. "You must not let Mrs. Dalrymple impose on you, Aunt Agatha. I would rather not say anything against her, but she has always been rather a pushing person."

Aunt Agatha's thin throat worked convulsively beneath the wide band of black grosgrain ribbon, which was considered more suitable in her peculiar situation than the ornamental velvet stripe of the honest but elderly. "I am sure she doesn't mean to be pushing, Victoria. She has a hearty manner, and she doesn't seem able, even with her past, to keep from enjoying life. But I really think she felt sorry for me and was trying to be kind."

The slightest quiver crossed Victoria's features. Only the husk of her mind was speaking, she knew, only the inherited covering of tradition and precept. Deep within, the core of her soul remained unconcerned and remote and faintly ironical. "I am sure I don't think you need her sympathy, dear Aunt Agatha. Surely she should have waited, don't you think, for the first advance to come from us?"

To Mrs. Littlepage's distress, Aunt Agatha's reply was more than sad, it was almost bitter. "I suppose it didn't occur to her that she could harm my reputation." This, unhappily, was one of the unforeseen results of the new psychology. Before the broadening of religious views and loosening of moral standards, poor Aunt Agatha would never have allowed bitterness to enter her thoughts. "She stays out later too," Victoria mused sadly. "She spends entirely too much time at soda-fountains. Besides spoiling her digestion, it makes her appear frivolous." Well, there was nothing she could do about it except proffer a tactful and delicate warning. If sixty-five wasn't a safe age, especially after so dangerous a past, then there was little hope that years would yield greater security.

"Don't you think, my dear," Virginius broke in, with a tinge of asperity in his level voice, "don't you think, my dear, that we may leave Aunt Agatha free to pick her own associates?"

"My advice was kindly meant, Virginius," Victoria replied in a hurt tone; for she knew that his asperity would have wounded her feelings if she had not been separated from him by that inward isolation.

In the pause that followed, Mary Victoria remarked soothingly, "I think Mother is right to warn Aunt Agatha not to allow unworthy persons to impose upon her good nature."

"But who is imposing upon Aunt Agatha, my dear?" Mr. Littlepage inquired in the tone of judicial authority.

"Didn't you hear what she said of Mrs. Dalrymple, Father?"

"I heard, my dear, but why should you be so ready to assume that Mrs. Dalrymple is unworthy?"

At this Mary Victoria stared at him. "Why, I thought it all happened, at least in the beginning, in Queenborough."

Mr. Littlepage frowned. "It is true that she made a most unfortunate marriage in her youth," he replied, while the advocate usurped the place of the judge in his manner.

"Didn't her husband divorce her?"

"Why, yes." He could scarcely deny this in the presence of Victoria's exact memory. "But, after all, that was as far back as the end of the century. She married again, and very well, after that."

"If it were only that!" sighed Mary Victoria, and continued with shining eyes and a lovely colour. "If there had been nothing else, we could have forgotten that because of her wonderful war record. But she has really been most imprudent in the last few years. Even in Europe she has become quite notorious, and it takes a good deal to make anyone notorious in Europe."

"Yes, my dear, I suppose it does," Virginius assented. An unnatural flush was spreading over his face, and Victoria tried not to observe that the purplish colour made his features appear swollen. "He ought to be careful," she thought, with wifely solicitude. "So many men of his age and build die of apoplexy." With this danger in mind, she lowered her voice to a note of admonishing tenderness. "Aren't you being a little imprudent in your diet to-day, Virginius? The doctor advised you to eat very lightly after that last attack."

Though Virginius made no direct reply to her warning, his expression was overcast by one of those sullen moods that she had learned to dread without understanding. "I think I'll have a glass of sherry," was his only remark, and this was flung carelessly over his shoulder to Randall, who was removing the bottle of Amontillado.

"Give Mother a thimbleful. She looks as if she needed it," Duncan said hastily, and while the words rang in her drumming ears, Victoria remembered that he was the only one of the family who ever noticed whether she looked well or ill. "With all his peculiarities, I believe he cares more for me than the others," she found herself thinking, while she raised the glass of sherry to her blue and trembling lips.

Then suddenly, without warning, that luminous veil dropped again between her and life. Time flowed round her and beyond her into an unconquerable vastness, and she knew that whatever happened or did not happen would not deeply concern her. Nothing was supremely important, least of all the intricate complications of human affairs. "If only this soundless tumult would end," she thought, with weary resignation, "and leave me at peace."

IV

A FORTNIGHT later, when Mrs. Littlepage was ready to admit that, however hard she tried, she could never really like her son-in-law, and to look forward with satisfaction to the day when they should discover the small but perfect house for which they were looking, Mary Victoria came to her unexpectedly one afternoon.

"Mother dear, would you and Father mind very much if we stayed with you awhile longer?"

"Mind, darling?"

"I told Martin I was sure you would be glad to have us; but he insists we ought to move the first of the year."

"Not if you are satisfied, my child. Not if you are both comfortable."

"How could we help being comfortable? After all those hard years abroad, I said to Martin this morning, it is like being in Heaven. Can't you see how he improves every day?"

"I do think he looks better."

"And he is getting on very well with his work. Think how much it means to him to have a safe place in Cousin Daniel's bank."

"Of course, it isn't really Daniel's bank, dearest. He is only the president. It does seem a good thing; but you must remember that the bank, like your father's law firm, employs a number of presentable young men who appear

not to have any future. I think that every time I go down
there."

"Well, anyway, it is only a start, and it is a nice place
to be in even if the salary is small. Then you and Father
are always so good about helping us. You are really growing fond of Martin, aren't you, Mother?"

"Really, dear!" Though Mrs. Littlepage met her
daughter's gaze without flinching, she felt a rheumatic
twinge in her conscience, which seemed to her to have
grown stiffer and more decrepit. For, being of an inelastic
habit of mind and body, she had, until the last few weeks,
found honesty easier than dissimulation, and now, whenever necessity compelled her to lie, she rose to the occasion
with more gallantry than grace.

"He is the kind of man who grows on you," Mary
Victoria said proudly. "The better you know him, the
fonder you will be of him."

"Well, that's good, dear. It is wiser not to reveal everything in the beginning." Surely Mary Victoria must
know her husband better than anyone else could—unless
you considered that unfortunate girl who had known
him entirely too well. Yet, in spite of this consoling
reminder, Mrs. Littlepage found herself wondering again
how love had ever attained its proverbial reputation for
wisdom. Surely, she repeated emphatically, Mary Victoria
ought to know her own husband—but did she? Hadn't she
been blinded from the beginning by the flames of that
ungovernable and disastrous passion? Nothing, indeed, in
the fifty-five years of her life, had astonished Mrs. Littlepage more than the completeness of Mary Victoria's infatuation. "I wonder if it can possibly last?" she thought,
with mild disapproval. "He is not worthy of it—but then
you never can tell about love."

Serene, conquering, Mary Victoria turned her lovely

auburn head and raised her eyes, which were as shallow
and as transparent as sunlight, to the stainless blue of the
sky above the bared maples. Candour, sincerity, and re-
sourcefulness, were in her smile and her voice. "He is
trying so hard to be everything I wish," she said, with the
imperious manner which had never failed, at least in the
Balkans, to overcome every masculine obstacle. "He is
doing his best to live up to my ideals."

"I am sure he is, dear," her mother assented warmly;
and feeling that something more than agreement was expected of her, she hastened to remark, "After all, there is
no end to the influence of a good woman——"

"And you can see that I influence him, Mother?"

"A blind man could see that, my child. He simply adores
you."

"If you think that now, I wish you could have seen how
dependent upon me he was in Paris and afterward in the
Balkans. In the first months he would follow me about as
if he were afraid I should vanish as soon as I got out of
his sight. It was only when I was with him, he used to say,
that he could keep his head out of the darkness. As soon
as I went away that black depression would close over
him."

"He must have been in a bad way when you met him."

"It was terrible." She lowered her flutelike tones and
shuddered, as if the recollection were too much for her
composure. "He had been tempted so often to make away
with himself."

"But why, dear?" It was Mrs. Littlepage's turn to
shudder; and she did so, in spite of her conviction that
God knew what was best for the world and acted accord-
ingly. Yet, conceding this hopeful faith, she could not dismiss the thought that, with all the moral endurance required to make marriage successful, a man who had

wished to kill himself, even in France, could scarcely be expected to stand the wear and tear of family life.

"Oh, you cannot imagine all that he went through, Mother. It would have wrung your heart to look at him when I first met him. He was in a hospital, and he had been suffering for six months from a nervous collapse. The truth is that he had starved himself after he went back to Paris. He knew a number of young Americans who were living there in a shiftless way, without any serious purpose, and he tried to drift on just as the others did. But he isn't strong, and he couldn't live without sufficient food and clothes to keep warm. In the end that kind of life brought back the trouble he had had after the war——"

"And then you met him?"

"Then I got Father's letter, and I started immediately to look for him. Oh, I can never be too thankful! It makes you believe that God really takes care of you."

"Poor fellow! He must have suffered," her mother murmured almost inaudibly.

"He went through hell, Mother, before I found him. That was what he told me in the hospital. 'I've been in hell,' he said to me, 'and you look as if the heavens had opened and let you out.' All the next few days I couldn't get the thought of his face out of my mind. He has a poetic face, hasn't he, Mother?"

Again Mrs. Littlepage assented. "Yes, he has a most interesting face. Suffering has refined without disfiguring him. That is one of the advantages that men have over women. Trouble is becoming to them."

"There is something about the way his hair sweeps back from his forehead that reminds me of Shelley—or, perhaps, it is Keats."

"I am not sure," her mother rejoined vaguely, "neither face is quite clear in my mind."

"And his eyes are remarkable."

"Quite remarkable," Mrs. Littlepage echoed, for an echo, she felt, was all that was left of her usual explicitness.

"I forgot to tell you how I was able to find him. It was through Henry Peyton, who had known him in the army, and had kept in touch with him because they were both from the same place. They moved in different circles here," she added frankly, "but you can't begin to realize, until you have lived in Europe, how little American social distinctions amount to over there."

Another murmur and a weaker one was Mrs. Littlepage's only response.

"It was touching to see how grateful Martin was for everything I said or did," Mary Victoria continued in the same fluent whisper. "Do you know that I was the first really good woman who ever came into his life? Of course, I don't mean his mother," she hastened to explain. "His mother must have been good and very unselfish—but she wasn't a strong character."

"Yes, dear, I understand."

"Then this girl Father wrote me about—— She wasn't at all the right kind of girl, Mother."

"I suppose not, my child. But you must remember that standards are very different now from what they used to be. It looks, indeed, as if we were living in an age without a middle way. While one extreme is trying so unselfishly to make the world better, the other is bent on throwing every moral restraint to the winds."

"But that doesn't explain Father."

"Well, you know how men are about women, my dear."

"She seems to have made him think that black is white. Have you ever seen her?"

"Occasionally in the office, and several times when she was ill during the war. She is very attractive-looking without being really beautiful. I wished to help her, of course, but I thought it unwise of your father to keep her in his office."

"Even now he won't let her go. Don't you feel that she is a designing person, Mother?"

Mrs. Littlepage sighed. "It is all beyond me, my child."

"I cannot tell you what a shock it was to me when I found out the truth," Mary Victoria said sadly. "Father would never have told me who she was. I should never have known the truth if you had not written to warn me against Martin."

"I acted upon impulse. Never for an instant had I suspected that there was anything between you and Martin. How could I have known when you were so careful not to mention him in your letters?" Mrs. Littlepage's voice dropped reproachfully, "And I thought I had your confidence."

"Oh, you had, Mother darling! But wasn't it simply hopeless to try to explain? How could you ever have understood until you had seen him?" Rising, she glanced at the clock. "I have just time to change my dress before I call for him."

"Would you like my car? I do not feel able to go out."

"No, I'd rather drive myself; but I'm so sorry, Mother dearest. Shall I tuck you in on the couch?"

"In a minute, dear. Perhaps you might stop for your father on your way home."

A troubled frown gathered on Mary Victoria's smooth forehead. "If you wish it, I will, of course, but I've almost a nervous dread of going to Father's office. I never know when I may run across that woman."

"Yes, that is disagreeable," Mrs. Littlepage's voice

sounded tired and listless. If only there were not so many needless complications in life! "Of course we mustn't interfere with her earning a living," she protested gently.

"Oh, I never meant that, Mother!" Mary Victoria flushed as she always did when there was the faintest suggestion of criticism. "Only it does seem that she might as well earn her living as secretary to some other man. Have you ever put it to him this way?"

"Yes, once, as soon as you came home. I felt that the situation was painful to us all, and I asked him if he couldn't find a place for Milly Burden with some other man of fine character. He seemed to think, however, that she was useful to him and that he should miss her if he sent her away. Besides, he has a fixed idea that he is largely to blame."

"To blame?" The word was a cry. "Why, Mother, he knows the truth."

"Yes, he knows, and that, he says, fixes the responsibility. He feels that if he had not interfered in the Burden girl's life, you would never have married Martin."

"He didn't understand. He was trying to help her."

"It is useless, my dear, to try to follow the workings of a man's mind. He insists that his trying to help her has given him an incurable distaste for interfering in people's lives."

"But a girl like that, Mother. You told me yourself that she never showed any signs of regret."

"I know that, Mary Victoria, and I know also that it is hopeless to argue with a man after he has formed an opinion. I doubt if your father is more set in his ideas than other men, but I have long ago ceased to try to change his point of view about anything. After all that has happened he insists that Milly Burden is a good woman."

"Good, Mother, how can he? As if Martin——"

"Don't ask me, my child, for I cannot answer."

"No woman would call her good," Mary Victoria insisted.

"And no man either, my dear, if she were his wife or his sister. It is her not being related to him or requiring anything of him that enables him to take that view of her conduct."

"But Father of all men! Why, I always thought——Are you tired, Mother? You are looking so pale."

"Just a little. I'll lie down now until it is time to dress. My heart has been giving me trouble ever since that attack of pneumonia. Will you let me have a little more air?"

"Oh, I am so sorry! Let me wrap you up before I go."

After she had settled her on the deep couch in front of the log fire, Mary Victoria tucked in the rose-coloured coverlet, pressed a kiss on her mother's cheek, and went over to open the window. "Shall I close the blinds?"

"No, I like the light." Her voice was scarcely more than a quaver. "I like light and air."

"Is there anything more I can do for you?"

"Nothing, dearest." The soundless and invisible tumult was swelling about her. "Rest is all that I need."

"Then try to take a little nap. I'll tell Luella to look in every now and then and see that you are all right. Don't think of stirring until I bring Father home."

Her confident step crossed the room; the door quietly opened and shut; and Mrs. Littlepage drew a breath of relief while she closed her eyes and sank down in the soft cushions under the warm rose-coloured coverlet.

Yes, Mary Victoria was more inspiring than restful. "Much as I love her, she always leaves me exhausted." Or was it that everything left her exhausted? Every discussion, even the simplest, like this motherly talk, left her tremulous and unstrung, with her soul and body gasping for air. Before that severe illness, she had been able to take a hopeful view of the most discouraging prospect and to quiet her thoughts by slowly repeating some magic formula. But of late, in the last few months, even her magic formula had failed of its efficacy. And outwardly, too, she was worn. Lines were in her face that had not been there last year. Grayish smoke was stealing over her chestnut hair; and it had become an effort to weave the old animation in and out of her words. For of all things moving on earth, nothing seemed to her now to matter so little as words. They were unreal; they were as insubstantial as shadows; they came between one and life. Closing her eyes to the sunshine, which quivered in from the window, she asked herself why the importance of living had flattened out as suddenly as a pricked balloon? "A few months ago I thought I had a full life," she meditated, "and now I seem to have nothing. Does everything resolve itself into the running down of physical energy? If only I were not so tired, I might care more," she thought, "but I have ceased to care, that is the trouble. I have ceased to feel that anything matters . . ." Time and space slipped away from her. Like a pale cloud, she felt them unwinding about her; she felt them dissolving and evaporating in a mist of light through the window and beyond into the transcendent blue of the sky. Marriage had dropped from her, too, with all the years and the crowd of withered husks she had once considered so vital. Her heart was throbbing with tenderness; but it was the tenderness of the past, not the present, and she realized suddenly that the loves which had stayed by her, even when she was unaware of their nearness, were the loves of her childhood. "Is it true that love is outside of time?" she asked, amazed and delighted. "Is it true that life passes, but the spirit of life is immortal?" . . . She was no longer middle-aged; she was no longer worn and discarded by time. Smothered in the rich darkness of memory, she was swept away by a sensation of lightness, by a torrent of ecstasy. "Why, I am a child," she exclaimed aloud. "I am not really old. It is all a dream, and I have never been anything but a child. It is absurd to think that I could live if I lost Mother. If I lost Mother and Rollo, there wouldn't be any life." She saw, through this rich darkness, the glimmering outline of her mother's head against the pale sunshine beyond the window. On her hand, hanging down from the couch, she felt the moist nose of Rollo, her spaniel. "Oh, I could never love anyone more than Rollo," she thought, "more than Mother and Rollo. But I have never lost them. They have always been here. It is only time that has gone on and left us . . ."

She was still dreaming, still submerged in that glimmering darkness, when the sound of a laugh in the street came dancing in like a shower of golden motes in the sunlight. So liquid, so vital, so joyous, was this melody that it awakened everything in the room to life, even the inanimate objects, even the chairs, the mirror, the pictures, the bowl of white and golden chrysanthemums. "There are some people so alive that it hurts," Mrs. Littlepage sighed wearily, opening her eyes. "Nobody but Mrs. Dalrymple would laugh like that in the street!" The laugh rippled and stopped and rippled again. Flinging the robe aside, Victoria started up and crossed the floor to the window. Outside, there was the long straight street filled with violet-blue shadows and the troubled sunshine of autumn. Shadows, dust, emptiness, and overhead the apricot-coloured light in the sky laced with the slender branches of trees.

In the first glance, this was all that she saw. Then, as if

some crystal globe of vision were suddenly shattered, there emerged out of nowhere the familiar red hat and amber hair and vague artificial lustre of Mrs. Dalrymple. Beside the curb the smart gray motor was standing; and on the pavement Aunt Agatha had paused for a last glimpse of her friend. "Why, she is with her again!" Victoria thought in surprise. "I believe they go to every moving picture together. Divorced for immorality," she added, as indifferently as if Mrs. Dalrymple were one of the imprudent ladies who make interesting history, "and not a day under fifty. Yet still golden, still gay and defiant, and still able to have her laugh at the world." Well, she also had her quality. Everyone praised her character in war, if not in peace, and surely a war record was something which no one (least of all Victoria, who had cut, hemmed, stitched, rolled, knitted, smiled persistently, and eaten sparingly, throughout the conflict) could wish to disparage. "Only," Mrs. Littlepage concluded, disturbed but still benevolent, "I thought that cooing had gone out of fashion even in the Balkans."

They had parted now. Aunt Agatha had turned away, grasping her black skirt, the long and proper skirt of repentance, and Mrs. Dalrymple had lowered her daring head and grasped the wheel in her large and capable hands. Then, just as she was about to drive on, her name was called in a genial voice and Mr. Littlepage appeared on the opposite side of the street.

"He must have walked up," Victoria thought quickly, "but why, why?"

Very gallantly, Virginius was lifting his hat to Mrs. Dalrymple. Very gallantly, like a man who feels young but remembers that he is a Southern gentleman, he was crossing the street in that faint sunshine, which cast a deceptively slender shadow behind him. "How well he looks," his wife said to herself, "How well he retains his youth. I am glad he walked up. The exercise has brought a glow to his face."

For an instant, he stood there beside the car, looking steadily at Mrs. Dalrymple, who looked as steadily, and even more alluringly, at him. Then something—was it a glance, a word, a sigh, a smile, or even a coo?—flitted between them. Something so soft, Victoria observed, more amused than startled, that it melted to air in a breath and was lost in the stillness.

"I must ask him what it was," she murmured, turning away as she saw her husband enter the gate. "Some men, I suppose, might still find her attractive, but Virginius is different."

V

EARLY in December, perfect candour demolished the glassy reserve of Southern tradition.

"You understand, Mother dear," Mary Victoria began, "why I wish to be near you at this time?"

"I suspected, my child."

"I was mistaken once, so I waited to be quite sure. But I feel almost too well to believe it is true. Not even for a minute has there been the faintest discomfort."

"My darling, I am so thankful!" Even in the burst of emotion, Mrs. Littlepage found herself recalling an old wives' superstition of her youth. "But she must not feel too well, poor dear. An easy beginning," they used to say, "makes a hard ending." Clasping her daughter in her arms, she told herself that now, if ever, was the moment for complete sympathy.

"Then you do understand, Mother?" Was it the composed voice or the gentle withdrawal that made Mrs. Littlepage turn away, wiping her eyes, and look out of the window? Why, she wondered, should she expect this discovery to change the nature of Mary Victoria?

"I understand," she answered, as soon as she could command her voice. "There isn't any place for you but our house. I could not bear it if I were not able to watch over you."

"But you need watching over too, Mother. You have not been a bit like yourself. There are times when you seem so far away that I wonder what you are thinking about."

"About nothing, probably, my child. I suppose it is because I am not so strong as I used to be; and I do feel sometimes that everything is too much."

"Isn't there any rest for you? Father would take you to Florida?"

"Oh, no, not Florida. I couldn't stand Florida." That senseless irritation again, and the exhausting effort to keep it out of her voice. Why was it that everything, even kindness, irritated her nerves? "It is just as if I were listening for some familiar voice in the midst of a tempest," she thought, "and every needless word that is uttered makes it the more difficult for me to hear clearly."

"It is so important for you to take care of yourself, Mother."

Mrs. Littlepage turned a pensive smile on her daughter. Then a quiver of nervous exasperation drove the smile from her lips. "Don't worry about me, my child," she remonstrated in a tone more impatient than she had ever used to Mary Victoria. "It isn't really important enough. All I need is time to collect myself. But, of course, I must watch over you as long as I live. After I am dead, I hope you will feel that you can turn to Louisa——"

"Oh, Mother, darling, don't talk about dying!"

"Never again, dear, only I wanted to tell you that Louisa is almost a second mother to you. And remember this is your home too. Don't think another minute about finding a house."

"I told Martin you would feel that way."

"Of course he understood."

Mary Victoria sighed softly, with the infinite patience that is the essence of wifehood. "Yes, he understands, but he has been longing to be in our home. Not that he doesn't enjoy being here, but you know how men are."

"Surely he must realize——" Mrs. Littlepage began, and broke off because she could think of nothing to add. For Martin, she told herself, was the last person who should have suggested that a change might be desirable. Certainly, if anyone had been made uncomfortable, it was Virginius, who so heartily disliked his son-in-law.

Sighing audibly, she turned to the couch, and drew the rose-coloured robe over her bosom, which, in spite of thirty-one years of wedlock, had remained virgin in sentiment. Though she had been a perfect wife to Virginius, there were moments when she acknowledged that in her heart of hearts she had never really liked men. She was fond of Virginius; she was faithful; she was tender in affliction; yet she had never, except for the few months of courtship, enjoyed him as naturally as she enjoyed Louisa. For more than fifty years Louisa had understood her more absolutely than any man can understand the woman he loves. Beautiful as this long association had been, it was fortunate, Victoria reflected now, that it had come to flower before the serpent of Freudian psychology had poisoned the sinless Eden of friendship. With Virginius, she breathed thankfully, life, on the whole, had been easy. Marriage, it is true, had been to her less a pleasure than an agreeable duty; but Virginius, since he had been born without a lower nature, was easily satisfied. "I did the best I could," she thought, and immediately there flashed across her mind the eternal wonder if, in other circumstances, with another love, life would not have been different? Even now, from some vast loneliness, she felt the spreading wings of her dream, of that desire beneath all other desires which is inarticulate and ever-lasting. Closing her eyes to the wistful December day, she heard that far-off thundering gallop of flight. "I am really a sentimentalist," she murmured to herself, "and I suppose sentimentality will die with me. But it doesn't matter so long as Virginius has been happy. Men are made that way," she added the more tenderly because she had never really liked them. "They are made that way, unobservant, complacent, easily satisfied."

Startled out of her reverie, she awoke, across an immeasurable distance, to the level tones of Mary Victoria's voice, which seemed to her as thin and meaningless as a whistling noise in the street.

"I wish, Mother, you would speak to Martin."

"Speak to him?" With a dazed mind, Mrs. Littlepage reflected that she was unequal not only to life, but to marriage.

"Tell him, I mean, that it is best for us to stay on until after my baby comes. I really believe that you have more influence over him than I have. There are times," Mary Victoria concluded, with a break in her calm voice, "when I think that my opinion means less to him than anyone's."

Mrs. Littlepage shook her head. "That isn't true, dear. Every wife feels that way, but it isn't true."

One of Mary Victoria's most endearing traits was that she never stooped to an argument. "You will speak to him, won't you, Mother?" was her only reply.

"If you wish it, dear, of course I will speak to him. But I have never felt that he liked me."

"Oh, Mother, he admires you greatly. It may be," her tone was hurt, "because you have never tried to conceal your dislike for him."

"But, my dear, you are mistaken."

"Oh, no, you do really and truly dislike him, and instead of making him hate you, as it would me, it has only given him a respect for your opinion. I shall never," she declared in a tone that was almost hysterical, "even pretend to understand men!"

"Well, I'll speak to him," Mrs. Littlepage promised, feeling that it was better to humour than to contradict a woman in Mary Victoria's condition. All her life, it seemed to her, she had been speaking to people for their good; all her life she had been trying to make the world better; all her life, in the words of her mother's chosen epitaph, she had done the best that she could. But, in the last few months, since this spiritual apathy had pervaded her being, she had become indifferent alike to public welfare and private reform. Flying beyond Mary Victoria, her gaze fluttered over the window-sill and sank down, like a tired bird, in the golden dust of the sunset. "Yes, I'll speak to him," she repeated. Nothing was worth to her now the protracted pang of a struggle with destiny. "Of course," she continued after a pause, "he wouldn't be so selfish as to try to take you away." But she was thinking, "How can he help being selfish when he has never thought of anyone in his life?"

"Aren't all men selfish, Mother?" asked Mary Victoria.

Mrs. Littlepage felt her gaze flutter back with trembling wings from the afterglow. "Most men are selfish when they are in love," she answered slowly.

"Oh, I don't mean only when they are in love, but even when they are not in love. Don't they always think first of themselves?" Her voice quivered to a flutelike pitch, and a flush of resentment stained the pearly texture of her forehead.

"Not your father, my dear. Your father has never considered himself; but, you must remember, there are few men to compare with him."

"But even Father doesn't always think of his family. If only he could realize how unhappy he makes me about that woman——" Her perfect equilibrium was shattered as if by a sudden blow, and she burst into tears.

"My dear, my dear——" Mrs. Littlepage murmured, and felt that her tone was wanting in sympathy. "You oughtn't to say that, Mary Victoria," she continued, after a pause in which she found herself gasping for air. "At least give him credit for generosity—for trying to do his best in a difficult situation."

"But he makes it more difficult, Mother. Oh, why can't he see it? He could be just as generous to somebody else."

"You can't make him see that. After all, my child, even the most generous men are seldom generous in exactly the ways we prefer." She sighed, without knowing why, and gazed dreamily at the bared trees.

For an instant Mary Victoria frowned. Then the frown disappeared, and she looked noble and wounded. "I shouldn't have cared before I married," she said, catching her proud upper lip in her perfect teeth. "Then I thought only of helping women to reform, and in Europe, where I met so many people of loose morals, I never let myself draw the line at a single one of them—not even at Mrs. Dalrymple. It is only since I've been married that I've begun to feel differently."

"A wife always feels differently."

"I don't think I ever realized how strong the hold of a bad woman can be on a man."

"No good woman ever realizes the strength of weakness until she has tried to combat it," Mrs. Littlepage responded. "That," she continued with a flash of insight, "has made it possible for women to erect a standard of virtue. Only upon that single principle have they ever stood together in defense of their rights."

Mary Victoria flinched. "Martin hates that word. He says people, even married people, have no rights toward each other, only privileges."

"Most men say that, my dear, except in the sacred matter of property. To understand all that a wife feels about marriage, I suppose a man would have to think in terms, not of sentiment, but of property. When you are older, and have become a mother as well as a wife, you will understand that men and women, even in marriage, do not speak the same language."

"Isn't it strange how two human beings can love without understanding?"

"Perhaps that is why they love," remarked her mother, with innocent satire. "Your uncle Marmaduke would tell you that love is a divine misunderstanding."

"But I like to feel, Mother, that I understand Martin."

"I am sure you do, darling. As for this girl, I should simply try to put her out of my mind. Men get over these affairs almost before they are begun. Especially after they marry a good woman."

"That used to seem unfair to the other woman," Mary Victoria murmured, "but now I see things so differently."

"Naturally you do. You couldn't be expected to know about men until you were married."

"No, I don't mean quite that, Mother dear. I should hate to think that I'd grown narrow just because I'm happy."

"Isn't all happiness narrow, my child?"

"It oughtn't to be. If I could help that girl in any way, if I could show her how to regain her self-respect, I am sure that I should feel it to be a duty."

"Don't let that idea enter your mind now, dear, when you need to think only bright and cheerful thoughts. There isn't any way you can help her. I asked your father about

it as soon as I discovered the truth, and he said she did
not wish to be helped. She has, it seems, a great deal of
false pride." Though her voice carried conviction, it
seemed to Mrs. Littlepage that her mind—no, something
deeper than her mind, perhaps her soul—had become
merely a rustling vacancy. And in this vacancy, all moral
problems, even the one of wayward women, were blown
like straws in the sultry wind of oblivion.

"They are so different to-day from what they used to
be," Mary Victoria sighed regretfully in spite of her advanced point of view.

"So different, my child, that we have been obliged to
change the name of our institution because fallen women
refuse to enter a Home for Unfortunates. We have found
it wiser to call it the House of Hope." A spark of humour
flashed from her glance and was reflected, beneath the
sadness, in her daughter's smile.

"That does sound more modern," Mary Victoria assented, "and it is certainly more American too." Her lip
trembled, and she added hastily, "What worries me most
is that men don't feel about women the way they used
to feel. Especially the men who were thrown with foreign
customs," and her mother knew that she was thinking of
Martin, "appear to take nothing seriously. When I said
something to Martin about the sanctity of marriage, he
asked me why marriage was any more sacred than celi-
bacy."

"He was only teasing you, dear. I suppose it does sound
funny to-day."

"Was Father ever like that?"

Mrs. Littlepage shook her head while she tried in vain
to remember if Virginius was like that thirty-one years
before. "Your father belongs to another age. He was
brought up to believe in the ideals of marriage."

"Well, it is a pity that ideals have gone out of fashion. When I married Martin I thought that I could become a power for good in his life. That is what Father used to call you when we were children."

"Yes, I remember," Mrs. Littlepage murmured; but she was asking herself if she were really the Victoria who had once, long ago, in some bloomless Eden of tradition, become the wife of Virginius? Well, she had done her best to live up to what a husband of the 'nineties expected, though she had found, as she so often reminded herself, that being an influence is very exhausting. "The only way," she continued, after a long silence, "is to go very slowly. Few men are influenced for good as long as they are aware of it. Even your father, and men were more sentimental in his generation, did not like to know that he was being influenced."

"But I hate deception. Oh, Mother, can't we ever tell men the truth?"

"Not often, my child, and never so long as we want anything from them. I'd go very slowly, if I were you, especially in the matter of forcing Martin to go to church with you."

"But it looks as if he neglected me. Father goes with you to St. Luke's."

"Naturally, my dear, he has always gone with me. But you must not make the mistake of judging Martin by your father."

"We've always been religious, Mother, and nice people in Queenborough go to church no matter what they believe."

"They used to, I know. Nevertheless, I'd go slowly, my dear. You will be much wiser not to insist upon anything, but to make every allowance for your husband's upbringing. Be careful, no matter how strongly you are tempted, not to mention this girl's name to him. Give me a little time, and I'll see what I can do with your father."

Though she had assumed the burden with her usual fortitude, there was an artificial brightness in the smile with which Mrs. Littlepage watched Mary Victoria open the door and disappear into the hall. "My task is too much for me," she thought, with a weariness that seemed to her to belong to the spirit. "I have tried to do my best, but my task is too much for me." As she lifted her eyes to the light, she was visited again by that poignant sense of the hallucination of all mortal experience. Ideals, duty, emotion, memory, the bare boughs, the brown earth, the glittering sky—all these things she could look through as clearly as if they floated before her eyes in some transparent medium. "It must be weakness," she said aloud. "I have never felt like this until now." And then suddenly, out of nowhere, illumination streamed into her mind. "It wasn't so easy as they think," she heard her voice saying above that soundless confusion which vibrated without and within. "It wasn't so easy as they think; but I did the best I could." Her thoughts, which had been clouded and dull, were transfigured by those sunken rays from the sky. Spirals of golden dust quivered and vanished and quivered again in her consciousness. "There is something I must tell Virginius and the children before it is too late," she added hurriedly, rising from the couch and touching the electric lamp on her desk. "I must try to remember what it is; for it is very important, and I must not die without telling them." With her pen in hand and the paper before her, she found that she was trembling with eagerness. There was, she felt, some secret of tremendous significance to divulge—only she did not know how to begin. What was the meaning of it? Why had she never thought of it until the end of her life? And why, having

thought of it, could she find no words that would convey
what she was longing to write? "It is about death," she
thought. "I must tell them what I have learned about
death." Yet what was it that she had learned? And how
could she make them understand if she told them? "It is
the only thing that is important, and it is the only thing
that sounds cannot express . . ."

"December 7th, 192—" she wrote, and after a pause
went on more slowly:

My dear husband:
I have known for almost six months that I have a very short while
to live, and my one effort has been to spare you and the children, to
keep you from suspecting. Nothing, I know, can spoil this last perfect winter, or perhaps year, that we shall all have together. But,
before it is too late, there is something I wish to say to you——

With the pen still in her hand, she looked through the
window to the fading light and beyond into the encompassing void. The illumination had died down as suddenly
as it had flared into her thoughts. Only hollowness was left
now, only hollowness where a few minutes before that
golden dust had quivered and vanished. "It isn't really
important," she said in a whisper, "or if it is, I have forgotten. After all, I am too sleepy to think. Another time
I may be able to remember what I wanted to say. Another
time, but not now."

Laying the pen aside, she slipped the sheet of paper
into a drawer, and turned off the lamp. Then, shivering a
little, she went back to the couch and fell asleep, under the
rose-coloured blanket, in the firelight.

VI

THE following night, when they were alone and not too sleepy after a small dinner at Louisa Goddard's, Victoria found an occasion to speak privately to Virginius.

"Mary Victoria is expecting to become a mother, my dear," she began with the slightest touch of concern.

"So soon?" Mr. Littlepage exclaimed. "I hope she is pleased."

"She is delighted. But it isn't so soon, Virginius. You forget that they were married last spring."

"Yes, it is hard to bear that in mind. Well, better late than never."

Mrs. Littlepage gazed at him reproachfully. "I wonder what has come over you, Virginius? You seem to grow more flippant every day that you live."

"I am sorry, my dear. I wasn't aware of it. However, if Mary Victoria is pleased, my attitude is of no consequence."

"That is just what I started to tell you. Mary Victoria has been worrying over your attitude. Of course, any worry is bad for her. An expectant mother ought to keep a cheerful outlook on life." She had had this phrase ready for hours, packed away in her mind as neatly as if it were a rolled bandage.

"Certainly, I hope I have done nothing to disturb her," Mr. Littlepage rejoined in the tone of formal apology.

While he looked at her despondently, she observed

again that his face had grown heavier and that his eyes were perplexed and troubled, as if he were trying in vain to reach a decision. This was what that unfortunate marriage had done to him. With the thought lodged in her mind, it seemed to Mrs. Littlepage that her whole world was revolving round a central enigma. "I am sure I don't know what is to be done about it," she said in a tone which implied that she knew only too well.

"Done about what? Are you still speaking of my attitude?"

"No, of Mary Victoria. She isn't, I fear, quite happy, poor child."

"Who is, my dear?"

"Well, we are happy, Virginius, at least in our marriage," Victoria replied patiently. "If only the child had waited to know her own heart."

"Well, she can hardly blame us for that. She didn't ask our advice, and it seems to me she has shown a decided reluctance to hear our opinion."

"We must not think of that now. What we must do now," Victoria insisted sweetly but firmly, "is to help her make the best of the situation and bring a happy child into the world."

There was an unwholesome flavour of sarcasm, she told herself sadly, in his rejoinder, "So we are to be offered up this time to the third generation?" A shiver of apprehension ran through her nerves, for she felt a presentiment that he was about to resist not only her moral influence but even her maternal infallibility. The sensation of rocking foundations, of a shifting world, attacked her while she stood there, with her ivory hairbrush in her hand, securely planted on the stable surface of American democracy, in which the superiority of wives is as firmly established as the divine right of averages. For an instant, her knees trembled, and she was thankful for the frail support of a Heppelwhite chair. Without a prop, either moral or physical, it seemed to her that she must give way beneath this endless burden of sparing people, of persuading them to do right, of being an inspiration for good. "If I had to do it over again, I'd consider myself more," she thought, without bitterness. "If I had to do it over again, I shouldn't expect so much of life."

"I sometimes wonder if we don't defeat our ends by placing too much stress on happiness," Virginius was saying. "When we flash so many searchlights upon an emotion, isn't there a danger that we shall extinguish the glow?"

"The idea has crossed my mind," Victoria admitted, "but surely it is natural to wish happiness for our children."

"Surely. I was merely wondering if we were doing our best to procure it. Weren't the older generations happier than ours? Certainly, they enjoyed life in a way that we have lost or forgotten."

"Perhaps. I hadn't thought of it. But, even if that were true, we can't step back several generations. All we can do is to pass on the best we have to our children. Just now, I confess, my first thought is for Mary Victoria. If only I can live long enough to see her contented——"

"Contented?" she heard her husband's slow voice repeating the word. "Does she really expect to be contented with Martin?"

"Doesn't every woman in love expect to be contented —or happy?"

"I hope so, my dear. But I should have imagined it would require more than love to create such an illusion in Mary Victoria's mind."

Victoria sighed and considered. It was incredible to her that Virginius, who had once been orthodox in religion

and an idealist in love, should have assumed what she
called in her own mind a metallic armour of cynicism. Was
this true of Virginius alone? she wondered, or did it mean
that wherever you scratched a cynic you found a disappointed idealist?

"Don't you think you may be a little too severe?" she
urged gently. "Martin seems to us unworthy of Mary
Victoria, but, after all, we must remember that she saw
him in Europe where everything is so different. He is attractive in his queer way, and it is natural for every woman
to believe that love, especially if it is her love, will work
a miracle in a man."

"Yes, I've given that up long ago. I confess that I have
never understood women."

"Oh, Virginius, not your wife, not your daughter?"

"All I can see is that Mary Victoria has plunged us into
an ignoble problem, and you tell me that she did it all from
the highest motives."

"No, my dear, I only told you that she was not swept
away by a selfish passion. She sincerely believed that her
love would make another man of him."

"Another man? I understood that she had fallen in love
with the man that he is."

"Virginius!" Mrs. Littlepage's voice was trembling
with weakness. "Do you realize that you are sneering at
the most sacred feeling in your daughter's life?" The
words, as she uttered them, seemed to her to float across
an immeasurable space, and to be spoken by some empty
husk of herself that she had discarded centuries ago.

"I am not sneering, Victoria. I am asking questions.
What is there sacred in Mary Victoria's mistaken belief
that she can perform miracles?"

"You don't understand these things, Virginius, but any
woman would know what I mean."

"Have patience, my dear, for I am trying to see light. I can understand Mary Victoria's being swept away by an infatuation; but I fail to comprehend why it should be noble for her to imagine that she could make a silk purse out of an ass's ear."

"You aren't often so harsh, Virginius."

"Perhaps not. Apart from anything he has done, I confess I can't stomach the fellow."

Again she looked at him with reproach. Never had she found him so invulnerable to that peaceful penetration which has proved almost as effective in marriage as in war. "I am not thinking of Martin, Virginius, but of Mary Victoria. As a mother, it is natural that I should think first of Mary Victoria."

"Yes, my dear, that is natural."

"I regret her marriage as much as you do. But, since she is married, and about to become a mother, don't you think it is more Christian to suspend judgment and hope for the best?"

"You are right, my dear," Virginius assented. "You are right as usual."

"Then you will do all that you can to protect Mary Victoria?"

"Naturally. Could you think I should do otherwise?"

"No, I couldn't, Virginius." Her weary voice rose on a triumphant note. "That is just what I said to her."

"Said to her?" He had turned away to the window; but at these disconcerting words, he wheeled round and faced her again. All his life, especially since his marriage, he had disliked argument when he was in pyjamas, because, in some obscure fashion, he associated them with unconditional surrender.

"That was exactly what I said to her when she asked

me if you realized how unhappy the thought of that other girl makes her."

He frowned. "I suppose she means Milly Burden. But I am not responsible for her. Martin is the man."

"Oh, Virginius, how can you?"

"Well, I don't mean just that. It is too late now to speak with any decision, and even at the right time I doubt if speaking would have done any good. But I can never understand the way women appear invariably to take the side of a cad."

"Not always, Virginius. Surely you have not forgotten my defense of poor Aunt Agatha and even of Mrs. Dalrymple."

"Yes, I give you credit for that. You have always been bigger than other women, even if, as Marmaduke says, you have expanded without shedding the husks of tradition."

"Does he say that? It is unkind of him." Already she was in bed, and the linen sheet, with its embroidered design of twin doves holding her monogram, was folded back over her bosom. For an instant, a retort trembled upon her lips beneath the shining film of camphor ice. Then, remembering the weakness of her heart and the secret martyrdom she was enduring for her family, she shook her head while the resentment in her expression softened to pity. "Do you think that is quite fair of Marmaduke?" she asked plaintively. "Have you ever doubted my willingness to befriend Milly Burden?"

"Good God, Victoria! Do you mean you would put her into your refuge?"

"No, I don't mean that. I could find a place for her in which she could earn her living and regain her self-respect without being a constant cross to Mary Victoria. The child tells me that she is afraid to go down to your office ——or to send Martin."

"There's nothing to bring her to my office, and still less, I hope, to bring Martin."

"It is impossible to have a serious discussion when you turn everything to ridicule."

"Who asked, my dear, for a serious discussion? Not I."

"But how can you fail to accept your share of responsibility? After all, you are the one who brought Mary Victoria and Martin together."

The clear flush in his face was stained instantly with a dark purple, and she thought fearfully of the men of his age who had dropped dead on the golf course and elsewhere. "I asked her to look for the lover of another woman," he rejoined, almost angrily. "I trusted her to be fair."

"You must have known, or I could have told you, that you were taking a grave risk. Did it never occur to you that Mary Victoria has some peculiar power over men? I sometimes think that her platonic attitude only makes her attraction the more provocative. But all the same," she insisted firmly, "I am convinced that she would never have fallen in love with Martin had he not made her believe that she was necessary to his salvation." Stout and wifely, in her chaste cambric nightgown, she watched her husband with a dispassionate gaze.

Mr. Littlepage untied the cords of his dressing-gown and settled himself wearily between the fragrant sheets. "It was a pity she ever gave up missionary work," he said, reaching for a small blue bottle and swallowing a digestive tablet. "In the Congo she might have saved whole tribes without being obliged to marry a single one of them."

"If you insist upon being frivolous, Virginius——"

"I insist upon nothing, my dear, not even upon the importance of frivolity in marriage."

"What I am trying to tell you——" Closing her eyes,

Victoria breathed a silent prayer for patience. "What I am trying to tell you is simply that Milly Burden would be much happier if she could go away and begin life all over again."

"Well, she'd go like a shot, Victoria, if it were not for her mother."

Mrs. Littlepage opened her eyes. "What does her mother do?"

"According to Marmaduke and Milly the lady's vocation resembles Mary Victoria's. She is engaged in reforming the world."

"What kind of reform, Virginius?"

"Her specialty, like Mary Victoria's, is character, though she differs, it seems, in confining her energy to female character."

"I could wish, Virginius, that you would choose some other subject for flippancy. But I wonder," she added thoughtfully, after a pause, "if she can be the very person for whom I am looking."

"She? Do you mean Milly? I am positive that she is not."

"I mean her mother, of course. Is she perfectly respectable?"

"So respectable, my dear, that Louisa is a fly-by-night beside her."

"I wish you would not take that tone, Virginius, when I am trying my best to think of some way to help the situation. Now, if you are ready to put out the light, I will take time to consider."

The light was put out, and turning on her side, Victoria considered long after her husband had fallen asleep. She considered first how dangerous a spirit of levity may become when it refuses to be controlled by religious beliefs, and secondly she reflected that Virginius (though he made little trouble about the more improbable articles of religion) was sadly lacking in earnest conviction. After this, she moralized upon Mary Victoria's unfortunate marriage, upon the infidelity and intemperance of the youth of to-day, upon the danger of another war in the near future, upon the general futility of the League of Nations, upon the comfort of established beliefs, and upon the moral value of a determination to look on the bright side and hope for the best. And while she lay there, in her luxurious bed, beneath the satin coverlet, which was scented with lavender, she was aware, without surprise, that these meditations were merely the formal patterns of inherited opinions. Like faded petals that enclose the living heart of a flower, they were folded round a radiant centre below the shifting surface of consciousness. They might wither, these clustering leaves, they might even drop away, and yet she knew that her deeper self, her hidden centre, would remain inviolable. "All these things have their uses," she thought, "but they are not really important."

And then, before falling asleep, she patiently mused upon the inspirational needs of Mrs. Burden and the broad but specific requirements of the House of Hope.

VII

"Yes, this is the best, this is the only way," Victoria repeated, as she ascended Mrs. Burden's steps the next afternoon. While she had walked from Juniper Hill, for with her usual sound judgment she had decided not to drive to the door, she had rehearsed the approaching scene, and had learned by heart the kind, but not too kind, words that she intended to speak. So mechanical had the phrase become on her lips that, when she found the bell beneath withered creepers, and Marmaduke unexpectedly opened the door, she found herself still chanting, "I have come in the hope that I might be of some help to you."

Cheerful, middle-aged, and still adventurous, Marmaduke glared at her, through enormous spectacles, with eyes that made her think of a cynical owl. In his shabby clothes he seemed to her, while her accurate glance counted the spots on his waistcoat, a mere bundle of deplorable habits. Then he removed his disfiguring glasses, and she observed that his eyes were as bright and blue as they had been in his youth and that the skin of his face and throat was still fresh and ruddy.

"Well, that's kind of you, Victoria," he returned, holding the door open with his crutch, while she passed in and stood looking up at him in the greenish light of the hall. "I am glad," he added in a genial tone, "that you do not harbour resentment."

Standing at the foot of the dim staircase, she glanced

round her with an ineradicable suspicion. "I have no re-sentment against you, Marmaduke," she answered sin-cerely, "but my heart has been weak since my illness last winter, and I doubt if I am equal to that long flight of stairs. However, I'll try," she added in a conciliatory tone, "if you'll let me go very slowly."

"As slowly as you please, Victoria. There won't be anybody else using the stairs this afternoon."

"Are you alone in the house?"

"No, but I'm the only lodger at present, and Mrs. Burden and Milly are content to be private. The maid of all work will not come up until she brings me my dinner."

Holding her black satin skirt as decorously as fashion permitted, Victoria climbed as far as the second floor. Though she dreaded to be alone with Marmaduke, she felt that urgent need of protecting him from his own nature which she entertained in regard to every member of the male sex. No matter how large in person or emi-nent in public virtues a man might be, she had never encountered one who was not dependent, even when he was unaware of it, upon the chivalry of women. It was this chivalry that prompted her to take advantage of any opportunity to win Marmaduke from his low ideals and his still lower acquaintances. "If only I could exert some purifying influence," she thought, casting an appre-hensive look over her shoulder down the dark hall. "If only I could make him see the real meaning of life." The real meaning of life! Eagerly, she grasped the phrase. Her mind, which was airy and spacious and honeycombed with platitudes, was suddenly illuminated by hope.

"I wonder if you would mind going ahead," she said at last, feeling safer with Marmaduke hobbling in front of her. "I am obliged to take my time on account of my heart, and you are so wonderful with your artificial leg."

It was only natural to suspect that a man of his character, especially when he was endowed with artistic insight as well, would be disposed to see more than he ought to see of any woman.

"I'm doing a portrait of Virginius now," Marmaduke said, while he steadied himself on the stairs. "Not a likeness, you understand, but a study in shadows. I wanted to catch those jolly purple shadows in Virginius's face."

Purple shadows! And of all unexpected corners, to look for them in the face of Virginius! "But there aren't any," she returned, with her still lovely and ingenuous smile. "I am sure if there had been, I should have noticed them. Virginius has always had an unusually fine complexion."

"No, you wouldn't have seen them; but by the time I've finished with them, you may admit that the shadows in a man's face are more significant than anything that he says."

What an unbalanced mind! What an ignoble vision! It was incomprehensible to her that any Virginian, born of the great tradition, with an inalienable right to enjoy the best people, should prefer to spend his time in the social backwater of Queenborough. With this wonder overshadowing her aversion from his indelicacy, she rejoined in a tone of gentle rebuke:

"At least you will not deny that I know Virginius better than anyone else could."

"Yes, Victoria, I am obliged to deny that." Though his eyes were laughing, his sensual lips, which always embarrassed her, as if they were improperly exposed by his beard, had become as grave as a philosopher's. "I admit that you know the husband; but the husband is very far from the beginning and the end of a man."

She looked hurt but forgiving. "I am satisfied that he keeps nothing from me. The thing that I am most grateful for in my life is that I have been able to make Virginius happy."

"Yes, you've done as much as one woman could, my dear sister."

A frown hardened her gentle features. "Are you implying that my husband is leading a double life, Marmaduke?"

"No, Victoria. I am implying that, like every other man, he is leading a quadruple one. Four secret lives aren't too many to allow a man when you consider the millions of predatory cells of which he is composed."

Though she entertained only a natural dislike for Marmaduke when he was absent, there were occasions in his presence when she understood, as she had once confessed to Louisa, why women so frequently murdered men. Not that she herself, she had hastened to explain, ever felt the slightest inclination to violence; simply that she could understand, at such moments, why other women had been unable to restrain their more choleric temperaments. Out of the depth of this comprehension, she remarked frigidly, "On the contrary, Virginius has been always as open as the day with me."

Marmaduke shook his head with the droll gesture that had made so much trouble for her as a bride. "Not with those shadows, Victoria. His guilty secrets are written in his face for any observant painter to read. Come up, and tell me what you think of my portrait. There aren't many occasions in life when a man wants the truth from a woman, but this happens to be one of them."

How could she, how could any woman tell, Victoria asked herself, whether Marmaduke was making fun of her intelligence or merely preserving his reputation as a buffoon? As she followed him up the staircase, which seemed to her dangerously insecure, she reminded herself that she had long ago resolved not to take him too seriously. Nevertheless, it was impossible to deny that the steep climb to his studio was strewn with conjectures. At the top of the stairs the band of sunlight was spreading, and in the middle of the studio Marmaduke, who had neatly whisked a decanter and a couple of glasses out of sight, stood waiting for her.

"You've never done me so much honour before, my dear sister. If I had expected you, I might have arranged a more flattering reception."

"Please don't bother, Marmaduke. What lovely sunshine!"

Standing there, while her eyes swept his pictures, she looked in vain for some object that she might admire without doing violence either to her womanly instincts or her religious convictions. Why, she found herself wondering, did Marmaduke, and indeed so many other modern artists, for the failing appeared to be general in art, insist upon painting only the more unpleasant aspects of nature? And apart from the mere indecency of his subjects, she doubted, as emphatically as Virginius had done a few weeks before, if the figures of even improper women, when they were undressed, were really as red or purple as he painted them. Moreover, what was the use, she concluded triumphantly, in painting a picture or writing a book that did not help to make the world better? "There's Virginius over there on that easel," he waved in the direction of the window. "What do you make of it?"

"Make of it?" Her reply was a wail. "Why, that isn't Virginius. You're painting raw flesh."

"You don't like it?" He was obviously disappointed. "You can't see a likeness?"

"There isn't the remotest suggestion of Virginius. Oh, Marmaduke," her vehemence ebbed in a murmur of pro-

test. "I can't see any good that it serves to go on painting
these things over and over. Of course," she continued, with
simple dignity, "I don't pretend to know much about art,
but I do love beauty." She closed her eyes as she spoke
because the brilliant sunshine clashing with these intemperate colours gave her a sensation of giddiness. Why had
she never suspected that so many violent shocks could be
wrung out of apparently insignificant tubes of paint?

"Do you?" Supporting himself against the table, Marmaduke smiled down on her as he waved a dirty remnant
of black cloth in his free hand. "Well, that's too deep
for me. I am not a philosopher, I am merely a painter. All
I am trying to do is to get in touch with some form of
reality."

"But do you believe that reality is obliged to be ugly?"

"I believe nothing. I paint what I see. If you choose to
call it ugliness instead of beauty, that isn't my fault. You
must blame it either upon an Act of God or a miscarriage
of nature."

"We were taught when I was young," Victoria remonstrated gently, "that truth is beauty."

"I know we were, my dear sister. That is a part of our
trouble."

She sighed with unresentful patience. "But, surely, you
cannot enjoy looking at such unpleasant subjects?"

"I don't know, Victoria. Candidly, I don't know. I suppose it all depends upon how much or how little you see
of an object. Most things aren't beautiful if you look
below the skin or the rind. Human beings are certainly
not, nor, for that matter, is human nature. On the contrary, pomegranates are beautiful even when you cut
into them; but one can scarcely go on painting pomegranates forever. I'd rather, if the choice is mine, take a chance
away from æsthetics to truth. After all, it is life I am

working on, not decoration. I am trying with every stroke
to get as far away as possible from all the smugness and
priggishness we were brought up to believe in. For the
last few days, I have been trying to see what Virginius
would look like if the old Virginia gentleman were wiped
out of his face."

"But isn't the quality you call smugness and priggishness simply what the best people everywhere think of as
religion?"

"Perhaps. That is what I am trying to find out."

"Oh, Marmaduke," she pleaded more sweetly, "what
good can possibly come from finding out what ought not
to be true?"

"I cannot answer, Victoria. I don't know anything. It
might, I suppose, shake us out of our moral complacency."

"But," she held to her principle with more than usual
tenacity. "Isn't there a chance that we may be complacent only because we know that we are right? After all,
hasn't Christianity survived the ages?"

His blue eyes were squinting in the sunshine, and a
smile of artless merriment puckered the carnivorous lips
within the silvery sheen of his beard. While her delicacy
shuddered away from him, he inquired pleasantly, "Have
you ever given a thought, Victoria, to what the shape of
a platitude would be if it assumed a symbolic form? If
you were drawing one, for example, would you make it
round, oval, or square? An oblate sphere? Or simply a
hollow square? No, I'm not teasing you, my dear. I am
really in earnest. After all, you are one of the few persons
I've known for whom I've never lost my respect. It is true
that your heart is very far in advance of your head; but
when you are remembered, it will be by the heart, not the
head, of the future."

The flush of indignation faded slowly from Victoria's

features. Even her early training, which had prepared her to soothe the tired brow and tame the predatory nature of man, had failed to anticipate the sharper thrust of intelligence. In her youth all that a lady needed to learn, after she had acquired the art of smiling above a wasp-waist, was the easier process of how to become an edifying example. As a bride, she had fervently longed to soothe and tame, as well as inspire, Virginius; and though she would have died sooner than admit the fact, the first year of her marriage might have been less disappointing if he had magnanimously cultivated a lower nature. Those were the months, before Duncan was born, when her beauty was in its angelic perfection, and Marmaduke had facetiously compared her to Una with a lamb in a lion's skin.

As she recalled this unseemly jest, her matronly expression became more severe, and she remarked coldly, "It is getting late, Marmaduke, and I should like to have a few words with Mrs. Burden before I go. Could you ring the bell and ask if she is at home?"

He looked at her in astonishment. "Do you mean that you wish to see Mrs. Burden?"

"Certainly. Why not?"

"No reason whatever. Only it seems a strange thing to wish."

"I understand," her voice wavered, "that she is perfectly respectable."

"She is more than respectable. She is estimable; she is an ennobling influence."

Though Mrs. Littlepage was always suspicious of Marmaduke, his description of Mrs. Burden impressed her as favourable rather than otherwise. "If she is indeed that, I am sure that she is the very person we need. Has she, are you aware, a particular vocation?"

"Only, I believe, for making the world better."

This again, in spite of his levity, might be considered encouraging. "It wouldn't surprise me," observed Victoria, who was hopeful but contained, "if she should turn out to be the ideal matron."

"Matron? Of what? Is it a Sunday school?"

"Please don't try to be funny. We are looking for an assistant matron for our House of Hope. It was founded by your mother, and used to be called, you remember, the Home for Unfortunates. We receive wayward girls after a first offense."

"Yes, I remember." He looked as grave, she said to herself with relief, as a judge on the bench. "But I doubt if waywardness would have the slightest attraction for Mrs. Burden. Why don't you try Mary Victoria?"

"Marmaduke!" The dark flush, which was far from becoming, stained Victoria's smooth cheeks and melted into the even waves of hair on her forehead. "There are times when you forget yourself."

"Unhappily, Victoria, I forget myself less often as I grow older. I still, however, hold by my opinion that waywardness makes a stronger appeal to Mary Victoria than to Mrs. Burden."

"Will you oblige me, Marmaduke, by leaving Mary Victoria out of our discussion. Though I regret her unsuitable marriage, I can still respect the purity of her motives. And now, if it isn't asking too much, will you tell me how I may find Mrs. Burden?"

"Oh, I'll find her for you, if you are determined. But, honestly, don't you think you have done Milly enough harm without this?"

"Harm? Why, I am trying to help her win back her self-respect."

"She has never lost it, Victoria. I assure you that she

has as much self-respect as you or I or Mrs. Burden could possibly help her to attain."

"But doesn't she know that, in the eyes of the world at least, she is a ruined woman?"

"My dear sister, she doesn't even suspect it. As far as she is concerned, the world might have been born amblyopic. Whether you realize it or not, being ruined is not a biological fact but a state of mind. It may sound paradoxical to any survivor of the nineteenth century, but Milly has proved to me that it is impossible to ruin a woman as long as she isn't aware of it. What really ruined poor Aunt Agatha—yes, and Mrs. Dalrymple, too—was not a fall from virtue but Victorian psychology. You—by that I mean public opinion in Queenborough and elsewhere—were inoculated with the Puritan virus."

She had reached the door, and after passing out into the hall, she remarked with a composure she was far from feeling, "I refuse to admit, Marmaduke, that moral principles are merely sports of the ages. No one could have pitied poor Aunt Agatha more than I; but the severity of her punishment almost fifty years ago does not justify us in lowering the standards of Queenborough to-day. After all, the world, even the modern world, must cling to something or perish. Even the extremest revolt of youth is scarcely more than a tempest in—in——" the triteness of metaphor checked the flow of her eloquence, and Marmaduke proffered softly:

"In a fruit-jar?"

"Yes, in a fruit-jar, if you are determined to be flippant," she assented, with dignity. "But, after all, you must remember that the future of American civilization is in the hands of the mothers. It is an affront to American motherhood to imply that it is unfaithful to its responsibilities."

She paused abruptly with the feeling that Marmaduke had pushed her back, politely but firmly, into the rustling void between time and eternity. "I am saying these things because they are the only words that I know," she thought, "but words are not real. Thoughts are not real. They are only the folded leaves of something that is hidden within."

"I dare say you are right, Victoria," Marmaduke replied, with a weary shrug, "and it is on this entirely appropriate note that I should like to introduce you to Mrs. Burden."

VIII

ALL that bright and windy afternoon Mrs. Burden sat before her fire and knitted one of the sad-coloured garments in which evangelical Christianity wraps original sin. While she knitted, her lean but active thoughts addressed the God of Genesis, and demanded some act of divine intervention in her affairs. For she had had, as she eagerly testified, a mean life from the hour of her birth; and after sixty-five years of complaining submission to the will of God, it seemed to her more than time for God to do something about it. Though she was familiar with the Book of Job and the inscrutable ways of Providence in Scripture, she still felt that she had been punished too long and too harshly for the transgressions of others. Even in childhood, for she had been a pious infant, and disposed to become an early example, she had attended church twice every Sunday and once in the middle of every week. Moreover, as she had not failed to point out, this devoutness had occurred at a stage of the world's history when attendance upon divine service exacted a robust constitution.

At the moment, so profound was her melancholy, she would have agreed with Mrs. Littlepage that being conventional (only she called it "keeping respectable") was by no means so easy as loose-living persons of the past had seemed to imagine. It is true that she had been blessed, among other favours, by the serenity of mind which is the spiritual property of those who are unacquainted with doubt. Yet the wonder grew, as years went by, that amazing grace, which has so sweet a sound, should appear to increase rather than diminish the struggles of nature. For even she had not been spared (though it was almost fifty years ago) the hopeless pangs of an unfortunate love. In April evenings, when the scent of lilacs drifted like rain on the silver air, she had walked with a lover among the tender whispers of the delicate green twilights. He was unredeemed; he was disreputable; he was a hopeless fugitive from the Blood of the Lamb; yet she had walked with him all those April evenings, and she had loved him in secret through the other months of the year. In spite of his sins, which were as scarlet, and his circumstances, which were beggarly, she might have been faithful to him, if only he had respected her. Everything else, even his poverty, she could have forgiven, if only he had respected her virtue. For almost half a century this thought had lodged there, driven by that old anguish into some obscure recess of memory. She could have forgiven him everything else, if only he had respected her. Sitting there by her scant fire, with her ashen skin, her upright old body, and her unconquerable spirit; sitting there in her attitude of bleak resignation, she felt resentfully that, though she bowed to the will of God, her life wouldn't bear thinking about. After almost fifty years (and God alone knew what those years had meant to her), there were recollections that still hurt her pride like the sting of a hornet. Those warm April evenings, when she put on her blue dress (they were wearing trains then, and a great many flounces), and believed she was being an ideal to an unworthy but infatuated young man. There were curls on her neck and an Alsatian bow in place of a bonnet, and there was not a thought in her mind that wasn't as pure as snow and a credit to any ideal. Walking out in the flushed light, and thinking all the sad and pious thoughts that came to her in the spring, especially when it was Sunday and warmer than usual, and she was close to an unconverted but attractive young man, who was in danger of losing his soul.

These thoughts were in her mind when she had tripped out into the road by the lilacs, prepared to spread the gospel and bring salvation to this young man, who was unworthy but loved her. For an instant, in the dying glow of the flames, these two memories touched and melted as shadows touch and melt into an empty embrace. All those ages before, in her blue dress with the flounces, wearing an Alsatian bow on her chestnut curls, she tripped down the pale road between white and purple clusters of lilacs. With the purest motives, she had walked out, suspecting no evil. Suspecting no evil from men, suspecting no evil from fate, trusting in God and the institution of marriage, keeping herself, in her blue dress, as remote as an ideal. Through all the wind and mist of time, she could look back and remember the warm scent of the lilacs and a white star shining down on her pure thoughts, which were occupied with the salvation of sinners. Pure as a lily she had walked out; and when they reached the first bench in the park, beneath the great elm that was cut down a few years ago (she could never understand, no woman could understand, how men enjoy cutting down trees), this young man had proved that he did not respect her. Yes, there were things in the past, there were April evenings, there were drifting scents, there were hopes, there were disappointments, there was love, there was bitterness, there was outraged modesty and rejected salvation—there were all these things in the past, and none of them would bear thinking about. Life was like that, she supposed. In spite of amazing grace and being washed in the Blood of the Lamb (Milly said it was horrible to drag blood into religion), life wouldn't bear thinking about. For her happiness had been a mistake. Her love had been a mistake from the beginning, and when, years afterwards, she had married a man who respected her, that had turned out to be an even greater mistake. But how could a woman know? How could any woman know that life wouldn't bear thinking about? For, though he still respected her, she had been deserted for a loose woman, after bearing seven children and losing six of them. He had deserted her for a loose woman; yet he had nothing he could complain of in his marriage except, as he had told her to her face, that his wife had never failed in her duty. But it was true. He knew it when he left her. She had never failed in her duty. And that also, though people who had no sense of duty were fond of saying otherwise, had not been easy. Doing your duty day and night by a man who respected you while he enjoyed loose-living women, had not been easy. But she had struggled on. Deserted, she had still struggled on and prepared her daughter for the hour of temptation. For there were lions in the path of all pure womanhood; and the station to which Providence had called her (though superior in right thinking to the profligate society that had ruined Miss Agatha Littlepage) was infested, as the preacher proclaimed every Sunday, with devourers of innocence.

Never, not even after forty-seven years, had she forgotten the prayer of thanksgiving for her own escape which she had breathed when she heard that the daughter of old General Littlepage had been betrayed by a Southern gentleman, who moved in the best circles but was married already. Married already, and therefore unable, as well as indisposed, to make an honest woman of Miss

Agatha Littlepage. For genteel conduct decreed that even the most prodigal Southern gentleman is unable to make an honest woman of more than one Southern lady at a time. Forty-seven years ago, yet it seemed only yesterday! It seemed only yesterday that she had tingled with horror and indignation and gratitude for her own escape from the snare of the fowler. "This came," scoffed her father (a plain man, and proud of it), "as a punishment for round dances and wine-bibbing and bare necks in the evening, and neglecting to hold religious revivals in the spring of the year." "This came," moaned her mother (a simple woman, and proud of it), "from forgetting your modesty and failing to spurn the brazen instincts of men." "This came," thundered her pastor (the voice of God, though a worm, and proud of it), "from braving divine wrath and embracing the frivolous dogmas and the Popish ceremonies of the Episcopal Church." For poor Miss Agatha had stooped to folly in an earnest age; and churches had learned politeness, if they had lost members, since the great elm was cut down in the park. To Mrs. Burden, who had survived the changing morals of two generations, and naturally took a mournful view of human affairs, there appeared a sounder logic in the severe decorum and the iron-bound theology of her youth. From her humble station, thankful for a decent obscurity, she had surveyed the higher circles of Queenborough, and had watched the unfolding of certain notorious scandals. Fearfully, she had watched. Fearfully and hopefully, she had watched for divine retribution. Miss Agatha, it is true, had been punished, however inadequately; but Mrs. Burden could only shudder in spirit when she recalled the ease with which Mrs. Dalrymple had safely wriggled past the wages of sin. But for that slipperiness (for hadn't she lived to enjoy immorality instead of paying the penalty for it like poor Miss Agatha?), Mrs. Burden might have kept her own incorrigible daughter straight in the path of duty and the pious fear of the Lord.

"I could understand it better if I had left anything undone," sighed Mrs. Burden. But, search the past as diligently as she was able, there was nothing, not so much as the merest shadow of neglect, with which she could reproach herself. What did it all prove in the end, she inquired now of an inattentive Providence, except that the severest upbringing is powerless to eradicate a paternal strain of depravity? Though the influence of home had been impeccable, Milly had no sooner started to work, or so it appeared to the morose vision of her mother, than she had rushed into sin. For the worst of it was, Mrs. Burden lamented over her knitting, that she had fallen not heavily, like poor Miss Agatha, nor even lightly, like the slippery Mrs. Dalrymple, but quite naturally, as if it were her own private affair. If she had been taught evil instead of good all her life, she could not, Mrs. Burden felt, have been ruined more easily. If she had been taught that life is a bed of roses, not a vale of sorrow, and that she herself was called to be a butterfly instead of a worm, she could not, in her mother's opinion, have flown more airily over the bottomless pit. And, as if her sin were not wanton enough, she had crowned her delinquency, mused Mrs. Burden, who was partial to dignified words, by her obstinate refusal to acknowledge her ruin or to remain where she had fallen. Boldly, in the most brazen defiance of virtue, she had risen again to her feet. "My life is my own," she had said. "My life is my own." Nothing more. That was her answer to the mother who had brought her into the world. "My life is my own." If she had ever repented; if she had confessed her guilty passion; if she had abased herself before God and her

injured mother, Mrs. Burden told herself that she should
have enjoyed lifting her up and leading her, with contrite
heart, to the throne of Grace. But, composed, capable,
defiant, Milly had taken up her life where she had left it
off, and the age had encouraged her! That, groaned Mrs.
Burden, was the bitterest drop in her cup of woe, the age
had encouraged sin, the age had encouraged hardness of
heart. An irreligious and licentious age had abetted depravity. In the sedate 'seventies a woman, even a
woman who was also, as in the case of Miss Agatha
Littlepage, a Southern lady, had known what to expect
whenever she felt a temptation to stray from the thorny
path of propriety. If anybody doubted that to-day, Mrs.
Burden reflected sadly, he had only to take a look at what
happened after Miss Agatha's fall. Even pure womanhood, it seemed, required stout doctrines and a heavy
hand to put the proper fear of God into its bosom; and
you had only to glance about you to realize that the world
had never been so well governed since the belief in eternal
damnation had been taken away. No matter how far-
sighted you had become from age and other infirmities
(Heaven alone knew what she had suffered from sciatica,
and her joints, too, had grown so stiff that she could barely
put on her clothes or hold her knitting-needles)—but no
matter how blind you were to things near at hand, you
couldn't help seeing that sin wasn't all that it used to be. It
had always been like that, her father used to point out, in
what he called, with his jocose manner, high society. Perhaps it had been; you could never tell where people would
end when they went after pleasure. Not that she had ever
bothered much with that kind of society, though her family, for that matter, was as good as the rest of them, only
more quiet. But she had heard things and watched, too,
in her day, and she wouldn't have been in poor Miss

Agatha's shoes for all the pride (which was false anyway) of those Littlepages. They had even taken her baby away from her, which was proper, of course, since it had been conceived in sin, and nobody had ever found out what they did with it. Sent it out of Virginia, some people said, though there were a few who went so far as to believe the fantastic tale of the old cinderwoman, Aunt Methuselara, addle-pate and half blind, who hinted darkly that she had found the body of a naked infant at the bottom of a barrel of ashes. Not many had credited that coarse version, however, and Mrs. Burden, though she suspected any enormity of people who drank mint juleps after church every Sabbath, concluded charitably that Aunt Methuselara's half-wit must have wholly deserted her. But, even if you declined to go that far, poor Miss Agatha had been punished severely enough to make her go in fear of sin all the rest of her life.

This, to be sure, was not contending, as some people did, that the child had been strangled the minute after it came into the world. This was not even contending (for Mrs. Burden governed her mind) that poor Miss Agatha ought to have gone to an asylum for mental defectives. Gossip of this nature had reached Mrs. Burden, but she had never stooped to repeat it. Still, it was useless to deny that, even with these extreme penalties suspended, the Victorian era was scarcely an age that one would have picked out for sinful purposes. Though a delicate sense of style refined the tongue, and Mrs. Burden had never heard the word "adultery" except in the Ten Commandments, she was perfectly aware that the American Republic has as little use for a repentant Magdalen as it has for a king's mistress. Even Mrs. Dalrymple, who looked as much like a king's mistress as if she had stepped straight out of profane history, had been obliged to seek

moral climes more congenial in profligate Europe. It
is true that she had held her head high, and had done her
best (though not so much as Milly) to brazen out her
disgrace; but in the nineteenth century, even at the very
end of it, a woman had at least known when she was
ruined. Many times in the last twenty years she had returned to fight the battle over again. Always a little
older, a little heavier, a little more painted, but still
beautiful in her vulgar style, she had returned to flaunt
her gilded shame in the presence of the stout matrons and
lean virgins of Queenborough. Several times on her way
home with Milly after divine service, Mrs. Burden had
beheld the flamboyant sinner vivaciously holding her
own in one of the Sunday parades from St. Luke's Episcopal Church. "It makes me blush to look at her," Mrs.
Burden had protested, and Milly had replied in her mocking tone, "But she is still very handsome. Wouldn't you
rather look like her than look at her, poor dear?" Well,
morals had crumbled with a vengeance, there was no use
denying it. Only yesterday Mrs. Burden had heard
(though she had refused to believe it) that the Home for
Unfortunates had changed its name because it feared to
wound the pride of the wayward. That was the home old
Mrs. Littlepage (and no wonder) had been so active in
establishing. Mrs. Burden had been told on the best authority (though she herself knew nothing of such places,
and would never think of entering one from vulgar
curiosity) that instead of keeping lost women down on
their knees, with a scrubbing-brush and a bucket of soap-
suds, the board of visitors went so far as to supply them
with many profane amusements. For weeks, after she had
first discovered Milly's guilt, Mrs. Burden had urged her
daughter to hide her shame in some such haven of rescue;
but Milly, supported by an unprincipled age, had relapsed

into her mood of solitary defiance. Only once had her
composure deserted her, and that was when she had
braced her courage to the point of borrowing money from
her employer. Naturally, he also had encouraged her, and
with a generosity of which Mrs. Burden suspected the
worst, he had received an unmarried mother (though
the encumbrance had been providentially removed) into
what had appeared to be a respectable office. Not only,
Mrs. Burden mused suspiciously, had he employed Milly
after her trouble, but he had even increased her salary
in a situation in which women are usually grateful for
the stale bread of charity. "She is as capable as a man,"
Mr. Littlepage had explained, for that was the way they
had talked in war time. "Any woman as capable as that
need never scrub for a living." But was it really, sniffed
Mrs. Burden, nosing delicately into the matter, Milly's
competence or her appearance that had worked on his
nature? For, to Mrs. Burden's constant humiliation, Milly
had been born with the sort of face that awakens evil
desires in unsuitable bosoms. Even on the girl's plainest
days (for her beauty was the kind that blazed and died
like a dark flame) she exerted, without the slightest effort
apparently, an improper influence over sober husbands and
dignified fathers. Not that many men required such an
influence, Mrs. Burden admitted, as she remembered that
April evening with the young man who had taken a liberty.
Yet, all things considered, it was a misfortune that her
daughter was not more subdued in appearance. For it
was a hard world at best, and a woman who worked for
a living could not afford to have a face that made men
think (so she had heard one of them exclaim) of moonlight on magnolia blossoms. Yes, she had had her trials,
Mrs. Burden remarked aloud, as she picked up her knitting, which had slipped to the floor, and not for a million

dollars would she consent to live her life over again. She had nothing with which she could reproach herself; she had done the best she could with her lot; but not for a million dollars in gold would she consent to live her life over again.

Sitting there, alone and very erect, by her smothered fire, with her head bent over the long swift needles, which moved with a monotonous click as the gray yarn unwound from the ball and was interlooped into stitches, it seemed to her that she was drowning in misery. No, not for anything that the world could give would she live her life over again. Yet she did not wish to die; she did not wish to grow old and wait there, at pause with living, until the wind whispered in the fading glow of the embers, the skein slackened, and the knitting-needles dropped from her hands. Already she could feel those dark dregs of age settling over her, while the past ebbed and flowed in the room and out again into the winter evening, into the world, into the universe. Yet she was not really old; she was not finished. There was life in her bones yet, she thought valiantly, only she had to struggle to keep on her feet, and being respectable was not so easy as it seemed to some people.

But the loneliness, she thought after a moment of vacancy,—the loneliness, that was the worst of life, that was the worst of being old and waiting for death. Not that she was really old, when you stopped to think of her age. Plenty of women were still active at sixty-five. Plenty of women still went after pleasure, and she had heard, though it was hard to credit this, that, since the Great War, some of these women even went after lovers. Well, thank Heaven, she had no need now, she had never had an urgent need, either of love or lovers. Though you couldn't have made her believe it forty-seven years ago, she was thankful now to have finished with all that. But she was alone too much, and she had reached the time of life and the state of mind when conversation is more agreeable than any form of activity. Yes, she was alone too much of the day, and the night also. That was what happened, she supposed, when you married the wrong man and were deserted but not made a widow. For she was deserted now all the time. She was lonely and neglected and rheumatic, though her life stretched back, beneath those dark dregs of age, to a girl in a blue dress with whom a young man had taken a liberty. Bleak, withered, austere, she was still a woman with whom a young man had taken a liberty. At one end of that slackened fibre, she knitted gray yarn with crippled fingers, and at the other end, she walked with pure thoughts in the April dusk, and a young man was taking a liberty. What was the meaning of it all? she wondered, interlooping the gray yarn on her knitting-needles. What was the meaning of it? Where was it leading? Two women and yet the same woman, and a single life. Which was her real self, the girl in a blue dress resenting a liberty, or the old woman by the fire, who was beyond love, beyond liberties, beyond everything but eating and drinking? You couldn't tell. No woman could tell which was real, the clear past or the dim present. No woman, not even the oldest, could tell what life meant. But it was the same life, after all; it was the same life, rippling, sparkling, or smothered there under that thick mound of ashes. It was the same life, and it was hers. It was hers, and what she had learned from it was that keeping respectable was not so easy as some people imagine—— *But not for anything that the world could give would she live her life over again* . . .

IX

"Poor woman, she must be lonely," Mrs. Littlepage
thought, as she drifted in on that spent wave of the past
which was still flooding the room. For the faintest sign,
the barest glimpse, of misery awakened in Victoria's
bosom an ardent desire to soothe, to ease, to comfort,
and, if necessary, to convert to some higher ideal. It was
not, as she often assured herself, that she ever wished to
meddle in another person's affairs. But she was so consti-
tuted that it was impossible for her to live in the world,
it was impossible even for her to sit in a room, without
observing how many objects needed to be changed and
straightened and put right before people could begin to
be comfortable. And so she thought, seeing Mrs. Burden
alone in front of the fire, which needed replenishing, "Poor
woman, I wonder what I can do for her!" It was this
benevolent impulse, she knew, this expanding and flowering of the maternal instinct into a vital sense of compassion, that made persons who did not understand her (and
Marmaduke, she admitted sadly, was one of these) imagine that she was sometimes without tact, that she was too
interfering, that she was never happy except when she
was improving something or somebody. No, it was not
really meddling; she was not always trying to manage the
world, she assured herself, while she held out her hand
and said in soothing tones, "I hope I am not disturbing
you, Mrs. Burden."

Mrs. Burden, who feared loneliness and enjoyed being disturbed, put down her knitting and struggled to her feet, with an apology for the appearance of the room and her simple manner of living. "When I was young, we never thought of not having a servant to answer the door-bell," she said, with a dismal smile, before she turned away to make up the fire.

"Why, I am sure it is all very nice," Mrs. Littlepage replied brightly, as she sat down in a rocking-chair on the opposite side of the hearth. "A fire looks so cozy on a frosty night. It must be hard," she added, glancing cheerfully round her, "to keep this big house warm in a snowstorm." Again she thought sadly, "Poor soul, her life must have been dreadfully bitter. How ashen and withered and hopeless she looks. It is all the more to her credit that she has been able to hold on to her religious conviction."

Had Mrs. Burden heard her visitor's thoughts instead of her words, she might have answered her remarks to some purpose and have told her more about religious conviction than any member of St. Luke's Episcopal Church was ever likely to know. For Kesiah Agnes Watkins, now Mrs. Burden, had been converted in the ages of faith when conversion meant something; and her father was an intrepid circuit-rider in the days when circuits were dangerous and riders men of stout bone and sinew. Yes, she was growing old (though sixty-five is still middle-aged), and she had known what trouble was in her life; but she could tell Mrs. Littlepage a thing or two about religious conviction.

"I hope you manage to keep your health, Mrs. Burden."

"I've always been strong, and but for rheumatism in my joints and that spell of sciatica last winter, I'd be as active as ever. I've had a mean life, if I do say it, and afflictions enough to try the patience of Job; but I've still a few things left to be thankful for."

"Well, that's a beautiful way to look at your troubles. It is so important, I think, to remember that we have always a few things left to be thankful for." Victoria's cloudless gaze dimmed while she laid a sympathetic hand on the ball of gray yarn. Not only a beautiful way to look at trouble, but the very vision she had tried to cultivate in the spiritless inmates of the House of Hope. How often in her Wednesday talks to the wayward had she reminded her hearers of the moral value that resides in a cheerful point of view. Certainly, the judgment of the ages has decided that optimism is meritorious in nature; and where it has few facts to support it, as in the case of saints or martyrs or minds that are poor but honest, it appears only to acquire a miraculous virtue. In Mrs. Burden's situation, which included poverty, ill-treatment, and disgrace, surely to continue to look on the bright side and hope for the best was nothing less than heroic. "Your faith must be a great comfort to you," she concluded aloud, and astonished herself by thinking immediately afterwards, "but these things are not really important. They are only words, and words are as empty as withered rinds."

Without moving her head, Mrs. Burden shifted in her chair, moistened her pale dry lips, and turned her opaque eyes on her visitor. Since she had never, within her recollection, been anywhere but in trouble, she was not impressed by the reminder; and it appeared to her, when she stopped to think of it, that Mrs. Littlepage had inaccurately defined her religion. "I don't mean that I've ever taken things lightly," she corrected, with a touch of asperity. "I know I've had a mean life, and a crooked one. There are times when it seems to me that my whole life was cut on the bias." Grimly, without smiling, but with what Mrs. Littlepage could only regard as a monumental patience, she took up her work, and the long knitting-needles clicked while the gray yarn interlooped in the firelight. How indestructible she looked in spite of her leanness! Gaunt, grizzled, dark-browed, and as inscrutable as a cedar-tree; yet with a humming vitality in her branches, as if life sang in her for a moment of time before it flew on into the whispering flames and the murmurous December twilight. "What an odd idea!" Mrs. Littlepage thought, with surprise. "I never used to think such incredible things. The truth is that everything has been different and nothing has seemed real since my illness last winter." Aloud, she replied gently, "There are times, I suppose, when all of us feel that our lives were cut on the bias." Her face was beaming with sympathy, and there was a quiver of happiness in her beautiful voice. Sweeping through her, and submerging all memory of the cruelties and contradictions of life, like some blissful rhythm and change of being, she was aware of this rising tide of compassion. Once again, she had found herself; once again, she was renewed, refreshed, and replenished, at some inexhaustible source which was deeper than thought and more real than words.

"I believe I can help you," she said softly, while a mystic joy, an infusion of sparkling energy, permeated her consciousness, spreading in rivulets of light, scattering a rainbow spray through her mind and soul. "Yes, I am sure I shall be able to help you."

"I don't know any reason on earth why I should have had so much trouble," Mrs. Burden was repeating, in an impressive monotone. "I have always bowed to the will of God, even when it was past understanding. I have always done my duty, and I have never failed to govern my mind properly. When I tell the minister this, he says that I must study the Book of Job and remember that God is trying my faith."

Mrs. Littlepage assented again, though more vaguely. After the milder view of Divine Providence that was presented to the best people every Sunday morning in St. Luke's Episcopal Church, she had grown a little flabby in spiritual fibre, and she found herself shrinking from the vehement doctrines of a less refined but more formidable theology. Nevertheless, she told herself, it was foolish to deny that the poor, and especially the afflicted poor, needed a firm foundation, and that the hope of immortality rather than the ease of the present contributed to a cheerful outlook upon death. "Poor woman," she thought sadly, "who could wish to destroy any beliefs that help her to bear her lot? How can we even imagine all the secret miseries she has had to endure?" They hung there, those secret miseries, like woven tapestries, before her; all the endless pinching and poverty and mortification of pride that composed Mrs. Burden's earthly career. No woman could look so bleached, so petrified in spirit, so ground down to powder in mind and heart, unless she had had the pleasure of living wrung drop by drop out of her body and soul. Pinching! Yes, this was the only word that expressed it. Nothing but pinching day and night, for half a century and more, could bring that drawn and sharpened edge to a woman's features. Her daughter's ruin, Mrs. Littlepage reflected, with an aching pity, must have been the last straw to her pride. Even with wealth to soften it (and there was no use pretending that wealth did not soften every affliction), disgrace was dreadful enough. And without the alleviation of an ample income, which did not bring happiness but made unhappiness far more comfortable, Victoria decided that misery such as Mrs. Burden's was one of the facts of life that you simply

could not look in the face. Was she in want even now?
Was she hungry? Did she need woollen garments or
sensible boots? In spite of Victoria's exalted mood, her
practical mind, which was securely tethered to philanthropy, was already engaged in a tabulation of details.
Food, clothes, fuel; these things were necessary to the
body, insisted her benevolent purpose.

"We were getting along nicely until Milly's misfortune," Mrs. Burden lamented. "After that, I had to give
up my place because I couldn't keep up my spirits. I was
matron for a church home for old ladies, and the old
ladies didn't want anybody about who couldn't act cheerful and brisk."

"Have you ever thought of going back to some easy
place? Mr. Littlepage tells me that your daughter would
be glad to leave Queenborough."

"She talks about it. There is a good position she could
have in New York; but what would become of me in a
big city? I don't know even a church in New York."

"Has she thought of taking you with her?"

"Well, she says not. She thinks she could go away by
herself; but I don't see what in the world would become
of her if she didn't have me to advise her. Not that she
ever troubles to take anybody's advice. She is her father
all over again. But good advice, as my poor mother used
to say, is beneficial even if nobody takes it."

"I am sure it is," Mrs. Littlepage agreed, with a smile.
It was natural, though unfortunate, she supposed, that
the poor soul should be so despondent. Not that she approved of levity in the poor. But such untempered melancholy as Mrs. Burden's was surely more Russian than
American in character. "Only I was wondering if it would
not be possible to find some congenial occupation for you
in Queenborough?"

"But what in the world would become of Milly if she didn't have me to look after her? Why, I often lie awake in the night worrying myself about who would take care of her if I were to die."

Mrs. Littlepage sighed and thought of Mary Victoria. "Such devotion is not usual in this modern age, Mrs. Burden."

"Oh, I'm not pretending that she's grateful for it. But you can't neglect your duty just because you don't receive the proper return."

"You are right, of course, and your attitude is commendable." As she rose from her chair, Victoria thought vaguely, "It is a weakness, no doubt, but I do find worldly people so much less depressing." Almost deprecatingly, she added, "Then, I fear, it is no use offering you a position as matron in our House of Hope? Or perhaps you would like me to consult your daughter about it?"

Mrs. Burden shook her head. "She doesn't realize how much she needs me. But I couldn't reconcile it with my conscience to let her go to New York alone."

"So many girls do that now," Mrs. Littlepage urged gently, and checked herself before she added, "even good girls."

"That's what she says. But I tell her she isn't like other girls. She has her mistakes to live down, and that makes her more defenseless."

"I wonder," Mrs. Littlepage sighed. "I wonder," and indeed she did. Though standards were not all that they used to be, she had observed that a guilty youth is almost as great a disadvantage in a business career as a virtuous middle age. "Do you think I might speak to your daughter?" she asked suddenly, embarking upon an impulse that astonished her only a little less than it displeased Mrs. Burden.

"Well, there she is now." Mrs. Burden raised her voice to a squeaking tone that was very painful to a sensitive ear.

The front door opened, and rapid footsteps approached. Suddenly a light flashed out into the dusk; the wind from the porch rustled and sighed in the hall; and a few brown and withered leaves drifted over the threshold.

X

"Poor Mother, are you still harping on the grave?" asked a defiant voice from the hall. There was the worldly sound of Marmaduke's laugh; and an instant afterwards, Milly came into the room with a pile of kindling wood in her arms. As she stepped over the threshold, the shadows parted and flowed away into darkness; and when she tossed a handful of sticks on the fire, a sudden wavering glow transfigured the depressing interior. "How vital she is," thought Mrs. Littlepage, while she held out her large, soft hand with a motherly gesture, "but she looks older and harder than she did before Mary Victoria's marriage." Seeing the girl like this, she could understand the spell that had been cast over Virginius. Not so beautiful, not nearly so perfect in feature as Mary Victoria, but more human and certainly far more exciting. The kind of woman, Mrs. Littlepage meditated, not without sympathy, who has power over men; the kind of woman whose every act, every gesture is instinct with vitality; the kind of woman who, whether she was innocent or guilty, used to be called dangerous.

"Mrs. Littlepage has offered me a place, Milly," Mrs. Burden explained, with an accent of proper pride, "but I was just telling her I didn't see how you would be able to get on without me."

"Oh, don't worry, Mother. I can manage." What a

voice the girl had! How charged it was, beneath its gay
derision, with youth and magic and a breathless longing
for flight! No really good woman could look so alive,
Mrs. Littlepage decided regretfully. Whether Milly's
bloom was natural, as it appeared, or artificial, as Victoria
suspected from the fashion of the age, it served definitely
to place her in a class with those other women who are
not all that they should be. And, apart from her rich
colour and her springtime glance, she was disposed of,
for philanthropic purposes, by the striking character of
her dress. That red cardigan, for example, the exact
shade of—Victoria cast about helplessly in her mind—a
carnal appeal! Though Mrs. Littlepage had never approved of severe measures with sin, she had always preferred the mildewed aspect of poor Aunt Agatha to the
meretricious glamour of Mrs. Dalrymple's appearance.
To resemble a ruin rather than a monument was surely
more in keeping with a true sense of remorse. "Only hussies
fall lightly enough to land on their feet," her dear old
grandfather, who prided himself upon a robust vocabu-
lary, had been fond of observing; and though she was
perfectly aware that a single fatal misstep may make a
Magdalen, it required, she told herself, both a slip and a
recovery to create a hussy.

"Are there any of us," she inquired sweetly and softly,
"who do not need a mother's love and a mother's
prayers?"

"What sort of home do you mean?" was Milly's disconcerting response. A stick of resinous pine had fallen
from the fire; and bending lightly, with a grace that would
have tempted the nimble male, she flung the wood back
on the flames.

"We are looking for an assistant matron, really more
of an adopted mother, for our House of Hope," Victoria

replied in the bright and helpful tone of her Wednesday talks to drooping daughters of joy.

"I think that would suit her. Why won't she accept it?"

"She feels that you would not be able to manage without her. But if you are really going away——" Dropping her sincere and earnest gaze before the mocking eyes of the girl, Victoria turned with a mute appeal to the older woman.

"I couldn't think of letting her go to New York without me," Mrs. Burden moaned.

"But I can get on perfectly well, Mother. I could take a little apartment by myself, and I'd be free for a few months. I'd be free," she breathed suddenly, in a voice that was tremulous with passion, with longing, with some indefinable joy of escape.

"Are any of us really free?" Mrs. Littlepage asked, with the patient wisdom of platitude.

"For a little while," Milly answered in that quivering tone. "All I ask is to be alone—to be free—for a little while, just a few months. As soon as I make a place there, Mother could join me."

In a normal girl, Mrs. Littlepage reflected, Milly's wish would have appeared far from extravagant; but what the poor child had happily forgotten was the tragic circumstance of her ruinous past. Since her innocence, being already lost, was no longer in peril, was she sufficiently prepared, through forbidden knowledge alone, to defend what remained of her character? "She doesn't," Victoria mused sadly, "realize what it means to a woman to have forfeited the respect of men."

Bending over her knitting-needles, which she picked up for protection, Mrs. Burden whimpered under her breath, "You'll be sorry when I'm dead, Milly."

"I'm sorry now, Mother. I've always been sorry. But I do want to be free."

"Perhaps when you say 'free' what you really mean is 'rested,' " Mrs. Littlepage prompted, with tactful inspiration. "Perhaps you've been kept too close in the office."

"No, I don't mean rested. I mean free. I mean free to go and come when I choose. I mean free not to be asked where I'm going, or where I've been, or why I went, or what I did there."

"That, my child, is nothing more than nerves," Mrs. Littlepage replied more patiently than ever because she perceived that there was infinite need of patience. After all, it did really look as if Milly needed her mother. Any young woman, with or without a past, who talked so wildly was in evident need of both mother and husband. "I am sure," she added inaccurately, "that you will find your mother ready to help you."

"If she had followed my advice, she would never have got into this state of mind," Mrs. Burden lamented, with bitterness. "I didn't know what nerves meant when I was her age, and I'm sure nobody ever had a meaner life, though I've always kept respectable."

"Certainly, that is very much to be commended," Mrs. Littlepage remarked in her charming social manner, which had never failed her in the hour of necessity. "You are a mother, I am sure, of whom any girl might be proud. Suppose," she concluded still brightly, "that you agree to think over the matter and let me have your decision. Remember, if I can help you in any way, either by advice or in a more practical form, I shall be only too happy to do it."

"Perhaps, after all, Mother will take that place for a few months," Milly was urging. "Just until I am settled——"

"You couldn't get settled without me, Milly. You haven't any idea how helpless you are about taking care of yourself or how dependent you are on me. I couldn't sleep at night for thinking of you in New York alone, with nobody to stand between you and temptation."

Mrs. Littlepage held out her hand. Really it looked, she sighed, as if there could be no solution. Though she yielded to no one, as she often said, in respect for the maternal instinct, she could not dismiss the thought that moderation, even in a divinely implanted attribute, is an excellent quality. With patient kindness, she shook hands; with patient kindness, she murmured "good-night"; and with patient kindness, she left the room and walked slowly out of the house into the roving wind, which blew from a mottled sky and smelled of dead leaves. She felt very tired, weak, and tremulous. The visit had taxed her physical strength, and yet she had failed in her effort to clear the way for Mary Victoria. She had failed, and she was shaken from her inward serenity.

As she reached the gate, the door of the house behind her opened and shut again, and she heard the startled whisper of Milly's voice. "Mrs. Littlepage, will you wait? May I speak to you?"

Turning hurriedly, she saw the red flash of Milly's cardigan and her pale forehead beneath dark wings of hair which melted into the twilight. Indoors, by the fireside, Victoria had been moved by the girl's sparkling vitality, but out here, in this ruined garden, surrounded by the blue dusk and the restless murmur of leaves in the grass, Milly's charm was subdued to an impersonal agency. It was as if she had ceased to be merely a wronged woman, and had deepened into a tragic experience, a vehicle of inarticulate passion.

"Why, certainly." After all, what other word could convey at once so much and so little?

"Won't you please, oh, please, keep that place free a few days longer? Perhaps I can persuade Mother, if only you will give me a little more time. It would make everything," the words rushed out with a desperate eagerness, "so much easier."

"I can understand that, but she doesn't look as if she could be persuaded. After all," this was uttered less firmly, "wouldn't you feel safer if your mother was with you?"

"Oh, I don't want to feel safe. I want to feel free."

"That is a wrong feeling, my child." The familiar refrain, for she had had much experience with girls who felt the wrong way, acted as a divine rubric upon the disordered processes of Victoria's mind. "You should try to curb such impulses and to govern your imagination. One danger of an unbridled imagination is that it so often leads to a nervous collapse."

"That," Milly rejoined in an emphatic whisper, "is also the danger of a bridled nature."

She was tremulous; she was unhappy; she had reached the breaking point of her strength; and Mrs. Littlepage, who was profoundly moved, was obliged to remind herself that these emotions might have been, but apparently were not, the outward signs of repentance. "You must cultivate a more hopeful view, my dear child," she urged, while her sympathetic heart overflowed and very nearly demolished the narrow boundaries of her settled opinions. "You must not allow yourself to brood over the past."

"It isn't the past; it is the present," the girl answered in her thrilling voice. "I want my life. I have a right to my own life."

Mrs. Littlepage, as a devout believer in the Episcopal Prayer-Book, could not go so far as Mrs. Burden in embracing the doctrine that we are all miserable worms in the sight of God. Still, though she had her doubts about the dogma of original sin, she had been brought up by indulgent but pious parents to regard life, as she regarded the chivalry to be expected from a Southern gentleman, more as a privilege than as a right. "I fear you have a mistaken point of view," she said, with gentle authority. "So many young people of to-day have lost sight of the fact that duty, not pleasure, is the chief aim of living. I always tell my girls," she continued on a higher note, "that, if we think enough of our duty, our happiness will take care of itself." If only she could instill this sacred precept into Milly's agitated bosom! But could any voice, however imperative, quiet, even for an hour, the tumultuous conflict in Milly's heart? "How different she is from other injured women," Victoria said to herself, with a fresh impulse of pity. Suddenly, without warning, an unsolicited heresy darted into her mind, and she found herself thinking, with a kind of weary astonishment, "I wonder why poor Aunt Agatha, or any other woman, ever consented to become a superstition?" A superstition! Was she actually going deranged? Or was there a grain of truth in the evil imagination that ruined women, like ghosts and goblins and warlocks and witches, vanished into the dark ages of faith as soon as the world ceased to believe in them? It seemed incredible; it seemed preposterous; but so many seemingly incredible and preposterous things were true nevertheless.

"I am not asking much," Milly was insisting in that tone of strangled emotion. "Only a few months or a year by myself. After being by myself, I could bear mother-love so much better."

Bear mother-love! What an idea! What an expression! Surely civilization was in imminent danger if the noblest sentiment of the race, and not only of the race but of all sacred and profane literature, had become a burden instead of a blessing to the young.

"I'll see what I can do, my dear child," she answered, with a manner of gentle rebuke. Then, before turning away, she lingered there on the broken flagstones, between the house and the gate, and asked her perplexed mind how a girl with an unfortunate past could have kept so gallant a look. The dusk was already closing in; but a transparent lustre still mantled the west; and by the wan light that fell from the sky, she could distinguish the glimmering radiance of Milly's smile. In a flash, she remembered that Virginius had always insisted upon calling Milly "a good woman." Though Mrs. Littlepage was by no means prepared to follow masculine opinion in such matters (and had observed, indeed, how often trouble came of encouraging men in that branch of philanthropy), she could not resist the indulgent thought, "After all, I cannot find it in my heart to condemn her." In the winter dusk, it seemed to her that passion enveloped, though it failed to ruffle, her passionless nature. She felt that she was being slowly suffocated by the despairing effort, the mute anguish, the deep vibration, of a thwarted desire.

"You must not lose courage," she said as cheerfully as she could while she thought anxiously: "How would it be possible to provide for Mrs. Burden without allowing her to have a doleful effect on our girls? Of course, I could arrange to pay her salary myself, and one would think that the gloomiest influence might be safely assigned to look after the laundry." Aloud, she added in a motherly tone, "My husband and I shall always be interested in your future."

"He has been an angel to me!" Milly exclaimed, with fervent gratitude.

Beneath the roving touch of the wind, a flush burned Victoria's cheek. Sincerely as she respected gratitude, and deplored the lack of that sentiment in modern youth, she could but feel that ardour like this was excessive. Her confidence in Virginius was unshaken; but she remembered that even the best husbands, who have no lower side to their natures, are seldom without their innocent vanities.

"Have you made your preparations to leave?" she inquired abruptly.

"Not until I can settle about Mother. That is all I am waiting for."

"Do you think you will be happy in New York?"

"Happy?" The word was so long in ending that it seemed to stretch and break beneath its burden of pain, of longing, of hope deferred, of mocking derision.

"I can never forgive him," Mrs. Littlepage said to herself; and without warning, the thought stabbed through her mind, "I wonder if she has seen him since his return?"

For an instant, the horror of the idea left her speechless. Then an impulse stronger than pity, stronger than anger, stronger than righteous resentment, surged up from the deep below the deeps of her being. Loyalty to her own, the oldest and most vital of her instincts, rose in the ascendant.

"The evenings must seem very long to your mother," she said in a voice that grew more reserved with each syllable.

Milly flung out her arm with a gesture of weary impatience. "Oh, the evenings are always long when you are waiting for nothing!"

"I begin to feel that the sooner you go, the better it will be," Mrs. Littlepage said sadly. "Even if your mother does not make a suitable matron for our home (on this point she felt very dubious), I can promise you that my husband and I will look after her. It may be better to arrange for someone to live with her here and attend to the lodgers."

Then, choking back her sympathy in the cause of her maternal feeling, she dropped Milly's hand from her gentle pressure, and turning away, walked slowly over the sunken flagstones and out into the street. Well, that visit was at last over! Painful, indeed, she had found it; for she felt that the struggle with Mrs. Burden had exhausted all the resources of her patience and her diplomacy.

Yes, she was very tired. Her limbs ached; her feet dragged; there was a flutter in her pulses that reminded her of the irregular ticking of a clock that is about to run down. "I must go straight to bed," she thought. "The doctor warned me against over-exertion. To-morrow, I must begin to rest later, and I must refuse to see anyone but Louisa." Even in the quivering state of her nerves, the image of Louisa brooded serenely above her stormy horizon. "If I find that I am too tired to settle this matter; if I am unable to help this girl without harming Mary Victoria, Louisa will take the problem out of my hands." Yes, it was an inexpressible comfort to remember that Louisa was always waiting and ready to help her.

What a dismal street it was in the twilight! Dark, insecurely paved with bricks, and swept by an untidy wind that scattered dust and leaves in her face. A chill penetrated her heart, and she thought, "Why did I come? How will it end? What is the meaning of so much unhappiness?"

It was at this moment, as she approached the corner, with a shuddering fear in her mind, that a man emerged from the thick obscurity into her range of vision, and she recognized Mary Victoria's husband. Hurriedly, without seeing her, he plunged again from the electric light into the shadows, walking, she observed quickly, more with the haste of an uncertain lover than with the leisurely step of a husband who knows what awaits him.

"It can't be. It is; but it oughtn't to be," she sighed in a panic of terror. "Oh, my poor child! Oh, my poor Mary Victoria!"

There was no thought left now of divided emotion; there was no thought left of any feeling except that vehement loyalty to her own. Pain as forked as lightning struck into her heart. "I must try to bear it," she thought in terror. "I must try to bear it no matter what happens. But not for anything in the world would I go through it again."

Part Third
FALSE SPRING

I

"IT FEELS like spring," thought Mr. Littlepage; and turning his head on the pillow, he looked through one of the open windows into a world that was transfigured by the swift pulsations of dawn. Beyond the glossy twigs of the maples, the sunrise widened in circles over the cloudless blue of the sky. "It is only January, but it feels like spring. It feels like what we used to call a false spring when I was young."

Within the last few months, he had argued two important cases in Washington before the Supreme Court; and this morning, after his second victory, it seemed to him that he was floating out into life, with the freedom of a tired swimmer taking his ease. "One case more or less, whether it is won or lost, makes little difference," he said to himself, with his gaze on the eddying ripples of light. "I have, on the whole, made a success of my career, I suppose."

Fragile, transparent, as softly iridescent as the rays from a jewel, the sunrise was stealing over the distant chimneys, over the quiet streets, over the dark network of branches, and over the tranquil form in the twin bed beside him. "Yes, it is only a false spring," he repeated, while the words enkindled the trembling gleam, the buried star of desire, that flickered in the profoundest depths of his being. "It is only a false spring, and we shall have our snows before April." Closing his eyes again, he thought, with a start of surprise over nothing, "Life! I wonder why people don't manage to get more out of life!" Coming and going, getting and spending! These endeavours were all well enough in their way; but were they sufficient for happiness? In the other twin bed, Victoria moved in her sleep and turned her smooth ashen-brown head on the pillow.

He had awakened with a sense of eager expectancy. What was the meaning of it? Had he been dreaming? Had anything happened last night? No, he remembered that he had gone to bed feeling rather more tired than usual, vaguely depressed, as if the best part of his life were already behind him; and now, after a quiet night (though he was aware that Victoria had been restless), he had opened his eyes on a world that was glistening with promise. "I must have been dreaming," he said aloud; and remembered that years ago as a boy he used to awake with the feeling that he was about to begin again some delightful adventure which he had left unfinished in sleep.

"There must have been something else," he thought urgently. "There must have been something more than I remember." While he searched his reluctant mind, the face of Mrs. Dalrymple was woven airily from the brightness of dawn. Quickly he closed his eyes; but when he opened them again she was still there, as if the effort to banish her had merely deepened her lustre. For days, for weeks even, he had seen her like this. In vain he had obliterated her image; in vain he had tried to subdue his riotous senses to the sober dictates of reason; in vain he had reminded himself that ladies of too liberal virtue are more alluring than safe, and that, in the pursuit of pleasure, as in the purchase of securities, the prudent Southern gentleman has always preferred safety to hazard. None of these arguments, however, had moderated the demands

of that eccentric appetite which persists in thirsting for
the unattainable and devouring what is bad for it. Only
last evening, for example, he had intended to avoid Mrs.
Dalrymple when he saw her on the other side of the
street. He had intended to avoid her; he had even started
to do so, when destiny, moving in the strangest manner
through his lagging footsteps, had swept him, out of the
easiest way, in her direction. And as soon as he had passed
within the sunny area of her charm, of her ardent vitality,
as soon as he had met the sparkling challenge of her smile,
he knew that, for the hour at least, if not for all eternity,
he was lost. Was it credible, he asked himself now, that
in his carefully entrenched middle age he should be visited
by one of those flaming passions that he had watched
pursue, and sometimes overtake, other men? Useless to
pretend that he could curb either his roving fancy or his
rambling footsteps! Useless to deny that he was hesitating, more or less precariously, upon the brink of a dangerous situation! Several times within the last month,
Mrs. Dalrymple had dropped into his office, with what
he could only recognize as the fabricated excuse of con-
sulting his legal opinion. More frequently still he had
passed her gate, and had naturally stopped to exchange
a comment upon the weather and other impersonal topics.
Yesterday, indeed, instead of leaving her as soon as
courtesy permitted, he had accompanied her into the house
and had glanced, in a dimly lighted room, over a few
harmless documents. Nothing had happened. Absolutely
nothing. Nothing that is, his accurate mind amended, more
imprudent than his careless remark, "You have made no
changes in this room," and her plaintive sigh, "Ah, then,
you have not forgotten!" What an extraordinary woman
she was, in spite, or because of, her romantic misfortunes!
All that sparkling vivacity, all that fragrant softness,

which some man had betrayed and some other man, no doubt, had enjoyed. A little over-blown, perhaps ("luscious," Marmaduke had called her) ; but far more satisfying, to a discriminating taste, than the closed buds of immaturity. In that dusky firelight, it had seemed to him that her loveliness was suffused with the immortal glamour of legend. She had become a part of a more effervescent world, of a more vital experience; and it was this increased joy of life that he was longing to share. He was longing to share it, though he knew that longings are bestowed upon man not that he may gratify but that he may resist them, and by resistance set an example of merit. And now, without resisting, without even evading, which was easier in practice, if less sound in theory, he drifted hazily into the wonder why light women are more tempting than their sisters of substantial morality? Not all of them, to be sure. There were, there must be, exceptions. But thinking only of charm, of that mysterious yet potent quality which disturbs the heart through the senses, if did appear that women who had forgotten themselves were the ones that men were long in remembering. Sterling attributes were, of course, desirable in the home. It would never have occurred to him to associate Mrs. Dalrymple either with the breakfast table or the twin bed; but, for the purposes of romance, it seemed that the lighter the woman, the better chance she possessed of adorning the unexclusive pages of history.

"Are you awake, Virginius?" inquired the morning voice of Victoria; and, as if in reply to her question, the door opened and Maggie sidled in with the tray of early coffee. Ever since Victoria's illness last winter, she had taken a cup of black coffee before rising, and animated by the marital instinct for imitation, Virginius had adopted this agreeable custom. At first he had urged her to have breakfast in bed; but the older Southern tradition had regarded breakfast in bed as the beginning of a decline, and a cup of black coffee, without cream or sugar, was the only indulgence Victoria permitted herself as a wife.

Large, soft, slightly rambling in figure but discreetly composed in expression, she sat up (while Maggie lowered the windows) and poured the coffee into one of the thin green and white cups. In her prim cambric nightgown, beneath the modest lavender bed sacque, she had not lost the natural sweetness and dignity of her demeanour.

"How pale, how tired, she looks this morning!" Virginius thought, while he reached across the intervening space and received the cup from her hand. Though she still wore a cheerful look (nowhere, not even at a funeral, could she have reconciled it with her duty to look cross or unpleasant), there were violet circles under her eyes and a fine network of wrinkles around her mouth. Seldom had she appeared less desirable; yet her good and gentle expression was still attractive and he told himself that she could never entirely lose the air of innocence with which he had first fallen in love. Inexplicable as it seemed, his lawless desire for Mrs. Dalrymple had increased his tender solicitude for Victoria. Never had he been more considerate of her in fancy than in those sanguine moments when he almost persuaded himself that he could be unfaithful to her in fact. In contradiction to all moral precept and most recorded examples, the mere prospect of infidelity had made him not only a happier but a more unselfish husband. What he needed, he perceived at last, was not more of marriage, but some ardent, though of course supplementary, interest in life.

"It is a comfort to me, Virginius," Victoria said, while she sipped her coffee, "to think that at last we have been able to help Milly Burden."

This magnanimity, so characteristic of her, brought a rush of tenderness to his heart. At the instant, he profoundly admired Victoria. He longed to tell her that he admired her, that he loved her; but, no, this, he knew, was impossible. He had been married now for almost thirty-two years, and every husband would understand that it was impossible to say things like that in marriage. So he responded simply, "Aren't you always helping somebody, my dear?"

"But this is a particular case."

"Isn't every case a particular one?"

"Well, I've seen her several times lately, and seeing people does make a difference. Except with Mrs. Burden. It was seeing Mrs. Burden that made me realize she wouldn't do at all for our House of Hope."

"Naturally. But if you pay her rent and leave her where she is, how are you going to find anybody to look after her?"

"Oh, that is all arranged. Louisa arranged it. She knows another very respectable woman who is almost as depressing, and quite as lonely, as Mrs. Burden. Together they ought to be able to keep each other company in the evenings."

Mr. Littlepage smiled at the pathetic picture. "You'll find them fighting like cat and dog before the end of the week," he said, "and Marmaduke interposing. However, it's all one to me so long as Milly escapes."

For a few moments Victoria pondered the idea. Then she said thoughtfully, "I have the queerest kind of feeling that we are responsible."

Yes, he might have known, he assured himself, with relief, that it was always prudent to trust Victoria's feeling. "That is exactly my own sentiment, my dear," he said warmly. "It is gratifying to me to find that you share my sense of obligation."

"Mary Victoria feels differently. She is convinced that she kept Martin from taking his life. It is impossible even to argue with her because she insists upon seeing an act of God in it all."

Mr. Littlepage sighed resentfully. Nothing, he was ready to acknowledge, could be more difficult to argue with than an act of God, not even the faith that persisted in magnifying every occurrence into a miracle. It was one thing, he told himself, to affirm a belief in the incredible from the family pew in church on Sunday morning, and quite another matter to assent to fables from one of the twin beds of modern marriage. "There are times," he remarked irritably, "when it seems to me that Mary Victoria's head was completely turned by the war."

"I don't wonder that you are annoyed, Virginius. Nothing is more annoying than an infatuation in somebody else. Perhaps when the baby comes she will begin to be normal."

"I hope so. If she doesn't, and he continues to sow his wild ideas, I think it would be well for them to move into a house of their own. I'd buy them a house to-morrow, if it meant not having to see him three times a day."

"Of course, while there's danger—and in spite of the way doctors talk about safety in childbirth, women do still die of it—but while there is any danger I feel that I should like to have her with me."

"Naturally, my dear. I am sorry to find that her marriage is turning out no better than we expected."

"I sometimes think," Victoria said wearily, for she always felt worse in the morning, "that she doesn't know how to manage him."

"Well, it isn't for lack of experience. Look at the way she managed men in the Balkans."

"Perhaps it isn't the same thing."

"No doubt you are right. Relief work may be quite as arduous as marriage, but I am inclined to agree with you that it requires less diplomacy. I should say, from my casual observation, that he is suffering from too much rather than too little managing."

"That is just what I mean, Virginius. You see Mary Victoria tries to rule him by reason alone; and reason, however admirable it may be, is the last thing men ever look for in women."

"Yet you, my dear, have always been guided by reason. It is, indeed, one of your most endearing traits. What could, for example, be more reasonable than your changed ideas about Milly Burden?"

Inherently honest, yet desirous of pleasing, Victoria hesitated before she opened her lips. Was her eagerness to place Milly at a distance owing to solicitude for the unhappy girl or to maternal anxiety about Mary Victoria? For weeks now she had remembered that absorbed figure driven by a dangerous impulse through the thick twilight, and with each recollection, she assured herself that it was only natural for a mother to think first of her own daughter. "After seeing their home I realized what a struggle she must have had," she said slowly. "People of that class are so harsh in their virtue. Her neighbours must have made it very trying for her in the beginning."

"She never told me. She's that sort, you know. But the old lady was with her, you see, and she must have been some kind of protection. Few landlords would dare to attack such a fortress of respectability."

"Respectable but so depressing. Just imagine how dreary it must be to live in the house with her."

"Well, people have managed to live cheerfully in the house with the doctrine of predestination. Some of us, you remember, never recognize duty until it is scraped to the bone."

"You mustn't call that duty." The words sounded so flat that they might have been spoken by a ventriloquist, and he told himself that Victoria had not put her mind on what she was saying. "I like to consider duty a part of religion."

There were times, and this was one of them, when Mr. Littlepage preferred not to consider duty at all; and so long as he was not compelled to think about it, he was willing that Victoria should decorate the idea in any fantastic art that she admired. "Of course, you feel that way," he assented before he touched on a subject in which he was naturally more interested. "I have come to the conclusion that we made a mistake when we let Mary Victoria go to the Balkans."

"How could we have stopped her, Virginius? Mary Victoria is very determined."

He sighed. "I fear she is. And, after all, if it hadn't been Europe, it would have been Africa."

"Yes, it was obliged to be some other country. She has that kind of idealism. I don't mean that she doesn't love America best; but, with all the other women working to improve things at home, she felt that there wasn't room for her energies. Motherhood will change all that, I am sure."

"And I suppose all this energy, which was too big to be exercised at home, will be devoted now to the reform of one poor devil. There are times, I confess, when I pity almost as heartily as I despise him."

"I don't like that tone, Virginius, though the idea has often crossed my mind that Mary Victoria never knows when to stop. Of late, it has been something of a relief to look at Curle."

"Yes, Curle will never get us into trouble, though he may make the world a desert and call it progress. But we must remember they are both good children, and so, for that matter, is Duncan. If he were not my son, I am inclined to think that Duncan would be my favourite of the three."

"I think that so often, Virginius, and I tell myself that we have much to be thankful for. Suppose we had had a daughter like Milly Burden!"

Suppose he had had a daughter like Milly Burden! His thoughts melted into a reverie, from which there was spun an airy vision of light and darkness, of tears and laughter. Daughters like Milly Burden were not plentiful, he imagined, and seldom, if ever, were to be found in well regulated families. Then, in obedience to a disturbing recollection, he proffered sadly, "But there was poor Aunt Agatha."

"Yes, there was poor Aunt Agatha," Victoria admitted. "But, even though I never believed it, the family insisted that Aunt Agatha was slightly deranged at the time of her fall."

For a moment he was silent, less from lack of an argument than because there are ideas a Southern gentleman does not introduce to his wife. Though it was impossible, he knew, for any man to live in the present age and remain in a state of innocence concerning the faults of biology, he still assumed that Victoria was impervious to the bolder misdemeanours of science. To be sure, Louisa, who had penetrated beneath the shallow surface of sound opinions, had discovered, to her satisfaction, that more than one indelicacy is required to make the most capricious of manias. But that was Louisa; and Louisa had travelled far since the artificial 'eighties, when spinsters, like husbands, had preferred sweetness to light. With Virginius, however, sophistication had never filtered through the interwoven fibres of prejudice. Stronger than theory, stronger than impulse, some ingrained moral principle asserted that an unbalanced mind was the only excuse for poor Aunt Agatha's early indulgence, and that prolonged remorse in a third-floor back bedroom was the only suitable remedy. "Undoubtedly there has been a great change," he conceded.

"But moral laws cannot change, Virginius," Victoria protested in the urgent tone which could be trusted to check Louisa's virgin dashes after an unbridled psychology.

"Perhaps not. Yes, certainly not," he replied, with an absence of earnest conviction. After all, was anything stable? How could a scientific theory, how could a moral law, be more stable than the perpetual flux from which it emerged and into which it returned? "It's a queer idea to come to a man like myself, a perfectly normal man," he thought anxiously, and reflected the next instant that the normal mind alone made these ideas abnormal. "Yes, I suppose you're right. They can't change," he repeated, without the faintest idea of what he was talking about. "Well, it's time for me to get dressed. You look fagged, Victoria. Why don't you have breakfast in bed?"

"No, I'm all right, dear. Just a minute longer before you go. I didn't like to worry you while you had that important case on your mind; but I have been very much disturbed in the last month about Mary Victoria."

"Is that so? I was under the impression that she had everything her own way as usual."

"You have been too busy to notice. I waited, hoping that I might be mistaken; but I feel almost sure that Martin is seeing Milly again."

This startled him out of the genial egoism in which he had awakened. In the act of stepping into his slippers, he paused and turned his benign but astonished face on his wife. "What makes you think so?"

"Well, most of all from his manner. Men may vary in courtship, though I doubt it, but they appear to have only one manner for infidelity. Then, too, I never told you that I met him, though he did not recognize me, that evening when I was coming away from Juniper Hill. He looked unhappy—at least his walk looked so. It was too dark for me to see his expression."

"Are you sure he was going to Milly?"

"No, I'm not sure. How could I be? But where else could he have been rushing at that hour on Juniper Hill?"

"I wonder," Mr. Littlepage mused aloud, while he thrust one plump white foot into his slipper, "if he can be seeing Milly again?"

"I'm afraid there isn't any doubt of it. He is the kind of man who wouldn't hesitate if he wanted to see her. Only to look at him, you can tell," she pressed in this point as if it were a needle, "that he has no sense of moral responsibility."

"He has certainly shown no signs of one. But he might feel, you know, that she is not without a claim upon him."

"How could he, Virginius, when he is married to Mary Victoria?"

"I am not disputing the superior claim of his marriage, my dear. I am merely reminding you that the seduction of a woman does constitute some sort of moral claim on a decent man. When there has been a child, the claim would appear to become stronger."

"Why, I thought you argued just the other way a few days ago about your Uncle Mark?"

Startled but undefeated, Mr. Littlepage frowned at his image in the mirror. "But that," he explained, with legal punctilio, "was the case of a mulatto child."

Victoria blushed as she remembered. Yes, she supposed the fact of colour did make a difference in the moral, as well as the legal, angle of vision. For Uncle Mark's elaborate profligacy had belonged to the immense area of knowledge that the mind of the Southern lady embraced without being aware of. "Of course I feel just as you do, Virginius," she said presently, for she preferred to evade rather than examine the intricate logic of right thinking.

"Well, it is a bad business at best," her husband conceded, as he wheeled suddenly away from her, in his flowered bath-robe, with the innocent air of an elderly cherub:

"His seeing her again," Victoria sighed, "will make a distressing complication. Poor Mary Victoria! I wish I knew what was best for her."

"Knowing what is best wouldn't help her unless you could persuade her to change her nature."

"And of course she couldn't do that. Like all young persons of to-day, she thinks she possesses the only infallible wisdom."

"That, my dear, is an undistinguished delusion, and confined to no particular era of history. Weren't we perfectly sure in the 'nineties that we could hasten the millennium by a study of the obscurer Victorian poets?" He was on his way to his dressing-room, but before he vanished as a husband to materialize, after an interval, as a pillar of society, he added impressively, "We must not forget that Milly Burden deserves every consideration. Though she has made mistakes, she is at heart a good woman."

Victoria, who had not a vestige of acrimony in her nature, assented after her fashion. "I don't doubt that she has her good qualities," she said gently, while she sank back on her pillows and turned her faltering glance to the bare boughs and the palely luminous sky. "After all, why should I care?" she asked herself suddenly, with a twinge of asperity. "None of these things really matter. Nothing of all this concerns me." For the last month, ever since her visit to Juniper Hill, she had felt that she was sinking into a windy hollow of space, and that about her there was only this soundless tumult. It was as if she moved through the world and played her part in a state of suspended animation. "I am not real. I am hollow within," she repeated, after Virginius had left her. "None of them has ever suspected it, but I am as hollow as a drum beneath the mask I wear." Again that shiver of exasperation ran through her nerves, and she added in a whisper, "If only the noise would stop. If only I could break through the confusion, there must be something beyond."

II

WHEN Mr. Littlepage came down to breakfast, he found his wife presiding over the early Georgian coffee service, which always reminded him of his mother. By the window Curle was briskly unfolding the *Morning Post,* while poor Aunt Agatha, who had acquired the habits of a contrite heart and slept little, was sprinkling an excessive amount of sugar over her oatmeal. It was one of the minor irritations of Mr. Littlepage's life that Aunt Agatha could not be prevailed upon to curb her fondness for sweets. Not only, as he had good and sufficient reason to know, was sugar injurious to the Littlepage stock, which was predisposed by heredity to various diseases; but he remembered that his grandfather, who preferred his whisky straight, had invented the maxim that every man digs his grave with his sweet tooth.

"I am sorry to see," he remarked pleasantly, as he drew back his chair, "that Aunt Agatha is so reckless in the matter of sugar. No, Randall, no grapefruit this morning."

Victoria shed a mild diffusive beam over the coffee-urn. "So long as she doesn't grow fat or impair her digestion, why should we interfere?"

"But she will suffer, she is obliged to suffer," Virginius insisted. "Haven't I heard my dear old father say a hundred times that too much sugar was injurious to everything by the name of Littlepage?"

"She hasn't felt any bad effects yet, my dear."

"She will feel them in time."

"Well, why not give her time, Father?" asked Curle with his buoyant air of "Don't knock, boost" or "Boost, don't knock" (to save his life Mr. Littlepage could not remember which advice came first). "My private opinion is that, if Grandfather had taken more sugar and less whisky in his toddy, he might have weathered the bad effects more easily. Are you afraid to try this batter-bread and roe herring?"

Mr. Littlepage frowned over his egg and dry toast. Yes, Duncan was right when he charged Curle with possessing every qualification for political life, even an aptitude for hypocrisy. As for the subject of their discussion, he regretted to see that she was reaching slyly for the maple syrup, and having finished her oatmeal, was preparing to invite dyspepsia with buckwheat cakes. Strange, that he should have lived in the house so many years with poor Aunt Agatha without observing that she had a disingenuous, he had almost said a stealthy, demeanour. Curle, on the contrary, dispatched his unwholesome but appetizing breakfast with the haste of a man who is on the point of flight or pursuit. The instant after such criticisms had entered his mind, Mr. Littlepage paused to ask himself if these were fair and impartial opinions, or if, for some reason so obscure that he could not fathom the source, he had left his genial morning mood in the bathtub? Certainly, he had awakened in an agreeable frame of mind. His impressions of the sunrise had been delightful and luminous. Not a cloud had darkened his horizon, not a misgiving, not so much as the shadow of a lean moral scruple. Then gradually, without his being aware of the process, the illumination had faded. Instead of that magnetic impulse toward activity, he had felt merely an increasing sense of defeat. The thickening medium of day; the interchange of ideas with Victoria; even the necessity of putting on his clothes and resisting his appetite at breakfast—all these tedious details, though harmless enough in themselves, had settled in an accretion of gloom over the surface of life.

"It would be wise for you to take a little more time with your meals, my boy," he remarked directly to Curle; for having observed Aunt Agatha's positive way with the maple syrup, he had reminded himself that advice was always wasted on a woman, especially on a woman who had received it so profusely.

"Oh, I don't bother about dyspepsia," Curle replied in his hurried tone, without waiting, his father noticed disapprovingly, to chew his food before he gulped it down. "Whenever I feel a pain, I swallow a pellet."

"That," Mr. Littlepage rejoined moodily, "is inviting dyspepsia." And it crossed his mind, though he yielded to no one in the sentiment of patriotism, that it was in keeping with the American brand of courage to invite dyspepsia with a panacea in one's pocket. "Where is Mary Victoria?" he inquired, averting his glance from the rapid impairment of Curle's digestion.

"The child isn't well this morning," Victoria explained. "I spoke to her on the way down and urged her to stay in bed. Martin," she added in a cooling tone, "never gets up until the last minute."

"I dare say he contracted that habit from literature; but it is out of place in a business career."

"He complains that he is unable to sleep at night."

"Do you know when he came in?"

Mrs. Littlepage looked appealingly at Curle, who replied in his breezy manner. "I let him in at one o'clock. He had forgotten his key. His key or his change is always in the other pocket."

"Did he tell you why he was so late?" asked Mr. Little-page, with a vaguely menacing air.

Curle laughed. "Yes, he explained that he had been out for a walk. It appears that he prefers taking his walks at night. No doubt he contracted that habit also from literature. Perhaps even," he added, with jovial humour, "from French literature."

It was unreasonable, Mr. Littlepage mused, to expect Curle to admire Martin. It was unreasonable to expect any man with red blood in his veins to admire a white-livered mooncalf, who wrote unwholesome books that nobody bought, and had lived long enough in Paris to lose the last shreds of American idealism. Curle, whatever his faults of breeding, and they were serious, was an American, every ounce of him. Moreover, in all the essentials of the code (including his respect for women and his antipathy to unwholesome books, and indeed to books of any character), he was a Southern gentleman of the permanent school. Well, there was comfort, however luke-warm, in the assurance that Curle would never cause him an uneasy moment. His younger son, he had long ago decided, was as safe as a Liberty Bond and almost as uninteresting. As for those nocturnal wanderings of Martin, Mr. Littlepage told himself that he was still conventional enough to disapprove of any midnight stroll-ing that took you away from your wife.

"I wish he would come home earlier," Mrs. Littlepage murmured anxiously. "It keeps Mary Victoria up so late, and she needs sleep."

"But I thought we gave them that upstairs sitting-room because he liked to stay up and she wanted to go to bed?"

"That didn't work very well. She says she can't go to

sleep until she knows he is in the house, and if she drops
off and he wakes her by turning on the light, she doesn't
close her eyes again. I suppose she got into bad habits,
too, like everybody else who went to Europe and didn't
come home as soon as possible."

"The trouble is," Duncan remarked, with his sardonic
smile, "that there isn't as much room for bad habits in this
house as there was in Europe. Some of them have to be
broken."

"Well, you can scarcely expect Mary Victoria to begin
as long as she is not feeling well," Mrs. Littlepage urged
gently. "If there are sacrifices to be made at this time,
surely Martin ought to be willing to make them. Aren't you
taking rather too much coffee this morning, Virginius?"

"Perhaps, my dear. Has it occurred to you, by the way,
that Martin is the sort of husband who has never discovered that sacrifices are expected in marriage?"

"Hush! They are coming. There will be some hot
coffee in a minute, Curle."

"Well, it is a fine morning," Mr. Littlepage observed
blandly.

"A very fine morning," his wife assented a little nervously. "I hope you had a good night, Aunt Agatha?"
Meeting poor Aunt Agatha's sharpened glance, she
thought irrelevantly, "I sometimes think she might have
had a mind if she had ever been allowed to use one."

"A very good night, thank you." Poor Aunt Agatha replied politely; for this was the answer she had made every
morning, in sickness or in health, for almost half a century. Sitting there in the winter sunlight, with her small,
keen features, her bent shoulders under a furry gray shawl,
her animated brown eyes, and her eager yet polite appetite
for sweets, she reminded her nephew of a fastidious
squirrel intent upon shelling a nut. Though he gazed at

her thoughtfully, there was little wonder, if any, in his mind; for she had reached the age when a woman, however piquant her reputation, has ceased to be an object of wonder to men. She had reached the age, indeed, he reflected, when all experience for a woman has withered to the small hard kernel of duty. So shadowy was the impression left by Aunt Agatha on her surroundings that when Victoria had once remarked to her husband, "Poor Aunt Agatha has had such an empty life!" he had replied, with inattentive kindness, "Why, I thought we had made her very comfortable. After all, women of her age must expect to make duty their pleasure." What, indeed, he had proceeded to reason, could be more in harmony with the ideal of pure womanhood than an imperceptible fading, at the proper time of life, from the ornamental into the useful, from the woman whom men admire into the woman whom men esteem? And when Victoria had objected in her mild but obstinate tone, "Esteem is good as far as it goes, Virginius, but you can't fill your life with it," he had retorted almost irritably, "Good women when they grow old have always done so, Victoria."

"Did you have a good night, dear?" Victoria began again, forgetting in her anxiety that she had spoken to her daughter upstairs. Then, without waiting for a reply, she continued with artificial brightness, "It is a very fine morning."

"No, I couldn't sleep, but it is a fine morning." Though Mary Victoria's animation was flagging, she smiled as bravely as ever. Would the time ever come, her father mused while he watched her, when the brilliance of her smile would be tarnished by years? She was looking a little drawn and sallow, he noticed, and when the smile faded on her pure cold features, he was reminded of the paling of the rich afterglow in a leaden sky. How much

of her conquering loveliness was owing to the merest accident of light and colour? At this hour, she appeared not
only ill, but, as soon as she stopped smiling, unhappy. Was
this touching expression the result of some physical change,
or was the fellow already making her miserable? Certainly,
no husband ought to wander alone at midnight when his
wife was for the first time, or even for the last time, in
Mary Victoria's condition. Even if Martin had not gone
to see Milly, he had committed the unpardonable affront
of roaming about the streets while his wife was waiting
sleepless for him in her father's house. While he meditated, Mr. Littlepage felt the flame of righteous indignation mounting within him. It was incredible to him
that any man who had made a failure of his life, and was
without the dignity conferred by an accumulation of property, should be able to make Mary Victoria unhappy.
Well-favoured, no doubt! Victoria, who was superior
to the magnetism of sex, had declared that Martin was
well-favoured enough, with his slender height, his flat
brown hair, and his brilliant eyes, to turn the head of a girl
who had resisted the fiery glances of Balkan blades.

With these roving thoughts in his mind, he watched the
anxious flicker in Victoria's look, and heard her ask her
daughter with grave reproach, "Isn't Martin going down
with your father, dear?"

"Yes, he was ready before I was, but he stopped to put
down a phrase that came to him in the night. He is doing
some short stories of Americans in Paris."

"It is a pity you can't persuade him to keep better
hours."

"I never try to persuade men, Mother dear. Think of
all the ages in which women depended upon persuasion,
and what did they get out of it?"

"I don't know." Mrs. Littlepage stirred wearily in

her chair, for it seemed to her that she had been sitting on edge since the dawn of creation. "I should think that they got a good deal out of it they wanted."

"That is the very reason I refuse to do it, Mother," Mary Victoria rejoined plaintively. "The old feminine way was insincere and indirect. I determined that our marriage should be founded upon perfect candour."

"Well, I am not going down in the car," Mr. Littlepage said, as he rose from the table. "I would rather walk on a fine morning." Ever since Mary Victoria's return, he had breathed the inclement air of perfect candour, and he told himself that to-day he preferred not to drive down the street in its company. There was much to be said, he felt at this particular moment, in favour of the imperfect feminine deceit of the past. Whatever its failings, he had found it more restful at breakfast, and less inclined to retard the natural processes of digestion. Though he was prepared, however reluctantly, to take his daughter's side against Milly Burden, he decided, while he acknowledged Martin's inattentive "good-morning," that moderation in a wife is second only to chastity. For the first time in his enviable career, it occurred to him that intemperate virtue is almost as disastrous in marriage as temperate vice. Passion, he supposed, explained, even if it failed to excuse, Martin's whole misadventure with life; but passion could scarcely account for the harmful moral activities of Mary Victoria.

"I hope your headache is quite gone," Mrs. Littlepage was saying sympathetically to Martin.

"Yes, it is quite gone, thank you."

"Virginius likes to walk to his office, but I shall be glad to drop you at the bank on my way to market."

"That's very kind of you, but I'd rather walk too."

"I should have thought you'd had enough of that last

night," Curle began in the aggressive tone he reserved for the nonconformist mind in general. "You looked pretty well fagged out when you came in at one o'clock."

"I get restless when I am writing, and I am obliged to walk it off. Sometimes I used to roam the streets of Paris until daybreak."

"Well, nobody roams in Queenborough. We have learned here that a straight line is the shortest way between two ends. If you don't look sharp, they'll think you demented."

An angry flash passed between the two young men, and then Martin retorted irritably, "I sometimes think so myself."

Curle laughed unpleasantly. "As long as you are the only one who suspects, it makes no difference. But be careful that you don't let the rest of us catch on."

"If only Martin and Curle would try to find a point in common!" Mary Victoria exclaimed. "Endless scrapping is so futile."

"Yes, scrapping is futile," Mr. Littlepage assented, "and even if we haven't a point in common, it is not impossible to invent one. Not many of us are able, like Duncan, to exist comfortably without points of contact." Silently he continued, "I wish I didn't dislike the fellow so heartily. I wish, if only for Victoria's sake, that I could put up with him." Was it Martin's conduct alone, he inquired sternly of his conscience, that made the young man so repugnant to the instincts of a gentleman? Many men of good social standing, even in Queenborough, had saved their reputations, he knew, in similar situations by deserting their lighter loves from the highest, instead of the lowest, motives. In the motive of desertion, as Victoria had so often assured him, there was all the difference between reform and dishonour. Any woman, she had explained with a firm and noble accent, could perceive the fine distinction between abandoning a woman without reason and forsaking a vice because you wished to profit by an example of purity.

"Will two clever men ever consent to agree?" The words floated to him in the bright, calm voice of his wife; and while he met her kind and charming glance, he comforted himself with the reflection that wherever she lived and moved and shed her sweetness of nature, there would be harmony.

III

As Mr. LITTLEPAGE stepped briskly across the street, it seemed to him that the variable moods of the morning had melted into a state of cheerful expectancy. Rain had fallen last evening, and the world sparkled as freshly as if it had been created at dawn. Overhead, beyond motionless boughs, the blue sky appeared to be dissolving in light, while pale clusters of shadows lay like a false spring bloom on the grass in Mrs. Dalrymple's garden.

After all, it was a good old world, Mr. Littlepage thought hopefully, slackening his pace as he recognized the sphinxlike shape of the Persian cat on the doorstep. Everything about Mrs. Dalrymple's house was disposed, with the lady herself, to appeal to the softer masculine moods. Wide, low, luxurious in setting, with its round white columns and its polished door beneath the fanlight of amber glass, the dwelling presided hospitably over its borders of miniature boxwood. Even the sleek Persian cat, striped like a tiger, reminded Mr. Littlepage of the purring grace of its mistress. Though the cat was too reserved in manner to attract his gregarious nature, and he felt usually the indifference of the Southern gentleman to any creature who could not make light conversation, there was to-day a fascination for him in the detached yet affable air with which the dignified animal rose at his approach. In the last few weeks, the world in which Mrs. Dalrymple lived had become a sphere of more intense and vivid reality. This was the world, he felt, that he had always longed to inhabit. After seeing Amy Dalrymple, he would forget for hours that he was middle-aged, and he would linger over his work with the feeling that some beautiful and satisfying experience awaited him. Then the warmth would die down; the endless tedium of life would envelop his soul; and he would recite all the proverbs that sanctify marriage and civilize the vagabond ways of the heart. After all, this would pass. False spring would be over. Desire, that hardy annual, must come to an end; and this sense of having lost something infinitely precious that he had never possessed would fade as inevitably as his desire. But, on this genial winter morning, slackening his pace before Mrs. Dalrymple's house, he felt, with a hurt and bewildered astonishment, that he was struggling against forces he could not understand. Why has it happened like this? Where am I drifting? As a husband and a lawyer he had respected all the institutions and practised all the rules that civilization imposed. After a sober and well-spent youth, just as he was settling into the evergreen monotony of the middle years, was he becoming the victim of one of those fateful passions that destroy husbands and make poets? In his office, with an engrossing legal problem before him, he could command his attention; but as soon as he passed out into the world, he was lost again in that restless undercurrent beneath the shifting surface of life. He had known Mrs. Dalrymple for many years; and after his first brief infatuation, he had dismissed her from his mind as a light and pretty woman whom a man might love for an hour and forget in the morning. Yet he realized now that no other woman, with the exception of Victoria in her youth, had moved him so long and so deeply. The age of love had come and gone, and through it all he had felt nothing stronger than pleasure or more

lasting than impulse. Life, he saw now, had marched by
him while he had lingered among shadows that he called
the things of the mind. It is true that he had been tranquil,
that he had believed himself to be satisfied. But now in a
week, in a day, in an hour, an ordinary, almost a common-
place woman, with nothing unusual about her except her
vitality, had changed the whole of existence. Well-preserved, no doubt, but cast in a shallow mould and already
beginning to break. In a few more years, the living ardour,
the vital warmth, which quickened his senses to this false
spring, would die away, with that transfiguring glow, into
ashes. When he thought of her this morning he could
remember nothing that she had ever said, nothing that she
had ever meant, beyond this eloquent response, this
extraordinary animation of soul. Yet so intense had his
hidden desire become in his life that it haunted all the
trivial actualities and made the rest of experience no more
real than phantoms.

Whenever he paused to moralize, which he did but
seldom, it seemed to him incredible that this adventure
of the heart should have happened to him and not to
Marmaduke, who was so obviously designed to be an
enemy to society. It would even have appeared ridiculous
to him had there been any circumstances in which a man
could appear ridiculous to himself. Everything, people,
objects, occasions, all reminded him of Amy Dalrymple's
smile. Frequently in the street he was arrested by a resemblance to her in some passing woman, in a walk, in a
carriage of the head, in a provocative gesture, in the gay
and musical notes of a voice. He had scoffed at youth for its
rashness, its vehemence, its lack of proper control, its
selfish preoccupation with a solitary emotion; and now,
at fifty-seven, in the fugitive sunshine of autumn, he had
plunged into the kind of catastrophe that only the young

and inexperienced can call happiness. Like this false spring in winter, like the blossoming plants and the hungry mouths of nature, or like that grim reaper of his mother's favourite poem, love appeared to demand all seasons for its own, as well as its peculiar time to fade and fall. What if, in the end, Louisa and contemporary literature should prove to be right, and the ideal of chivalry should be preserved only as a psychological fossil? Louisa, who had gone as far, he decided, as it was safe to go without puncturing the balloon of civilization, had reduced all the ancient perils of society to the white-slave traffic and the predatory instincts of the male. Though this point of view interested him as an argument, it was repugnant, he felt, to every civilized sentiment. For, in common with other men, he was cold to the white-slave traffic; and he clung stubbornly to the belief that, since man is not responsible for his own nature, he had probably suffered more than Louisa from the harmful instincts of the male sex. Moderation, he sighed pensively. Would good women, of whom his world contained so generous a share, ever learn the value of moderation? Yet, surely, even in its extremity, virtue commanded the respect of every right-thinking mind. Moreover, if respect were a sentiment that ruled the world, or even rocked the cradle, he knew that Louisa, not Mrs. Dalrymple, should be the proper dispenser of his delight. Compared to Louisa's gallant baying at shadows, he could not deny that Mrs. Dalrymple's voice was as frivolous as the coo of a turtle-dove. Only, like every other legitimate son of Adam, he preferred a coo to a bay.

He was approaching the Vigilant Club (that stern-fronted building had started this train of reflection), and just as he reached the gate, the imposing door opened, and Louisa, bearing her portfolio, tripped down the steps.

Catching sight of him, she called his name with her wonted enthusiasm.

"Oh, Virginius, I am so glad of this opportunity! There is an important matter I wish to consult you about."

Here, he reflected, while he grasped her hand, was one of the most deserving women of his acquaintance. Here, indeed, was a woman so superior that his regard for her was as unenterprising as his respect for the Ten Commandments. Tall, slender, still handsome for her age, and as erect as a moral principle, she smiled at him with that mingling of good sense and good humour which ought to have been, only it was not, as alluring as coquetry. Beneath her smart black hat, her waving iron-gray hair shone with a silver gloss; her eyes sparkled with pleasure through her discreet glasses; her firm brown skin, in which even the wrinkles went upward, looked not so much youthful in texture as impervious to age. Everything about her was bright and positive and earnest; and he observed, with an inward smile, that her features wore an expression of faint surprise, as if the mysteries of Babylon had left her in a state of perpetual astonishment. For a reformer, he considered her unusually good-looking. Her face was not, like Mrs. Burden's, an act of God, but was still agreeable enough to tempt any man, if there existed one who did not think that he was too young for her. For some years now she had been the only thorn in his comforting theory that bachelors make themselves while Providence makes spinsters. In spite of her intelligence, Louisa had received, he knew, at least half a dozen dubious proposals of marriage, as well as several desirable offers of an established position and an ample income. Even from the chivalrous angle, it was impossible to think of her as discarded by life. First and last, he admitted, she excelled as a good sport;

and he was sufficiently generous to admire a good sport even in the inappropriate disguise of a spinster. It was true, as he promptly amended, that her type was not the one he preferred. Her whole appearance, fine, distinguished, and slightly inquisitive, was not formed, like the rambler-rose of Mrs. Dalrymple's face and temperament, to attract the despoiler. No, Louisa appeared, he summed up hastily, exactly what she was in character, a woman of independent spirit, who knew her world and was capable of finding her way.

"I had planned to see you this morning, Virginius. For the last few weeks, ever since that first visit to Mrs. Burden, I have not been easy in my mind about Victoria."

"You mean——"

"I mean she has been over-exerting herself. This trouble about Milly Burden has been a great strain on her. Victoria gives so much sympathy. She never thinks of herself."

"It would be better sometimes if she did. I'm afraid we've got into the habit of taking advantage of her unselfishness."

"She has always been so energetic; but ever since that attack of pneumonia she has not seemed like herself. I wish you would try to persuade her to be more saving of her strength."

"I'll try, of course, though she won't listen. There isn't anybody in the world whose advice means so little to her as mine," he added on a playful note.

"I am sure you are mistaken, Virginius." Sadness had stolen in a brown mist over the sunny hazel of Louisa's eyes. "She thinks you are the most wonderful man in the world."

"That, my dear friend, is her only weakness." His tone was still light, for he was always a little embarrassed by Louisa's clear but short views of life. Though she was not wanting in humour, she seemed unable to apply its sharpened edge either to persons whom she admired or to principles that she respected. Standing beside her in the tempered sunlight, which glittered over her like varnish, he studied her intelligent features a moment before he continued. "But you are right. The time has come when she should begin to think of herself."

"No one realizes that, Virginius, more than I do. Even as a child," she added, with a quiver in her competent voice, "from the first winter after her family came to Queenborough, I have always adored her."

"Everyone has adored her." A flush darkened his smooth skin, for, unlike Louisa, who blushed only at facts, he was more sensitive to words than to deeds. "It may be because she exacts so little. I sometimes think that she is the least exacting woman on earth."

"It is a great happiness to hear you say that. No man ever had a better wife, and I am sure that no woman ever had a truer friend than Victoria has been to me."

"She is devoted to you. Yours has been a wonderful friendship, and it has made me ask myself, now and then, if men really know anything about women."

As she nodded over her portfolio, he thought irrelevantly of a sparrow pecking a crumb. "Not about women in themselves, only about women in relation to men." Then her tone lost its authority, and she said in a whisper of agitation, "I'm afraid this affair has been almost too much for her. It is not only the tragic circumstance of Milly Burden. I think the greatest blow has been the discovery that Martin is seeing the girl again."

"She didn't tell me until this morning."

"That was like her. She was afraid of distracting your mind from those important cases. But I know that she has been very much worried over it."

"I wish you had gone with her to Mrs. Burden's, Louisa."

"I didn't know of that first visit until after she came home. Once or twice since then we have stopped at the house for a minute; but we have never noticed any sign that Martin had been there."

A look of distress sharpened his features, and it seemed to her that his face was suddenly refined and ennobled. "Yes, I'm afraid you're right. The whole thing has been too great a strain on her."

"The strain and shock together. You know how she feels about Mary Victoria, especially at this time, and she has got the idea into her head that the child's happiness is threatened."

He frowned. "If it wasn't ruined before it began."

"You and I feel that way." Her complete sympathy enveloped him.

"Even Victoria must understand that no marriage could endure on such a—a rotten foundation."

"She does understand it. That is a part of her anxiety. Mothers are made that way. They suffer again in the life of every child."

"In a lecture you would call that an extension of the ego."

"But this isn't a lecture. It is——"

"Oh, I know what it is!" he had begun, in his whimsical vein, and with scarcely a change of tone, he added after a pause, "And I used to consider Mary Victoria a sensible girl."

"No girl is sensible when she is in love," Louisa replied; and he asked himself, with a twinge of irritation, if she had merely repeated one of Victoria's soundest platitudes? Why was it, he inquired almost resentfully, that everything he knew or thought or examined, persons, opinions, objects, all issued from Victoria, like rays diverging from some vital but passive centre of experience? Nothing that she said was ever original; yet it was always repeated as a proverb, with the accent of authority. Though at middle age she herself was neither beautiful nor interesting, she was, it appeared, as much admired as she had ever been by the best minds. Was this because she was so sensible in her views that she had become in time the voice of established conviction? Or was it because when she spoke of herself as "advanced" in her opinions, she meant always advanced in the right direction? Ah, that was the word he needed, there was the label! Since she was advanced enough to be modern and conservative enough to be safe, she had become a power for good in the community. All the forces of progress that still feared the strange and the new had assembled behind her.

"Well, it looks as if Mary Victoria would have to come to her senses," he said, with decision. "If the fellow is unfaithful to her, the sooner she discovers it, the better it will be for her."

"She might at least be spared," rejoined Louisa, whose courage, unlike his, was equal, in conversation at least, to the extremity of birth, "while she is expecting a child."

Her colour did not change while she watched the becoming flush mantle Mr. Littlepage's suave features. If he had looked into her straight and narrow mind, where every idea, old or new, was neatly labelled and placed in its proper category, he would have surprised merely a bright wonder that men should be so timid about facing the facts of life. "That is what makes Victoria so anxious," she explained fearlessly. "A shock at this time might be so harmful."

"She is right of course. She is always right." Though the words were as much as any paragon of wisdom could

expect from a man, there was a ruffled sound, the merest
hint of annoyance, in his agreeable voice.

"She never admits that Mary Victoria has a fault,"
Louisa reminded him. "One of Victoria's most beautiful
qualities is loyalty. She can see no flaw in anyone that she
loves."

This also, he admitted readily, was nothing more than
the truth. Praise, however superlative, never sounded
effusive when it was lavished upon a good woman. He had
won a perfect wife, he told himself once again, and the
fault was in his spiritual part if he longed for something
more—or was it something less?—than perfection. As-
suredly, he had everything that any husband has a right
to expect; and yet, as he had sufficient reason to know, any
husband is uncertain alloy rather than pure metal. There
was, for example, the attraction of mystery. For mystery,
though frowned upon by reformers, is still an indestructible element in the desires of the heart.

"You and I," he said sincerely, "can find no flaw in Victoria." Then, dropping his gravity as easily as if it were
a handkerchief, he added in the softer accents of chivalry,
"You ought to have married, Louisa. It is a great regret
to me that you could not make allowances for Marmaduke's temperament."

To his astonishment a vivid blush stained her cheek.
What was there, he wondered, in his harmless remark
about marriage that could embarrass a spinster who had
confronted so unflinchingly the naked fact of birth?

"We should never have suited each other, Virginius,"
she answered in her gentlest voice. "As it is, I have been
quite happy. I do not feel that I have missed anything."

"You are too fine a woman not to have made some man
a good wife." How windy that sounded, how hollow. Yet
it was the sort of thing, he insisted defiantly to himself,

that every unattached woman expected from a married man a generation ago.

"I have been quite, quite satisfied," Louisa repeated, as if she were determined to convince him of the truth. "You and Victoria have meant more to me than I can ever make you believe. Your children have been as dear to me as if they had been my own."

Gratitude moistened his eyes as he looked at her. "You are a noble woman," he answered, with feeling. "I cannot think what Victoria and I should have done without you. From the beginning, as she often reminds me, you have been a rock to lean on."

Again that girlish flush dyed her smooth brown skin. "I would do anything in the world," she responded, "for Victoria and you and the children. But you must not think that my life is not so full as I wish it to be."

"Mustn't I?" He smiled playfully. "Well, you ought to have been a man, Louisa."

Her dark eyebrows sprang up in amazement; but she retorted good-humouredly, "And you ought to have been a woman, Virginius."

He frowned. "Do you mean that I am too fussy?"

"Not in the least. Do you mean that I am too bold?" Then, while he was searching his less nimble mind for an answer, she continued with the moral earnestness which was, in his opinion, her most pronounced feminine attribute, "Please try not to be flippant. It is a very serious situation."

"Then you and Victoria must handle it. I am not at home in serious situations."

"We have done all we could, and apparently it isn't enough. The only thing now is for you to speak to Milly Burden."

"Speak to Milly? Why, I speak to her fifty times in a day."

"But not about Mary Victoria's husband."

"No, thank God, there are other things to be said."

"But you will," she pleaded urgently, "speak to her now?"

His frown deepened. "I am willing to speak to her, but I haven't the slightest idea what I could say."

"Well, you could warn her—couldn't you?—that she is pursuing an unfair and dangerous course?"

Still frowning, he broke into an angry laugh. "Has it ever occurred to you that she might retort, 'Dangerous for whom'?"

"Is it impossible to appeal to her moral sense?"

"I have never tried; but there again she might reply that you can't grasp a moral sense by both ends."

"I have never known you to be so sarcastic, Virginius."

"I am not sarcastic, I am merely honest. These different accents have a way of sounding alike."

Louisa glanced swiftly away, and then back again at his look of ruddy indignation, which was very becoming. "After all, he is your daughter's husband, Virginius."

"That isn't my fault. Mary Victoria married him, I didn't. My advice, even as a lawyer, was not consulted."

"But the fact that she is his wife means a great deal. Doesn't the whole structure of society rest upon the institution of marriage?"

"I used to think so; but that was before I discovered that it rests much more firmly upon the institution of hypocrisy. Have you never, in the last forty years, changed your opinions, Louisa?"

She looked at him anxiously. "Oh, often, but never about moral values. I regard marriage as reverently as I used to do. In spite of the emancipation of women, I believe you have changed more than I. The shock of Mary Victoria's marriage did a great deal to upset you."

"More than anything that ever happened," he confessed, "more than the war, more than poor Aunt Agatha's past. You see, I had pinned my faith on Mary Victoria's goodness. I don't mean on her virtue alone, but on her honour, her unselfishness, and her sense of fair play. I imagined that she was what other women might become after they had helped men to solve the problem of—yes, of sex."

"And you think now?" The question was uttered with a sigh; for Louisa also had known her hopes and her secret disappointments.

"I've stopped thinking. But I can't see, when I look round me, that you have invented anything better than the wasp-waist and the perfect lady."

"You mustn't judge every woman by Mary Victoria, and you mustn't judge her too harshly. She was desperately in love, you know."

"Then you've simply come round again in the old vicious circle. You are fair to each other until you both happen to want the same man. When you fall in love, you still fight it out in the jungle. No, it seems to me that poor Aunt Agatha was more civilized. She was too genteel— too proud, if you please, to fight over a man."

Louisa shook her head. "I can't argue with you, Virginius. But you must admit that your Aunt Agatha is better off to-day than she was in the Victorian era."

"She has escaped from solitary confinement to the moving picture. But does that mean anything more than that she is too elderly to be dangerous? What about Milly Burden to-day?"

"Why, she has fared very well. In the nineteenth century, you could never have kept her in your office. Even to-day, you couldn't have done that if Victoria had not been an angel."

"I grant that, especially what you say of Victoria. The trouble is, I suppose, that I am still too much of an idealist. When youth was in the saddle, I expected, or at least I hoped, that it would ride toward the dawn."

Louisa's face softened. "Yes, you are an idealist. But isn't it unfair to ask of the good women who are really helping the world, the women, I mean, of ennobling influence, like Victoria and Mary Victoria, that they should encourage the others, who are—who are——"

Again that angry tone ruffled his voice. "You may be right about Victoria, and even about Mary Victoria, but you are wrong about Milly Burden. She is one of the best women I know," he asserted defiantly. "There is something about her that reminds me of you."

To his astonishment, and he reflected that women, even the more sensible ones, are indeed unaccountable creatures, Louisa failed to resent the comparison. Instead the shadow of a smile crossed her face, and she asked with interest, "And what is that something, Virginius?"

"I can't tell exactly what. A kind of—well, a kind of steady courage in facing reality. She is the bravest woman I've ever known."

He had expected not only dissent, but imperative contradiction, and he was puzzled, an instant later, by the softened wonder in Louisa's expression. "I can't understand you, Virginius," she said presently. "You talk almost like Marmaduke."

"Perhaps we have more in common than I imagined. We both inherit wild roses and snowy landscapes."

She looked bewildered but emphatic. "Don't you think you may need a change after those hard cases? Now that you have won them both, couldn't you take a rest?"

"Oh, I am resting. All I do in the office is to put my brisk young men to work." Then, changing his tone, he asked abruptly, "Is Victoria really disturbed?"

"She is anxious, and I think fearful that a break may come while Mary Victoria is in this condition. Of course, everything has looked darker since she discovered that Martin has been visiting Milly."

"Well, I refuse to credit that even now. Milly is an honest woman, and she is no longer infatuated. She told me only a few weeks ago that she hated the very sound of his name."

"My dear Virginius, she may do that and still be in love with him. The trouble with you lawyers is that you try to reduce love to logic, and it has never been done since the dawn of creation. This isn't a point of view, you must remember, but a mortal passion. It is neither old nor new, for it is an everlasting purpose."

"If you wish it," he said impulsively, "I will ask Milly if she ever sees him."

"Well, ask her. As long as she has nothing to lose, she may tell you the truth."

"Oh, I can trust her to tell me the truth," he replied, with a stronger confidence in his voice than he felt in his heart.

IV

ALL day, while the energetic young men of the firm asked his advice or obeyed his commands, Mr. Littlepage sat in his private office and meditated, in the lull between cases, upon the problems of life. Instead of decreasing, it seemed to him that these problems, especially the more sentimental ones, which might naturally be expected to diminish with age, had thickened like shadows in the declining sun of his years. Not only had his autumnal romance absorbed all the glamour and beauty of youth; but since his significant talk with Louisa, he had suffered from an aching pity for Mary Victoria. Judge her as harshly as he dared, she was still his only daughter, and he was paternal by nature. Though none of his children had given him the companionship that he craved, he was the last man in the world to discard the obligations of blood. Well, life was like that, he supposed, and the obligations could be depended upon to outlast the pleasures. Had any man, had even Methuselah, ever really had what he wanted? Women, perhaps, won their way; but this was because they expected less from mortal experience, as well as from the opposite sex. They accepted life as it is; they were the only pragmatic philosophers. Victoria, for example, had acquiesced in foregone conclusions; she had been content with what came to her; she had never defied the tyranny of appearances that wars against happiness. Yes, Victoria had known how to live.

Except for the loss of her children in infancy and this disastrous affair of Mary Victoria's, she might have been perfectly happy. Even Mary Victoria's marriage, he suspected, had not appeared hopeless to her until she had watched Martin rushing at twilight in the obscure direction of Juniper Hill. And yet, in spite of Victoria's alarm, he told himself that Martin's adventure may not have been serious. In the good old days, when people had proper ideals and marriage was respected, men had stolen or rushed, according to their habits of mind or the elasticity of their arteries, in the pursuit of every glittering delight; yet nobody, least of all the unfaithful husband, had considered that any institution was menaced. But, menaced or not, he decided at last, he could do nothing about it.

Late in the afternoon, when Milly brought him a pile of letters, he looked at her with an unspoken question, while he entreated the law of precedent to provide him with an auspicious beginning. Every minute that he wasted made the task, he knew, only the more difficult; for when he looked back, he was reminded that Milly had never responded successfully to even the most delicate interrogation. At the first direct question, he was prepared to see that soft, inscrutable reserve spread in a silken mask over her features. Only her eyes, strangely living and defiant, would still flicker like blue fires beneath her winged eyebrows. To be sure, his mission had appeared simple enough in the keen, dry air of Louisa's intelligence. Asking questions, however impertinent, was easy to a mind, undeterred by moral weakness, that enjoyed doing its duty. Here in his office, however, with Milly sitting there so quietly, his resolution was no longer as clear as sunlight shining through glass. That transparent certainty, he realized now, had sprung, not from his own, but from

Louisa's unshakable purpose. With his dignified head bent over his desk, thinking, thinking, while he played with his pen, he knew that he could never speak aloud the question that was gnawing its way through his thoughts. Yet all he had to do was to look straight into Milly's eyes and ask quietly: "Do you ever see Martin? Did you see Martin last night?"

Lifting his glance from the paper, he said suddenly, "It feels like spring, Milly."

She looked beyond him and over the bare boughs to the western sky. "Yes, it feels like spring."

"You ought to get out of doors. You look tired."

"I was up last night. Mother had neuralgia."

"I am sorry to hear that. Is she better?"

"Yes, she's all right. It was the kind of neuralgia that comes when she is in low spirits."

"I hope she has had nothing new to depress her?"

"Nothing new? No, there isn't anything new. She is still worrying because Father didn't do his duty to her."

"Well, I'm glad she wasn't worrying about you. I thought, perhaps, you had told her you are going away."

Milly looked at him gravely. "Oh, that isn't new. She has worried over that for the last year."

"Do you really think you are going away, Milly?"

Her eyes left him and wandered again to the sky. "I am going as soon as I can," she replied slowly.

"You want to get away, then, as much as ever?" Was he nearer her secret? Did she suspect that he was sounding her heart for the violence of her old passion?

"Oh, more than ever!" her voice quivered with longing. "I want to go more than ever."

"Is there, my child, a particular reason?"

"Isn't there," she hesitated, with suspended breath,

while her gaze clung to the sky, "a particular reason for—
everything?"

He took up his pen, wrote his name at the end of a
letter, and remarked with a smile, "I am taking things
easy to-day."

"You ought to, after all that work. It was wonderful,
winning those two cases."

"Yes, it was fortunate, but I can feel it, somehow."

"That is because you are tired." Her face had softened
with interest, and he thought how lovely she would be
if she were happy. Poor child, she had been over a rough
road. It was unfair; it was deplorable; but Victoria had
said that there was nothing they could do except send
her away and provide for her mother.

"Yes, I am tired," he admitted presently, "but after
this I shall begin to take things easier. I refuse to drop
dead from overwork as so many men of my age are
doing."

"No, you mustn't," her voice was gentle, and she seemed
attentive, but there was, he thought, a shimmering vagueness about her.

"You ought to take up some other interest too, Milly.
Have you ever wanted to try golf?"

"No, that wouldn't help."

"What would help, my dear?"

"Oh, I don't know." The light died in her face, and
she looked away again. "Nothing, I suppose."

"I'll do anything to help you," he said, with genuine
emotion.

"Well, help me to get away. All I want in the world is
to go away."

"We are helping you. Mrs. Littlepage will look after
your mother, and I've already arranged about that position in New York. Much as I shall hate to lose you, I'll

do everything that I can. After all, it may be for the best."

"It is for the best, if only Mother will see it."

"Perhaps, after a while, she will be reasonable. The old must learn that they cannot stand in the way of the young."

"She cries about it all the time when she isn't crying about something else. I may have to go without telling her."

"Well, wait a few weeks. Give her a little time, and she may take a more cheerful view."

Milly shook her head. "No, she'll never take a cheerful view. She never has in her life. She thinks they are wrong."

"That is unfortunate," he conceded, though he was aware that the concession went no deeper than his throat, "but, after all, she is your mother."

"Does that give her the right," Milly demanded passionately, "to ruin my life?"

He looked vaguely troubled. "I thought you had forgotten that old senseless charge. Milly. At least, you owe her some consideration for having brought you into the world."

"I had no choice. I did not ask to be born."

"You are unreasonable, my dear. Didn't she look after you and bring you up when your father deserted you?"

"Oh, he would have taken me, but she wouldn't let him. He used to send us something as long as he lived. Of course she did her duty," she continued recklessly, "but I despise the word 'duty'!"

He frowned and shook his head. "I don't know what the world is coming to, my child. Have you really no spark of affection left for your mother?"

For a long moment, Milly pondered the question. "I am sorry for her," she said at last, "but I don't like her. I never liked her, not even when I was little."

Mr. Littlepage gazed at her with startled wonder—
or was it horror?—in his expression. "Your own mother!
It seems incredible. But so many things that I once thought
incredible have become mental habits with the younger
generation."

"I should hate to think that she was in want," Milly
said thoughtfully, after a longer and deeper reflection.
"I am willing to work for her, but I cannot live with her.
If I knew that I should never have to live with her," she
continued in a voice of desperate calmness, "I might even
begin to be fond of her."

"In a measure I can understand," Mr. Littlepage replied, with his judicial manner. "In any case, it is useless to
pretend that family ties are as strong as they used to be."

Milly looked at him so steadily that he glanced, in his
turn, at the western sky. "Haven't family ties," she asked,
"always made more trouble than any other thing in the
world?"

"I don't know, my child." She had drawn his gaze back
to her. "In my youth we were taught that only monsters
were without family feeling. No matter what the family
was, the feeling was supposed to be there."

She laughed. "Well, perhaps I am a monster; but even
if I am a monster, I am real. I know you can't force yourself to love people. You can only pretend."

"Much of the old family feeling was, no doubt, a sham;
but I dare say it was useful in creating an illusion of stabil-
ity. But did you," he asked more sternly, "never love anyone but this unworthy young man?"

Again she pondered his question. "I loved Father when
I was little, but he couldn't live with us."

"He deserted your mother most cruelly. A decent man,"
Mr. Littlepage declared, with warmth, "does not desert his
wife, especially when he has nothing against her."

"Nothing but duty. He couldn't live with Mother's duty. Nobody could. Even I couldn't; and I've been so unhappy that you would think I could live with almost anything."

"Yes, you have been unhappy," he assented, with feeling, "but you are wrong to insist that your mother ruined your life. Wasn't that your own doing?"

Milly's lips closed more firmly, while that deep blue flame in her eyes flickered and died down. "No, I didn't ruin it," she answered slowly. "I didn't ruin it."

Though this shocked him, he was prepared for her unreconciled attitude. After all, people to-day were more hopeful about everything, he reminded himself, than they used to be, even about ruined lives and eternal damnation. Perhaps Marmaduke was right, and the Victorians had made too much fuss about souls, especially lost ones.

"I've always believed that you are a good girl, Milly," he said, with stronger sympathy but weaker conviction.

She looked at him gravely while she fingered her pencil. "Mother wouldn't agree with you. She used to tell me about a murderess who was hanged in sixty-something for killing three persons, and she never failed to remark, 'but she wasn't a bad woman.'"

"I know," he returned a little grimly. "They used to feel that way. However," he added in a lighter tone, "I still think you a good girl."

Her lips twitched in mockery. "You mean because I've never forgotten anybody but myself?"

"Yes, I suppose it is something like that."

"Well, Mother thinks exactly the opposite. According to what she was taught, you may hurt anybody you please, you may even commit murder and be hanged for it, but you are still an honest woman so long as you haven't forgotten yourself."

"Is anything sacred to you, Milly?" he asked abruptly.

Her face grew stern. "Truth would be, if I could find it. Truth that you could really believe in, not just shams and labels."

"Well, it wouldn't matter if you were happy. But you aren't happy."

"Oh, I'm happy." The flame leaped up again in gay derision. "Isn't everybody happy?"

"Some are happier than others."

"I know," she said, with sudden earnestness. "The happy ones are those who have found something worth loving." Then rising from her chair, she stood attentive, composed, competent. "Is that all?" she asked in an expressionless voice.

"Yes, that is all." Looking at his watch, he remembered that he had promised to drop in and advise Mrs. Dalrymple about her future. He thought of the friendly and cheerful room, warm in colour, fragrant with cedar-logs. He thought of her, as she awaited him, soft, glowing, submissive, with her hair that was still golden, her eyes that were like dark flowers in moonlight, her fruity mellowness that reminded him of the bloom on a sun-ripened peach. Ah, there was a woman who knew men! There was a woman who had made of love a delight, not a disaster! There, in that glowing room, was rest alike from moral indecision and mental exertion!

"Yes, that is all," he repeated in a tone that was vibrant with hope. Not until Milly had taken the letters and closed the door after her did it occur to him that he had never asked her the one question he wished her to answer. What he knew of Martin's infidelity was exactly as much as he had known when she came into the room.

V

MRS. DALRYMPLE was alone when he entered, and while she rose from her inviting sofa and trailed toward him in a tea-gown of pale yellow chiffon, he breathed in the intoxicating perfume of her emotion. Ah, if only woman had consented to remain the delight and the relaxation of man! Everything in the room was soft, restful, flattering to masculine vanity, and kind to the tarnishing flight of the years. In that fire-coloured glamour, Mrs. Dalrymple's charm was still magical. While he held her large white hand, which was a trifle too plump but as soft as a flower, he heard, above the tumult in his heart, the restless flames murmuring like a far-off cluster of honeybees. A burning sweetness, an effervescent delight, rippled from his touch to his senses. From the harsh complexities of modern life, from the fleshless bones of moral problems, he was sinking back deliciously into the dreamless slumber of pleasures that are not too important. It was agreeable to discover that nothing, least of all the bidding of conscience, which decreed that his duty was elsewhere, had altered in Mrs. Dalrymple's company. For the hour, he was living again in a man's world. Mrs. Dalrymple, notwithstanding her war record, was still a woman whom one desired but did not respect. What a help, what a support are definite classifications, he reflected, as he sat down beside her, and defended his masculine courage from his legal precaution. Had Mrs. Dalrymple been a good woman, had she been even a perfect lady, serious complications might have ensued. Not only might a sense of duty have preceded him in her affections, but the solid burden of responsibility might have dampened, if it had not extinguished, the pure delight of his senses. It was encouraging to remember (though he was chivalrous at heart) that he was not responsible for what happened, that he was not even involved, except remotely, as the husband of some other woman. For, as every gentleman of the Victorian era was well aware, he could not become involved, except remotely, with a woman who had first forgotten herself with somebody else. All that was expected of a man, if he were profligate, was to enjoy and forget, or, after the habit of Mr. Littlepage, if he were temperate, was to enjoy and regret.

Sitting there in that rosy glamour, he found that instead of profiting by the occasion in a way which would meet the requirements of contemporary fiction, he was seduced into a meditation upon the perishable nature of woman's attraction. At a distance, he had longed passionately, with all the heated fervour of youth, for this moment; but basking now in the warm firelight, he told himself that he had no intention of being faithless to his vows of monogamy. Once again, in spite of his vehement desires, he found that habit, as a controlling motive, is superior to impulse. Once again, he said to himself, with his sombre eyes on the ripened fruit of Mrs. Dalrymple's bosom, he was doomed to hesitate and fail on the very brink of fulfilment.

While he hesitated, Mrs. Dalrymple, who had decided long ago that the tastes of Southern gentlemen are languishing, raised her eyes to his flushed features and began to coo in her most mellifluous notes. "If only I could make you realize how much you have helped me."

"I wish I could have done more," he responded sincerely. "Anybody could have given you that advice."

She bowed her head, and the firelight danced over all the amber waves, from the gleaming crown to the fluffy little curls that protected her ears. "I believe I'd rather have them too fast than too slow," she was thinking, "slowness always makes me so nervous; but it is perfectly true that the faster they are, the quicker you lose them. No matter what anybody tells you," she mused more deeply, since Mr. Littlepage showed no sign of hurrying his impulses, "no matter what anybody tells you, nothing compares with stinginess when it comes to holding a man. No sooner have you bound one to you with ties of generosity or pleasure or gratitude, than some woman with real stinginess appears, and all your labour goes for naught. The trouble with me is that I've cheapened myself from the most generous motives. It has taken all these years to teach me that no man ever put the proper value upon a bargain." Sighing, she continued presently to herself, after a glance at her companion, "If I had my life to live over again, I'd make it a rule to give away nothing. Nothing! Not an old dress, not a bad penny, not even a kiss."

"Anybody could have given you that advice," Mr. Littlepage repeated suddenly, which was exactly what he had said five minutes before. Slowness had been always, she told herself, the peculiar flaw in this kind of love-making. Well, perhaps, for all she had heard to the contrary, this might prove in the end to be merely another blessing in disguise. If he had not been so slow in the past, this affair might be already over and done with, and then, in the hour of her greatest necessity, she might have been left stranded for lovers. Slow but sure! Had not those restful traits been paired off in a proverb? And after fifty, no matter how well-preserved, a woman knows how to appreciate staying power in a lover.

Cheered but not enlivened by these reflections, she said aloud in her softest accents, "You can't imagine how much it has meant to me. Even more than your advice, your wonderful sympathy has helped me to hold up my head."

"Well, you must keep it up now, my dear lady. There isn't any reason you shouldn't. The world isn't so harsh as it used to be."

"But I never forget. No one to look at me would dream I have a deep nature. People think that I am volatile because I dance and go to the movies. They don't understand that I am only trying to escape from myself."

Indeed, indeed. He looked down at her compassionately while he patted her hand. Such sensibility, no doubt, was old-fashioned, but it was also very feminine. Even though he preferred the light to the heavy touch in love-making that involved no serious responsibility, he was genuinely moved by Mrs. Dalrymple's confession. Strange, how he had misjudged her! Strange, how he had misjudged anything so obvious as her old affection for him!

"You have been very brave, I know," he said gently, while pity broke out in a moist heat over his forehead.

"I can't tell you," she murmured presently, "how much it means to me to find that you haven't forgotten."

"No, I haven't forgotten." After all, he thought as he looked at her primrose-coloured draperies, women are more graceful in tea-gowns.

"When I went away twelve years ago," she said caressingly, while she insisted in an inaudible but more positive tone that you frightened men away if you began to talk about yourself, "I thought that you no longer respected me."

He shook his head in denial. "I am sorry. I feared that
we had made a mistake, but I blamed only myself."

She sighed and wiped a tear from her lashes. "I was
weak, I know, but I felt that you were so strong." Was
that really too serious? she wondered. Or would the
epithet "strong," which she had found so efficacious in
turning rabbit souls into lion hearts, quiet the moral
scruples that were now making trouble?

"I blamed only myself," he repeated, which was true
as far as it went. A pleasant fire ran through his veins
and flickered out in that obscure region where conscience
resides. More years than he liked to remember had flown
since a woman had sighed because he was too strong for
her; and Mr. Littlepage, who knew his own weakness,
felt that strength was the attribute in which he preferred
to excel. Looking down, in fear rather than reproach, on
Mrs. Dalrymple's curls, and listening to the soft, irregular
pulse in her throat, he found himself regretting the lost
capacity of youth to yield to temptation. "I suppose I'm
not cut out for a philanderer," some detached, ironic spectator in his mind thought as clearly as if it occupied a box
at a concert. "After all, few natural bents are harder to
overcome than a fixed habit of fidelity." In his private
office, or between the cool linen sheets of his twin bed,
he had believed himself to be a match for any occasion.
But here, in this rosy enchantment, where temptation, as
it seemed to him, was almost too free and bold to be
tempting, he admitted reluctantly that he was inadequate
to the exacting, if silent, demands of a guilty passion.
Though he still desired Mrs. Dalrymple, he was content,
at least for the present, to desire her less as a happy lover
than as a disappointed idealist. For, in common with the
best masculine taste of the great tradition, he preferred
sin on the stage and elsewhere when it was treated in the

grand manner, with an orchestral accompaniment. Without musical or at least dramatic support, he felt that it left one entirely too much at the mercy of one's appetites; and appetites, though useful in evolution, are superfluous in the finished product of a Southern gentleman.

While he reclined there in the firelight, stroking Mrs. Dalrymple's hand, which reminded him of a particularly large and fine magnolia blossom, the idea dawned slowly upon him that his respectful manner of love-making was not giving complete satisfaction. Though the last thing he wished for was a costly, or even a complimentary, affair in his life (having too often arranged the fruits of such intrigues), he was still as sensitive as other men in his vanity, and it wounded him to have any woman imagine that he was deficient in a lower nature. For the first time, it occurred to him to regret that a woman with a past, however stimulating to the emotions, could so seldom be anything else. The changeable moods of man were familiar to him; but he told himself now that the failure of the *grande amoureuse* was in variety. He had never known a woman with a past (except the unwomanly Milly) who seemed to him to have even the weakest grasp upon either the present or the future. Frailty was, no doubt, very attractive; a broken heart made an irresistible appeal to a chivalrous mind; but, since change is the only permanent law of our nature, Mr. Littlepage reflected that even frailty might be expected to harden and broken hearts to become whole again. Certainly, such a sanguine view of tragedy was more American, if less romantic. A passive attitude, even in repentance, he told himself, was not only out of place in a march of progress, but impressed the citizens of our Republic as antiquated and incompetent.

"If only I could see more of you." Mrs. Dalrymple's

inviting tone broke in upon his meditations like the amorous note of a dove in the spring. Had she, once again, she questioned mutely, lost sight in her folly of the timid nature of lovers? Had her restless vitality overleaped her discretion and her expert knowledge of men? Well, after all, even if he were the only one on her hook, she reminded herself, with robust but homely wisdom, there are as good fish in the sea as have ever come out of it. Though she told herself that she was prepared to fall in love with him, if the prospect appeared sufficiently promising, she was under no delusion as to what the venture might hold for her. For she had observed that the law of diminishing returns rules in love as in everything else. Like most of her married lovers, Mr. Littlepage, she surmised, would probably prove to be just rather than generous in illicit relations, and as careful as other unfaithful husbands to keep the more durable presents within the family. Yet, knowing these things, she sighed again, in obedience to some deep instinct that was older and wiser than knowledge, "If only I could see more of you, I should have something to look forward to."

"Couldn't you," he asked gently, "take an interest in some good work? In some—cause or charity?" Much as he disliked philanthropists, there were situations, he felt, in which one was compelled to resort to desperate remedies.

She shook her perfectly arranged head, which had been arranged, she reminded herself, not for philanthropy but for adventure. "I never took any interest in such things."

"Nor do I. I don't like reformers, but, after all, you need something to occupy your time. As Duncan says, we cannot have a world war every day."

A sigh escaped her. "Ah, I haven't any life now. I live entirely in the past."

"But that's a mistake, my dear lady. The past, however painful, is over and done with. You are young yet. You are as attractive as you ever were. You look every whit as handsome to me as you did the first time I saw you."

Turning slightly, she enveloped him in one of the celebrated smiles of the 'nineties. "I was a beauty—why shouldn't I say it?—in another period. We had hearts in those days."

"And they were broken," he answered in a troubled tone, while the moist heat cooled to chill dampness on his forehead.

Her eyes, as glimmering as twilight, dwelt on him tenderly. "What else, my dear, are hearts for?" she asked, with a delicious revival of last-century archness.

"What else?" he repeated daringly; and reflected that if only she could sustain her sprightly mood, the evening might become more agreeable. Smiling into her dangerous eyes, he thought of all the ballroom floors and other public places where Mrs. Dalrymple had held court, as a crowned queen, in the early 'nineties, and he thought also, though less cheerfully, of the long procession of Southern gentlemen who had vied with one another for the honour of holding her bouquet when she danced. That was, he hastened to recall, before the noisy scandal of her divorce; for, after the judicious retreat of her first lover, Southern gentlemen had flocked to her not in processions but in single combat, and had shown a disposition to seek quiet corners rather than crowded ballrooms. And then, gradually and imperceptibly, tastes had altered, and the late-Victorian ideal of beauty had gone out of fashion. Vanished also, or surviving with a faded splendour, was the brilliant archness, the irresistible coquetry, which had turned the more nimble or less solid wits of the nineteenth century. Yes, the truth was (he perceived this in the very

act of denying it) that she had had her long and glorious
day and was now ending. Never again, except in the de-
lusive pages of fiction, would the great Victorian ideal
inflame the emotions and the imaginations of men.

"I thought once you might teach me that." Her up-
raised eyes challenged him while the playful tone of her
voice smoothed away his alarm. "If only I could see you
now and then."

"Of course, you must see me. It is always," he added,
fearful yet resigned, "a pleasure to see you."

"Queenborough has changed so much that I feel like
a stranger. So few of my old friends appear to remember me."

"Then you must make new ones. I told you how highly
my daughter praises your war record."

"Yes, she was kind to me when we were in the Balkans
together. But I wasn't thinking of the younger generation.
That is friendly enough. Only the women I used to know
have never forgiven me."

He smiled consolingly. "They will when you begin to
look as old as they do." This was the kind of thing, he
told himself, that every woman of her age and experience expected. For the conversation was flowing again
into the old channels, and nothing more, he knew, was
required of him than a willing surrender to the warm
and slow-moving current. "After all," he continued, with
his whimsical humour, "you must confess that you never
cared much for women."

"No, they didn't seem worth bothering about. I suppose you would call me a man's woman. That may be the
reason," she added gravely, visited by a flash of penetration, "why I had so few friends when I needed them."

"But men still befriended you." Though he tried to
make his voice steady, he could not subdue the nervous

tremor that afflicted his mind. After a quarter of a century, his conscience still accused him when he remembered her loneliness while the storm broke over her head. Such a lovely head it was then and even to-day; so high, so proud, so like a golden rose in its airy grace. To be sure, he had done more than the rest to protect her; but had he, in the face of his accusing conscience, done all that he could? While her guilty lover had dashed for the storm-proof shelter of marriage, the beauty that allured men for pleasure had failed to hold them, Mr. Littlepage mused, in the hour of adversity.

"Are men ever more than fair-weather friends to a man's woman?" she asked, with the capricious gaiety he had never forgotten.

"You know that is not true," he answered, while his reverie warmed and melted beneath her sprightliness. "You know that is not true." Something—was it the transforming glow of the flames or the misty radiance in her eyes?—awakened the living memory of that August evening. As he lost himself in that summer darkness, the old desire and the old ecstasy drummed again in his pulses. "You know that is not true, Amy," he repeated heavily, as if he were in a trance or asleep.

In another instant he would have embraced his illusion. In another instant he would have held out his arms to that misty radiance, to that startled surprise, which tempted and eluded him in her face. But, while he reached toward her, in the very flash and pause with which she surrendered, a trivial incident, as insignificant as the turning on of a light in the hall, shattered the crystal globe of the moment. A bell rang; a step passed; and he heard a messenger asking a question.

Collecting himself with an effort, he looked at his watch.

"It is late. I must go," he said, but his voice was thick and clotted with longing.

With a gesture, she seemed to put herself in order, to smooth her shining hair, to reassemble her faculties. "Must you really go?"

"What else can I do?"

"But you'll come again?"

"Oh, yes, I'll come again. Haven't I," he asked, with playful evasion, "always come again?"

"After twelve years?" she sighed, and he thought that she looked suddenly older and more tarnished. The glow had wavered down in her eyes, but they were still dark and unfathomable.

"Oh, it won't be twelve years this time!" he exclaimed in a mood that was more tender than thunderous. "It may be to-night."

"If you cared, you wouldn't go," she said breathlessly. How intense women were, even the lightest, the loosest! Why were they never satisfied to turn from one thing to another, as every man in the world was able to do?

"But I can't stay. Amy, you know I can't stay."

Her eyes were wet as she looked at him. "Will you promise me to come back to-night?"

"If I can, if I can possibly arrange it, I will come back to-night." Did she really care for him, he wondered, oppressed by the responsibility, or was she obeying some general law of woman's impulse to cling? What illogical memories women possessed! What disastrous loyalties! True, he craved the lost flavour of youth; true, he longed, in safe places, for the perilous fires of romance. But he knew now, beyond any doubt, that the only romance he needed was the kind that did not give serious trouble. Prudent rather than possessive, he kissed her clinging lips, and turned quickly away.

As the door closed behind him, Mrs. Dalrymple gazed pensively into her most becoming mirror, which hung over a vase of yellow roses on a graceful Heppelwhite table. While his steps still echoed from the flagged walk to the gate, she sighed with weary resignation. "I shall probably never see him again." Then, more in pity than in resentment, she added sorrowfully, "I don't believe he has a spark of true manhood."

VI

OUTSIDE, in the cool violet dusk, Mr. Littlepage waited patiently while his brief flare of passion faded and died. He was glad that he had escaped; and yet had life, he questioned regretfully, ever meant to him anything more affirmative than an escape from experience? Had he ever lived intensely except in those imaginary shadows cast by actual adventures? Well, he had been true to his ideals; and though he had been true to his ideals, a profound melancholy descended upon him. Far overhead, above the living gleam in the west, he saw pale flowerlike clusters of stars, and he thought disconsolately of spring, time, eternity, which flowed there into emptiness. Standing in Mrs. Dalrymple's garden, he was visited again by an aching sense of the evanescence of happiness. And not only of happiness but of all animate and inanimate forms—of the street, the houses, the trees, the inaccessible heavens, and the secret recesses of his own changeable nature. After all, were the meshes of the actuality in which he was struggling more permanent than the afterglow in the sky or this false spring of the heart? Suddenly, while he lingered there, imagination played its old trick in his mind. "Nothing is over," he thought hopefully. "She is still here, and I may see her again. I may see her to-night."

He walked slowly between the borders of boxwood, and passed out upon the pavement just as Martin Welding turned the corner with his rapid stride, which always left an impression of flight. For an instant, so strong was his dislike for his son-in-law, Mr. Littlepage felt a temptation to retreat behind Mrs. Dalrymple's gate. Then courage overcame discretion, and he advanced with the most careless manner he could bring to his aid.

"Well, Martin!———" His greeting had begun briskly, but before the bleak despair in the young man's face, he broke into the startled question, "Is anything wrong?"

Stopping so suddenly that he was obliged to catch hold of the gate, Martin asked bitterly, "Is anything right?"

"You look as if you were suffering."

"Do I? Well, I was wondering how long I could stand it."

"Are you in pain?"

"I am in hell, if that interests you."

"It doesn't interest, it distresses me."

In the waning light, Martin's features wore a drawn and ravaged look, as if he were devoured by an incurable malady. His skin had always seemed lacking in health to Mr. Littlepage (for all skins that had remained long in France appeared to him unnatural); but there was more here, he told himself now, than the result of sleepless nights and an over-indulgence in absinthe and bad habits. Even to Mr. Littlepage, who had little use for the twilight zone of psychology, it was evident that Martin's ailment was some obscure and mortal distress of the soul. "He stayed too long in Europe," Virginius thought, and remembering Mary Victoria's triumphant mission to the Balkans, he added hastily, "nobody ought to stay too long in Europe unless he has the moral fibre to stand it." From the first it had been clear to him, and to the rest of Queenborough, if not to Paris, that Martin was wanting in moral stamina.

"I am sorry." The young man's burning eyes stared

back at him from a face that was swept bare of expression. Why was he suffering like this? How could anyone suffer like this when there was no visible cause?

"Why don't you tell me about it and let me help you?" the older man asked with all the sympathy that he could summon.

The merest flicker of gratitude shone in the sullen misery of Martin's look. "The trouble is that I have come to the end of my rope. I am wondering how much longer I shall be able to stand it."

"Stand what, my boy?"

"Stand the whole thing. Stand life, stand marriage, stand women."

Mr. Littlepage frowned. "But this isn't normal," he said sternly. "This isn't rational."

"Well, what am I to do?"

"You should see a physician."

"I've seen dozens of them since I met Mary Victoria."

"And what do they say?"

"That I'm not normal, I'm not rational."

"Then, it seems to me, you will have to believe it."

"I do believe it, but that doesn't make it easier. I am still that way no matter what I believe."

This was serious. Moved in mind as well as heart, Mr. Littlepage repeated to himself that this was indeed serious. In the whole of his career, he had never, until he was thrown with Martin, encountered the erratic vision outside of a court of law (except, perhaps, in the case of poor Aunt Agatha), and he was attacked now by the superstitious terror an unbalanced reason inspires in the completely reasonable mind.

"I didn't know it was as grave as this," he said gently, and with an effort to be reassuring. "Well, we must find a cure. We must waste no time in finding a cure. You are positive," he inquired suspiciously, "that you realize the tremendous—yes, though I dislike exaggeration, I feel that tremendous is not too big a word—debt of gratitude you owe your wife?"

"Oh, I realize that. Good God! Do you think that I realize anything else?"

"Have you asked yourself if you have done everything in your power to make her happy?"

"I can't make her happy. I told her that in the beginning. Nobody can make another person happy."

"Have you tried?"

"I've tried to do what she wished. What is that accursed bank but trying to do what she wished?"

"That, of course, is one of her ways of bringing you back to a normal existence."

"But I don't want to be brought back. I can't be brought back. I was never there."

"I fear that is true," Mr. Littlepage sighed, "but at least you might make an effort to govern your faculties. It looks to me," he added presently, "as if you were in for a nervous collapse."

"Then it has always been that. The trouble with me is that I ought never to have been born, and everything I've ever done in my life has only made that more evident. But so long as I had to be born," he continued, with passionate resentment, "I might just as easily have been born in some other part of the world. Could anything but a machine survive this mass production of mediocrity you call progress?"

"No doubt there is a grain of truth in what you say," Mr. Littlepage admitted, not without sympathy. "I sometimes tell myself that in Queenborough there is no living to-day, there is only progress."

"Oh, Queenborough isn't any worse than the rest of

America. What you call the American spirit has left itself but one outlet, and it has paved that with concrete."

"Well, even if that is true, you will feel better about it when you have recovered your nervous equilibrium. If only you will try to help us, we may have you all right again in a few weeks. But we must spare your wife all anxiety."

"Her anxiety doesn't do any good. It only makes matters worse."

"Are you sincere, then, in saying there is no other woman?"

"I've had enough of women. Can't you understand," he demanded bitterly of his father-in-law, "a man's wanting to get away from every woman on earth?"

"Yes, I can understand," Mr. Littlepage assented reluctantly, and he felt, indeed, that he could. He had known hours, even days, when he had longed to escape to some desolate polar region of the mind, where woman, even as an ideal, could not hope to survive. "The trouble with America," Marmaduke had said, "is that woman's influence is too heavy."

"If you do," Martin was responding in a quieter tone, "you are the only one who knows what I mean."

"But you were in a desperate situation, weren't you, when Mary Victoria found you?"

"God knows I was!"

"If you felt that way, why did you marry?"

"I hoped Mary Victoria could change me. Aren't men always hoping they can change their spots? And wouldn't you," he inquired, with a sardonic laugh, "have believed that Mary Victoria could change anybody?"

"I suppose I should, if I had been in love with her." As he looked sternly into Martin's despairing face, Mr.

Littlepage felt that his resentment was swept away by compassion. This was his weakness, he reminded himself, to understand and to pity the failures of life. "I know how he has suffered," he thought. "I might feel that way myself if I had had to begin life in poverty and with an unhealthy imagination." Life! There it was again, with its cruelties, its frustrations, its beauty, its splendour, and its unconquerable isolation. There it was, and at its worst, we could, he meditated, do nothing about it. Beyond the young man's tormented youth, he looked into the sombre dusk of spring in winter, and beyond this, he looked still farther into the starry vastness of space. "Most men have felt like that at least once in their lives," he replied.

"Even if they have, that doesn't help me," Martin said, with a strange rasping sound in his throat. "I tell you I am suffocated by the artificial life I am living."

"Can't you think of your wife? Isn't she in even a worse plight? For God's sake, be a man!"

"It's no use. I am not that kind of man."

With his eyes on those wasted and unnatural features, Mr. Littlepage softened his tone to one of gentle commiseration. "Well, we can't settle anything here. You will have to collect yourself before we decide on a way."

"There is no use," Martin said grimly. "I tell you I am smothering."

"Try to stop thinking about it to-night. Come in with me to dinner, and to-morrow we will consult Dr. Buchanan. Don't get the idea into your head that we are unsympathetic. You are an ill man, that's the way I look at it, and the most important thing is to build up your health. Why, I came near having a nervous breakdown myself after the war, and but for Buchanan I might never have recovered my grip. What you are suffering from, my boy, is simply lack of proper control. You've got the fear of life in your mind, and you must put up a stiff fight not to give in to it."

"I've seen Buchanan," Martin answered, "but he cannot do anything. Nobody," he insisted stubbornly, looking past his father-in-law as if he were staring into the face of a spectre, "can do anything. You can't argue with me because I don't accept your premise. I don't accept a single one of your fundamental beliefs. Perhaps I'm rotten inside, or I may be as ill as you think. Either way doesn't make it any easier for Mary Victoria to manage me."

"I wonder," Mr. Littlepage asked, with discernment, "if the trouble is not one of too much managing? Some men cannot stand being made over."

"I don't know. I don't even care. But you're right about one thing. Some men ought never to marry."

"Those same men," Mr. Littlepage observed in a tone of rebuke, "ought to keep clear of women."

"But they seldom do, and I didn't. They are the very ones that women, especially good women, wish to try their hands on."

"If you cannot be a man, at least don't be a rotter. There's no sense in this attitude. There's not a particle of reason."

"No, there isn't any reason," Martin assented. "I am not looking for reason."

"Then give it up for the present, and come into the house. I'll brace you up with some old Baumgartner before dinner. You haven't been drinking, have you?"

"No, I'm not drunk. The kind of stuff you get here doesn't do any good."

"Well, come in now and stop thinking until you've had your dinner."

"Did you ever," asked Martin abruptly, "feel that you

stood on the outside of everything and watched the world sliding by?"

"Yes, I've felt exactly that way. It is nothing more than the warning of tired nerves." But was this true? Mr. Littlepage demanded of himself, with astonishment. Were his moments of ecstatic vision only the hallucinations of an unbalanced mind? "There's no use standing here," he continued. "It's getting late, and Mary Victoria will be anxious. Just try to convince yourself that there is nothing unusual in your condition. You can't find anything so strange in this world that somebody else hasn't thought or felt it before you."

"I wasn't coming in. I was going for a walk," Martin muttered irresolutely. But there was no heart in his resistance, and he yielded, almost without a struggle, to the firm grasp of his father-in-law. "It is foolish to lose patience with him," Mr. Littlepage was thinking while he hurried the younger man across the street and up the steps of the house. "A man so far gone as this isn't accountable."

The door opened as he inserted his key; and with his first step into the hall, he found that the scent of roses and the glimmer of firelight from his library restored the lost pleasure of living.

"Wait for me in the library," he said cheerfully. "I'll be down as soon as I speak to Victoria." While he turned away the thought played in his mind, "Victoria will know what ought to be done. Victoria will know how to deal with him."

He had reached the top of the stairs, and was about to enter his wife's sitting-room, when the door opened, and against a stream of rose-coloured light, he saw the pallid features of Mary Victoria. "Oh, Father, I can't wake her! I've tried and I can't wake her!"

Frightened as she was, he saw that she was still com-

posed, still capable, still mistress of herself and any
emergency. While he rushed to the couch under the hanging lamp, he heard her imperative voice at the telephone;
he heard her summon the doctor; he heard her ring for
the servants; he heard her give the order to send for
Louisa. In one instant, as if by the flash of a signal, she
had brought method and purpose into the crisis; she had
banished, or at least subordinated, the aimless impulses
of the heart. With respect and not without repugnance,
he watched her draw aside the rose-coloured robe and
apply to her mother's vacant form all the restorative
treatments she had learned in the war. Only when she
had convinced herself that treatment was useless, did Mary
Victoria replace the robe, draw aside from the couch,
and burst into tears. "No one in the world," she cried in
anguish, "could love her as I do!"

"I know, my darling, I know," he answered, folding
her in his arms because he could not bear to meet the
stricken look in her eyes. Why was it, he wondered even
now, that he could never reach, that he could never touch,
the real Mary Victoria? Why was it that, clasping her
in his arms, resting her wet cheek against his, he was still
separated from her by that vast isolation of spirit?

Standing there, in the shower of rose-coloured light,
Mr. Littlepage gazed down on the tranquil form of his
wife. Already the violet pallor of death, the unconquerable finality of the grave, enveloped her in an impassive
remoteness. Her face, which was turned slightly away
from him, in the direction of the half-open window, was
as delicate as porcelain and so luminous in expression that
a faint phosphorescent gleam edged her profile. In the
minutes—or was it hours?—since her death the look of
virginal wonder and surprise had returned to her features. "I forgive everything. I understand everything,"

her lips, which had closed in that magnanimous smile, might have murmured. And this smile, so bright, so distant, so noble, reminded him of nothing more human than the smile of a spring meadow or the flashing curve of a river in sunlight. He had neglected her, he told himself; he had wearied of her goodness; he had trifled, in the way of less fortunate husbands, with love and lust. Only an hour ago, while she lay dying, or perhaps dead, he had been faithless in spirit; he had been unworthy of her fidelity. Only an hour ago! Only an hour ago, when she was lying there alone, with that comprehending yet faintly ironic smile on her lips.

VII

THE next Sunday afternoon, two days after Victoria's funeral, Mr. Littlepage returned from Rose Hill cemetery, where he had carried fresh flowers, and sat down, alone with his grief, in his wife's sitting-room. For in his active life, assailed on every side by the vocal optimism of industry, only on Sunday, after the morning service was over, could he find an opportunity to indulge his sorrow at leisure. While he sat there, bowed over her desk, where her letters had been arranged in neat piles by Louisa, he clung to his grief with the desperation of a man who realizes, in the hour of his sharpest distress, that life is inexorably ordained for the living, and that time, like an impalpable dust, is sifting in from the world outside and obliterating the most passionately cherished remembrance. Bitterly, he reproached himself. Bitterly, in his heart, he reproached Mrs. Dalrymple. Bitterly, with the very accents of grief and despair, some derisive voice in his brain whispered that reproach is even more fugitive than delight. No matter how deeply he suffered, no matter how unfalteringly he clung to his dead, nature would restore itself in the end, and this colourless dust of minutes, hours, days, would filter in from eternity and settle in a thick deposit of time over his memory. Though he longed with all his soul to suffer and remember, he knew that both this longing and his aching heart were born of an insatiable hunger for life.

Beyond the west window, which was half open, as it had been on the afternoon of Victoria's death, the dark gray wings of pigeons were flashing like curved blades against the changeable blue of the sky. On one of these swift wings, the thought darted into his mind, "There won't be another day as good for golf in many weeks." Then, resolutely averting his eyes from the sunshine, he intoned mutely, as if he were summoning all his faculties in a ritual of commemoration, "I was not worthy, but I loved her! I was not worthy, but I loved her!"

In the adjoining bedroom, he heard the footsteps of Louisa moving to and fro, while she sorted and arranged for charitable purposes the more intimate belongings of his wife; and these slow and steady sounds throbbed in a monotonous undercurrent beneath the mournful refrain of his words. "I was not worthy, but I loved her! I was not worthy, but I loved her!" Out of some shadowy region of memory there emerged the face of Victoria as he had first loved her, serene, passionless, poetic, confronting the world of illusion with her air of innocence and surprise. This was her look when he had fallen in love with her, and this was her look, only more magnanimous in its remoteness, when her lips had smiled at him in the sleep from which she had never awakened. Between these two supreme moments of his life, what was left except an encroaching futility? It was as if all the weariness of age, all the disappointments, all the thwarted desires, had been buried beneath that slow accretion of years. Yet he had loved her. Even when he had neglected her, even when he had been faithless in heart, he had still loved her. In his early manhood, he had believed that love meant loyalty, that it meant benevolence, that it contained some perennially living seed of kindness and self-sacrifice. Now, looking back, he realized that this was an error. Either an error or one of those artful impostures with which the elderly, who know better, encourage the dangerous illusions of youth. For love, he understood now, was not loyalty; it was not loving-kindness; it was not even tenderness. You might love a woman and yet deceive her; you might love a woman and yet betray her; you might love a woman and yet destroy her. You might do anything in love, he saw at last, with a pang of agony, but cease to remember.

"I never really understood her. I never really appreciated her goodness," he said in a whisper, as if by forming the words with his lips he could leave a deeper impression. "She must have endured anguish this last year, while I never even suspected that she was dying." Day by day, night by night, they had been together, and he had lacked the sympathy or the patience to discover her secret. How brave she had been to the last! How brave she had looked lying there, and how lonely! He suffered again, as he had suffered in that false spring dusk, face to face with the inscrutable mystery of Martin's despair. Within four walls, bound together by the indissoluble bonds of affection, interest, and habit, he had never known, he had never even seen, the real Victoria.

The footsteps in the adjoining room began again, like echoes in some broken chords of his memory. They drew nearer, as he listened, paused for a discreet instant at the threshold, and lingered there as if some reverent preparation were needed. Then the door opened slowly and softly, and Louisa entered with a sympathetic murmur and crossed the floor to Victoria's desk. Her eyes were red and swollen, and her thin, firm hand, with its heavy veins and polished nails, trembled with weakness. "I found this note in her desk, Virginius. It was hidden away in a drawer."

He reached for the sheet of paper, while his questioning gaze, the look of a child that is hurt, travelled from Louisa's helpful hand to her quivering features. By virtue of some natural aptitude for a crisis, she had been able to enter into their grief and make their desolation her own.

His gaze fluttered over the paper, and for an instant he hesitated. "Do you think I had better read it, Louisa?"

"I should if I were you, Virginius. She would wish you to see it."

Glancing down again, he saw that there were only a few lines, written in a rapid and infirm hand, as if Victoria had been overcome by emotion.

December 7th, 192—

MY DEAR HUSBAND:

I have known for almost six months that I have a very short while to live, and my one effort has been to spare you and the children, to keep you from suspecting. Nothing, I know, can spoil this last perfect winter, or perhaps year, that we shall all have together. But, before it is too late, there is something I wish to say to you——

Before it is too late there is something I wish to say to you. Nothing more! The last sentence was slightly blurred, as if her hand, he told himself, had failed her, and she had waited until her strength should return. No words that she might have written, no act, however exalted, could have moved him so deeply. Faced with that discovery of her mortal illness, she had forgotten herself, she had thought only of him and her children. And it was in these last months that he had wronged her in his heart, that he had betrayed her devotion.

"I knew she would wish you to see it," Louisa repeated. "She suffered a great deal, but her one thought was to spare those she loved. I have never seen anyone with more courage—or perhaps fortitude is a better word—than Victoria showed——"

Stunned into silence, he looked upward, over Louisa's neat gray head, as if he were worshipping at the shrine of some tutelary divinity. Crowned, radiant, incomparable, a new Victoria, one whom he had never even imagined, had flowered there, out of the throbbing light of his vision. Nothing in his life, not young love, not marriage, not fatherhood, not religious devotion—none of these emotions had ever plunged so far beneath the shallows of consciousness. All the beauty of Helen adorned with the meekness of Mary could not have transformed him so utterly as this miraculous visitation of pity and terror. For this Victoria in heaven, who resembled the actual Victoria as little as a star resembles a glowworm, had won at last his unalterable fidelity.

"You were more deserving than I, Louisa," he said in the furtive and hesitating voice in which a man utters the unutterable. "You are the only one of us who was worthy of her." For this sudden apotheosis of Victoria had absorbed all the light and colour from his field of vision, and had left the smaller human figures drained of vital significance. By that act of silent heroism, which had cost her so little, Victoria had triumphed over every rival she had had in the past and over every rival she might have had in the future. In the presence of this stainless legend, Mrs. Dalrymple's allurement had wilted like the crumpled wings of a butterfly. At the funeral, he had caught a glimpse of her charming head in the distance, and a gust of repugnance, almost of physical aversion, had swept through his nerves. Yes, this was the kind of thing that must stay by a man until the end of his life.

"You were a perfect husband, Virginius. She told me only a few weeks ago that the greatest satisfaction in her life was the thought that she had been able to make you happy."

"But I wasn't worthy, Louisa!" The cry rushed out in a torrent of anguish.

"You mustn't think that, Virginius." Louisa laid her comforting hand on his shoulder. "You mustn't let that idea begin to brood in your mind. Victoria would never have wished you to nurse your grief. She didn't believe in selfish grief. She has said to me so often in the past, 'Louisa, I hope to leave only happy memories!'"

His eyes were looking inward, and there was a strange clear light in them. "Happy memories. That was why——"

"Yes, that was why."

"She knew all the time, but she was perfectly cheerful."

"Oh, yes, she was perfectly cheerful. Even as a child she had the sunniest disposition."

"I could bear it better," he said suddenly, while the idea flitted through Louisa's orderly mind that men never stop being children so long as there is a woman to look after them, "I could bear it better if only these last few months had been different."

"Different?"

"I mean if I'd thought more of her. Do you know I have a terrible feeling that I never really knew what she was, that I never really saw her until she was dead."

"That is taking a morbid view of your grief, Virginius. You remember how Victoria disliked morbid views of death."

She had taken off her glasses to wipe them, and now, as she returned them to her reddened nose, her features appeared to settle into their usual composure. Though her devotion to Victoria had been deep and genuine, the precise equilibrium of her mind had not been disturbed by her

sorrow. For her, death had softened rather than magnified
Victoria's virtues. She beheld her now, not as she had
seen her a few days before, good, gentle, incapable of
malice, and hopeful by nature rather than intelligence,
but finished, harmless, undissembling as a dove, and
blindly at the mercy of life. Yet this, she told herself, with
accurate judgment, was an error of sentiment. Living
or dead, Victoria would triumph. Because she was one with
the doves of life, at least in the mind of Virginius, her
memory would remain invulnerable to disaster. Or was
this also a mistake? Would she be preserved from oblivion, not by merit alone, but by the benign embalming
medium of circumstances? To Louisa's startled horror
some small, malicious demon of irony spoke suddenly from
the primitive jungle of consciousness. "Was it because she
felt her way instead of seeing it that she reached everlasting remembrance? Or was it simply because dulness,
if it is sweet tempered, will outwear every form of activity?"

Amazed, helpless; for even in a mind as neat and frugal
as Louisa's thoughts are not numbered, she said hurriedly, while the cold glitter of her eyeglasses transfixed
his grief:

"Try to do what she would have wished, Virginius.
We must both forget ourselves and think of Mary Victoria."

He assented without animation. "I suppose people are
obliged to forget. That is the worst part of death. No
matter how much you want to keep the past alive, the
business of living is too much for you. You can't keep
rust from settling over anything that is motionless. In remembering Mary Victoria, we shall forget Victoria."

"No, not forget." She was firm about this, for such an
idea was not only fruitless but morbid. "Don't you re-

member that when little Edward died soon after he was born, Victoria would not let herself give way and brood. She told me that you said to her then that life must always be for the living."

"Yes, I remember," he replied, vaguely consoled. Few women, he mused, a moment later, possessed Louisa's infallible touch on a wounded heart. In the last few days he had reminded himself so often of Victoria's description of her as "a rock to lean on." He had even reproached himself for the flippancy with which he had dismissed her in the past as a sterling character, but one of those women, in spite of Marmaduke's long wooing, whom men did not marry. Now, in the hour of affliction, he was beginning to realize that, even in marriage, there is much to be said in favour of a rock-ribbed foundation.

"I don't know what we should have done without you, Louisa," he said gratefully. "Especially Mary Victoria. You are like a second mother to the poor child."

A tear trickled down Louisa's nose under her glasses. "Well, I've always been that way, Virginius. Victoria's children are as dear to me as if they were my own. There isn't anybody," she added, "not even you, who will miss Victoria more than I shall."

"I know that," he assented, and felt suddenly very close to her. "Well, you must help us all you can. You must tell me when I am wrong about Mary Victoria. There are times when I feel that I scarcely know her."

"You'll get over that," she said reasonably. "She would have been more like Victoria, if there hadn't been any war." Then she leaned down and patted his shoulder. "The best thing you can do now is to go out and take a walk. You're beginning to look sallow, and you can't bring back Victoria by neglecting your health. Go out and get a breath of fresh air while I finish putting these things

died, he seemed to be in a blind alley. I advised him then to see Buchanan in the morning, and but for——for what happened that night, I think we might have made him listen to reason."

"I was wondering," Louisa remarked, with the composure that somebody, she felt, was obliged to preserve in a crisis, "if he could have meant more than he said. Wasn't he once before, when he was in Paris, on the brink of——?"

Her question was never asked, for Mary Victoria broke into a sobbing so wild and unrestrained that Louisa was frightened into compassionate dumbness. Accustomed to the girl's arrogant cheerfulness, she felt a pang of remorse because she had believed, especially since she had seen her in the presence of death, that Mary Victoria was lacking in genuine emotion. As she bent over her now and watched the long, convulsive sobs shudder through her relaxed body, she thought, with a flash of sympathetic understanding, "It must be her condition. Being that way seems to upset women dreadfully."

"I couldn't bear to think that. Oh, Father, I couldn't bear to think that," Mary Victoria moaned. "Help me to find him, Father. I shall die unless you help me to find him!"

"If only I knew where to look, my child. Try to be calm. Try to tell me all that you know. Why do you suspect that he has gone to another woman?"

"I don't know, Father." She stood up, wringing her hands in anguish. "I don't know, but I must find him! Oh, won't you help me to find him?"

"Try to be reasonable. Try to think of us, to think of your child."

"I will, if only you will help me to find him. I must find him before it is too late. I want him back. I don't care

what he does or what happens, I want him back. Oh,
Father, won't you help me?"

"Then tell me just what he said. Louisa, is there anything you can give her?"

"Oh, no, I don't want anything. All I want is to find
Martin. He said he was going away, and that I must not
expect him to come back."

"Was that all? Every word?"

"That was all. I thought he had gone to Milly Burden.
I never dreamed that he would—— But—— Oh, I see it
all now. I see what he meant. Aren't you coming, Father?
Aren't you coming with me to look for him?"

"I'll look, dear. I'll do the best I can." But, even
while he was speaking, the ugly thought had occurred to
him, "Isn't death the only solution? Is there any finality,
except in death, for a situation like this?" Horrified by
that flitting shadow of evil, he said with compunction, "If
you will try to bear up, daughter, I'll promise to do everything in my power."

"Then we must start," Mary Victoria said, with passionate haste. "We mustn't lose a minute, if we hope to
find him before it is too late. Oh, Aunt Louisa, won't you
give me my hat? I left it somewhere in the hall."

"But you can't go, dear. You are not well enough. It
might do you harm."

"I can—I must." Reviving suddenly, Mary Victoria
was animated by flaming resolve. Light streamed back
into her eyes; colour flowed again beneath the leaden
pallor of her skin. "I can. I must," she repeated desperately. "Oh, Father, can't you understand that I shall die
if I have to sit and wait?"

Mr. Littlepage looked helplessly at Louisa. "Ought she
to go with me? And where, anyway, are we going?"

Louisa, having found Mary Victoria's hat in the hall,

was trying to place it at the exact mournful angle on the girl's head. "Wait a minute, dear, I must smooth your hair." Then, after repairing Mary Victoria's injured appearance as well as she could, she turned to confront Mr. Littlepage with her imperious sagacity. "Of course she oughtn't to go, Virginius, but what are you going to do about it? If she doesn't go with you, it will be the first time in her life that she hasn't done what she wanted to do." Then, with her watchful glance on Mary Victoria, who was already hastening across the room, she added in a warning whisper, "I suppose it is safer not to cross her."

"Couldn't you reason with her? She hasn't the slightest idea where she is going."

"Oh, yes, she has, Virginius, she is going to save Martin. As soon as I made that unfortunate bent in the situation, it provided her with her direction. She is going to save Martin from his own nature, which is exactly what she has been doing since she first met him."

Irritated by her sepulchral whisper, he replied almost angrily, "All the same, you might try to reason with her."

Louisa shook her head. "You can't reason, Virginius, with salvation. All you can do is to follow her in the hope that she will never lose anything else that she wishes to keep."

He glanced at her in despair, but before he could summon an indignant protest to his lips, Mary Victoria cried urgently from the hall, "Oh, Father, won't you please hurry! This isn't any time to stop and discuss things."

While he obeyed her, he asked sharply, "Have you any idea, Mary Victoria, where you are going?"

"I am going to Milly Burden," she replied in a tone of impatient anguish. "I am going to ask her if she knows where he is."

Again he turned to Louisa. "Can't you stop her?" he

pleaded, with bitterness. "Women must not do things like that."

"If you were ever to stop her, Virginius," Louisa answered sternly, "you ought to have started trying twenty-six years ago. But I shouldn't let a theory of behaviour bother me," she added consolingly. "Behaviour isn't nearly so important as it used to be."

He flushed darkly. "Mary Victoria," he said sternly from the threshold, "I refuse to allow my daughter to go to another woman and ask for her husband."

Turning in her steps, for she had reached the head of the staircase, Mary Victoria gazed back at him with incredulous eyes. "I am obliged to find Martin, Father," she answered, with tragic forbearance. "Nothing else on earth matters to me if only I am in time to save Martin."

"Have you so little pride that you will go to another woman to look for him?"

"You can't understand, Father," Mary Victoria reasoned, with patience. "Pride has nothing to do with it. I must go to him wherever he is. I must try to save him no matter what he has done. If you would rather not go with me," she added in a throbbing voice, "I will go by myself."

"God help us!" Mr. Littlepage exclaimed more in anger than in supplication; and then, with one last moving appeal to Louisa, he asked, "Will you tell me what I am to do?"

"I think," Louisa replied as gently as she could, "that the best thing would be to order the car."

Mary Victoria, who had started down the stairs, turned to call back over her shoulder, "The car is waiting, Father. We can leave it as soon as we reach Juniper Hill."

"You may as well start," Louisa remarked, as he flung a helpless glance in her direction. "And I shouldn't worry

a bit if I were you about her going to see Milly Burden,"
she added, following him to the staircase. "Nobody minds
a thing like that any longer."

To this she received, as she had expected, no audible
reply; but it seemed to her that Mr. Littlepage's shoulders were very straight as he descended the stairs, and
his pace had not slackened a few minutes later, when,
turning to a front window, she watched him cross the
pavement and step into the car. "He hasn't been the same
man since Victoria's death," she meditated sadly. "Some
men seem never to fall in love with their wives until they
have lost them and can fit them into a halo. By the time
he is through with Victoria," she added presently, with
her unfailing shrewdness, "nobody will be able to recognize a single feature. Well, I suppose it makes him happier, and whether it does or not, there isn't anything to
be done about it."

As the car vanished in a haze of sunshine, her thoughts
passed, with astonishment, from Mr. Littlepage to Mary
Victoria. Yes, Virginius was right. This was the kind of
thing that no woman, at least no woman who was a Southern lady, could have done in the last century. Never, not
even if he had been her lawful husband, not even to save
him from his own nature, could Louisa have run after
a man. Even murder in a just cause, as long as it
did not involve a sacrifice of proper pride, would have
been easier for her. The women of her age had waited
silently for what they wanted, spinning their intricate
webs with the eternal patience of nature; and when what
they wanted did not come because he was caught elsewhere, they continued to wait and spin as long as the
gossamer threads held together. "I wonder which way is
best?" Louisa speculated, for hers was an inquiring mind.
"Is it better to cling to modesty until you lose every-

thing else, or to waste it like scattered rose-leaves in the
long pursuit of delight? But what is love, after all?" she
asked suddenly, "and who has ever found it by seeking?"
On the pavement the faint sunshine glittered and vanished
and reassembled in a pattern of silver. An old torment,
the torment of hope and of long waiting, shuddered back
from her heart into her nerves. "I could never go through
it now," she thought, with a start of wonder because she
had ever survived it. "No woman of to-day could go
through it and live." Yes, she could not agree with Virginius that the world had changed for the worse. Being
a woman, she knew better. Being a woman, she knew
what she could never bring herself to tell him, that the
modesty of the past was a false, not a true, deity, and delighted in sacrifice. No, it wasn't worth it, she said in a
strained whisper, as if someone were listening; it wasn't
worth it, at least to women. Nothing was worth all the
deceit, all the anguish, all the futile hope and ineffectual
endeavour, all the pretense and parade, all the artificial
glamour and empty posturing, of the great Victorian tradition. For an instant, so relentless was the clutch of the
past, her heart struggled like a wild thing in the beak of
an eagle. Yes, she knew, and Virginius did not. She knew
what it had all meant to women. She had lived through
the ages of waiting, and she knew every throb, every
ache, every pang, every quiver. She had lived through it
all. For her heart had cracked and broken as quietly as
the hearts of all perfect Southern ladies broke beneath
the enamelled surface of beautiful behaviour. And now,
cool, composed, indulgent, self-contained, and easily
amused, she watched with sympathy the liberal manners
of the new century.

VIII

Moving in what seemed to him an unnatural dream, Mr. Littlepage left the car at the corner of Juniper Hill, and followed Mary Victoria over the cobblestones to the opposite pavement. Though he had reached the age when, according to all the schools, man seeks comfort rather than adventure, he had been shocked into self-reproach by the suddenness of Victoria's death, and he was lingering now in that inhospitable region between despair and resignation. Obstinately, in spite of Louisa's sensible advice, he clung to his grief and remorse. Obstinately, in spite of Mary Victoria's distress, he reminded himself that the loss of Martin, even if he were lost forever, was a trifle compared to the loss of Victoria. Yet he had observed, not without resentment, that Mary Victoria, who had borne her mother's death in deep affliction but with quiet fortitude, had shuddered into a tragic victim when this man, who was in every way ignoble, had tried to abandon her. "You can't reason about love," he thought indignantly. "It is love, or what they call love, that makes most of the trouble in life."

Looking round as she walked, Mary Victoria sobbed under her breath, "Oh, Father, promise me you will find him!"

"Don't worry, my child, we will find him," Mr. Littlepage replied consolingly, and he added angrily to himself, "He isn't worth losing."

A sigh floated back to him as Mary Victoria quickened her pace. "But, Father, I want him!" And this sigh, so mournful, so ardent, was inexpressibly moving. While she had lain sobbing in his arms, Mr. Littlepage had felt that his heart was flooded with tenderness. Now, however, following her in her eager pursuit, he was conscious that his inner mood had chilled into compassion. If only women had been satisfied to remain protected, how much pleasanter the world, even this changing modern world, might be to-day! If only they had been satisfied to wait in patience, not to seek after happiness! For it seemed to him, while his mood, if not his heart, froze into resentment, that there could be nothing nobler in women than the beauty of long waiting and wifely forbearance. He was old-fashioned, no doubt, notwithstanding his advanced views in other fields than those of woman's sphere; but surely it was not too much to insist that the true feminine character had never flowered more perfectly than in the sheltered garden of Southern tradition. Never had woman appeared more desirable, never had she exerted a finer influence upon manners and customs, than in those legendary periods when she had disposed her limbs in the classic posture of waiting.

"Mary Victoria is going the wrong way about things," he mused bitterly. "If only she could believe it, she would stand a much better chance of getting what she wants if she would be content to go back home and sit down."

At this point, his meditations were faintly ruffled by the intrusion of poor Aunt Agatha and her attendant train of shadowy figures, who had all, to judge from their subdued appearance, waited somewhere with infinite patience. Well, of course, every rule, however sound in principle, has its exceptions. Poor Aunt Agatha was not only an exception, but, surveyed through this disfiguring modern

atmosphere, almost a catastrophe. To be sure, she must
have won whatever life had assigned to her by staying at
home; for even her fall, which happened so long ago
that it had receded to some dim island of allegory, had
occurred, he reminded himself, before the Southern lady
had plucked even the most immature apple from the
forbidden tree. In his early youth, when nymphomania
was less literary than it is to-day, he had heard elderly
ladies, who were always interested and usually well in-
formed, whisper vague warnings against poor Aunt
Agatha's moral contagion. But, even then, he insisted to
his harassed mind, while he joined Mary Victoria's bold
pursuit of the fleeing male, Aunt Agatha had been sheltered, she had been protected. It would become, he moralized, a deranged world indeed, if women should begin to
track down men in their wild happiness-hunting. Mary Victoria, he knew, for all her reckless chase, was pursuing
Martin less for pleasure than from benevolence. She was
animated as always by a lofty purpose, not by a discredited instinct. Before him, in the triumphant flesh, he realized, was a living example of the steadfast dignity a sense
of duty confers. If women were ever to grasp this simple
truth, what an endless opportunity for destruction awaited
them. Toying whimsically with the idea, for there is safety
in the whimsical that does not slip into a tragic abyss,
he thought with idle malice, "They may ruin as many lives
as they please, if only they will consent to ruin them from
the highest motives. . . . His mind, overshadowed by
grief for Victoria, retreated suddenly into itself as into a
darkened chamber. Life again, the invincible Adversary!
He was alone with it there in that inner obscurity. Without light, without longing, without joy, without hope, he
was alone with it forever. Even love could not save; for
what did he, what did anyone, know about love? Far

away, as faint and thin as the music of distant chimes, he
heard the voice of Mrs. Dalrymple grieving because love
is not kindness.

"I must not let myself grow morbid," he thought. "I
must not begin to take a dark view of life. Louisa is right.
That is a poor way of showing respect for Victoria's memory." Lifting his eyes from the pavement, he gazed up
at the silvery blue of the sky, where small white clouds
were sailing in fleets. On the still, soft air the sunshine
quivered and paled; the winter branches looked as
insubstantial as mist; and over the sky and the sunshine
and the glimmering boughs there hovered the impalpable film of a dream. "It is not real," he told himself,
with a start. He didn't know why, he didn't know how;
but it was not reality at which he was looking. It was not
reality in which he struggled and suffered like a bird in a
net. "Perhaps I am too complex," he thought. Or was he
too simple-minded? Some day, when he was old and his
active life was well over, he might begin to explore the
secret labyrinths of his own nature. He might even try
to discover why he had seemed to live like a pointed flame
in those instants of release—or was it communion? But
not now—not yet, not so long as the imperative needs of
time and space still enslaved his desires. Well, no matter.
All he knew at the moment was that he had been born
out of his proper time, that he did not fit into his age. He
did not belong with poor Aunt Agatha, who was too tender; he did not belong with Mrs. Dalrymple, who was
too brittle; he did not belong with Curle, who was too
vulgar. Yet, in the end, he speculated idly, Curle and his
kind might be the only ones to survive. In the end, they
might wear out all the softer and finer strains of human
material. Was that the victory toward which our civilization was moving so proudly? Well, no matter. . . . This

dull resentment against noise, against size, against ugliness, might be nothing nobler than the approaching rigidity of age, the slow hardening of arteries that had once been as elastic as youth. It was his fault, perhaps, that everything except his sorrow seemed trivial and meaningless. Modern life especially appeared without dignity and even without direction, an endless speeding to nowhere. Man, he told himself, may have flown to the stars, and broken light and air to his harness; but he was no nearer happiness than he had been in the past. He was no nearer the everlasting answer to Why? Whence? Whither? . . . Even Curle, who never left off speeding and, as Marmaduke once said of him, "could see the cheerful side of a corpse," was not happy. No, Curle was not happy, his father repeated cynically after a moment; he was merely full of noise and rushing wind and the urgent impulse to live faster than anyone else. With intense irritation, Mr. Littlepage recalled that Curle, who had sincerely loved his mother, had translated his grief into renewed speed and increased production. Straight from the cemetery, he had rushed on in search of a monument; and not until he had procured the costliest memorial that could be crowded into the populous family plot, had he been satisfied to turn back to his parades and his old cornfields. Well, no matter. . . .

"Is this the house, Father?" asked Mary Victoria, as she stopped before the sagging gate, under the dappled boughs of an old sycamore which had escaped the political axe.

Beneath the tree, an Italian organ grinder was encouraging a wistful monkey in a romantic burlesque; and while he doffed his little cap and assumed the immemorial posture of chivalry, the eyes of the wistful monkey asked, "Why? Whence? Whither?"

While he felt in the pocket of his waistcoat, and held out a coin, Mr. Littlepage spoke a friendly word to the organ grinder, who was playing a sad, gay melody.

"Did you bring him far?" he inquired, not merely to be kind, but because he was interested for the first time since he had entered the shadowy desert of sorrow.

"We came a long way, a long, long way, sir." The words attuned themselves to the air, or was it, as Curle was fond of saying, to the infinite?

"Do you treat him well? Why does he look so sad?"

"Oh, I treat him well, sir; but he is an artist. It is a hard world for artists, sir, whether they be men or monkeys."

A hard world for artists! "Yes, we should keep to facts, especially if we are monkeys. The world belongs to facts. Here is one for you." Taking out his pocketbook, he selected a generous note, and unfolded it slowly. As he gave it into the withered little claws, the monkey doffed his cap again and replied with a flourishing gesture. "He needs a new cap," Mr. Littlepage said.

"Yes, sir, he has a new cap, but he likes the old one better and won't give it up."

"Aren't you coming, Father?" Mary Victoria called impatiently from the porch.

"Yes, I'm coming, dear." As he opened the gate and went up the walk of sunken flagstones, he glanced back over his shoulder, and saw the wistful eyes of the monkey still following him. Why? Whence? Whither?

"The idea of stopping, in the midst of our anxiety, to play with a monkey," Mary Victoria remarked in the tone of a woman who is exasperated but still mistress of herself and her surroundings.

"I wasn't playing, daughter. That monkey has something I have always needed and never been able to find."

"I shouldn't choose this time to joke, Father." As she lost her temper, she held the more firmly to her patience.

"My dear, I never felt less like joking in my life, nor, I feel sure, did that monkey. Don't you think I'd better go in alone?"

"I must speak to her. But I've already rung twice, and nobody has answered."

"Perhaps they are all out. Or Mrs. Burden may be putting on her Sunday dress. If they keep a maid for the lodgers, she is probably out walking with her young man."

Mary Victoria's only response was to ring for the third time more emphatically. Then, after a long pause, she said with annoyance, "You speak as if you hope they are out."

"I am not sure that I don't. Have you tried the door? In this part of town doors are not often locked." Pushing her gently aside, he turned the handle, and the door opened on the fine old staircase in the darkened hall.

"They may think it strange if we go in," Mary Victoria remarked, peering cautiously into the wan green light of the house.

"Nothing is strange in this neighbourhood. Marmaduke will know where they are. I'll run up and ask him. Are you able to come?"

"I've never been up to his studio. How far is it?"

"Two flights, long and steep."

She shook her head. "I am not equal to a climb like that. You go up, and I'll sit on the porch and wait."

"You look pale, daughter. Are you sure you don't mind being left?"

"Oh, I don't mind being left. I don't mind," she said, with a strangled sob, "anything in the world." Then composing herself with a gesture, she added, "But look inside first and see if anybody is there."

Obediently, he glanced into the rooms until he came to the kitchen, where he found a smouldering fire in the stove. Returning, he said in a tone of relief, "Mrs. Burden is probably visiting one of the neighbours, or she may be upstairs in Marmaduke's studio. It isn't likely that she would leave her house empty for more than a few minutes."

"Uncle Marmaduke may have left the door open."

"Well, he may have, but I doubt it. However, I'll go up and ask. Would you like a glass of water?"

"No, I don't want a glass of water. I don't want anything."

Her eyes filled with tears, and she turned away from him to the melancholy garden, where the leaves of autumn were still lying in windrifts. With a pang in his heart, he told himself that she was thinking of all the emptiness of the future, of all the emptiness of other winters without a noble and engrossing purpose in life.

"Shall I go up now?" Hesitating and irresolute, he felt that in ascending that staircase and taking Marmaduke into his confidence, he was beginning a search that must end in disaster.

"Oh, go, go. Why don't you go?"

"I don't like to leave you, my dear. Somebody might come."

"What does it matter? What do I care?" Her nerves quivered in her voice; and turning away, he went as quickly as he could into the house and up the dark flight of stairs.

IX

WHEN he reached the second floor, he could see the afternoon sunshine streaming down from Marmaduke's studio; and mounting rapidly, he found his brother still encircled by his depraved riot of colour.

"I was going up to your house a little later, Virginius," Marmaduke said, as he balanced himself on his wooden leg and held out his hand. "Few persons admired Victoria more than I did. There was more in her, I believe, than she ever suspected. Her convictions stood in her way, but convictions always stand in your way, if they are strong enough."

"Everybody misses her," Virginius replied coldly, because he could not bear to hear Marmaduke talk of Victoria. "But I came to speak about Mary Victoria. Her husband has left her."

"Well, what did you expect?"

"I don't know what I expected, but not this. Mary Victoria is broken-hearted."

"She doesn't know when she is well off. What excuse did he give?"

"None. That's the worst of it. At first she thought there was another woman. Now, she fears he may destroy himself."

"By another woman, do you mean Milly?"

"She means Milly. I don't mean anybody."

"What do you fear?"

"Well, I talked to him the evening I—we lost Victoria, and I think the chances are that he has made away with himself."

"Poor devil!" Marmaduke said, with a sigh. "I suppose he's a cad and a rotter; but all the same I have a lurking sympathy for him in my heart. When you turn a man with a face like that loose in a woman's world, you might more mercifully hang him."

"Haven't we always known that a man's face doesn't matter?" Mr. Littlepage inquired, with asperity.

"No doubt. We've always known a good many things that are not true. I tell you a chap like that, looking as if he had stepped out of a sad legend, hasn't any better chance than a—than a rabbit. Not than a hare with the hounds after him."

This was, in Mr. Littlepage's opinion, an ignoble view of life; but, within the last few days, ignoble views of life had not seemed to him worth resenting. So he said merely, "He has one of the best wives in the world."

"I can well believe it. The best wife sometimes smothers a man."

"I remember he used that very word when he talked to me. He even asked if I couldn't understand a man having had too much of women?"

"You couldn't, I suppose?"

"On the contrary, I told him I could. Any man, no matter how happily he has been married, can understand that much of life. But it didn't sound as if he were pursuing Milly again."

"No, it doesn't sound that way, but a man's protestation does not always accord with his practice. He has been seeing Milly, I know. I met him coming out of the house last night."

"Oh, you did!" Mr. Littlepage exclaimed blankly.

"Well, I dare say it was too much to expect him to be decent; but I did hope Milly had come to her senses again. It looks," he prophesied gloomily, "as if the whole world were going to ruin."

"We've been going that way for several million years, my dear brother, and we haven't apparently got any nearer our destination."

Mr. Littlepage frowned. His nerves, which had been on edge ever since Victoria's death, slipped suddenly beyond the control of his will. "I believe it's love that has gone rotten," he said, while his lower lip protruded angrily and the purple flush Victoria had dreaded mantled his face.

Marmaduke assented. "It wouldn't do any harm to try pity in its place for a while. Pity is a finer sentiment than love, and it might build a better world in the end than love ever imagined."

But this frail philosophy only exasperated Virginius. "I am too old to begin experimenting with either sentiment or philanthropy. What I want to do is to save Mary Victoria and Milly, if it is not too late."

Marmaduke's gaze roamed through the window, and beyond the old sycamore, to the thin sunlight that was dissolving over the river. "I believe Milly is saved already," he answered. "If to be saved means to become something more than the helpless victim of life. As for Mary Victoria, I am not sure that she can ever be saved until she has first been destroyed."

A quiver ran through Mr. Littlepage's mottled features. "If you have the heart to stand by and watch my daughter ruin her life over an unworthy object, I haven't," he said bitterly.

"I confess I'd rather not watch it, Virginius. I am not sufficiently pious to enjoy seeing people suffer. I don't even enjoy seeing them go to prison, and I am sure I could never have borne the sight of a burning. My heart, or at least my nerves, are so unredeemed that I am not able even to justify the ways of God to Martin. It seems to me a poor sort of Providence that tracks down a wild creature with an automobile and slaughters it with a machine gun."

"Do you think of Martin as a wild creature? He seems to me nothing more dangerous than a flabby failure."

"He is a failure, I admit; but I still maintain that Providence should be a sport even when tracking down failures. That will, no doubt, impress you as impious. Perhaps it is. But I cannot get over the feeling that the poor fool never had a chance to be anything but some woman's purpose in life."

"Naturally," Virginius agreed more quietly, "you can't help feeling sorry for him. But we must remember that he owed everything, including his life, to Mary Victoria."

"That was where the trouble began. He owed her too much."

"She still loves him devotedly."

"You can't blame him for that. He did his best to destroy her illusion. The truth is that she could have done twice as much with him if she had loved him less and liked him more. Ever since he was born, Martin has had too much love and too little liking."

Mr. Littlepage sighed. After all, Marmaduke was speaking from the shallows, not from the depths, of experience. "Sometimes a man may have both," he rejoined uneasily; for he would have died sooner than ask Marmaduke how much he knew, or imagined that he knew, about love. "Have you never seen them united?"

"Not often. I can recall only one woman who has been able to give both in equal measure, and that is Louisa."

Mr. Littlepage started, and his unnatural colour faded slowly. "But was Louisa really in love with you?"

So mocking was the flash in Marmaduke's glance that it enlightened his brother even more quickly than the derisive note in his voice. "Are you as blind, Virginius, as you pretend to be?"

"Blind?" The word cut like a blade. "Do you mean to imply——?"

"I imply nothing. Are you too wise or too dull to understand why Louisa has remained single?"

"I am certainly too dull, if you mean——"

"Have you looked at her almost every day for thirty-odd years and yet never seen what was as plain as—as —well, as the nose in her face?"

"She has absolutely, if that is what you mean to suggest," Virginius faltered, "given me no reason to think that she was—that she was——"

Marmaduke chuckled. "Good God, man, do you imagine I could have stayed in love with Louisa for thirty years if she had not been in love with somebody else? But she wouldn't have given you any reason. Trust her for that. Louisa plays the game, even if she is a Victorian virgin."

"She was always devoted to Victoria," Mr. Littlepage answered resentfully. "She was Victoria's best friend."

"She probably loved Victoria better than she loved anyone in the world. Louisa is the kind of woman with whom friendship runs deeper than love. There were women like that born even in the same year with Amy Dalrymple—or with Aunt Agatha."

Mr. Littlepage was still justly incensed. "If you had not lived abroad so long, Marmaduke, I should feel obliged to resent your insinuations. It is little less than an insult, not only to Louisa, but to Victoria."

"Louisa would not admit that. Even though she is a virgin and unviolated, she has learned something since Babylon."

"I have the highest regard for Louisa," Mr. Littlepage remarked stiffly, "the very highest regard and admiration."

"Well, so have I," Marmaduke sighed softly. "You must remember that I have loved her almost as long and as hopelessly as she has loved you."

In the deep despondency of Mr. Littlepage's mind there was a sudden discreet flutter, as if a flock of startled birds were settling to roost. "I refuse to admit that, Marmaduke. Such a suggestion is an affront to Louisa's sterling character."

"My dear Virginius, there are circumstances in which a sterling character is not only admirable but essential, and a long and hopeless passion is one of them. Without a sterling character, it is impossible to be hopeless and still love on."

Out of the flutter and confusion in Mr. Littlepage's mind, there emerged first a puzzled wonder and then the diffused light of complete understanding. Surely to have inspired a passion, however confined by virtue, in a sterling character, such as he knew Louisa to be, was a higher tribute than the awakening of wanton fancies in ladies of looser habits and softer natures.

"I must go down," he said abruptly. "Mary Victoria is waiting for me." There was a new note in his voice, and before hastening to the stairs, he paused an instant and looked with compassionate eyes at his brother. Incredible as it appeared, he had never realized before that Marmaduke was an old man. The years had not mellowed him; they had merely driven and twisted him into this mood of sardonic defiance. Standing there, in the last flare of day, he looked, not only tough and seasoned and crippled, but invulnerable alike to time and chance and desire.

"Well, good-bye, old chap," Virginius said softly, as he began his long descent of the stairs.

When he passed the second turn, a view of the open front door and the outside world floated before him, and he saw that clouds were gathering in the west, while a round red sun, spotted like a tiger-lily, was dropping slowly into the river. As he approached the door, the sound of muffled voices reached him, and one of these voices, he recognized, with a start of dismay, as Milly Burden's.

"Yes, I am going away." There was a running cadence of ecstasy in the words. "I am going away into the world!"

"I thought you might help me to find him," Mary Victoria answered, as her father stepped out on the porch. Glancing indifferently round when he laid his arm on her shoulder, she added in a composed but suffering tone, "He is so ill that he hardly knows what he is doing. I thought he might have come to you."

"He did come," Milly said with a strangely absent air, as if she were listening to some faint music. "He did come, but he didn't stay. He had to go on. Something was driving him."

"He didn't ask you, then, to—to——"

As Mary Victoria's voice wavered under her anguish, Milly caught up the broken sentence, and finished it with an air of defiant candour. "To go with him? No, he didn't ask me. He thought he wanted me," she added, in what seemed to Mr. Littlepage, in his anxiety, a less brazen tone, "but he didn't—not really. What he really wanted was loneliness."

"Loneliness?" exclaimed Mary Victoria, and the echo was a sigh of despair.

"Do you know where he went?" Mr. Littlepage demanded; and it appeared to him, as he asked the question, that every circumstance, even Milly's unhappy passion, had changed since he entered the house and went upstairs to Marmaduke's studio. Even the air had grown colder; a wind, with a sharpened edge, was springing up from the river; and the heavy clouds were drifting down over the red and black sunset.

"He didn't tell me," Milly answered slowly, "but he is going as far away as he can. As long as his money holds out, he said, he would go on. Maybe he will have to stop in France, but he was hoping that he might get as far as the Himalayas. He wants to find a place where there are high mountains and snows that never melt and nothing else except loneliness."

A long shudder quivered through Mary Victoria's body, and over her lowered head, Mr. Littlepage said sternly: "Well, it is a good riddance—so long as he is going alone."

"Oh, he is going alone," Milly replied, with that quiver of joy—or was it cruelty?—in her voice. While he looked at her in anger, he told himself that he had never seen her so overflowing with life. The blue of her eyes was deeper and richer, and the April radiance shone in her smile and in the vivid bloom of her lips. "She looks as if she were in love again," he thought moodily, "but, in God's name, who is it this time?"

At her words, Mary Victoria had drawn away from her father's arms, and she stood now, noble and proud and very lonely, against the boughs of the old sycamore and the dark sunset. Broken but undefeated, she put out her arm with a magnanimous gesture; and looking into her face, Mr. Littlepage felt that the lost adoration and romance were ebbing back into his heart. Once again, his memory dissolved into a glowing mist and flowered anew in the image of a little girl with auburn curls on her shoulders and bare, sunburned knees above her white socks and black slippers. "I want him to be happy," she was saying, in a tone of exalted emotion. "If you can make him happier than I can, I am ready—I am willing——"

For an instant, Milly stared at her with a flame of surprise in her face. Then she answered quickly, almost fiercely, with a hard little laugh (the laugh, Mr. Littlepage told himself, of youth that is lost in its own selfish concerns), "But I don't want him. I thought I wanted him until I saw him again, and then I knew that I didn't. He doesn't want me, he wants loneliness. And I—oh, what I want is something worth loving!" Catching her breath, in that defiant laugh, she cried the words over again, as if the very sound of them filled her with joy. "What I want is something worth loving!"

"Well, I hope you'll find it, my dear," Mr. Littlepage said coldly; for not only did he marvel at the curious appetite of youth for disaster, but he disapproved of her unbridled desires almost as much as he deplored her lack of feeling for Mary Victoria. "But I doubt if you will, and even if you find it, you probably won't know it. As for Martin," he concluded in a tone of deep disgust, "we cannot lose him so easily. If we wait, he will come back."

"When he finds loneliness," Milly replied indifferently, "he may find also that it is not what he wanted. He may even find," she added, with the shrewdness of instinct, "that it isn't any more satisfying than love."

Holding Mary Victoria in his arms, Mr. Littlepage felt that all her gallant spirit, which had conquered Martin as well as the Balkan kingdoms, was oozing slowly away. Her erect figure appeared to shrink and falter beneath a burden that was too intolerable to be borne. Even her voice, when she spoke, sounded as if it were crushed by despair—or was it repugnance?

"It makes no difference now," she said, sinking back from her supreme gesture of sacrifice; for what sacrifice, however noble, can be confirmed when it is wasted? "No matter what happens, it could never be the same thing again." A gust of pain, or perhaps of anger, darkened her eyes, and Mr. Littlepage wondered hopefully if she were at last seeing Martin, not in the glow of her illusion, but by the chill dawn of Milly's awakening? "Are you coming, Father?" she asked, as she descended the steps to the walk.

"In a minute, dear," he replied, and turned back to Milly. "So it is all arranged, and you are happy?" Looking round nervously, he saw that Mary Victoria was standing in the desolate garden, with the withered leaves blowing about her feet.

"Yes, it is all arranged. Miss Goddard will look after Mother. She said Mrs. Littlepage asked her to do so."

"I know." That was like Victoria. She never forgot anything, least of all a chance to do a kindness. "But the chief thing is that you are happy."

"Yes, I am happy. Nobody who hasn't been as miserable as I was last year could possibly be so happy as this."

"Just because you are going away?"

"Just because I am free. Just because I am free to begin everything over again."

Everything over again! Oh, that insatiable appetite of youth for disaster! "Well, you know now what life is."

She laughed with the old gay derision at circumstances. "But the whole world is mine, and in the whole world there must be something worth loving."

His face hardened. "Then you have not yet had enough? You are still looking for love?"

She shook her head, and he felt that all the tragic splendour of youth was in her face. "Not love," she answered, and her voice, so rich, so vibrating, was like the sound of wings in the air. "No, not love alone, but something worth loving!"

He smiled sadly. "Well, I hope you will find it, my dear, and when you do find it, that it will be better than loneliness. If it isn't, you know where a friend will be waiting as long as he lives. But I shall see you to-morrow?"

"Oh, yes, you shall see me to-morrow. I am not going until the end of the week."

With a last pressure, he dropped her hands and hurried down into the garden. The wind was driving the leaves in flocks after Mary Victoria, and it seemed to him, as he picked his way over the broken flagstones, that the advancing dusk was saturated with the taint of despair. "If it is any comfort to you, my child," he said when he had caught up with her, "you have every reason to feel that he will come back in the end."

A sigh escaped her, and was lost in the melancholy rustle of the wind in the grass. "Doesn't everything come back," she said, "if you wait until you have stopped wanting it?"

Perhaps. He didn't know. He wasn't sure. Even in the practice of law, he had avoided, as far as possible, the problem of fugitive husbands. "Well, you must try not to lose courage," he answered cheerfully. "After all, the important thing," he added, with a vague idea that his words were an echo, "is to bring a happy child into the world."

At this imperative summons to duty, her drooping shoulders became straight again. "That is all I have left," she replied in the familiar accents of noble determination. "Even though I have lost love, I may still become a power for good in the life of my child."

Touched in his most sensitive, if not his most rational part, Mr. Littlepage drew her hand through his arm and patted it softly. Nothing, he meditated with a quizzical smile, could temper the moral principle of Mary Victoria. "The best thing we can do," he said gently, "is to go home and let Louisa look after you."

"Yes, Aunt Louisa will know what I need," Mary Victoria assented. "One of the last things Mother said to me was that if anything happened to her before my baby came, I must let Aunt Louisa stand in her place. As if anyone could!" she added with a sob. "As if anyone could!"

Mr. Littlepage was still patting her hand. "You will find," he said gently, "that Louisa is a rock to lean on in trouble."

Then he let her hand slip from his arm; and turning back for an instant, his troubled gaze crossed the river and lingered on the last faint gleam of red, which, even while he looked, was smothered by the darkening drift of the twilight.

THE END